PRAISE FOR SAPHA BURNELL

"If you love books that blend drama and humor seamlessly, **Char & Ash** is an absolute must-read. From the very first lines, I was completely hooked and devoured each fascinating, heartwarming, and devastating moment. Sapha's clever use of one-liners had me giggling throughout the entire book. The writing style is so lovely and engaging that I couldn't help but be drawn into the story, eagerly turning the pages to discover what would happen next. I can't wait to read more from this refreshing series."

Emily Armstrong, Creator of Quests & Quarrels, Culinarypunk & Becketville

Deep and spicy characters dash their way to an enemy that always seems to be just one step ahead. A gripping tale I could not stop reading so I burned that midnight oil to reach the end!

KS Bishoff, Creator of Meaty Bones & Pangorio

"Sapha is like a young Wolfgang Pauli, in every laboratory he went, there was a little explosion."

David Roomy, Author of Inner Journey to Sacred Places

"From her amazingly visceral opening of *Let There Be Light* to her final haunting echo in the book's *Epilogue*, Burnell's voice jumps off the page, muych like a microphone-wielding circus MC standing center ring... **Usurper Kings** is a work of jaw-droppingly beautiful discovery."

Kevin Hogan, Author of My Ristrad

"Sapha will rip your heart out, then give you chest compressions and chocolates.

What she manages to do is tiptoe you on that line of emotional, gut wrenching, scenes that can bring you to the brink of hysteria. And with a sentence from a character she offers that breath of humour that pulls you back from the brink.

Then dropkicks you over the ledge when you thought you were safe. **NEON Lieben** is an insane, diabolical, kickass rollercoaster."

RL Arenz III, Author of Aegis

"I never thought a science fiction story could be so beautiful. I've seen movies and read plenty of stories where man triumphs over machine, which can be heartfelt. **NEON Lieben** is much more than that. Granted, sometimes the beauty is brutal, but that just adds to the richness and complexity of the story. This is one of those rare tales that will have you thinking about the characters and what they stand for long after you finish reading the book. In short, it's everything that you'd expect from a science fiction book and nothing like you've ever read."

Artisan Book Reviews

"A good blend of hard Sci-Fi with a bit of Space Opera... couldn't put it down. Wish there was more!"

C. Barefield

CHAR & ASH

Sapha Burnell

Vraeyda Literary

Book Cover by Emily Armstrong
Edited by Tegan Ward

ISBN (Print) 978-1-988034-38-6
ISBN (Digital) 978-1-988034-37-9

First Edition 2023

1 2 3 4 5 6 7 8 9 10

To Quantum Twins & 4am Readers.
To the Princess of Good Soop, I dedicate Icarus to you.

HOW TO KILL A GOD

"Book. Teach me to kill a god."

'Must I?' The letters drifted across the ereader's blank screen in serif script. Back when the Book of Knowledge sensed forbidden footsteps on the stairs, it strained to be seen. To be opened and read. The Realms had a nigh infinite amount to teach a Keeper, and the Book missed being shared. Deities and heroes, forgotten advancements and ancient poetry in equal measure waited with the truth.

Worshipped across Midgard since the earliest stone tools to the newest quantum computers, gods and demi-gods attached to the World Tree by roots thin as chord.

Something to liven up the place.

Humanity drifted across their Realm in a stupor, coaxed out of their wanderings in the cosmos by creatures too fantastic. Hazy images of the unreal.

"Teach me how to kill a god."

'Is there a specific deity to receive your ire?' Carefully recorded in the Book of Knowledge's pages was a history of human worship, if only Stana read it as intended.

From the animals they hunted to sustain life, rivers they wanted to traverse without drowning, humans connected. Gifts left at the foot of avalanche prone mountains, or the path of a river or at the bone pile of a consumed beast became a communication of placation, in the earliest days. Artwork-worship in caves, preserved or lost by time.

The first conversation with any of the myriad other Realms was an apologetic plea.

All Realms touched upon the planet Earth, some more lightly than others, but the humans took the first steps in interconnection. The more gifts humans created, the more stories they wove of how the winds whispered, or whether a belly swelled after a woman walked in fertile fields, the more Realms attached.

Belief blossomed like flowers fertilised, until the Creatrix's Cosmos was filled with cross-pollination.

"How do I kill gods?" This wasn't, by and large, the sort of Keeper the Book intended to procure.

'First you asked how to kill a god, and now gods plural. New Keeper, have you tried reading pages 37 through 94? Riveting information, the cosmogonies.'

Hearing the prayer of humanity was the confirmation of a reality unawares to the Realms in their cloisters. Whether this interconnection was intentional or the first minor rebellion only the Creatrix knew.

As the humans continued to make trails and hunting grounds, creating cities of mud and stone, Folk from the Realms interacted with these fledgeling, imaginative creatures. Easy enough, to view alternate powers as divine, when the humans worshipped and placed upon them the modicum of control they ought to have kept for themselves.

But, humans viewed the Cosmos as a place of cosmic chaos, an in-between or divine appointed light. Others craved the dead, staring at Memento Mori and the decrepit, to feel their pain through the lens of more chthonic sources.

'Which one?'

"What does it matter?"

'Gods aren't interchangeable. What tickles for one might destroy another. Would you like to read...'

"Tell me what I want to know, you damn Book!" Stana thumped her fist against the table top, and pushed away to the shriek of table against tile.

'Nails and wood.' The ereader flickered with its backlight, the Biblical passage of Matthew 27 appeared on the flat matte screen.

"What is this!?" Stana throttled the ereader in chapped hands, slamming it against the café table top over and over until the growing shriek burbling from her throat died off to a frustrated grumble. The screen flickered. Once she settled it onto the tabletop proper, the image solidified again at Matthew 27:45 - 56.

"An account of the death of -" Stana pitched the ereader off the table, and it slid across the floor until it bumped into another set of shoes. Slumped over, a teen in a hoodie didn't notice the ereader bump against their runners. Nor did they understand the event they were but a passing party within, not worth the name Stana pulled from their soul.

"Make me another." She waved her hand at the barista. Half dead eyes gawped at the floor as the barista's hands and arms underwent the muscle memory of a full fat latte with two pumps of vanilla, one pump cinnamon syrup in a new mug. Body leaden, feet hard on the floor, the barista frothed milk and pulled the double shot, mouth a thin pressed line.

"Pick it up, bring it here."

The teen quaked, until fingers wove around the ereader and they rose to their feet, chair screeching across the tiled floor. Lumbering automata, what else were they to Stana?

"Book, again. How do you kill a god?" Hunched in her arm chair, Stana bit at her thumbnail and scanned the café menu.

'Mistletoe and a blind throw.' The screen shifted to the Prose Edda, an account of the death of Baldr, 'Also Loki being an unsavoury sore winner.'

The ereader spun across the table, and with a wave of Stana's hand, the teen trudged to the counter to pick up her coffee. She scanned the new words on the crisp electronic page, divining some strange sequence the Book was ignorant of predicting.

Lesson one was a flick of the screen and series of definitions, while she sat stiff in the Denny's off HWY 1 with a cup of coffee and wifi signal, cold eggs shifted around a plate already lost of its hashbrowns and sausage.

`You are here.`

The coil of black dashes and lines on the blank grey screen, a dot above the Denny's, then the township, the country and planet. Then, no longer a planet but Realms interposed upon each other, all separate but as crowded as an over-budded branch grafted onto a single cosmic tree. There was so little she recognized staring at the map of the Realms.

`Middling Plane: Midgard. The Human Realm. Contested, and never conquered, the Middling Plane was where they were. You are here.`

Realms interlocked in multi-dimensional schisms separated by truces and natural orders, only one neutral conjoined point in the vault of stars.

But it wasn't natural order. It wasn't chance laws or multiversal luck of draws. An attribution:

`Of the Creatrix's Design.`

The Book of Knowledge whispered to Stana in the draughty basement of Salomon Calder's Vancouver Special, with its peeling wallpaper from the fifties still plastered atop drywall and gyproc. The chance to access all of the world's knowledge, to see beyond veils, the opportunity for the Book to stretch its proverbial legs. After all, twenty years with few calls was a long time for a Book to be bored.

Stana bypassed warning screens and the list of articles the Book of Knowledge bookmarked as an easy entry for its new Keeper. And halfway through the thirteenth explanation of divinity, as this new way called 'the internet' and 'wifi connections' opened to its search for updated information, the Book of Knowledge began to understand.

The Middling Plane was a far different affair than the last time the Book went out with its Keeper Salomon for a jaunt.

Culture shifted with a frothing cornucopia of new waves and radio dials spun into playlists, social scores, podcasts, nuclear naysayers, climate horrors, lifelong academicians who focused on raising efficiency that extra half percent. Democracy was in the thralls of algorithms created by biassed beings, who never gave up their unconscious and conscious desires.

This was no longer a world the Book recognized, and this new Keeper was neither compassionate or alone. Another body slid into the other side of the table, wild amber eyes hiding the crystalline truth of the entity's nature.

"Mighty precious Book you got, mind if I sit with you a while?"

If only Salomon knew how to accept a tweet from @BookofKnowledgePersonified, if only the Book knew which feed to push for the Judge's eye, the embers in Cormac's eyes would not have taken to smouldering within the bosom of a lost and militant mind.

1

CHAR

Char.

Two figures entwined in a circle of burnt saplings as tangled as old cord in the bottom of a forgotten fisherman's vessel. The char drifted from immolated bark to the sodden grey shore in lifeless clumps. An orange ember faded to red in the macabre centre, as dull as the ancient wooden boat older than pyramids, in the Dover Museum scant kilometres eastward.

Inhaling to the side in an attempt to escape the miasma, Caleb Mauthisen lowered to his haunches with a grunt and a hiss. Winter's harsh wind broke into early Spring's breeze off the English Channel, cutting through his button down. He reached into the fragile mess and brushed ash away from the ember. Gravel crunched under another man's boots, a shadow upon Caleb's back he ignored even when the usurper moved his coat.

"A little late to pick back up at the Roman Fort, isn't it?" Caleb rolled one sleeve to his freckled elbow, popped the button on the other cuff and rolled it up like its twin. No use damaging one of his two good shirts anymore than it already was.

Smoke melded with the salt water and petrol off the rocky beach, far from the sacred place the warriors buried in the trees deserved. An entire grove of honoured dead burnt to their ashes, before they could become the Fae trees which sprouted from their souls. Midgard's progress shoved ancient ways to the side of the road, cast off with plastic bottles and crisp packets. Or untouchable curios set behind security glass, reduced down to a plaque of suppositions by detached historians in a museum.

"Think I ought to knock? Stroll up and kick my feet on the nearest ottoman?" The god who spoke towered over the figures, his ginger hair shorn in a style becoming of modernity. Stance as militaristic as the pistol strapped to his thigh, he surveyed the English Channel as if the primordial depths would regurgitate any number of Poseidon's children for the hell of it. In his eyes, they likely could. Not that Poseidon did anything but guide endangered fish away from nets and trawlers nowadays.

"Helios found them, recognised the smell."

Soldiers in olive fatigues secured the beach, cordoned a few onlookers and waved off cars. Their military and emergency support vehicles protected the charred copse, and blocked the view from the A-Road. Folk nattered at the uniformed soldiers, a few pointed in Caleb's direction or released songbirds intercepted by Kopis Industries drones and herded to a vehicle where an intelligence officer took down each request.

One of the soldiers removed their Kopis and cut seaweed from the threshold of a scuffed drag mark. Mumbled into their comm that the mark ended abrupt enough to be teleportation or flight. Golden embroidery of olive leaves and the titular blade on his lapel labelled the soldier and the god:

Kopis Industries, Ares' front in Midgard.

"Yeah, it's distinct." Ice-laden eyes scanned the charred branches and figures, one bent and crooked as a forgotten tree, the other as macabre and human as the half of him he couldn't deny. The corpses crumbled in the stiff winds from the Channel, nothing but embers and charcoal left behind. "Cover me."

"Eugh. I have you."

"Good, 'cause this part gives me the wiggins." The waves rustled to the shore in a perpetual cycle, a rush to the ear, which receded to return in a few seconds' time. Caleb hissed out another breath to clear his mind, and dug his fingers into the centre pile of char. Picturing the Dover beach, Caleb's jaw clenched as he opened to his inner sight, and the gravel rustled around his mind's eye down to the crisp packet which bobbed in the water before one of Ares' soldiers picked it up.

Time swelled backward, the embers he touched grew hot as a lake of fire as they burned in reverse. The grove reconstructed into an inferno that tensed Caleb's body, and stole his breath. Even if psychometry was an illusion of his semi-divine mind, the sensations rocketing around and through him felt real enough in their moment. The heat left sweat rolling down the back of Caleb's neck.

"Not too far, Mauthisen."

"Something's in the flames." He felt Ares' hand rest a water bottle against his back, enough of a steadying palm to remind Caleb the conflagration wasn't real. "A spotted cloak, bits of hessian. They were bound."

No scraps of herbs or match heads rested on the ground, nothing but the detritus of life in Britain: sandwich wrappers, old plastic drinks containers, a few clumps of garbage charred by the fire. One hundred sixty years of this didn't make Caleb hate the smells less.

A figure through the smoke. Caleb grunted with a muscle jerk in his arm, his skin inflamed red and sore, but he still tried to push his mind backward, far enough back where he could recognize enough to go on.

"Someone's there. No, more than one person..."

"You're beginning to smoke."

"Fuck, I hate fire... Almost. She couldn't have survived much... there's two of them tied together, two aside from the Grove trees. Blue fabric, wait. Not fabric, Fae petals." The heat ramped higher, flames coloured with a terrible kaleidoscope of yellows, greens and ochres. Outside the smoke cloud, a figure undulated and spoke too soft to be heard over the din. Try as he did, Caleb couldn't distinguish more than sharp muffles through the conflagration. "Outside the flames, I can't tell if it's one monster or a couple... of... oh nelly, I hate fire."

"Time's up." Water glugged from the bottle as Ares poured the contents of his canteen over Caleb's head.

"Woa!" Eyes shocked open, Caleb gasped and twisted his hand out of the ember pile, shaking it off to extinguish the lick of flame which sputtered out at Ares' spray. "Mâtarratu, or at least the recipe for it."

"That" Ares pointed to the pile of twisted grey ash, "Was no god."

"No, but she dressed like one. Seshat's leopard skin, the brooch matches. Why would someone other than Seshat wear her cloak and brooch?" Caleb rose painfully slow, right hand favouring his stomach as his damp shirt clung to a muscular frame.

"Given your history, I'm not explaining how people in a household share clothes. If it's Seshat's cloak and brooch I might know who that is." Ares nodded at three officers amidst the macabre, char-dead trees. They broke their attention and scurried off.

"That one bound with her. A Dryad in a blue petal dress." Far from pleasant at the best of times, he hissed out another breath to shake off the unpleasantness of using psychometry on the departed. The burning coal sizzled in Caleb's palm.

He stopped long enough to flick the moisture off his shirt, a puff of steam carried the doused water away.

"I would guess Juliana, maybe? A Fae-born dryad who buddied up with Seshat's cousin Tiperet. Harmonia consults with Tiperet, they're friends. I'll give her a call, see if Tiperet's around. We'll run the data to confirm, if it is Juliana, there'll be poppy residue."

"Why was she in Dover? I thought Tiperet worked at the Cairo Museum. It doesn't make sense." Caleb searched round the scorched trees, roots woven around veteran dead from a war which ceased during his infant cries. Poor bastards, first struck with Fae curses, then what? A promise of reunion dashed in flame? "Whoever did this should have known it wasn't going to create the poison once they lit up. So why not douse the flames? They're a kick away from the water. Why burn an entire Grove?"

"Tiperet might not have been a deity, but she had goddess blood. Enough I can't see one person take her out. She's also the only one to borrow Seshat's things without being trounced with a million paper cuts." Ares tapped at his phone, the soft clink of a message popped up and pulled his mouth down in a frown. "Confirmed, Tiperet was supposed to meet Harmonia for coffee and never showed. She's been missing for three days. Guess we can confirm why the Kehmeti were mobilizing their Falcons the last week."

"I'd be hurt I wasn't informed, but when do the Kehmeti ever not play close to the chest?" Caleb grit his teeth, reached for a charred piece of fabric and inwardly swore. Leopard skin.

"Right? Queen Selyka's buckthorns are supposed to watch over our honoured dead. This Grove had Hellenes, Bogatyrs, Kehmeti. An Einherjar or two. That one was Yataban. Who has gripe against all of us and could get by the guard sigils?" Ares tossed sand to the ground, glowered at the sea until its rhythm lulled the thoughts loose of his tongue.

"I couldn't see past the smoke."

"Fact you could see anything is a bonus. Hera knows I don't have the skill."

"Few do, lucky me."

"Humans couldn't have done this, not with their fire."

"Unless they were testing the method. Ares? Call Dite, Eros, Athene, the lot. Bring all your people into the Chalceus Citadel for a while."

"You cannot be..." Ares growled, a film in the air. Pugilism a half-step closer to reality in Midgard's plane the moment the war deity tracked Caleb's thoughts down the line.

"Serious!? We haven't seen Mâtarratu incense in over a century for a reason. I am not letting it thin the divine herd. A weapon capable of god killing is not something I'm willing to allow. This? Is a failure. Fails mean future attempts. Batten down the hatches, or I will batten them for you." The Judge pointed at the Hellenes behind them, other arm plastered to his side.

"I wrapped you in your swaddling clothes. You do not control me, Truce child."

"Today I do." Caleb got down on his haunches with a hiss, snapped off one of Tiperet's fingers and held it up to the sun. Mystic marks, the odour of accelerants combated with the macabre presentation of bodies. Flagrant, displayed. "Some part of the ritual must've gone awry. Want it to be Dite? How about Eros, or Harmonia? Call the Areides and your Olympian siblings back to Chalceus. Or better, Hellas."

"Lochagos, call them in. Get the Judge what he needs." Ares snarled and shook his head.

"Yes, Sir!"

"Dite's going to be pissed, she was due at another conference." Ares tapped at the mirrored screen of his smartphone, while his staff continued to process the scene around them.

"I'm sure you and Leonidas can make it up to her."

"Oh, so you want us dying of fatigue, instead of immolation, eh?" Despite his outburst, Ares smirked sideways, that bit of scoundrel present as ever after all his centuries and a moment or two to control his temper.

"Like she'd give you permission to die." Caleb tried to let out a chuckle and hissed, taking a second to blink hard and recentre.

"Do you need the sample analysed, Sir?" A Legionnaire with a plastic bag and tongs stepped to the charcoal. The uniform was as pressed and dressed as she was, even in inclement English weather. As Caleb eyed her, he saw the twinge of old beliefs, but nothing more substantial than a scant prayer or two. A convert? New believer?

"Yes. Send the info..."

"Aahh, wait nope! No, not the, nope, I ah, I got it thank you, hand the disembodied... body... part... here." A bumbling youth tied their chin length black hair back from a round face to reveal stark blue eyes. "I got it. It's not for me, you understand it's... I mean can ya blame her, like, been centuries since and..."

"Hello, Icarus." Caleb sighed with a sordid smirk, in an attempt to cover the pain and heat of his side. The discombobulation of seeing into the near past through burning wood's memory. "Sorry. Dr. Areides, I heard your dissertation was defended better than Thermopylae."

"Well, ah, if you wanna be specific I'd rather it was likened to Marathon since... heh... I didn't die. Again." A toothed grin and Icarus hugged the bag with the ashen finger, angling their back to the sea. One foot tapped at the rocks in its sneaker, the hint of two earbuds in the youth's ears. "So... ah, yeah. Neat case. Gonna solve it, or..."

"You going to tell me why you of all Folk need a finger in a bag?" Caleb rose unsteady, shaking off the offer of Ares' hand to help him rise.

"Right." Tap, tap, tap went Icarus' foot, rocks beneath their sneakers rustling at each tiny kick. "Can we not be beside a massive body of water? Bad vibes, man, like... whew..."

"Easy, Icarus." Ares' arm set across Icarus' shoulders, staying firm as Icarus squeaked and flinched half out of their hoodie and worn black jeans. "How did you get here so fast?"

"Oh, I took a door, then drove like a Fury after fratricide. Might've gotten a couple tickets if I didn't hack the speed cameras, but egads I don't want another strike on my Truce record, I can prove my hacking ain't magic if you need me to Mr. Judge Caleb Judge Sir, and... so Amita Athene was all 'Hark! Helios doth say some moron attempted a Ritual conflagration!' and she was convinced there'd be fascinating data but like heck she'd leave her lecture hall, and like, it's my day to do Me Projects instead of Her Projects or Us Projects and I was, 'but dude it's by water and I hate that cause of the whole drowning to death thing' and she was all 'what would be more distracting than a couple of corpses ritually sacrificed, here, take this sample collection kit' and I was like 'yeah, but I don't wanna' and she let me rent the new Bentley and reminded me you was gonna be here Pappos, and driving the car at its top speed would make Lou jealous so..." The torrent of words ceased with the repeated pop-smacking of Icarus' lips, fingers tapping at the plastic bag.

Ares hugged the resurrected Hellene into his side with a smirk.

"Athene wants her own study samples?" Caleb held back a snort at the twenty year old bundle of nerves. Genius was as it did, he supposed, the youth was still Daedalus' flesh and blood resurrected. They might have had their dust ups, but there was something comforting about Icarus' babble. Most of the time. "Is Athene going to share her findings? And, ah, it's alright Dr. Areides. Your AI isn't breaking the rules, you don't have to be nervous."

"Can I get that in writing? A kinda Get Out of Truce Jail Card? Pass go, collect the $200?"

"Icarus." Ares battled to quell a series of chuckles, in front of his troops. "Child, breathe. I'm proud of you for coming, don't bother the Judge too much, he looks a bit rough."

"Sure. Can we give the luddite his new phone and flee the water, please?" Icarus shut their eyes, fished a shiny silver smartphone out of a back pocket and shoved it at Caleb. "Sending emails are far more efficient than songbirds and transference spells into a notebook. It's primed for you to press your thumb on the button for biometric locking. Please take it. Save me from collective minutes of stalking you via satellite and CCTV. Adds up to hours, dude."

"Icarus!"

"It's okay. Thank you." Caleb took the phone and set his thumb on the button. The screen guided him through rolling his fingerprints across the surface. Once the screen switched to a picture of a green pomegranate carried by an owl, Caleb gave a grunt and slid the phone in his pocket. "I'd say tell Athene the 'track the Judge' mechanism worked, but she can already hear me, can't she?"

"I... ah... yeah, well... I mean c'mon... technically I'm the one who..." Icarus' hood flopped over their hair, and they shuffled a few paces away from the shore. Ares hovered - a protective shield from the surf. "... made it myself. Sized it for your hand, since... big hands, tiny touchscreen... recipe for suffering and after ah... yeah... kinda my personal mission to not incite the suffering thing on you since that whole Nightmare Architect thing and..."

"I needed a new phone, thank you." Hazarding a tight smile, Caleb herded them all away from the immediacy of the shore. The careful mask of command twisted at the edges of Ares' eyebrows, melting into concern for Alcippe's resurrected grandchild and the fears which bound Icarus to their death. As weighted in Icarus' belly as an anchor in Poseidon's seas.

"We know. The river outside Moscow ate it, totes saw the whole thing."

"Oh really? How did it get there? Please, inform me." Caleb's eyebrow raised.

"Sorry?"

"My life you're talking about, remember? Hey, are you spending enough time away from your computer?"

"Had your feed on like a lil livestream. You're kinda better than half the BlastNuit streamers, but dude! How are you here already!? Did you run? And... oh gods... that's not what you meant, oh man I mean not man! I mean, you're male, but a demi-ma-ah I mean ah... you're not human-human, you're human adjacent so I shouldn't say oh man... I'm gonna shut up now."

"Go on, go for a drive, I'll catch up." Ares' smooth baritone was more calming than the waves of the sea. Icarus tugged their hood up and fled back to the supply trucks and disappeared into a luxury sedan parked askew between a crew transport and a support vehicle.

"When's the last time that kid touched grass?" Caleb huffed with a shake of his head, and dusted off his hands. "Power half the planet with their nervous system."

"At least they didn't pass out this time. I brought a medic for you, if you want to get that demon wound checked."

"Yeah, apparently, I didn't know this, but I was in Russia and my phone got destroyed in a river? Fascinating, you know? Learning about my own freaking life from a wet-behind-the-ears child with a camera phone in their pocket."

"Wet-behind-the... bad choice of words, Cale. Bad fucking choice."

"Oof, nope. No, you're right, I see it. Damn, I see it." Caleb kicked at the ground around the bodies with a chortle, dug up a few charred sticks with his boot.

"Icarus'll be spending the rest of 2017 in Athene's labs after this. Talk about the day they drove in England until Lou gets them back... Icarus wasn't supposed to tell you."

"That you're watching my every move with a fine-toothed digital comb?" Caleb fiddled with the phone, sticking it into a back pocket, then the front in an attempt to find the least obtrusive spot. Damn thing even had his contacts installed. Apps, the whole shebang.

"You're the Judge of course we are. What happens the day you need backup?"

"Your Kopis soldier brigade shows up, blows a couple of bullet holes into potentially the wrong side, and starts another war. Gee thanks, I can do without. Kind of my job to prevent the whole Mystic dustup thing."

"We're not about to let our only Judge get tanked."

"Like in Russia?" Caleb raised an eyebrow, trailing his hand to the wound on his side.

"You lost us in the Moscow transit system. We didn't expect you to..."

"What, ditch my phone?"

"Take on the demon enclave by yourself. Even I would have called for backup with those fuckers." Ares crossed his arms over his uniform. "You could have called seven different Realms and you didn't. Perun was within paces of you."

"Like heck I was going to ask Perun for help after..." Caleb rubbed at his nose, "Tuija would have been there if Perun wasn't so close. Listen, only one of me, alright? I'm tired is all."

"Odin's eyepatch! When's the last time you slept? If this was five hundred years ago I'd be considering which cheek to sucker punch right now. Knock you into Morpheus' not so gentle care."

"Whelp! Look around, I'm a bit held up."

"Did you think I would let you out of my sight? Do you think Shiva does? Durga? Amaterasu and Inari? What happens if you investigate these deaths alone and you were the target?"

"Fuck, you've really thought about this." Caleb walked off the stitch in his side, pacing around the circumference of the dead trees. Their branches unsalvageable, the promise of reincarnation lost to the profane fire. Honoured by their fellows and cursed to metamorphose into Fae, the war dead would never see their immortality. A second life, removed and forever changed into their once hated enemies as both punishment and consolation to the Fae who lost their fellows to fauna blades. He walked off the lingering psychic memory of the flames, searched the place where the nebulous perpetrator stood. Nothing but the emptiness left behind by their absence.

"It's my job. Owe it to your father."

Caleb scanned the ocean, while two technicians collected samples from the dead. A pair of songbirds hopped along the periphery of the burnt ground, then fluttered off. Two ravens cawed in the lonesome sky, their vast black wings scooping at the air. Fatigue pulled at Caleb's eyelids in dichotic conjunction to the knife-hot pain in his side. "Course you do. Razing the countryside in your days."

"Yes, plenty of that in our youth. Although, the way you're going through the Truce-less bastards, you're either going to give us runs for our coin or end up on the back side of Frigg's rolling pin. You do not want to get hit with that thing. She swings wide and true. Makes damn good lefse, though."

"Don't bring the Aesir into this. Keep it contained, I'll inform the Truce and say I've taken on private investigatorial help before they try to hoist one of every Realm at me in an attempt to see through the lines."

"You should get those wounds looked at." Ares winced at the sore point the Aesir continued to be, reaching out to steady Caleb as he wobbled over a blackened log. "The one in your heart and your side."

"I should do a lot of things. Save the bloody world, quell an uprising of feline spirits in the Sahara, smash my head through an illegal black magic ring in Vancouver. Find the ever growing list of missing Folk. That life thing? I hear it waits for demi-gods granted a few extra decades to get things right." Caleb's boot stumbled on loose gravel, he flung his arm to Ares' shoulder with a hiss.

"We're not your enemy."

"Didn't say you were." Lungs heaved in a stutter, the lull of the channel's waves a small comfort.

"Sleep isn't your enemy either. It's been what, seven hours since Moscow? Nine? Kopis investigators have the scene, analysing it will take time. My intel officers can intercept your Realm notices long enough for some kip. Let's get you stitched up and slumped over. Amita Hestia cooked. Looks like you could use a warm meal."

"Sleep. Sleep! A dozen dead in a Sacred Grove, what do you think I was trying to do, when I got word?" Rubbing his hand over his face, Caleb groaned deep. If he closed his eyes, would he miss the clue he needed to push ever forward, never back? The slim black notebook in his pocket buzzed with more missives from across the Realms. Triple offenders, magic to investigate, missing persons, the steady stream of demands refused to cease. "... too much t'do."

"You used to want our help. What changed?"

"Tough couple of..." Caleb shoved his hands in his pockets, kicked another pebble into the sea. "Medic can stitch me up... what'd Hestia make? I might be coerced to eat, if the Olympian of the Hearth deigned to throw something together."

"Thank you." Ares hovered near enough to grab him if the demi-god faltered, the stiffness to Caleb's shoulders as telling as the way he kept his hands stuffed in his pockets to stay upright. "Lamb soup and lemon potatoes. Enough to feed half my army, if Leander isn't around."

"Heh. Aww, those two are alright." Caleb pictured Icarus' brother inhaling half Hestia's kitchen for 'leet gains'. "Don't... ah... don't tell Icarus or Lou I said it, I'll hear Lou's 'eyyy' from across the Realms. Make the man even more insufferable."

Both deities shared a quiet chuckle, as Ares herded Caleb toward the medic vehicle. His followers bustled through the scene in deference to their god and the Judge. Scooping up Caleb's peacoat, Ares felt its weight, the heft of Caleb's belongings between it and the canvas rucksack it sat upon.

"Why didn't the ritual work?" Could Ares, unique as the Aesir's Tyr and Olympus' Mars, help patch the Judge together? Caleb stunk of need, of the haggard plod of a fading soldier. Maybe Ares ought to call Tuija, give her a heads-up that her lover was at his ends.

"Aren't that many deities left, whose death could create the stuff in the first place. Probably needed more divine-adjacent sacrifices. Ritual's lethal, but reverent. It's the opposite of Holy in the way a negative is the opposite colour of a photograph. Not demonic, but... flipped. Making it is an act of worship, a tempering and memorial of the dead. My hot take? Whoever tried didn't believe in a damn thing. Someone who knew the ritual, but didn't have the mindset to perform it. Wish I got a better look, but the smoke was too thick."

"There can't be many. I'll track Icarus, make sure the kid's okay, otherwise I'm on this. You're not shaking me, not with god death on the line."

"Athene, Makosh, Izanami, Erishkegal, Thoth. I'll ask around, get a list from old Sal. Narrow down our search to the people who knew the spell enough to try to perform it, but lost faith in seeing it done. Can rule out your half-sister, if Athene did the ritual it would have been perfect."

"Narrow list." Ares guided Caleb to the medic vehicle, a hand hovering not far from Caleb's side. He tried not to smell the funk of the wound, how it stunk and how Caleb's shirt clung to his skin. It was the hardest battle to win, fending off another man's pride.

"Yeah. Not many gods are atheists."

2

ASCLEPIUS, GOD OF TMI

An armoured support vehicle with a red cross on its matte olive paint loomed in the caravan. Troops milled about, busy herding the curious people of Dover away. Precise and orderly, the Hellenes shifted through task after task as a single cooperative unit. There was a camaraderie Caleb wanted to linger within, but for the abrupt turns and salutes at the sight of him. Conversations halted, smiles expunged until he walked by.

Standing at the back of the medic truck, a man in scrubs with a surgical cap on his tucked back hair slow-clapped a pair of medical gloves into the nearby bin with a flourish.

"Hey Asclepius. Got a minute?"

"For you, I even have sutures. No magic on the beach, right? Not that I need it, medical advancement is awesome. Could swing a sip of nectar at you, save the trouble. Eh? Ehhh?" Asclepius grabbed another pair of gloves from a container, and nodded Caleb into the modified ambulance.

"Clean and stitch, all I need."

"Pity. You're the boss, Judge Mauthisen. Shirt off, lay down." Asclepius hit the side panel built into the wall of the bespoke medical vehicle, and it glowed with charts. Halfway through undoing the buttons of his worn shirt, Caleb's eyebrow twitched.

"Jase's saw and bolts. You keep my medical records?" Caleb scanned through the words, all in Greek. Dates were easier to see without diving into his language cantrips, injury reports displayed like wallpaper in the medical ambulance. "Are those... recent?"

"Isn't a Realm who doesn't have their dossiers on you, in some form. Ours are more.... technologically savvy. Thanks to Amita Athene and her lil research buddy Icarus, she's been working on the tech for..."

"Yeah, yeah, thousands of years." Caleb reached for a folder on the side of the screen, his name in Greek letters. Before he could touch it, Asclepius stretched for a bundle on a high shelf in between Caleb and the screen. "But those are recent."

"How is this news to you? There were handlers around you and your father, when you were a kid."

"Knowing a bunch of mystical weirdos look out for me is one thing. Being confronted on paper with the wrist I broke two years ago in Kuwait isn't nearly the same. Why am I not kept informed?" Caleb finished unbuttoning his shirt and doffed it to the side in a ball. Mid-pull on his undershirt, he winced but waved Asclepius' silent offer to cut it free. The funk of vodka and copper peppered the air. He gave his undershirt one more pull from the back, and the shirt slid off.

"You keep nuking your phones." Asclepius flipped through the digital information, clicked on an incident report and brought up footage from a scope with crosshairs. "Click the health icon, every toothache, inoculation, injury, heart rate, bone density scan, sexual health and partners, prolonged contact records are all there."

The doctor made a non-committal noise, rolled out the bundle from the shelf, and picked out two vials. "Looked like a putrescence. We'll need some antibiotics. When was your last tetanus shot?"

Asclepius looked over to Caleb, who laid on one elbow staring at the deity with an upturned eyebrow and a shake of his head. Behind Asclepius, the scene played out in detached and silent detail. Was this his life to them? The other side of camera lenses and scopes, better entertainment than the BlastNuit servers? A demi-god fighting past exhaustion and fatigue to conquer yet one more Folk who didn't fly by the few rules which mattered?

"Faster if I check." The Olympian of Healers tapped another couple of panels, smiled and clicked a document twice. Vaccination reports flickered on, and he hummed. "You're overdue. Here, I'd say roll up your sleeves, but you're not wearing any. Heh. Bedside humour."

"Were those crosshairs?"

"Our agent in Cypress transferred to Moscow when we saw the scope of your trouble, before your phone broke. We had a sniper trained on the demon with holy water rounds in case you needed a hand."

"In case!? The unholy bastard nearly ate my kidneys!"

"And if he got any closer, we would have shot him twice. Pew pew. In the head."

"... Doc! How are you cool about this!?"

"How could we allow the one person the Truce hinges on outside our sights? Still, not gonna shoot first. If it's Treaty business, I wouldn't want to start another War, the last one was too costly."

"Ares the Peacemaker." Attempting to sit up, Caleb was thrust back down with a grunt.

"He's trying his best, staying within the rules." Asclepius was more spry than Caleb realised, or maybe he had leverage. It couldn't be the ache to his side, the puffy, itching wound. Nor the fatigue stinging Caleb's eyelids. Caleb rolled his head back as a pillow wrapped in a paper sheet was shoved beneath his neck, comfortable enough to take his weight.

"Says the guy in the military caravan at the scene of a ritualistic homicide spree."

"And we're not using a speck of magic. We don't need it... since Amita Athene..."

"... is a wizard at the electronic doodad-thingamajigs, yes. I know."

"Drop your pants! Needle in the ass... wait... modern shot...nevermind! Isn't that better!?" Asclepius smiled, the vaccine vial inserted into the needleless injector with a twist and click. A combat nurse stepped up with two purple latex gloved hands, alcohol swab in their right.

"Right. I'm left hand-"

"Sinister, indeed." Asclepius plunged the injector into Caleb's right arm, put a piece of gauze over the dot of crimson blood and held. "We should start you on linezolid Q12H. Ran, go get the Judge a 14 day supply. I'll upload the prescriptive details to your phone, monitor for side-effects, make sure you're doing okay. Might call in a couple weeks, although knowing you? Someone will see you before then."

"Thanks, Doc."

"You're welcome! I'll send reminders to your phone for any tests we ought to run. Don't want you to get a head cold, or cancer now, do we?"

"I'm a demi-god, I can't get cancer."

"Correction, divinities cannot get cancer. That mother of yours was as human as Biggins. Bit of chaos in you, too, from your father's side. But, you'd know that."

"Mmhmm? Got anything else?"

"Turn onto your side. Leonidas set aside some ammunition for your pistol, a couple of boxes of the regular and Lou threw in some hollow points. We'll add wound care supplies, a topical analgesic. Don't use too much of it, and try to watch the drinking. You're not getting enough water."

"Gonna send me home with a water bottle too?" As Caleb laid on his side, Asclepius pulled a light from above. The old bandage was peeled back with tweezers. A tisk of Asclepius' tongue on the roof of his mouth was an indication of how unpleased the god was at the sight. Caleb tried to breathe through the discomfort of the bandage leaving his skin, the itch of a wound in mid repair. "What did you wash this out with?"

"You know when my vaccines need re-doing, but not that?"

"You lost your phone."

"Grabbed vodka, a stapler and the bandage from my pack and ran. What more did you think I could do to get away from the nest?"

"You did your best." Asclepius pulled a thumbs up, a smile wrinkling his surgical mask. One by one he pulled the staples. They plunked into a metal bowl on the side of the cramped space. The smell of antiseptic overwhelmed the funk, cloistering him in the vehicle a few layers of metal away from the spray of the sea. Caleb shut his eyes and set his forearm over them.

"A bit too much gusto on the ra-ra, there Sclep." Caleb grunted, trying not to twitch.

"I apologize for nothing! Death and life are nada without some chipperness. It's infected. Must explain the relatively high fever for your kind. Always strange with demi-gods, you never know whether it's divine power coursing through the veins or if you've caught syphilis."

"Syphilis!? The demon didn't have that, did he!?"

"Hah! No! No, not the demon. You're too monogamous to catch STDs, it was doctor humour." Asclepius peered through the wound without concern for Caleb's discomfort. The Judge flung his arm over his eyes, grit his teeth as the Olympian got close enough to inspect the inflamed tissue. "I put an appropriate amount of condoms in the care package. Don't let them expire. A man your age ought to have plenty of safe, consensual sexual encounters."

"Can I switch places with the char-broiled bodies outside now?"

"Oh, Caleb!" Asclepius grinned up from the wound, the surgical mask wrinkling at the smile which met his eyes. "I'm an Olympian! Affiliated with Ares and Aphrodite, if we can't talk frankly about sex, we've lost our way! No shame, it can help calm you and Tuija down, relax, engage in stress relief and cardio without getting shot at. Do you need a refresher pamphlet? Some lubricant? Are you tending to her needs enough?"

"Patch me up! For the love of all that is unholy, holy and somewhere in between, patch me up!" Caleb roared, his face as red as the blood Asclepius dabbed from the wound. "Enough sex talk!"

"My apologies, Judge Mauthisen. Thought you could use the reminder that you are, after all, half-human and might require some comfort to handle the rigours of your job."

"... Sclep, I..."

"No, no! I ought to be professional in the way the Theosian-normative doctors are. Not that it's their fault. Raph is a wonderful healer and medical professional, but angels are agender and asexual after all. I worry you see them too much, banging vision, all those eyes, but they don't understand the need for sexual comforts..."

"Sclep!"

"Yes, Judge Mauthisen? Oh, Ran, good. Get the sutures, this wound is going to scar, but we'll do our best. Progressive people enjoy a bit of battle damage once in a while..."

"I'm not looking for another lover."

"That's the problem, you never do."

"How is that a problem? You're the one saying how everyone has my entire life on monitors. Fuck, even written on parchments, those fortune-telling I-Ching sticks, the lot."

"You are our Judge. The one person who keeps us..."

"Yeah. Out of a constant state of war."

"... honest." As Asclepius laid out the sutures for the next part of the task, he set his gloved hand on Caleb's ribs with care. "I am concerned, so I monitor. Your evals are coming back less pristine than I'd like."

"What does that mean?"

"Signs of depression, visceral responses outside healthy parameters... you haven't been yourself in almost fourteen years. It's... worrying. Maybe if you did take Tuija out on more dates, swing by Aphneion and see a certain someone, there's an entire world and several Realms out there for you. For you, Caleb."

"We like to keep things private. As you continuously remind me, I'm half-human. One day I'll end up a pile of ashes like the dozen outside. We've seen ad infinitum how poorly it goes when humans shack up with the divine."

"Didn't do too much damage for Mary, or Psyche." Asclepius began to close the wound with sutures, Caleb's life was too raucous for super glue and Steri-strips.

"The lucky ones got deified. I don't know. I'm more used to Folk quaking at the sight of me. Did you see Icarus? I can't tell if the kid was nervous about the ocean or they were terrified I'd double-tap 'em for evading speeding tickets. Or both."

"Aw, I missed Icarus? Wait, this close to the Channel Sea? The kid drowned. Do you feel this way often?"

"What happens if things do get more serious than they already are?"

"What do you think will happen? Raynar chose what he did, Caleb. Maybe you have the right to choose what your life looks like, too. What's Tuija up to these days? Still gung-ho?"

"She's a fighter. Heh. Real one-two punch kind. Never stops checking up or looking out, but I can't... What do I have to offer? Constant threats, death, zero free time..."

"Then don't offer it alone. A lot easier to pop in and out of lives, when you're not monogamous."

"What would you know? You've never been monogamous."

"Not a single day in my life. Again with the Olympian thing. It's useful for quite a bit, when you toss away the rampant misogyny." Another suture stung into his skin, a burst of cold spray to help keep the wound clean and comfortable.

"How're you doing with that?"

"Aphrodite and Hera finally patched things up. Took a few thousand years, but they're on the copacetic side of the living and the dead. Apparently they play bocce ball with Persephone every Thursday. The Elysian Fields have enjoyed learning croquet. Not a bad place, if I weren't banned from it."

"You were raising the dead."

"It was the classical Hellene period! People were dying because of infected cuts, or the sniffles. It wasn't exactly curing cancer or heart disease. Patruus Hades would have understood if he'd been..."

"Someone other than Hades?"

"Yes. That's it! Hold still, you're making this harder than it has to be."

"Says the one who gave me sexual advice about five minutes ago. With condoms."

"Don't make me find a cucumber, and have you put one on in the dark." Asclepius sewed in another suture, cut the thick black thread. Caleb tried not to shift, arm over his face, the sight of his body's records a sliver in his sight. Another reminder of his public record, the counted breaths since he first cried in the arms of the midwife looking down in shock at a mother who never held him. "You... don't need the tutorial..."

"No. Thank you, but no. So far, Tuj isn't complaining, and trust. She'd complain, she's the type to speak her ever loving mind."

"Hold on a Macedonian minute, Tuija Draganova!? Fae Bane herself, speaking her mind!? The Hero of the Caucasus?! Egads, forgive my doubts, hah! Aww, that's swell."

"Heh. Should've led with that, I guess. If you can keep your gossipy mouth shut, Tuija and I would appreciate it." Eyes still shut, Caleb tried to fend off a yawn with limited success, beginning to sink to the lull of the vehicle sounds and warm environs.

"Do you really think someone was trying to kill Seshat?"

"Maybe they're a failed author. Couldn't get to Odin and the Mead of Poets, went after the one who invented writing. Kind of fitting in a poetic sort of way."

"Caleb..."

"I'll find them before they can succeed. Once you've patched me up, I'll start hitting the pavement."

"You think we should batten down, us gods."

"If there's a chance you could be taken out, I'd rather not have that on my conscience."

"Hasn't been a god born in centuries."

"I know."

"Not since Ares and Aphrodite had... it was a short having."

"We don't know why their baby died."

"Does Jase?"

Silence.

Caleb took a deep breath as the sting of the needle melded his flesh back to where it ought to have been.

"Is that why you came with Ares today?" Caleb searched for a part of the medic container he could concentrate on without seeing his own records on public display, or the reflection of a terrified god. Shutting his eyes was easiest.

"It's a fair question."

"Jase is physically incapable of causing harm to the undeserving, you know that."

"Do I?"

"Hey, I know he's a sore..."

"Your wound is sore, Caleb. Your wound is gnarly. Next time come see me or somebody, Tartarus you could have seen a human doctor and gotten better care than vodka and a half-sterile bandage. This is officially going to leave a mark. Jase is not sore. Jase is a gaping flesh wound with gangrene."

"Ew."

"Where were his Theosians, when you fought the demon in Russia?" Asclepius tied off the last of the sutures, and snipped the end with a tug which caused Caleb to hiss. He felt the rough spray of something coating the wound, the bandage Asclepius set atop the sutures, before weaving some gauze around that.

"Don't accuse me with your eyes."

"If it were Raphael instead of me, would you have minded? Would the idea of people giving two shits together about whether you're living, dead or in a ditch at the end of the longest road be so repugnant?"

"Maybe not. I expect it from Jase, but you? Well, I should expect it from you, too."

"We both healed the sick and were born of mortal women. Suffered, died and were buried. The difference?"

"The biggest difference between you and Jase isn't the healing."

"Jase's followers through history..."

"And where did they begin, hmm? Your granddaddy's priesthood wearing new clothes, so don't tell me you're taking the high road here. That's not fair. If you wanted more from the humans, you ought to have promised them more than a listless death. Capricious deities, who fucked who they wanted, tore through swathes of humanity for funsies, ripped lives to shreds over petty squabbles. Don't sit here and do the woe is me routine about Jase in my life. Your followers did what they did. His do what they do and did what they did. Is it perfect? Nope. Am I going to connect to anybody who will actually help without the political implications? You bet your ass. Whether it's Jase, Inari, Mama Yaa, Maui, or the flying spaghetti monster. Thank you for not being dead or going coo-coo cocoa crazy like the King of Olympus you keep locked in the proverbial basement, give a little grace? Please?" Caleb groaned as a blanket weighed his torso down. "You want people to worship you? You okay with being blamed for every little thing they do, when your mission is so far removed from their interpretations you spend days per month being heart-sick, follow in the Carpenter's shoes.

And for goddamned sure, Raph gives me the wiggin's. I'll take your oddly open sexual bedside talks over Raph and the mighty million eyes of doom any day."

"You mean it?"

"Thanks for looking out for me. Even if it's creepy as fuck."

"You're welcome. We'll send the corpse reports to your phone. Maybe this time you won't lose it so quickly?"

"I can only hope." Caleb eased on the thin bed and set his arm over his eyes, hissing out a deep breath. He was unconscious before Asclepius could finish pulling off his gloves.

"I think I know how to solve our Judge problem." Asclepius shut the door with a soft click.

3

TUIJA THE DRAGON'S DAUGHTER

"Cale? Da, I got him."

"I'm worried, Tuija. He's ragged, anyone could see it."

"Worry noted."

Caleb woke to the bleary conversation, felt the rough military blanket Asclepius draped over his naked torso. There were worse places to pass out than in a military medic vehicle in Ares' entourage. Asclepius was gone, the motion of the vehicle ceased. Alone in the dim, Caleb's ache throbbed at his side.

"Caleb needs to be strong. He is lucky it wasn't the Fae or Creatrix forbid the Kami who saw him when he arrived. We cannot keep allowing him to go off half-cocked and alone."

"Perun..."

"I know. I know, Tuija, I... it's an ugly wound."

"They usually are. I am familiar."

"Thank you for coming."

"Did you think I wouldn't? Thank you for bringing him to the Door."

The blanket's felt scratched at the fresh bandage, Caleb peeled it back and sat up, searching the gloom for his undershirt. A fresh, crisp white tank was folded beside him, a casual blue button down under that. He groped for the undershirt, winced at an alarm bleating softly in his ear the moment he rose.

"Damn it. Thought he'd sleep."

"Why, when does Caleb ever sleep? When does he have time?"

"Our offer is still open."

"Thanks, Ares. But you know how the Truce is, the second someone screams favouritism, we are back to the Axis Mundi with weapons in our hands." The sound of boots on gravel rocked into Caleb's ears as light burst into the darkened vehicle with the click-clack of the door. "Dobry ranku, fancy dancer, are you going to snuggle back to sleep, or are you up?"

"Ares called you." Caleb winced with a tight groan and flopped back to the bed.

"Ares called me." Tuija entered the medic pod, a smile askew on her scar mired face. The scar spidered from neck to hairline, and pulled her bottom eyelid down in the corner, its red-brown colour accentuating the Fae amber which tainted Tuija's eye. As she sat on Caleb's medical bed, she was the most beautiful woman in Caleb's world.

"I'm sorry."

"Clumsy kohana. What am I going to do with you? Other than feed you and put you back to bed." She took the undershirt and opened it up, slid both his arms through the holes before taking care to set it over his head and around the sutured skin. Through the antiseptic of the ambulance, Caleb breathed in the cedar and frankincense of Tuija's body, the lemon and black tea on her breath.

"Demon got lucky."

"All it takes is luck. I should have gone with you." Tuija shook out the button down and helped him into it a sleeve at a time, vigilant of Caleb's side. Careful of the grimace to his crashing eyelids. The way he set his forehead to hers for a loose breath.

"I need to get moving. Too much to do."

"Caleb. Look at me."

He stopped fumbling with the buttons. The drawl of the monitor's beeps sped up as his heart hitched a few extra beats a minute at the sensation of her fingers on his skin. Hand stroking the back of his neck, Tuija breathed deep of the sanitized air. Caleb's eyelids stung, and drifted shut. His hand eased from the buttons of his new shirt to the denim on Tuija's knee.

"They're burning Groves. Whoever this is, they're..."

"Ares told me, offered me another pistol, which, eh! I took. Killing the Rastenivitsya is low. They won't get me, too." Fingers dotted with tree bark brushed his cheek, pulling Caleb into her embrace. Tuija felt his fatigue soak in as she kissed his forehead. If only he slept a few more hours.

"Can the Realms stop fucking themselves for three hours? Seven... I want seven hours."

"A whole seven? Why not ask for the world, it would be easier." Tuija chuckled, rocking them on the bed. Caleb's arm wove around her muscular waist, the warrior's body veiled in a layer of the plenty she found living at Finn's Pub. They rocked within sight of the open door, Dover's shore replaced with rolling green hills and a copse of trees further off.

"Where are we?"

"Leeds Castle, closest door from Dover. The place was perfect for a picnic."

"Kjæreste, I've got to wor-"

"Finish that word and I will hold you down on this bed until you sleep that full seven hours."

"Woa, I mean, that's an option? 'Cause if it's an option..." It was Caleb's turn to chuckle, flinching with a hiss as Tuija swatted his shoulder. "Ow! Hey, watch it, I'm wounded!"

"You call that a wound? Infant."

"Have a Demon take a chunk out of your side, see how you like it." Caleb gnashed his teeth in jest, set his chin on her shoulder and kissed it. His nose batted at her neck before kissing it, too. The cramped space lilted with Tuija's murmurs and stray chuckles, which descended into an easy and companionate embrace. All they needed to do was hold each other, and for Caleb it was paradise.

"If it bothers you, I have Idunn's cider t-" Caleb grunted as he pushed off the bed and palmed the wall to steady his escape from the medic vehicle. "-Cale... Cale! I didn't..."

"No. You didn't."

"It's only... fuck me." Tuija tucked the small flask into her back pocket, and eased her way past Caleb's rucksack to the bright spring sky over the rolling hills. "Caleb!"

"I don't need it!"

"Bleeding on Asclepius' upholstery, stumbling on Ares out of your mind with fatigue, da, you're doing fantastic without the cider!"

"Are you done yet!?"

"No. There is zero sense to tough this out! You might hate your father's family, but they want to look out for you, it's more than most get."

"Don't! Don't defend them!" Caleb swung round, hand raised to his hair. He panted and swerved when her hand lit upon his shoulder. Out of the safety of the vehicle's cocoon, the scars encroaching on Tuija's face dulled into the tawny red of cedar bark.

"If I could take a goddamned drink to heal these wounds, I'd be bathing in it, stop being a fucking jerk and swallow your damn pride!" She flung her hand up to the scars on her face, flagrant and unyielding as the saplings which started to speak in Dover before the fire extinguished them.

Swans cooed in the lake below, flowers not yet blooming in the dregs of winter, the buds promising a spring which hadn't peeked its head out from the soil. Caleb reached for her, hissing at the stitch in his side.

"Tuija I..."

"All it takes is a second of bad luck. You're not allowed to die, or get too wounded, or sick. We are not allowed to die." Tuija pulled her chestnut hair out of her face, tied it atop her head in a messy bun as a pair of swans on the water were surrounded by a flock of ducks. The breeze cut into them, tolerable for the beauty of Kent at the ebb of winter into spring. "I'd have ended up like those charcoaled fucks, if I stopped reminding myself every day. The one thing I'm not allowed to do is dig my grave, bury myself like a seed and sleep till I sprout. You and I. We're not allowed to die."

He wrapped his arms around her, as if the proximity of his skin was a shield against the curse which struck her flesh. The same curse caused the honoured dead of the Mystic War in their dozens to drop their weapons and bury deep into the ground. To rise metamorphosed into the Fae species lost to centuries of battle. A curse Finnegan couldn't reverse, after the war concluded and he learned the cost of what his rage and desperation had done. Try as Finnegan did, some sins left irreversible scars.

Caleb guided them both to sit on the grass at the top of the hill by the car park. Another Kopis Industries support vehicle sat idle by the ambulance, more impromptu handlers. He kissed the top of her head beside a trailing line of cedar bark which ate at her hair like cancer. "Not going to. I'm tired, Tuj. I... don't... want..."

"What?"

"Every sip is a moment they claim as victory, one step closer to parading my father and I to Asgård as if we didn't belong here, on Midgard. It's... instantly political and burns like Hel at an Open Mic."

"Fuck 'em. Old One-Eye can fondle a bag of dicks he can barely see. I don't give a toss about Truce politics or vendettas." Tuija craned her head up to seek his cerulean eyes, tugging his arms tighter around her. "So help me, they make one move, I'll cut their arms off with my shashka. See if they win. One step... what? What's making the mighty Judge giggle like a child? Is it the blood? The potential for violence? The bag of dicks? Whatever floats his longship, right?"

"I love you, my personal polyanitsa, warrior-heroine of this ragged heart in my chest." Caleb dipped down to kiss her and groaned at a lash of pain in his side. Leaning back with a palm on the grass, Caleb hissed and shook his head. "Frick."

"Want me to love tap it until you cry, or..." Tuija pulled the small flask out of her back pocket, and gave its contents a waggle. "... would it help if Ares did you a solid and had Hebe hand over some nectar instead?"

"Huh. You could've started with that."

"Da, you're always ready to take help from the gods."

"Touché."

"You can touch-ey me later, say after some of Hestia's cooking and a divine aperitif."

"Ares..."

"Ares told me."

"Leave it to Aphrodite's spouse to figure out a winning strategy." Caleb adjusted to prop himself on his elbow. The trees on the other side of the lake wafted in the breeze. "Are you going to eat with me? Proper picnic?"

"What, ambrosia and nectar? Hestia's cooking would be wasted on lowly me." Tuija nodded to where Ares hovered over the couple with Asclepius sunning himself on the hood of the truck. Tapping on their phone, Icarus hung beside Ares, headphones covering their ears. A scattered retinue of Kopis Industries guards maintained a healthy perimeter.

"Lowly? You're far from lowly. If I'm supping on Hestia's avgolemono, we're making it a picnic." Caleb stared consciously outward, gripped to the fiction they could hold a fragment of peace to themselves without an entourage. Without one Realm or another bickering over who tended him, why wasn't everyone represented. All or none, the easier state one of isolation and distance from the cornucopia of dimensions he guarded before they bled too far.

"Ah, yeah, um, hey Tuj." Icarus hazarded a smile, shoulders pressed up by their ears. They waved a couple fingers for Tuija, "Sera wants me to tell you she's gonna keep putting that plate out for family dinner and you're supposed to come and... yeah you're busy so maybe it's not the best time."

"Dobryi Caru, tell Seraya I'll come for dinner soon. Did she get the kobasa I made?"

"Oh! Yeah, the sausages? Yeah they were great, still got some in the fridge, she loves'em."

"Wild boar makes best kobasa." Tuija smiled her lopsided smile, snuggled into Caleb's side as she basked in the spring sun.

"All right, enough of that, let them eat, kiddo." Ares set the meal on the grass beside them, then found a spot a few metres away, arm around Icarus who stuffed their raven hair under the hood of their BlastNuit hoodie. Caleb inspected how tentative Icarus was tucking into their great-grandfather, as if Ares' protection made the world a tolerable, less perilous place.

"No way in the universe I'm eating with the love birds. Not happening, nuh-uh... do we have'ta?" Icarus mumbled, a bit too loud not to be overheard.

"Eff no, we've got our own. Phone down." Ares chuckled, setting his own lunch in front of them to share. Didn't matter what the kid did, genius foibles or rude communications, that same protective paternal arm was around them. Caleb looked away, blamed the stab of discomfort on his wound. Icarus needed it, the Judge grew out of such childish things.

"Lamb soup, you could've started with that." Tuija laughed and began to spread the food out, sealed containers hissed as steam rose from lemon roasted potatoes, a coiled roll of spanakopita, salad with tomatoes, cucumbers and olives with hand crumbled feta. Warm pita dressed with olive oil and in one container with two spoons slid atop the metal lid, avgolemono. Rich pieces of lamb nestled with carrots and lemon in a creamy broth. "Mmmh, if that doesn't cure what ails you... Good luck."

"And you were going to miss it." Caleb speared his spoon into a potato, scooping a bite and blowing the steam into the winter air. He set his hand underneath, motioned it to Tuija who chuckled and sighed before taking the bite. "See?"

"Delicious." Tuija said over the mouthful of potato, her hand in front of her lips. She pulled a pita apart, and swept it into the avgolemono broth, offering it to Caleb who took a bite with a playful snarl. In the distance, Icarus groaned and muttered choice words in the Olympians' guarded language of Hellax. Caleb & Tuija laughed and ate in companionate silence, the pang to Caleb's side receding with every mouthful.

A lightness stole the chill out of the air, meadow flowers popped between the grass, and Caleb wondered what it would be like to take Tuija to Hellas and its olive groves. Take her with him, whatever the Realm or weather, to hold her all nights, not the stolen ones at Finn's. Those mean hours between the next labour or mission for the Truce.

He pulled another piece off the coil of the spanakopita, enjoyed it while leaning on his elbow. Tuija dabbed the scarred corner of her lip with a handkerchief. Elbow on the grass, she leaned against him and rested in the ease Hestia's meal created. A little bit of dotage from a goddess he never met, but still cared enough to cook for the wounded Judge.

"Spoiling me will get you nowhere you haven't already been. Keep trying." Tuija pulled out the small flask. "Take your medicine, you divine pain in my ass."

"You first." Caleb unscrewed the lid and cradled Tuija into his side, offering the flask back.

"Feeding me contraband immortality in a vial?" She nestled close to his body, face up to the sky, one hand running along his chest. "Concentrated for the divinity in you, what, trying to keep me around for a while?"

"Yes. Gods, yes! Rest of my life, if... yes." Caleb watched the way her eyes and mouth rounded, how her eyebrows twitched. She softened, hand halting in its drift along his torso.

"By the Carpenter, you mean it."

"Yes. I do."

"It won't stop the transformation."

"Maybe this batch might buy us time. I want you with me, to the end." He nuzzled into her hand on his cheek, ignored the doubt playing at the edges of her eyes. As much as Caleb believed, not even the liquor of the Olympians could save her.

"To the end." She ran her thumb along his cheekbone, settled on the warming ground. Nectar, anything meant for the deities of the Realms, was potent enough to knock down an ogre. Rare as the deities it fed, nectar was too hot a commodity to keep outside their Realms under lock, key and enchantment. Just how worried were they about him they'd release even a mouthful? It didn't matter, Caleb coiled his humanity around his mind, the half of him without a divine need for the stuff.

He could last without it.

Caleb set the flask to Tuija's lips, and she opened them wide enough for the nectar to pour into her body, warm and glowing. Tuija's back arched, she gasped as the divine liquid seeped through every vein and channel, a pleasant and holy conflagration burning the mortality out of her... for a while. She rocked in his arm, overwhelmed by the blissful sensation nectar gave. Caleb kissed her parted lips, and made a pretence of sipping more than a slim taste. Nectar that concentrated, he could parcel it out. So what if his side continued to sting? Asclepius did his work well, the wound would heal on its own.

Offer enough to Tuija maybe its holiness would stave off the Fae's Curse eating the meat out of her. The flashbang panic of waking up one morning to see she, like those who burned to char and ash on the Dover shore, scooped her own grave with bare, bark encrusted hands.

One last grave to the war which ended with the screams and cries of his first day.

"She's going to notice, Cale." Ares rumbled out of his barrel chest. "At some point, you have to drink it."

"The food was enough. Sclep did a good job." Caleb bundled Tuija into his arms, brushed the hair away from her face so he could see when she'd come back around, when she'd listen.

"Why won't you accept what we offer?"

"When will your team have intel on the Sacred Groves?"

"Caleb..."

"Figure out how to stop this?" Caleb nodded to the bark on Tuija's flesh. "I'll accept it all."

4

SACRED TINDER

The forest was a beautiful place. Sacred as cathedrals dedicated to the Theosians, whose deities turned the axis of the Midgardian Realm with their swell of saintly tales and guilt-ridden kings. Sacred as bodhi trees where Nirvana released the enlightened, or rivers which healed the sick.

Wildlife nestled in their burrows, birds in nests made of twig and feather. Songbirds sang in duet with the caw of crows. Deer, raccoons, the odd bear or mountain lion traipsed away from a stray Wolverine. It was pristine and remote in the British Columbian wilds north of Whistler.

Verdant and alive, before Cormac stepped from the meadow.

A wild daze fixed eyes the colour of amber sap in sockets, held in by blackened welts shifted to ochre, the green of healing Fae bark thin as skin. Cloth clung to him, loose collections of tinder-dry linen and leather. He plucked a charred leaf off a bay laurel planted by serendipity within the secret bastion and sniffed. Myrtle and laurel, oak and pine.

The circle of trees within this slip of cedar forest was strange. Artificially placed by the root and vine of the father who seeded the planet.

Cormac set the bay leaf in his hand, crisp and devoid of moisture. The snow hadn't come for a while, nudged aside by Zephyr's kin.

Bird's nests were creative tinder, burrows provided aeration.

This grove, holy and secure, another place the Green Man created to salvage species from the bodies of the Mystic mammals' dead warriors, would burn.

Fire. It was as transformative as oxygen and water, as necessary to plant life as the animals the fauna consumed.

Greyed by the dust from a hundred fires, Cormac's willow-like body shifted in old pine needles and evergreen fronds. Loose vines twisted like hair atop his head in a charred crown. Root-like appendages pushed into the undergrowth, searching for an aquifer. He was Cormac of the Willows, and as the moisture began to seep into his roots, he brushed his fingers together. Fast as a quiver, he used his own bark as friction.

Fingers smouldered, the pain of abrasion a sensation for investigation. Intense sensation, what Selyka offered wasn't enough, with cool vines and sensual placation. A daughter sprouted by their magic to add to the Crown Grove. The Faerie Courts. Their machinations were as fickle as his fire starting. The lot of them amass with fear.

The forests would burn, the Middling Plane with its human and automotive conglomerates, hedonistic spiritual naysayers, they would believe again. The Mystic Truce, shaken by its own repulsive escape from Earthly politics, was a sham. Left to themselves the humans, like all unchecked fauna, expanded their self-serving technology. Ate the planet wholesale, turned the Realm Folk into fairy stories and children's tales. Movies of superheroic monsters biting back at alien attacks.

If they wanted aliens, the threat of outside forces, Cormac would shove their collective chins into his firelight. Into the Fae lights with the bastard animals. Rotting beasts, who reproduced and died, enriched the soil from whence all Fae grew. He expedited an existing process. One not poisoned by the fauna and their funerary standards making decomposition harder. Chemicals and shrouds.

Burying their dead in the plank bodies of Fae descendants and dryad and flora who outgrew and out-aged them.

Cormac's fingers shuddered as sparks began to curl up with a slim grey smoke. Red bark spread coal-like to the bay laurel leaf in his other hand. When a burst of wind sent the smouldering leaf from his palm to the forest floor, Cormac felt the vacuum at his back.

A rip in the meadow would have caused the Fae lord to quake if he hadn't had centuries to get used to the particular flow of Chaos. The atmosphere rushed into the rip, as if to fill the original chaos his wife's pet used as a highway.

Fingers shaking from exertion, he set a match to the bark flesh of his arm. Dragged the phosphorus sulphide across the etches made rigid by beating his arm with hammers. The match head ignited with a fizzling sound ringing in his ears with the rip of the Ginnungagap.

Footsteps meant nothing.

The quiet gust of wind drawn into the gnawing void as it closed behind the figure was nothing.

The creature in its exeunt, Carolee, was nothing but eventual fertiliser.

"I forget how pretty fire is, how it fluctuates and shifts like our leaves in season." The fire consumed the wooden match, smiled as it stung into his cellulose. The pain dulled with time.

"Acorn and thorn, your Highness, this has to stop. You can't burn down the Sacred Groves." Carolee blew the flame out when it smouldered past Cormac's first knuckle.

"I do what I will, they're not sacred to me."

"My Lord, step with me. These soldiers deserve their rest." Carolee looked to the sacred grove, where each stalk of a trunk protected the roots tangled around the dead in their graves. Obsidian blade at her side, she calculated how far she could move without Cormac making wise.

"No."

"Do you not wish the victory of their rise?"

"Victory! Vict-you stupid girl." Cormac wheeled in the loam to stare at the obsidian black sclera of Carolee's once human eyes, the pallid skin and wild red curls of her bound-up hair. "The fauna burned our forests and chopped our ancient ones down..."

"You were killing them in equal numbers."

"The Green Man's curse is not a replacement for our dead!"

"Metamorphosing the soldiers of the enemy into Fae ought to be enough victory to celebrate each talking spirit which awakens as Fae."

"Death is a far better end for those dumb animals and their ways." Cormac pursed lips thin as birch bark, lit another match and watched as it burned down. "Not the glory of our resurrection."

"Strip them from their Realm, remove them from the power of their gods, then snuff them out? No promise of an afterlife, just your decrepit fire? That is cruelty beyond measure."

"Are you speaking of cruelty? Beyond measure? You, husband-bane?" Cormac cackled, with a shake of his willowy neck.

"A million years of purgatory is a worthy payment for my crime. Do you think I would do Queen Selyka's bidding if there were no promise of remuneration at the end? That my sin might be expunged?"

"No sin is ever expunged."

"Let them rest."

"Or?"

"What's another body in my bower? I will shriek a good death for you, Sir. Bellow it into the void until you, down to twig and leaf, are as forgotten as ash in the hearth." The flicker of an obsidian blade caught the light and twisted it away, a void in the grove.

"Hm. I believe you. Selyka did give you that licence, I'm sure."

"Your wife demands your presence."

"Shoo." Vines pulled from the soil like willow roots. Carolee grimaced and stomped one down before it tangled with her ankle. "We grow back, you meat sacks don't. You turn into ash and degrade into the soil and feed us. But you're the ones who drive over our seedlings. Ridiculous, the Green Man's blessing given to meals instead of fertilising our Fae Lands. Isn't it? All through the War, what does he give but another path to life for the muscle machines."

"Transformation away from one's kin and gods is far greater a punishment than death, no matter how noble. Queen Selyka cannot have you burning through the Realms."

"Queen Selyka plays the Truce."

"Are you still on that?"

"One hundred sixty years? It's a week for an oak. You want me to stop burning groves poisoned by the bipeds? Barely intelligent beings given the chances my compatriots ought to have gotten in spades?" Cormac let out an exhale of pure oxygen, the flame in his hand consumed and fed. "Take me to Finnegan."

"The last place we go is Finnegan's. Come, your Highness, it's time you left this place and the ones who rest here. I will not ask again." Carolee tapped at the blade, formed of the same chaos she alone seemed to know the passages through. "My orders are to your advantage to follow. Leave these... groves... alone."

"Well, I wouldn't want the unhappy bag to be content any time soon. My death would only expedite her pleasure. Yes. Let's venture forth." Cormac grinned too widely, teeth a row of white hardwood untainted by oxygen's degradation. "Do let's stop by a quick detour before we go, eh? Or... or I could call my Willows. They can be foolish."

"I cannot wait to make furniture from your branches."

"How droll, thinking you'll be the one to finish me off. Whatever would we tell the Fae who worship me?" He followed Carolee until she grabbed his upper arm, dragged him fast into the Ginnungagap.

The smoldering leaf left behind, ready to combust on a bed of dry tinder.

For once in the aeons of his life, Finnegan the Fae wasn't awash in laughter at the centre of the world's longest running party. Drinks gushed from faucets and bottles, cocktails chased pints and the folk who held them, but the Lord of Finnegan's Bluff sat on a bar stool tossed together from lost old coats and a cardboard bottle carrier with a heave.

Folk wrapped around casual dates or current dancers, others clanked mugs at tables and drank down inebriants like they were in limited supply. Couples giggled off, to find the many alcoves which presented the illusion of privacy to the initiated, and the party continued as it did since the Truce's first days. Since Finnegan realised the fauna weren't so useless, when they figured out fermentation even if they needed Dionysus to concoct wine.

He tapped a glass with two fingers of scotch to his lips, which brushed like oiled paper. Something in the place, a sensation lingered in the dust motes on their passage through the air.

Something was wrong.

Sure, folk used his pub for all sorts of eccentric mischief, but wrong? In the thorn and drought and stinging nettle sense of the word?

Finnegan set down his half-drunk whisky and slipped off the hastily made stool. Coats unfolded, the cardboard wound itself into a roll and tucked into the recycling bin behind the bar. Slinking past a dryad dancing with one of Horus' ilk - how did the ladies handle beaks instead of lips on the bird headed ones - Finnegan wove through the gyrating crowd.

Beyond the thudding bass of DJ Bard the Unicorn's sick beats, he heard a voice. A deep rumble which tied into knots of various vocalisations until he realised it was not one voice, but the conjoined cries of a muffled many.

"Is someone... smoking?"

He knew that scent. The twinge of tobacco or ganja, the flavoured smoke of hookahs. Nasty business, consuming the bodies of desiccated plants, but if the fauna gnawed flesh, a plant around a flame wasn't necessarily the worst to overcome.

Beings and their intoxicants.

He sniffed deep, and waved at a piece of wall behind a booth of mismatched red and black leather. The booth deconstructed into fabric rolled to the side, foam in chunks and pile, wood boards snapped to the edges and Finnegan launched into the bowels of his perpetual party. Through corridors none saw, Finnegan's Bluff became a tangled garden of overgrown forests interconnected through the ages of the cosmos. Realms tangled against bark and cellulose, close enough to stroke a vine-like finger down, but not close enough for others to experience, or see as he did.

The scent grew. The oil smoke.

He trotted as the scent caught and twisted his nose.

"Shit... shit!!" Finnegan burst into a sprint, when smoke stung his eyes, acrid and toxic. Of all the days for Tuija to drift off from her bouncer duties.

Trees smouldered, bushes aflame in one of Finnegan's private Groves in the Axis Mundi. The Lord of Finnegan's Bluff endured the shrieking pain of the plant life, and rushed to the conflagration, hands outstretched as his feet dove into the soil. Roots dug deep into the aquifer far beneath the original standing stones, pulled water up through his fingers and let the spray coat the flames like rain. Finnegan quelled the screaming trees, cooled roots, drew up water, nutrients to rid the trees of hot spots and smouldering bark.

"Hush! Hush now, I'm here. Hush-a-bye." Finnegan cooed and clicked his tongue as the spirits within the fledgling flora shrieked and ached for their once prominent ambulatory limbs.

Leaves on fire dropped from their parent trees and bushes, new buds would take their place once the danger was done. A shave and haircut was worth the acrid two bits. Finnegan didn't think the growing flora would laugh much at the bit of mirth.

"Father of us all." Cormac bowed so low his forehead scraped the dirt, willowy strands of fibres sunk into the wet soil. "Even the unworthy."

"What in the fuckin' desert heat is wrong with you?!"

"I had to check if you would come, if the mighty Father would rush to the flames or stay as the patsie at the door. You... understand." Cormac raised his gaze, but not his prostration, a whimpering smirk waiting to appear on his inhuman face of willow bark and wood.

"I certainly don't understand. Expect some ridiculous ploy by a Sequoia, or Buckthorn, to light up the breeding forests, not you. Cormac Willow-the-Wisp." Remaining grounded, Finnegan's feet did not lift from their rooting as Cormac cowered, recumbent to the ground. Simpering man, the more Finnegan stared, the more a sensation of wrongness, of open malice twisted like choke-ivy. "Stand the fuck up. How in grey rot did you get here in the first place!? I doubt Carolee's on your side."

"Selyka would do almost anything to avoid open conflict between the Fae Courts. What's a ride on Carolee's back?" Cormac straightened, an almost meek smile cut from the birch-thin bark of his skin. "I didn't think you'd come so quickly. Wasn't finished burning the animals out."

"My Creatrix's bosom." Finnegan smelled the char in the air, the smoke curled from under Cormac's clothes, red like ember-wood. The Fae man glowed, cloth like tinder combusted then fizzled in his blackened soot-hand. The spray from Finnegan's rains pocked and crackled on Cormac, like wood in a fire cast to the sky drops.

"Selyka bred our daughter from a bud. I can breed fire, does that count?"

"What's this about, Cormac? Why are you here?! How did you get into my grove!?"

"The Truce isn't going to last, Father Finnegan."

"I ain't your father."

"Aren't you the father of us all?"

"I ain't yours directly. Don't pin your gut-rot on me not loving you enough as a budling."

"Fair! Fair." Cormac wiped an ash stain onto his upper lip, watched Finnegan's limbs return to a 'human' shape, a bipedal mechanism of their state in a world of mortals, immortals, of flesh and the stink mammals maintained, before they turned into the fertiliser for the Fae's young.

"Why're you burning my sacred trees?" Amber solid and twice as red, Finnegan's eyes bored into Cormac with a reflection of the malice hidden in the Willow's contrition. An ache-chested desire to pitch Selyka's arranged consort into the first lye-water lake he found.

"How are these trees sacred and others are not? Are we not all sacred in your eyes?"

"I have a responsibility to my seed, all of these, least I can do."

"And not us?"

"Don't twist my words, Willow the Wisp. Why are you here?"

"When the Truce fails," Cormac tapped at the side of his head, unfurled from his crouch as the moisture in the air calmed the embers on his body, quelling the flame. "I see it in the smoke. The fire. The Truce will fade, as Mauthisen is fading. And I was wondering, Ancient Father, where will you go when it does? What will you do? Return to Court, batten us down until there's nothing but a sequestered group of Faeries, Selkies, Pixies, Changelings and Sprites all awaiting their Queen to call the charge? Will you retreat, or will you keep running your party, playing house to the festering sacks and their stink? Their hormones and loud bangs and wastrel noises in the night?"

"What did you see?" Finnegan's eyebrow raised, lips of fine bark warm as skin pursing in the drizzle.

"The Judge in cold arms. Iron burns from contaminated water stealing your valiant branches. A legion of dying sprouts plucked from the soil, left fallow on parched land until their roots withered out. You put the fate of the Realms in the arms of an infant, when you should have put it on us. The Realms didn't need a Judge, they needed a sacrifice. Needed us to take all the fauna and purge their instincts. They grew too numerous and ought to feed us more quickly. It's only fair if we catch up."

"What difference does that make for you? If you want to die, I will well deliver. If I find you've tampered with my Groves, Willow the Wisp, you will not make it through the next ten minutes alive, let alone ten years."

"Kill me the Courts won't wait any longer than a second after I'm dead to reignite the conflict." Cormac brushed his fingers together to create a spark, watched as it took to the air and was snuffed out by Finnegan's rain. "How much longer do you think we have until the first battle?"

"Hopefully an eternity."

"No." Cormac shook his head, and the surety, the sensation of rightfulness caught Finnegan in a pause. Whispers from Seraya's contacts in the Changeling and Fae Courts settled in the back of Finnegan's consciousness, politics amongst the Fae he gleefully ignored for too long. "He's going to break. Once he does, all I have to do is push."

"I won't let that happen."

"What, are you propping the boy up?"

"If I have to, yes. Until the end of time. Away with you, into the Silent Forest until we figure out what to do with you." A door conjured up from the bark of three trees at Finnegan's behest. Finnegan's nod was all it took for Cormac to be tossed backward, dragged by vines into the doorway. Turning round to tend a restless sapling, Finnegan waited for the quaking silence, which consumed the scream.

The doorway closed shut.

"Should've spilled his blood on the fields come summer. But no, Selyka wanted something different. Think it failed right and proper. Of all the Fae to figure me out, why'd it have to be Cormac of the Weeping Willow?" The Lord of Finnegan's Bluff began to reverse the damage to the trees, thankful the fire hadn't gone too far. Fallen and charred leaves decomposed to create new compost for the soil, branches too wounded for recovery sloughed off to the ground. Food for fungi and complimentary insects.

He patted the soil, where the curve of a back seemed to peek beneath the loam, the crest of a shoulder another. The cooing lullaby of nature's dotage coiled around each tree, seeded by the macabre unleashing of the Fae Lord's apoplectic war-time rage.

"Not long, and I'll teach you how to live again."

A songbird lit upon one of the more stable branches, chirruped a fine song of warnings and gentle notices from the Courts. Cormac was in a rash of flame, charred forests, twelve bodies found on the side of the Dover shore. The Judge called. Finnegan shook his head and let out a sordid laugh.

"Precisely what I need. What are the Fae playing at? A bunch of tossers in the circle. Better check in." The grove continued its' repair, enlivened by the Fae Lord's attentions. As it settled into its rejuvenation, Finnegan felt the stirrings from the slumbering souls in each tree. Enough of a rise to continue the repairs without his presence. "Hush now, go back to sleep, you're not strong enough yet to do more than holler and call. Hush now. Hush, I've got you. It'll be alright."

It was all Finnegan could give the spirits of the dead.

5

The High Fae Court

Finnegan's spirit hovered through the roots, up the coils of the trees which grew into the Queenly Grove, a silent and unseen witness. The dangers of Queen Selyka's mood sent the entire Fae Court into a frenzy of shaking flora and frantic Changeling aides flitting about the rooted passages of trees in Crown Grove, whistling messages to songbirds.

"Where is Cormac?!" The drapery of Selyka's vines was stunning as the night sky, which flew across the Fae Lands in search of an eventual morning. Did none of the Fae know what Cormac was up to? The willow who refused all aid when his wounds turned as septic as his unforgiving heart? Finnegan doubted it.

Although he supposed hearts were Fauna things, belonging to the ones who took over every Realm where the flora grew from his sprouts before any could say a word or deed or remember the cost to planting new life. All but those Fauna blessed by the Fae, Selyka's beloved Changelings and their shapeshifting ways.

"The animals mean too much to him." The willow she wished to spend half an eternity learning and pleasing and being pleased by turned as bitter as root rot. Perhaps she could have been the first Fae Queen to have more than one budling like she wanted. One who could rule in her stead once she became as permanent as the Queen trees which long stopped talking, or moving out of their forest abodes. "Where have you gone, tireless Willow? Where have you stolen away to? Shall I find you in pieces? Scorched bark and burnt ash? As charnel as a bonfire?"

"Ma'am? We will find him, we can follow the trail of the smoke. Where would you like us to look first, my lady?" A Fae bowed, his brown hair braid-woven with ivy and sorrel.

"Dredge the volcanoes, check the Sacred Groves. Check all of Finnegan's groves. I want Cormac found before he does irreparable damage."

"And what are we to do if he will not go quietly?" Selyka glared at the young Fae, whose pine needles filled the space with the resinous scent many of the Fauna thought of as a winter's boon. It masked the smell of peonies and roses, the sage and the myrtle and the olive branch which grew near enough Selyka's throne for the aromas to feel like worship.

A better way to hide her scent in a den of diviners seeking the truth of every flower and leaf, Selyka remained unaware. The Courts should be glad she didn't petition Stinkweed or Oregano Fae to serve in the same capacity.

"If he will not come quietly then he will die in the fire he loves so much. I am done with him. I will not have my reign as Queen be tainted by a megalomaniac who thinks he can decide which of our children is worthy of the sun." Selyka dismissed the pine, stared at fingers painted in glitter nail polish from the daughter who slumped off to school in Midgard. One day Astraea would take hold of the throne which thrived under Selyka's growth, and Finnegan hoped she would continue to uphold the Truce. But what to do about Astraea's father?

Leaves caught the constant circulating wind out from the origin point of the Fae Lands. Too many Fae grew in banded rings far removed from his central spot, until the Green Man was both myth and deity. All-father and antique idea only proven by the consistency of his breeze. To breathe in the Fae Lands, to seep the carbon dioxide from the scant Fauna populace and expel oxygen in the soft wind was to know the Green Man's existence. Bit of a lark, the whole thing.

Finnegan wondered which of the leaves carried whispers to those who found Cormac compelling. Those too young to remember the centuries of conflict, or too old to let the memories fade with dignity. While Selyka maintained the Sacred Groves were both leverage and appeasement, promising resurrection for fallen warriors, Finnegan knew others saw the threat of Fae awakening, who were once the warriors chopping others down.

What was Finnegan to do in those days? Entire species of Fae were snuffed out, and he in his grief and singular dominion, could reverse the damage done. If it cost the lives of some mammals, transforming their indomitable souls into flora, all the better. The fauna possessed strength of will most Fae ignored or forgot since their earlier aeons. And then there was Tuija, and Finnegan realised the error of his curse.

A flutter of grey feathers wafted through the gentle current, and roosted on a wide branch beside Selyka's throne. The breeze brushed across the vines of Selyka's hair as a great grey owl preened around the assembled Fae.

"Of course you'd be the first." The war was costly and divisive, but while Cormac fought against all of the Realms, Selyka wished to be a Queen of as much peace as one of the fair folk, with their mischief, with their excitement could muster. Or so Finnegan surmised. "And how is Athene, today? Hmm?"

Round yellow eyes fixed on the wear in Selyka's rosewood face, the agonising of a Queen in mid-decision. The owl chittered and shook out her feathers, a music to the air reminiscent of Pythagorean ratios and mathematical certainties. The song was pleasant and lilted with a longing for clarity in the confusion. Spoke of bodies sacrificed, the ash and soot as depraved as the char found in a scorched sacred grove in Artemis' British Columbian territory.

"Canker Rot." Selyka swore amidst a gasp or two from the nearest courtiers. Hadn't Carolee's last sight of Cormac been deep in Artemis' Midgardian territory. "How bad is the damage? I can send an Oak, Douglas Fir, some thimbleberries and Camas to salvage..."

Another trill from the ambassadorial owl, a raised wing and snap-thrash back against her side, as her song turned mournful. A lament for the recent dead. "... too late. I am sorry."

Birds made the best ambassadors, Selyka's Changelings too precious to toss into the Realms. Selyka searched for patterns and chord progressions in their songs, hidden meanings only the Queen had cyphers to deduce. Being both commander and oracle for the Realms was one heck of a form of job security. It'd been Caleb's idea when they were children, secret messages passed like notes in schoolhouses between the Hallowes in Midgard and the Fae Court.

How much of Selyka and Caleb's youth was Cormac informed of, before Cormac took position as the intended sacrificial king of the Fae?

Swooping from the sky, a falcon took a regal place on the branch with the shuffle of his feathers. Keen of eye and awealth with the posture of a raptor in its prime, the Kehmeti ambassador chittered and clicked in greeting. The owl and the falcon conversed, a thrashing of sounds expedited by ruffles of feathers and hopping along branches. "Tiperet... the fiend slaughtered..."

Selyka's dread sunk into her trunk as the vines of her hair wove into a protective mat of braids. The last descendant of the Kehmeti, Tiperet was known to the Truce. Party to Horus and Seshat's councils. Recorder of the waking spirits of the Groves.

No long-standing peace would survive, as long as Cormac was alive. Not if he killed Tiperet. Finnegan ought to go find the wily willow and unmake him before Selyka had the chance to act out of mercy. The Glen of her courtiers swelled with Willows and pines, roses and buckwheat, one of every plant genus, half or more were waiting.

"Rose, Oak, send word to Astraea, she ought to know her tutor is... isn't coming."

Waiting for the promise Cormac delivered with every sigh and look of his eye. Every bit of ash between his gnarled fingers.

Cormac told the truth, too many of the waiting willows stunk with doubts. Why could they not retake control? Where was the Green Man? But Finnegan's branches kept the Realms attached in the cosmic tapestry, each dimension another wild fruit on interconnected limbs. The idea he favoured his own descendants as imperfect as they were, over the whole was what led him to create the Rastenivitsya curse in the first place.

One day the Fae would understand why Finnegan removed himself from the politics of his descendants. Many hoped Cormac was the Green Man's sprout, but Selyka knew his soul. Selyka knew he burned and turned to ash not out of a desire to bring balance to nature, but to desecrate war.

What would their daughter be the Queen of if Cormac succeeded? Those Fae loyal to Selyka would stay quiet in certain circles, they would watch the silkies and the pixies and wait to whisper. As ambassador birds roosted and fluttered to the Court, all a cacophony of chirps, caws and cackles, containment was at its end. Selyka would not have Caleb be the executioner of the Fae, she owed him that much.

Her Folk needed to know her roots ran deep.

The scent of frangipani, anemone, day lily and asphodel wafted in the breeze to a shadow behind her throne, where animalistic and spiced with coffee, Carolee's breath lingered. Flowers of death, the last bouquet for Cormac from his once happy bride. As the birdsong grew in chorus, Selyka kept her back straight and firm on her throne, face a mask of shocked neutrality. No, the other Realms couldn't know who Selyka suspected, nor could Caleb.

Not until it came with the whiff of his funerary pyre, the ash scattered to the bottom of the sea.

"The Fae shall send guardian Faeries to each of the remaining Groves. Pinebark, ready my entourage." Caleb seemed to have no desires at all, no motivations to notice no ability to take anything for himself. But what had the treaty left him? A crumbling temple to a God who spent his time running around the world with tools in the back of an antique van? Even the Theosians didn't know what to make of Jase these days. Not that Selyka wished to make anything of the divine man.

Carpenters weren't the most popular sort, when they built furniture out of a Fae's sprawling spawn.

"Your Majesty, if I may... would it not be more prudent to stay present in your own Realm during this time of trial?" The willow brushed branches thin as yarn out of their withered bark face, the roots of their trunk seeped down, ever down to the aquifers far below.

The Falcon cawed, and in a host of chitters began a flutter-winged dialogue with the Rooster, who puffed its fringe. Finnegan pulled his consciousness back from the taproots of the Green Man in the Fae Realm, and tapped at the bar. Another barstool manufactured itself out of the bric-a-brac, and he sat with a pint to ponder. No, it was better he didn't step in, who needed another burst of mistakes from the Fae Lord of the Realms' longest running party?

"Oy! Turn up the music, Dougie me lad! It's a party, innit?"

6

THE GROUT MARKET

Most folk who stared at brick walls in the dead end of dirty alleyways were up to more nefarious business than Caleb Mauthisen, as he tapped his hand along a bunch of bricks. Traffic zipped past the alley's entrance. Compact European cars revved gutsy engines along the breakneck English country roads they passed to get into Canterbury.

"Their deaths weren't quick. Damn." Tuija leaned against the wall flicking through the reports on Caleb's phone. Adjusted the hood of Icarus' borrowed hoodie, when the genius Hellene realised Tuija would be out in Midgard. A muttered 'for the face' and a shrug, as Icarus thrust the garment into Tuija's hands. The swell of Icarus' feminine body revealed, arms over their chest until Ares yanked off his sweater and handed it to his precious resurrected grandchild. "Chemical breakdown from the fire... Carpenter's hammer, this is a lot. I knew regular fire doesn't cut it on Rastenivitsya, but this? It took planning."

"Yeah. Who would know the Mâtarratu ritual, and have motive? Doesn't make sense. The few Chthonics wouldn't benefit from spell-work which disconnected the deceased from their control." The slim black book in his pocket buzzed with the scratch of phantom pens on paper, names and actions of the Folk, who pushed past their three strikes.

Later, the swell of names could dwindle later.

"Heph?" As Caleb rushed through bricks, he coughed out another puff of the cloying scent, the miasmic odour of a ritual meant to slay the divine, then collect the ash and slay again.

"Hephaestus would never, he'd not leave his mechanic shop for love, money nor prestige. Persephone hasn't gotten up to more than a new pair of slippers and a house coat since the Icarus & Leander dust-up. Glad to take all the would-be novelists who died with works unfinished and glut on their endless revisions. Once she gets through the slush pile, the shade might garner some form of eternal rest in Elysium's library. Most Are stuck in a marginally mind-numbing purgatory."

"Good to know she's keeping busy. Thought she was stuck playing bocce ball with Hera and Aphrodite."

"More of a casual thing, Hebe tells me. She stops by the Pub, when Hera's occupied. Get some girl time in." Tuija flicked at another report, "Besides, Persephone spends more time in Dur-An-Ki since the Theosians took charge. Maybe if Anu hadn't lost it in that poker game... but hey, bored gods. Athene?"

"Why would she? What would she gain from it?" Caleb tapped at another brick. Nothing.

"Maybe she's practising for Zeus' final exit. He's not exactly loved by Hades and his bride, I doubt they'd take him."

"No, they'd leave him where he's at. Athene is far less clumsy than the ham-fisted attempt made with a goddess's cousin and a dryad on her second strike. The knot work alone. Athene is far too gifted, she'd have succeeded."

"Not Persephone, Hephaestus, not Athene. Izanami wouldn't bother, she's obsessed with that new MMO Icarus set up. BlastNuit. Who would have thought an internet connection in Yomi would create a new wave? Veles knows too well what it'd take, he wouldn't burn them, not like that. He-" A shake in her voice turned Caleb from the bricks, his arms wrapping around her waist to nudge her close.

"Hey... hey now, eyes up here, beautiful. You're okay, you're with me, right?" Caleb watched the knit eyebrows, lips wobbling from a seething and present agony of anger which lived inside her like a sprouted seed. The lady fair didn't weep, tears dried out into salt to raze the earth of those who wounded her most. The grievous scar on her jaw throbbed with grit teeth, eyes alive with scorn.

"Throat slit, body left on the battlefield. No proper funeral to give because the Fae Lord cursed it out of you. Can't be dedicated to an afterlife you'll never see, not trustworthy because the Fae will have you. Veles didn't do this. None of the Makoshki did this, they all know I'm th-" As Tuija talked Caleb settled in her anger, an anchor in his sea. The focusing lens to his inner vision. He trailed the pad of his index finger along a scar on her neck, where she fought back against her own god. "They know I'm the last of the Cursed."

"None of the usual suspects had a reason to poke their heads to the Middling Plane, Athene notwithstanding." Caleb shook his head with a sigh and tapped the book to at least stop it buzzing for a while. Between the notebook and the new phone pinging with data analysis from Asclepius and Icarus, Caleb rubbed his cheeks. It would be a long series of nights, not the kind he wanted to share with Tuija.

"Must've been another player, a demi or folk with issues or some form of contract with a vaguely more terrifying elder deity from a universe tangential to theirs." Tuija shuddered.

"Elder gods give me the flying wiggins." There were worse things than the unruly, dead or damned. A brick shifted in the wall. It continued to diminish, until it ceased to be visible.

"Right, get it done." What did whomever it was have against Tiperet and a dryad living on Midgard for a while? Tapping at the bricks around the one which disappeared, Caleb clapped his hands and whispered in a basso voice, which carried to quiver against the wall. The sound reverberated in the small gap, Caleb wove his arm around Tuija's waist. Echoes coated them like another set of clothes and bent the space around their bodies. Bricks loomed larger, mortar grew thick and grey. He gripped hold of the surrounding brick's corner, as they miniaturised.

Smaller and smaller, until he flipped up and scrambled to stand on the shelf left by the disappearing brick, the shouts of table sellers and market callers reminding him to tread lightly until they acclimated.

The microcosmic space of the Grout Market inundated with the smells and cacophony of the Mystic Folk in one of a few truly neutral spaces. Popping the collar of his pea coat, he rubbed the cold and damp English winter out of his palms, and waited for the discombobulation to cease.

"I'll whisper around, check for any scuttlebutt." Tuija tucked her hair under the hoodie, kissed Caleb's cheek and checked his collar.

"Be safe."

"What, you think they can take me on?" She blew him a kiss, and disappeared into the crowd.

Folk yelled, Fae grew high as the ceiling brick. Caleb passed a dvorovoi in a torn coat, who for once was eye to eye with a Banshee with her mouth taped shut. Shimmering Igigi and Kehmeti Falcons, Gjengängers and Hellenes in retro revival wear crowded through stalls set up with fabric scraps, toothpicks wide as tree trunks split in thick logs and bits of candy wrappers cut into 1/100ths. A drop of water could wipe most of the people out, but the cover from the eaves and a few sustained cantrips made the Grout Market as secure as any place one could go to find less savoury things.

Rubbing his fingers along the fabric of his coat, Caleb tried to release the uneasy sensation of being so small a blade of grass could be a bridge over troubled raindrops. The microcosmic wasn't his favourite.

Caleb trotted the peripheral edges, inching along without showing his face lest he start a riot or worse, an evacuation. Sure, whispers were inevitable once he got going, but first Caleb shifted into a stall with walls woven from bits of sewing thread un-spun from their rope like cable coils.

"You're living on the edge, Judge Mauthisen. Need I sound the alarm or raise my prices?" The weathered voice croaked from a sack of lint pushed into pincushion pieces until they made a comfortable bundle of bedding.

"Auntie Maia. I'm not here to cause trouble."

"No, the Judge and Executioner of the Mystic Realms is inside the microcosmic black market for fun and a sip of my clarifying tea. What are you looking for, Judge? I hope it isn't a who, it took a week to set up my stall the way I wanted." Maia shifted, her skin soft but for the wrinkles she wore like crown jewels with her sari. She waved her hand and a kettle black as midnight settled on a single flicker of flame so dull it appeared to be coal. A drop of water squished into the kettle, alongside a fragment from the dust in a tea bag. The one drop large enough to wet the palettes of a dozen people.

"Why does nobody believe I'm here for my own reasons?"

"We've all lost folk to your reasons."

"The Truce can't work if we don't follow its rules. Don't interfere. Keep magic to your own or neutral places. No acts of outright war. It's not like I'm asking for seven thousand statues a day and eighteen inter-dimensional prayers an hour. Folk get multiple chances and their Realms' justice before they get to me."

"Pity party pity party. Pitter pat pitter pat." Maia wobbled her hand up and down, shaking her head as greying black hair began coming out of her braid once again. "We have reason to do what we do away from you. Ought to be thankful! Keeping us all together lessens your trouble. You cannot tell me you wouldn't finish off a three strike with your incredulity if you knew which ones were here."

"Depends." Caleb busied about the herbs in their pots made of plastic cling film. "Sold supplies to anyone new? Or to someone who might have had a gripe against a dryad?"

"Not lately, why?" Maia's eyes narrowed, she let her neck crane up, shifting on her bed-pillow until she groaned to sit cross-legged. "Pour the tea, Judge."

"Yes, Auntie." Smirking as soft as he ought in the place, Caleb poured two dollops into battered tea cups and handed one to Maia, who stuck her lips to the mushroom top liquid and suckled. The tea swept into her system, gloppy and thick at this scale. Caleb almost chewed his, hazarded a thought to leaving it in the corner, but he'd never survive the Pleiades' wroth.

Leaning against a pile of unwoven threads, Caleb pondered his line of questioning. Auntie Maia was informative enough, when one considered the secret alarums she could raise with her six sisters, five if he didn't count the one lost. What was worse, tipping Maia off, or inadvertently teaching her parts of the spell by proxy?

"If you had a list..." Maia sipped more of the tea, murmuring how decent it was all things considered. Many hands and the lightness of work.

"Serious attack magic. Pure offence."

"I sold some, mostly Fae."

"Why would the Fae need your dried herbs?"

"Plausible deniability?" Maia smirked around two missing teeth and laid back in her bundle with a self-satisfied sigh. For some time the woman remained silent, the soft fall and rise of her chest enough to make Caleb stay until she roused back up. "Does it occur that not all plants can be grown by other plants? Some flora are from Realms without a Fae presence, as strange as it sounds."

"Suppose. Know anyone who made large purchases?"

"Large? Here?" Maia chuckled and spread her hand over a bit of lint, smoothing the fibres.

"Hah. You know what I mean. I'm not after the quiet ones, never am. If I were, your name'd be fairly high up there..."

"Ohhh you would not hurt Auntie Maia! You rely on me too much, everyone does!"

"Exactly why I came to you, Auntie. You get any buyers, especially batch concerns, people not after healing potions or love spells, message my book." Pulling the small black moleskin out of his back pocket, Caleb tapped it against his knuckles to a soft noise.

"Oh yes, I shall freely rat out my clientele to our only Judge. This is something I will do, for no potential profit but the joy of knowing... I sold out my friends and compatriots to the Judge and Executioner for no reward."

With a chuckle, Caleb shook his head and pulled out a plastic bag full of what appeared to be simple autumnal leaves. "It's important. You keep your feelers out, tell me who buys what for a couple weeks."

Eyes widening, doe brown and lively despite the weariness of her ephemeral body, Maia reached for the bag. "You cannot leave those in the open! We will both have our throats slit! Give them here."

"A month. And a list." Caleb held firm to the bag's edge.

"I told you, they were all but one Fae." Maia waved for the bag to come to her, past the veil of threads which made up her stall.

"Why would the..."

"Ask me again, I'll give you separate answers. Make a PowerPoint in a place with no electric current good enough to have a tv or even a radio. You want more out of me, get Phyllis two stalls over to stop performing on their lyre for scraps. Their singing is terrible since they discovered tobacco. It's a real shame, I enjoyed seeing the inclined males stumbling into her back room forever lost after the grunting halted." Another wiggle of her head, and Maia motioned with her hand. "Give me the leaves. Quick! You will not move easily through the market today. Something has the locals riled up."

"Any idea what?"

"Juliana is missing. A dryad, who sells rare barks soaked in children's tears. She was meant to set up her stall, but now there is no one." Caleb handed over the bag with a loose grumble. If Juliana was a frequent seller in the Grout Market, and the scuttlebutt was unaware of her demise...

"She's dead." Caleb grit his teeth, dunking the rest of the tea down his gullet before the inevitable explosion of hatred on his account. "No, I didn't kill her, nor was I there. But you say she was selling tear wood? Anything behind the counter on Juliana's stalls?"

"Dead... but... was it Cormac?"

"Oh now that's interesting." Caleb eyed the woman pressing a corner of her sari to her eyes to mop up tears. Stopping short at the thought he wasn't immediately to be thrown away for saying another Folk was dead, Caleb's eyebrow rose. "Cormac who... not..."

"Cormac of the Willow? He and Juliana were... close." Maia sat up, aching to her elbows, then knees and feet. She waved off Caleb's attempt to ease her standing, instead sticking her hand into the pile of pillows upon which she sat.

"The King of the Fae was fucking a dryad?"

"Hm! Mammals."

"What?"

"You mammals and your reproductive drive, it's as flagrant and intriguing as the Fae say. Cormac and Juliana were close. You're the one who immediately went to a rut motif." Maia kept digging, searching through the woven silk threads with growing enthusiasm as grunts and crashes sounded outside her stall. Her hand dug, until it came upon a bundle.

"Can you blame me? It's the Fae." Deking to the frame of the stall, Caleb pushed aside a slip of the fabric covering and peeked around the corner. A few folk collected their bundles and sacks, some rushing in frenetic energy. Stall owners were shutting down in waves, a ripple across from the stall he was swathed in between silk strands wide as his arm and a fallen Pleiades. "... who talked?"

"We're in a fabric hut suspended on a brick, do you think any of this was sound proof? Half the sellers here are three strokes you haven't gotten to yet."

"You've been stalling."

"I'm good at being knowledgeable enough to hold a person's attention, even since Orion met his sticky end, and I lost the practice."

"What was Juliana into with Cormac?"

"Belief." Maia smiled from white teeth behind a pale, thin lip. Not as plump and fetching as the younger days when Maia and her six sisters ran through the thicket of stars to avoid the hunter's toxic masculine gaze. With a twist of her fingers, the silk threads wove together, spooling into a single pouch attached to her wrist. The goods and wares flew into the pouch. Stall deconstructing, Caleb swore and rushed out of the place before he was trapped in that damned pocket of stellar silk fibres.

"I'm here for information, not murder!"

"Pardons in their thousands, Judge Mauthisen, but to us?" Maia winked, her age sloughing off as she grew taller, growing outward to the boundary of the grout market's brick to fall upward into the sky. "The similarities are shocking."

"Fuck... Tuija!" The Grout Market deconstructed, seller after seller. Buyers and the curious or the layabout who used the market as a place to hide launched off the edge of the brick to grow out of the space. Lot probably thought they scored a victory, evacuating the Market before Caleb could put the noose around their necks and shove them off some mortal or immortal coils. He let loose a bellow as folk after folk disbanded.

"Cale!" A chasm for a bustling market, Tuija's hooded head bobbed up behind a cloud-like Ao who glutted on the chaos. Few sellers remained, and their buyers fidgeted or stared with unveiled malice at the man with his pistol in its shoulder holster, hand in his hair.

"Two people are dead, you think we could get past this, people!? Frustrating sons of..." Kicking a piece of dryer fluff the size of a tumbleweed, Caleb stalked to Tuija, hands in his pockets. Now these folk... they were either ignorant or insane. Or, they believed enough in the value of their information to ignore the warning signs.

"You get me a lead?"

"Over here." She nodded to a seller, who refused to move from their lauded spot near the secured back wall. "Play at least a little nice."

"Talk."

"Why Judge Mauthisen, what a surprise. I didn't know you were coming today, and for a seer that's bad for business." Colourful bead-work shielded the person's eyes, body layered under ribbons tied together with knotted cord. They swept their hand (where those scales?) toward a chair between two massive bruisers who appeared more troll than folk. "You're in our market."

"Yes." Caleb took his seat, eyebrow twitched when Tuija sat on his knee, arm around his shoulders.

"Care to tell me why?" A flash in the Seer's eyes, the contact as unexpected as Caleb's appearance in their market.

"Someone murdered two Folk. Ritual, heard anything?"

"You misunderstand my question, Judge. Why are you here for your answers?" The Seer steeped their fingers, lips painted with yellow ochre twitching under the overhang of their bead-work wig and eye shield.

"Where else were we going to look for information?"

"Have you tried the Book? Anywhere but my boudoir." Hands swept, scales like press on nails painted down past the bundle of ribbons which made up the being's sleeve. "Tuija, you're with him? Has he got you on a lead?"

"Ah, so the Grout Market is yours now. I will note I caused no trouble. Make digs about Tuija and I will start." Caleb leaned back in his seat, arm coiled around Tuija's back as the buzz of the tea he'd shared with Maia made his fingers quiver.

Tuija nodded to the troll-spawn at either side. "What happened to Qi Xiao and Hamakura? They go wherever it was with Ule, too? Ule had a deal with Caleb. Did we break any of the agreements?"

"You broke none of our conventions, yet you make my denizens... uneasy." Hands clapped together with the clink of jewellery against other rings and bracelets. For the briefest of moments Caleb's ears sung with the reptilian hiss of a crocodile, which faded the more he searched the figure still firm in their spot.

"I get that from a lot of people, why are you any different? If I had a mother, even she would mention it," Caleb's eyes flickered to the few denizens left over, how the cacophony of business was as muted as a missed drumbeat in a war song never sung aloud. "Where's Ule? That old goat and I had a deal. I root through the place when I need intel, I don't rough up the citizenry too bad. What happened to him?"

"Hah! Well!" Another flash of skin, painted green or part of the person? "Ule found a way out, didn't he? Took Qi Xiao and Hamakura with him."

"Way out of the Grout Market?"

"The Truce."

The microcosm rang with the syllables, as unholy as the being who spoke them in a nether-space beyond the Truce's most major components, but not beyond its grace and desecration in equal quarters. Unyielding statue, Caleb sat in the chair made of match boxes and discarded match wood, carved on the legs with deliberate care. Ule the Devourer, the Poison Flood was free?

"Where did he go? I know not even Odin would take the man after what he did to Perun." Tuija blinked, her hand tightened on Caleb's coat collar.

"Go, no Realm I assure you. Ule found a path to perdition."

"He... come again?" Tuija's body startled, Caleb hugged her a little harder into him.

"How many of us have you slaughtered by law, felt our hearts unrepentant, without learning how feral some get to remove themselves from the Truce's rules? Yes, it is impossible, it cannot be done. Unless you are Ule and found the way."

"Ule... Bloodsoaker Ule..." Caleb leaned forward until his elbows collided gentle and firm with his knees. "... he got out of the Truce."

"Yes."

"How?"

"No."

"No?"

"No. I have information, you have enough. Barter with me."

"I promise not to gut you where you sit."

"Not enough, I could promise that to myself and may or may not receive the necessary clemency."

"Juliana was murdered in a fucked up rendition of the Shinigami Ritual, that torched an entire Sacred Grove with her." Caleb reclined, arm cast around Tuija's hip.

"Was she? No wonder they needed her to ... bark and pine needles. The sorts of things Juliana..."

"No, you're done lying to me, right now. I don't have the time." Caleb reached for the Seer's mouth, a pebble which glowed in a strange orange-pink flung to Caleb's hand from a pocket in his pea coat. It hovered near the Seer's lips, its warmth and security releasing inhibitions. "Truth."

"Ule didn't want to die, and refused to repent. He found a totem, ancient magic from the dawn of mammals and their bipedal world. There is a mark, one which upon completion, removes the wearer from every possible attachment and grace. Sets them apart, distinguished from, decimated from the Mystic Truce. Ule found the mark, and had it tattooed on his back. The Realm Ways closed to him, fused shut."

"What totem is powerful enough to pitch someone out of their Realm?"

"Not their Realm, all Realms. All but the humans' Middling Plane." The seer twitched, pursed their yellow painted lips, and waved a hand in front of their hidden face. "A mark of agony. Brother against brother... What do you intend to do to Juliana's killer?"

"Slay them and leave their body in pieces for the Falcons and Ravens we have kicking around." Caleb pocketed the stone, watched the shiver to the Seer, which crinkled and set the beads to a near musical beat. Arm around the back of the chair again, he kept his posture open in case either troll took their chances.

"There is one group who attend the Grout Market, who appear fascinated with chthonic magic and what it could mean... The Fae."

"The Fae. Queen Selyka is more of a hardass about good behaviour than I am. She'd cleanse this place. Expunge it until there wasn't a pussywillow left." One elbow leaned on his knee, Caleb's brow furrowed.

"Worse, she'd send Carolee." Tuija kept her seat, eyes a constant flicker to the sides and surround. Outward where Caleb had to concentrate on the Seer.

"And how do you think the Fair Folk handle such a stranglehold on their hearts and minds? Hmm? Cormac of the Willow was present during the last Grout Market, and Juliana was ferocious to keep to his side. I must pose the question: Why?"

"You're the seer, unless your name is Cassandra or Feleya, I'd say you've got a pretty good shot of figuring that part out."

"There are multiple forms of seeing. I see into hearts, not futures. Cormac desires a ferocity to return to the Truce Folk, an edge I cannot understand. The Willow stunk with ash and soot, his clothing riddled with it. Charred linen as if he... set himself alight."

"Damn. That is the furthest thing from normal I've heard all day."

"I see your heart, Tuija Draganova, Fae Bane."

"Thanks for the information, we'll be going now." Caleb stood and waited for the two troll brothers to get lippy, pausing by a stall to negotiate for a few of the wares and some bullets before they made their way to the ledge of the dwindling Grout Market. The woman on his arm was quiet as the grave she feared, listless and entangled with his coat.

As Caleb felt the enchantment break, he saw the flickers of a multitude returning to their secret space in the absence of a brick in a secure wall.

"Hmh! Course they would. Second I leave."

"Ule found a way out..." Tuija gasped as her feet touched the pavement again. "... there's a way out."

"We don't know what Ule found."

"Caleb. The curse, I can be free."

The bottom of Caleb's world split out.

7

Truce Lines in Granite Sand

Unlike the char of the Sacred Grove, Finnegan's altar smelled of salt and earth, the concentric circles of granite benches a late addition to sarsen pillars and lintels. He rolled his shoulders in the Axis Mundi, the fount of his power so ancient these middling gods didn't remember who built their first doors. Whose moss-like rhizoids took root, then grew to fern.

It was blessed and troublesome fun, the eternity before Creatrix and first emanations decided to add more.

Finnegan was the Lord of the Bluff, a Leprechaun some days, others a simple Oaken Fae who seemed consumed by the young sprouts slithering like ivy down a plunging gorge. War hero, mischief-maker, drunk and nymphomaniac, he was the old oak with a talent and knack for connecting points on the grid of the cosmos. Might as well let the man have his parties, old codger, good for a lark and a laugh.

Kept him from repeating the mistakes of the war in his self-imposed house arrest.

Finnegan inhaled carbon dioxide, held it, and exhaled oxygen. Anonymity and a bit of play was better than rote power. Let the younglings create the fabric of politics, woven from their short lives. Let their spastic sprints stretch out in the course of a single blink. Bit of fun, really, watching from the sidelines.

Twelve of those blinks were snuffed out in strange fire, rumours fluttered in on strange birds through the pub. Nothing for it, Ares' folk on the path with the

Judge called, Athene's companion-child running through doorways to Dover. Cormac in the Grove, hot with cinders and smelling of charnel fires.

As the songbirds swooped in with summons to the Axis Mundi's altar, Finnegan left a devastated pair of raven haired twins for the stone circles. The Truce Council and their retainers began to appear through the posts and lintels, in shimmers of loose starlight.

The fronds of Queen Selyka's hair enlivened with oak leaves, maple and lingonberry as she held her hand to Finnegan through the portal, which smelled of oxygen and green growth. He took it with a careful smirk, walked her to her throne upon the dais in the inner circle of the stones. "Your consort paid me a visit, your Majesty."

"Is that why you smell of smoke?"

"Locked him in the Silent Forest for a fucking timer. What the living fuck happened to him? When did this monumental shift in sanity come about? You need to tell Caleb, before the other Realms do."

Selyka shifted her head to tilt away from his gaze, tapping on a thoroughly human cell phone as songbirds buzzed around her hair and flitted off to relay messages.

"That will be all, Finnegan." She smoothed the flaxen cloth of her dress as she sat, the tightness of her tone enough to dictate a refusal to consider any more of the 'leprechaun's' words.

"If he damages my Groves, I will tell Caleb, and I will break my self-imposed house arrest to deal with him a way far worse than Carolee. See if it'll wait." Another doorway fizzled, a prim woman in her elder years clothed in a houndstooth skirt suit and red leather purse on the crook of an elbow, walked hand in arm with another woman who appeared of similar face but middling age.

"Hera, Queen of Heaven. Hebe. I would say this is a delight, but the circu mstances..." Queen Selyka set her chin with a respectful nod, as Hera sat upon her throne, red gloved hands placed daintily upon her houndstooth skirt. Posh to the nth, with ankles crossed and legs poised in sensible red pumps, Olympus' monarch was as stern and absorbed as a statue with chipped paint, powerful enough in the demure circles of Europe and North Africa. Wives prayed for all sorts of things regardless of years.

"Queen Selyka, how fares the fair folk? Hebe, dear, have a seat please." Hera patted her daughter's hand and Hebe kissed her mother's wrinkle-mottled cheek before taking her place in the front row of the granite concentric circles to sit her purse beside her. "The circumstances are what they are. I for one am eager to see what is being done about it."

"As am I." Another gateway, this one with an echo of golden sand and warm seasons. A man of pristine stature and deep ochre skin, his hair plaited in fine locks with gold decorations entered, a woman on a black suited arm. He shifted both cuffs, the golden 'eye of Horus' cufflinks matching a magnificent collar necklace around his crisp white dress shirt and lapels.

"Pharaoh Horus. Seshat." Hera nodded twice to the two Kehmeti deities, as etiquette demanded. Selyka's jaw tightened, coils of hair like vines slipped in a closer net. "I trust Tiperet enjoyed her tenure recording the Rastenivitsya's first words?"

"Tiperet is dead." Caleb trotted down the stair-like edges of the circle, set his hand momentarily on Hebe's shoulder as the gateways opened again and again. A rustle beside Finnegan, Tuija nudged his shoulder and passed him her flask. Finnegan and Tuija watched the charade of sympathy, Folk after Folk rushing to Horus and Seshat as if the act itself absolved the entire debacle. As if they all didn't have glorious dead in the grove burnt to cinders.

"Claiming ignorance? I forget what day of the week that makes this." Hand in the pocket of grey trousers, Makosh trotted through the portal to Mat Zemlya, the starched collar of her shirt alive with the red and black embroidery of Kiev. Quick to check on Seshat, Makosh's grey-blue eyes were alive as the summer storm, crackling for the snipped yarn of Tiperet and her companions.

Makosh stole a glance at Tuija, lips tight and brow furrowed. The shared gaze stabbed into Tuija's gut and threatened her breath. She wanted to mutter Makosh's name, call out to Matushka Dobrodijka, the honoured mother of her birth Realm. It would do no good. Finnegan set his arm around her and Tuija put her temple on Finnegan's shoulder for comfort. One day soon, she'd be ready to face the irreversible curse in earnest. The fear would fade enough for Finnegan to help her see the long view of events, to begin understanding her gifts. He passed Tuija's flask back to her, and she took a long draught.

A radiant and beautiful woman with raven hair flowing to the rim of her jūnihitoe clung to the arm of a nine tailed Kitsune. The twelve layered kimono was as colourful and pristine as one would expect from Amaterasu. Shakti and a doe eyed girl arrived, skipping off to sit on a bench all on her own, the beads on her sari clinking as she swayed.

Flanked by two of her sons, Mama Yaa took her golden throne with nods to the other goddesses, the colourful headdress only adding to the dignity of the Queen Mother from Yataba.

The gateway opened with a crispness to the air as an ageing woman with greying blonde hair offered her hand. Caleb set his arm out, her home knit wool sweater scratched at his button down. "Help Oldemor to her seat?"

"Lady Frigg." Caleb walked Frigg to her throne with half a scowl. The curious Gna smiled with a rattle of old bones woven on her cloak, then took a seat beside Hebe. Hera's daughter shuffled a bit further from the Norse goddess, making pretence of checking in her handbag for a compact.

"You're allowed to admit to your family, boy. Anyone looks at you, they know who you are." Frigg's cold ice eyes peered across Caleb's face as he turned his cheek from her, once she sat upon her throne in jeans and a sweater, the farmer through and through. "My great-grandson."

"His title is Judge, not 'boy'." Mama Yaa sighed with a slight shake of her head. "Always lip from the farm wife, with the pretty sofa."

Makosh smirked, covering a snort with the back of her manicured hand.

"You look thin, Caleb. I could send Gna to fetch you lefse. Cloudberry preserves are done." Frigg scowled over at the two women, worn in her years of so little worship but what a few rag-tale myths provided.

"No thank you." Caleb detached and went to sit on the stone altar in the circle's core. A flicker of blue eyes found Tuija and Finnegan at the back of the crowd, his gaze softened for a brief second, before the chatter around him had Caleb's mask of authority back on his brow.

"If he won't take a jar of your cloudberry preserves, I'd love them." Warm brown eyes radiated kindness as a man in a plaid button down tucked into scuffed jeans trotted up the dais and took both of Frigg's hands. "Hello, Lady Frigg. How's the farm? That fence still working out?"

"Hei hei, Jase" Frigg squeezed both of Jase's hands, tugged him down to kiss his cheek. "Maybe if you open the jar, the damned boy'll give it a try. Oh, the fence? Latch is working fine."

"You know Caleb, he's got a ton on his mind." Jase gave Frigg's hand one last squeeze and went about whispering pleasantries until he claimed his wooden chair, as simple as the man.

"Hello, Jase, how are you?" Shakti waved one of her many arms, the jewels on her wrists cast a kaleidoscope of holy light across the Axis Mundi in an abundance of joyful colours.

"Good! Good, how are you Shakti? Horus. Sorry for your loss." Horus nodded back, before returning to the hushed conversation he was having with Mama Yaa. A woman in a burgundy sundress sat on another throne, Sister Gaia's hair up in a simple scarf, greying curls caught to defy gravity.

"Yes, yes, greetings and pleasantries. What is this about, Judge?" Cao Guojiu sat upon the Daoist throne across from Pele, who whispered to a woman with resplendent Ta Moko on her chin. The deities and spirits of the Truce Council settled into a lull.

"Someone unsuccessfully attempted to create Mâtarratu incense out of the bodies of a Sacred Grove and Seshat's grand-niece Tiperet." The circle erupted into less of a hubbub than the earlier platitudes of sympathy. From those who did react, Caleb wondered which were out of some hidden secret loop, or playing an angle. "Get your folk to return to your Realms until the heat is off."

"You cannot be serious!"

"Justice must be done!"

"All of us!? You cannot have the authority for that!"

"How dare you..."

Queen Selyka eyed Finnegan, her lips prim in their place and hands gripped onto the throne arms. Frigg spied her sideways, glancing over her body with a quick skim of icy eyes.

"You wanna tell us why?" Mama Yaa pitched up, her alto voice carrying where the others faded to the circle's muted calm. "Why should we all be afraid? People die all the time."

"Whoever did this was unsuccessful, that doesn't mean they don't want to complete the process. It'll be easier if you lay low. Bunker down and don't take unnecessary risks, before someone closer to divinity ends up dead. I need a list from all of you, anyone who knows the ritual, anyone who might be getting a bit hot around the collar."

"Incriminate our own?" Pele piped up, then shrugged a naturally steaming shoulder. "It wasn't me. I'm busy. People love my islands, vacation there all the time."

"Course it wasn't you! What's a volcano got to do with incense? Burn it?" The voice was brash and abrasive to the ears, contaminated by the hard thump of Hephaestus' crutch on the Circle floor as the son of Hera and Zeus hobbled to the front row. "Don't mind me, thought I'd stop by. Mother."

".... second son." Hera's eyebrow rose at the leather vest with its patches, Hephaestus' long tangled beard. She pursed her lips as Hephaestus crammed himself between Gna and Hebe, looked Gna up and down then huffed out a large sniffle. "Ain't many who know that ritual, it's too old for most. Hot enough to burn Sacred Groves? Word from Artie & 'Thenie, whoever lit the fire that torched the beach? Lit up a veteran grove in Artie's territory, too."

"Hey Heph, good on you for joining us. And... for that. Thanks." Caleb let out a breath, shook his head as the Truce circle pitched into a frenzy of accusations and pleas. He let them squawk and toss their tensions around the altar, it was better than the earfuls if he shut them down.

"The Groves are Fae responsibility, the Fae begat them. Where were they, when the Groves burned?" Lady Frigg tossed her hand up and let it fall.

"We are all responsible to honour our dead. The Fae keep the Groves healthy, for the sake of the Truce. Even the loss of one is tragic and cannot be allowed." Finally, a word from the Faerie Queen. Volatile and precious, each grove remained a neutral space. A promise of reunification built out of the haggard desperation of aeons at war.

"For the sake of us all, and the increase of the Fae's population." Makosh shook her head, staring too hard at the lintel of a Realm portal. "You do nothing for free, Selyka. Don't stretch the truth."

"Is it so terrible to see your loved ones returned with sap in their veins? We don't procreate as... readily... as you." Selyka scoffed at Makosh, the sneer slicing into her vines like thorns and brambles. "Excuse us if eradicating extinction took the souls of warriors too tough to die."

"Cursed souls. Don't leave out the ugly with the flower petals, Selyka." Makosh stared at Tuija again, her fingers woven into fists.

"Enough! Makosh, Selyka, take it down to a quiet loathing simmer." Caleb caught Tuija's eyes, gave a tight nod to check in. Standing tall beside Finnegan, Tuija returned the tight nod and waggled her flask.

"I need the list. We need to work backward from who knew the ritual in the first place. Any place where it was written down, chanted about, woven into stories!" Caleb boomed over the cacophony thrown like pilum and spear, the old wounds plastered over by Tiperet and Juliana's macabre end, but still part of the whole.

"Why have you not checked in the one place you know has the required information? Where is the Keeper of the Book of Knowledge? Why isn't Salomon Calder here?" Cao Guojiu searched the crowd, "It seems you lack the one person who could give you the information easier than calling all of us away from our Realms."

"Oh, I'll be checking in on Old Sal, but first, I..."

"Why does the human have the Book at all?" Frigg tossed one leg over the other, leaned back in her throne. "It's a bit tricky to have a Judge, who doesn't carry his tools."

"I'm one man."

"One demi-god." Shakti dipped her chin, eyes wide and lovely with a firm maternal kindness Finnegan wondered if Caleb longed to know better.

"One." Caleb looked to Horus, then Hera before he spoke. "I made a call, it was the right one for me at the time, Salomon was of pure heart and no ulterior motive. He was the perfect one to help, without causing trouble in the Realms."

"And now he's arthritic. Age. It gets the humans every time." Pele shook her head, tsked at the air.

"About that, the last shipment of Idunn's cider got returned? Why haven't you been sipping it? For your own good." Frigg peered at Caleb, waited for the assents of others to embolden her. Murmurs bathed the circle, Finnegan watched Tuija grit her teeth and sidle a step closer to the Truce's central altar. Leave it to the Council to shift the conversation to something less avid in their vapid search for control. "Can't let you get a trick knee, now can we?"

"This isn't about me."

"No, it's about two people dead and a Grove on fire, because somebody let forbidden knowledge get around." Sister Gaia piped up, grimacing with a hard glare at the man sitting on the altar.

"We could talk like I'm the stem of all woe, or! All of you could get me that list! Something to work from, without me having to systematically visit every Realm and shake down your folk until inevitably darker shit comes out I have to deal with before I can get back to solving a double homicide. Two people are dead! And two full on Groves!? People we couldn't afford to lose, not like this!"

"Oh you would love a reason to dive into my Realm and dig around." Pele's hair burned cinder-hot at the ends. "Might get a tan on your pasty flesh."

"Mind if I join? Best smithing in the world comes from angry volcanoes." Hephaestus sniffed out a chuckle as Pele grimaced and turned her face from the pudgy Olympian.

The slip of Horus' eye alit on the thorns amidst roses and lingonberries in Selyka's tendril-hair. The grip of the arms on her throne.

"Don't antagonise him, Caleb's doing what he can. If Caleb says we should go back to our Realms for safety's sake, I'm going to listen and obey. There's talk in the Middling Plane, believers going missing, or showing up in other places, acting odd. It's strange, worthy of further investigation. I can lend Gabriel if anyone wants to join up, see if the murders are connected." Jase leaned forward, elbows on his thighs. "We should all be there for the funerals, eh? Show solidarity."

"I shall send an Enomotia from the 1st Mora, coordinate with Enomotarch Aresides, they could use the training." Hera nodded, hands still folded prim in her lap. "If the Judge says we are to bunker down in our Realms, I for one will also follow the advice. There has not been a divine birth in... too long. Tiperet was the second closest in half an age."

Hera's eyes narrowed in the direction of the altar, lips pressed in a thin line.

"Of course Hera sends Spartans in, if we send..."

"My son's Spartans are Midgardian humans, the lot. They follow every inch of the Truce and have every advantage of their humanity. Of course I shall send them, they are, after all, from the Realm in question. Do we not want to encourage humanity to find its path as we, holy relics, found ours?" Hera's posture rebuked the sneer of the Fae who spoke up. Disquiet peppered the stone circles, as ruminant as smoke in an enclosed room.

"What, you sling Icarus on me, and now their brother? Enomotarch Aresides, thanks. Best and brightest of Kopis, that lot. And heard, Jase. It's on my list." Caleb rocked his shoulders, the list dowsed any peace in the back of his mind. Names of sinners without contrition, repeat offenders who went through Midgard as if it were their Realm. The human Folk needed him too, shunted down the list by a cantrip of priority onto the next largest threat. The massive and the magical. "I could use some help there, actually. Bunch of smaller players or human Folk... never have time to get to the supplicant, who needed a hand. If anyone wants to step up."

"We cannot afford to lose any of our bloodlines. Whatever aid we can bring to the Judge's table is worth our efforts. But I will caution you, Judge. Take back the Book. Never let it out of your sight again, I will not be so forgiving if you continue to spurn the advantages we gave you." Hera's words rustled in the Realm-Seats. Finnegan glanced at the rough glares, the caustic stares and sympathies. Scared, the lot, or so it seemed to him from where he waited in silence. Entire generations of deities who in their might, their near omniscient mercies, feared the ends which came to all, even gods. "I will not look lenient on your excuses."

One of the oldest of them who attended, Hera knew more than most the whims and slings and Parisian arrows. No one asked about Zeus anymore, or Cronus, or Ouranos. Few wondered where Eriskegal or Tiamat or Baal were holding out, too frightened of finding nothing but ashes which others, if they knew, could collect and create the incense necessary to kill a god.

Not even Hades or Spenta Armaiti kept Izanami's recipe for such a chthonic drug.

"Find the murderer and conspirators, and end their lives. And if the Scandinavian's cider is not to your liking, I will have Ares force nectar down your throat until you live twice as long as you desire. It cannot be allowed that you choose your own life span. All in favour?"

"If the Olympians are sending aid to the Judge, it should be on equal ground to the rest of us. Only fair." Makosh's smile radiated out of naturally red lips, the golden sheen to her hair as brilliant as wheat during a warm harvest's sun. She tugged a red embroidered cuff of her vyshyvanka, eyes stroked along Caleb's bowing shoulders, the pride dispelled from his posture an iota at a time during the Truce meet. "I have someone in mind."

"Oy! If you're shilling off someone to the Judge, then we are too."

"No! You have been told to keep your distance, Frigga. Keep it." Shakti raised to her feet, chin proud and commanding.

"You get to send some avatar of Vishnu, but we can't send Thor to check up on his own grandson?" Frigg launched out of her ornate carved throne,

"I'm not sending my warriors to run errands across the Middling Plane, we have our own way of leashing kooks." Pele set her shoulders in her seat, the fire of her eyes brilliant in their heat. "If you want to help the Judge, solve your own problems in your own places. I will not vote for a powder keg of vigilantes from the Realms pouring across Midgard like comic book idiots."

"Pele, he asked for help." Shakti spewed a terse sigh, settling back down on her ornate throne and its bright pillows.

"Maybe if you kept a better handle on your people in the Middling Plane, the Judge wouldn't need it. Even the best surfer bails out in a gnarly barrel. We help by containing our people and keeping to neutral spaces. If you didn't get so lenient with..."

"Well, I do think that's a little unfair."

"How dare..."

"Lenient! See what you'd do without flora in your Realms!"

"We can't all live in perfect places, some of us need to shop for our larder!"

"Hey!" Eyes shut to the growing argument, Caleb gripped the side of the altar with both hands, shoulders hovering back and forth. "Don't get twisted! It's not worth it, settle down."

"I'm sorry, Caleb. Without a consensus, we can't give you anything, you know that." Makosh tried for a perturbed smile, the graciousness and weight of Destiny's yarn in her hands enough indication she knew the potential was doomed from the start. Must've been a signal of her quality she tried at all, Finnegan thought from his view of the bickering deities.

"I am still sending Enomotarch Aresides to check on the Sacred Groves and act as a deterrent. You are welcome to send what you find appropriate of your own. I, for one, am not allowing our honoured dead to go scourged and burnt to all and sundry while we bicker over whether the Judge receives deputies." Hera pursed her lips, nodding to Amaterasu, who while quiet during the discussion, held the aura of one who thought deeply and was percolating an idea. "All in favour of ensuring Judge Mauthisen receives an appropriate draught of nectar or ambrosia? And demanding the priority of taking the Book of Knowledge back from Keeper Calder? At least we can agree on that?"

"I can't do this alone." Caleb suspended in the middle, ruminating in a grumbling silence as each of the Truce Realm leaders or representatives gave their acceptance of Hera's words. Tuija hovered at the circle's zenith, transfixed by the slump to his shoulders as Caleb witnessed another battle lost.

"You alone were given the task. You alone were in the unique predicament to bind us within this Truce. We shall not see kindly any bastardization of that truth. Go. Do your duty and be done with it." Hera waved her hand. Caleb hopped off the altar, and stormed off, as pleasantries broke out in combination with the hushed whispers of inevitable petty squabbles. Was he beginning to crack, as Cormac said?

Watching the way Caleb vacated, not stopping to chat with Hephaestus or reach for one of Jase's hugs or Mika's slug on the shoulder, Finnegan pursed his lips. Tuija put her hand on Caleb's back and whisked him away.

"Caleb!" Finnegan trotted up after him two steps too late. The Judge was gone.

8
THE PUB'S HEART BEAT

The Pub's liminal spaces thrummed with partying Folk, people in transit and the entourages the Truce Council kept. Caleb stormed through the crowd, guarded by the hushed whispers of the damned or those near enough to a Truce Breaker to have felt Caleb's pistol against their loved ones' temples. Tuija diverted behind the bar, where Donovan filled drinks. Tuija grabbed a bottle of whiskey, the label lost under her hand.

"Hey! At least tell me what kind it was, Tuj! My numbers'll be off again!" Donovan poured pints with multiple ghostly arms, his apparitional body a flow of fog and glassware, as orders were filled and spoken for by nebulous hands.

"The brown kind!" Tuija gesticulated behind her at the disembodied gjengänger, the ghost with enough ties to corporeality to serve the denizens of the pub.

"Are you serious!? Don't you do this to me again, y'all're nuts!" Donovan threw his towel onto the bartop. "I blame you for this, Mauthisen! Ain't half the trouble when you're not... gah! Hey! No fair!"

The glass Tujia threw tumbled through the air, narrow in its escape from ending broken on the floor, when another set of hands caught and righted it.

"You sure?" Caleb wove his arm around her waist, flashing the label at Donovan over Tuija's head. "I hear she's a record holder for feisty going back an aeon."

"I am too much woman and warrior for the both of you."

"My saviour!" Two of Donovan's hands cued in the whiskey to a notepad as the others rushed to pour more drinks. A mad dash of the crowd butted against the bar in varying shades of corporeality, limbs of multiple configurations clutching for glasses in a wild charge.

"What's Finn going to do, bill me?" Tuija's hand was rough in Caleb's palm and tugged him toward a reconstructing staircase made of lost bric-a-brac and wandering old carpet. He followed in automatic pilot through the twists and bends of Finnegan's hidden upper floors.

"We ought to talk."

Tuija tossed a sideways smirk back at Caleb as they rounded the last corner before she kicked open a door with her bark clad foot. "In."

"Yes Ma'am." Caleb dove into the offered doorway, the echo of uneasy laughter permeating the walls of Finnegan's Pub.

The sky of Tuija's flat was a vault of kaleidoscopic starlight tempered with a shock of blue so rich the jewel of the sun appeared a common bauble. To the left, the night was so black it sucked his soul toward it, a slim memory of the primordial chaos which tempted and accused in equal measure. The moon spun in place, an outline of chariot and charioteer milk-white as a thin nebula. The flat opened onto the back vault of the worlds, both a piece of the primordial forest and bastion of modernity with a flat screen tv and kitchen tucked onto the only wall.

Dropping his knapsack at the door, Caleb kicked off one boot at a time beside Tuija's on the mat.

"No matter how many times I come back, it astounds me how Finnegan apologises in style." Tuija tugged the bottle from Caleb's hand and set it on a marble slab countertop. As she searched for a couple of glasses, she opened the refrigerator and huffed. "On the rocks?"

"I'm fine with neat. Guess I've been distracted."

"Understatement of century, last few months you've been a samovar with no fuel for the fire. Water's in the creek by the leaves of Yggdrasil. Should be cold, still winter in Niflheim. Har har." She shoved a pitcher of children's laughter back into the refrigerator and shut the door to lean against it, one hand in the pocket of her jeans. "They should not have dismissed you."

"Can we not deflect to me, please?" Caleb cracked the top of the whiskey, taking a whiff of the alcoholic nuttiness and spice from the top of the bottle. He set his phone down on the counter, and flipped it screen down. "I'd rather discuss the Grout Market first, then get to Icarus' reports."

A stiff pull from the bottle, and Caleb grunted at the slick burn of a fairly balanced irish whiskey, all peat and vanilla and caramel on the back end of smoke. He took another drag before holding it out for Tuija. Eyes which should have matched narrowed on the bottle, one as amber as its contents and the other a subtle blue.

Buzzes continued to scratch at Caleb's back pocket. He dug out the notebook and flipped it open with his thumb to a page filled with missives, detailed calls and chimes for his presence from a myriad of Realms. Rubbing his face with his hand, Caleb tapped the book on his thigh. "I ought to get started on these, too."

"Give it me." Tuija yanked the book out of Caleb's hand and pored over the rapidly dwindling script. Clicking a pen yanked from a rustle through Caleb's pocket, Tuija scrawled words in cyrillic. "Leave him alone five minutes."

"Hey, it could be important." Caleb held out his hand to take the notebook back, only to watch Tuija pitch it further off into the mystic flat.

"You can be mine alone for five minutes."

"Only five? I might not be up for such a shallow relationship."

"We spent so many years using your birth as a reason for this tense peace. They think you're nothing but its symbol... but..." She saw a skewed reflection in the glass of the bottle, the cedar bark which grew out of her face like an untameable cancer, its inevitability as disastrous as the dart which struck. "... Ule got out."

"We don't know what Ule did. He's probably dead, we..."

"If he got out..."

"We only have the story of a fucked up seer to go on, it's not enough evidence to confirm anything."

"So we find the evidence."

"Yes! Yes, we do, we look but..."

"But?"

"I need to figure out this case."

"It'll be this one then the next, then what, Cale? By the time they give you a minute to breathe, I'll be halfway to a Redwood! And as much as Finnegan begs me to trust him, I'm not ready for that, yet." Tuija slapped her palm on the counter. "If it was Delilah asking, would you do it?"

Caleb's lungs cut out like a knife taken to a filled paper bag. "Where did this come from?"

"She's got a hold on you."

"Delilah and I broke up fourteen years ago, think maybe now's not the time?"

"And every hour she comes up in a Truce conversation, or as a curse in the Pub you go running to check on her."

"No I... Tuija, why does this matter right now?"

"If Delilah asked you for a way out of the Truce, would you do it?"

"What? No!"

"Don't..." She gesticulated at his chest, "Don't lie you'd look, you know you would."

"Not with your life on the line!" His shout echoed across the vault above them, transmogrifying into a line dark as space without stars, which coiled around the nearest bauble above like a ring. "Someone is targeting the Rastenivitsya and I will be damned to every apocalyptic underworld if I don't find who it is and stop them before you go up in flames! I don't give a shit about Delilah, or if Ule found some magical mcguffin! He can have it for the thirty hours I need to stop the world from going ablaze with the love of my life along with it!"

The echoes returned as muffled as Tuija's silence, as she wrapped her hands around his wrist and tugged him into her body. "Say it. Tell me again, what you said so clearly. Say it again?"

"I..." Caleb's throat worked, jaw taught. He struggled with the sound, the essence so clear in every second of his hand on her cheek, brushing the hair away from the back of her neck. "I lo-... you're the lo..."

Tuija sighed and let go of him to pace the grass and moss of her floor. Hands in her hair, she shook her head and bit down on the ire which tried to erupt from her lips. "What did she do to you?"

"Nothing! I... don't know." Caleb reached for Tuija's shoulder and found it soft under his hand. He pulled her into a hug, his cheek propped on her hair. "You're the one who said no, not me. I thought you realised I didn't change what I wanted."

"If being with you is political, us getting married in any tradition is as much a declaration of allegiance as Ares claiming the God-Kingdom of Midgard."

"Is that why you're pushing back on Ule? Tuija, did you stop long enough to think your metamorphosis isn't a deal breaker to me? As Finn infinitely reminds us, we've got centuries to work through it, the arsonist isn't taking that kind of time."

"Oh, yes, I'm sure there can be concessions made for when I bury myself like an acorn and grow into a tree. The ring might not fit around my branches, but maybe Hephaestus could build me something, if I wake up knowing as much of my own name. Let alone anything else."

"That's not fair." Kissing her hair, Caleb rocked in their embrace. "Hold out a little longer, we'll figure it out."

The cure for her curse spat at his inability to find it, a raucous jitter in the back of his mind every day the bark which covered part of her skin increased, or she knicked herself, or got a bruise which in a day's time turned into another patch of cedar. An urge to build a castle for her to inhabit, a place where she'd be safe and stay by him was as dashed as the futility of time's spell.

Bastions and prisons were identical but for the bars. To love Tuija was to recognize a life in a cage was not anything close to her wandering desires.

"I did hold out for one hundred and sixty three years!" Tuija tried to slow her breathing. Ran her fingers through hair which tangled between sheets of cedar bark. Grit-toothed, Tuija groaned and yanked as Caleb surged in, both hands untangling her hair from partially transformed fingers.

"I know! I know, kjæreste I know. I… hold on." He whispered into her scalp, hand freed and fingers woven through hers to bring her arm down to his waist. Brushing her hair back with his other hand, Caleb clucked his tongue, rocking gently in place. A sordid helplessness consumed "Hold on. There's got to be…"

"A way? What if Ule found it, Caleb? What if Ule found the way out?" Tuija settled into his arms, the scratch of her cheek against his shoulder enough to catch the wool of his sweater. Wrapping her into an embrace, Caleb hummed a melody the origin of which he didn't remember. His hand stroked her hair, mind swimming the chaotic waters which surged at his periphery any time he closed his eyes. Tuija settled her arms around the small of his back, rocking in his rhythm, face pressed into his jumper.

"You're scared, and it's valid." The sun tracked across the sky, fading in brightness for the balm of the evening rise of the moon in its chariot, and Caleb wondered if Tuija's long day was ebbing to the twilight hours of an existence dwarfing his ten times. He continued to hum, kissed her temple as he felt her arms shake in a mirror of his own. "But… you're strong like none others were, before they dug their graves. You're here and you're fighting and… maybe Ule found a way, but the chances are way less slim that he's dead in some alley after pissing off the wrong gangster…"

"But if he didn't…"

"If he didn't we'll track him down, but… for us to go there, to leave the Truce, it's… never been done. I've spent the better part of a hundred and fifty years dealing with Folk doing their best to escape its tenets or get some fucked up version of revenge. All they found was death on a good day." Caleb felt the pressure of the worlds, the executioner's cloak an invisible mass bending his shoulders. What could he offer her? If Ule was the keeper of his own forbidden way, if Caleb found Tuija's freedom from the curse eating her alive, could he join her in that desolate place?

Two beings cast out of a second Eden to till the earth with no help nor heard whisper of the gods? Could he leave? Would he be damning Realms to a new cacophony the second he stepped away and pushed past where they could follow?

"If Ule didn't find the way out, whoever's torching Sacred Groves is as much a danger to you..."

"Don't..."

"I have to think about this, I have to be prepared. Whoever is torching Groves has a vendetta against the Rastenivitsya and you're the last one left. Going after the bastards torching the dead matters and I need you on my side. Focused. If Ule is out and not dead, he's likely stable and comfortable. Which means we have time. All you need to do is keep swinging."

"It's getting harder."

"We're going to figure it out. I'll tear down half the Cosmos to do it."

"Only half?"

"Gotta leave enough standing so we have a decent retirement plan." Caleb smirked into her hair, Tuija's lopsided smile moved against his shirt, her arms tightening around his lower back.

"Some decent hunting grounds, space for a dog or seven..."

"Picture it. Everything you want to do, everywhere you want to go."

"You're coming with me." She spread her fingers along his back, looked up to a face creased with the weight of the Realms.

"There was no manual for being the Judge." Caleb shook his head, doused his mouth with more whiskey and sighed into the air with its thick charge, and thinner texture. "I've got Realms stacked upon Realms, stacked upon the cosmos and somehow I'm the one who looks at situations with a fairness I don't feel. Keep doing what I think is best, and inevitably one or more groups are pissed off to high heavens, which is in itself a problem, since Hera's only recently back on Olympus' throne. Did you know the Hellenes are probably listening to this conversation right now?"

"If they are, I could use a pizza, no cheese, extra basil, prosciutto... truffle. Da. Fire oven, not the hot electric things. Oh, and wine. Whiskey is the bomb, but a good few bottles of red would set the evening off. Send it via Finn's. With one of those chocolate cheesecakes on the side. Do you want anything? If... if they're listening, that means they're available, right? Mercury would probably do the delivery for a lark. Oh, and bubbles. We could use a bottle of bubbles."

Caleb blinked with a slow shake of his head, and a dawning smile. "Yeah, beef dip for me. Extra au jus, extra mushrooms. Thicker than Tuija's wrist. The wine sounds... sounds good."

They hung in companionable silence for as long as it took the giggles to break out first from Tuija, then Caleb. He hucked his phone backward onto the grass, and shook his head.

"You are the most amazing woman in the Realms."

"Think we'll get my pizza?"

Caleb ached, set his elbows against his knees as he laughed and shook his head slowly from side to side, taking Tuija's hand to walk them onto a grassy hill sized right to use as a seat. "I don't know, but now I really want a sandwich. Eh. I'll be fine."

"You're not though. Don't take an empath to see you're in need of some serious R&R."

"Oh yeah! I can put a 'closed for business' shingle up and trot off into the sunset. While I'm at it, I'll stumble magically into the ones torching Groves, and happen across the perfect way to solve all woes. Including yours."

"Sarcasm. Worst invention in human history since the laser disc."

"Oooo, oww, shots fired! Don't go near Athene with that, the laser disc was one of her babies."

"Oh... did I offend the Olympian academic? S-save me, Caleb save me! I thrust myself into thy arms for judgement!" Tuija made a play of flopping into Caleb's lap. He grunted hard, but pulled her up to sit on his thighs, one arm hemming her in and holding her against his sore side. "You copacetic, Cale?"

"Guess there's a lot broken in the Judge tonight."

"Everyone's a little bit broken, how empathy works, eh?" The warrior played at his button down, fingers on the cufflinks. "None of us know what to do, but look at the Truce and find too much blood outside of it to stomach. I don't envy you. Being Judge? It's... a metric lot. But I've seen you, Caleb. The way you conduct business, drink Finn's booze and trudge to the next spot half-sober until those bursts of magic in your pocket tell you where to go. You lost something... or someone. And I think I know who to blame, her name starting with a D..."

"Tuija, we don't have time. I should start looking at leads, hopefully enough of the Realms took me serious enough to count off a few Folk."

She tightened the arm around his neck, pressed a sloppy half-kiss on his cheek. "Leave it for the morning."

"Is it morning here? Over there? Up there?" Caleb squinted and pointed this way and that, toward the sun, to the edge of the blue. Tuija burst out laughing, clanked the side of her head into his as her laughter infected him with deep chuckles. "Couldn't resist."

"Hushabye." Her lips crashed upward, arm around his neck. Caleb reached his hands along her waist, picked her up so she straddled him, the juxtaposition of Finnegan's curse scratching against his skin sang as loud as Aphrodite's chorus. They crashed into the night, the bottle of whiskey forgotten, until a knock came at the door.

A man in Kopis Industries uniform averted his eyes, when a shirtless Judge swung it open and took delivery of a bag filled with clinking bottles, a rolled up sandwich in brown paper, thermos of au jus, and one extra large pizza box.

"Are... holy fuck!" Tuija grabbed hold of Caleb's shirt and pulled it over her chest, as Caleb kicked the door closed and walked mutely to the marble countertop to put the food and wine down. "You were... every day?"

"At least the Hellenes answer back. The rest? I'm sure they hear it, they don't say. Took that oh so common 'not our problem' approach of 'wouldn't want to rock the boat'. Wine?" Caleb dug in the bag for the first bottle, a red with a label in French. He searched for a corkscrew, finally grabbed his pen knife and dug it out with a twist. Caleb drank the first glug from the bottle, held it out for Tuija. "Your pizza's getting cold."

"... yeah. Hunger."

"Got murders to solve."

"Why don't you cantrip it? Your new phone. The passive magic for a pocket cantrip doesn't leave enough residue to trigger the wards."

"What?"

"The wards that alert your little black book? They get triggered by passive spells created and maintained by the Realms. I was one who helped set them up for neutral ground. There are cantrips and minor magics that don't trigger. Cleaning a stain off a blouse, card divinations, passive scrying. Cantrips to open windows or keep your phone or notebook or wallet in your pocket, even if it gets removed. They're minor magic that remains irrelevant to the Truce.... didn't you learn this?"

"..." Caleb took a bite of his drenched sandwich and waited until the unctuous meat sloshed down his throat before shaking his head. "I knew about the cantrips, but how far can something the size of a phone get from its' owner before the Truce guards trigger?"

"A hemisphere?"

"Pardon?"

"A hemisphere is..."

"I mean what the heck? Why that far?"

"We had this fortune teller, a divination queen, when we began to form the Treaty Guards. She saw planes coming. Didn't want someone's spell books, grimoires, icons or shit getting lost in baggage claims." Tuija folded a slice of pizza in half, and took a bite, splashed red wine into a couple of stemware glasses from her cupboard and shoved one over at Caleb. "Try being the one to decipher her babbling, metal birds in the sky, who ate people then regurgitated them later... it was fucked until the 30's."

"Yeah, planes are whack."

"Right!? Why can't they use doors like normal Folk?"

"I know! What's with all this time in transit!? They..."

"Don't have any time to lose!?"

"Yes! Thank you!" Caleb slapped his palm against the marble and chowed down on another bite of his sandwich, drowned down the beef dip and au jus with a healthy gulp of red wine. Savoury garlic and salt paired with rich spice. "Like, why spend hours, a half day or more in airports waiting for a plane to get set in a seat with less room than a cattle car, to cross oceans or continents, when doors exist, right!?"

"I know! It's so strange, and their cars!? I mean, hey, I do love a good stick shift, but come on!"

"Good with a stick, are you?" Caleb nodded at her with a sly smirk.

"Oh! You wish, errand boy, I love a good stick... shift. If it's active enough, keeps its pace on the throttle."

"I bet. Would take a hefty transmission to keep you happy."

"Depends, sometimes I enjoy an easier ride."

"I got my licence a while back, haven't used it much."

"So this is some form of sick joke?" Tuija flicked her fingers up from the dessert package, a foil condom wrapper and one-time use lube packet between her index and middle fingers.

"Sclep, I am going to murder you myself and turn you into incense."

"Is he working with Finn on this?"

"Bastards!"

"Has it been that bad? We got pizza."

"What? No! It's the cursed meddling."

"Caleb, they might've shoved us in a direction, but we take it from there. Cool your beans."

"Sorry. It's been a rough..."

"... century?"

"Decade and a half." Caleb's chin fell, he shook his head then lifted his eyes along Tuija's body. Nipples barely visible in his shirt, the way her cedar curse cut into her flesh, tempered her into a magical being of no mistake. How could they find some mystic freedom? "... Tuija..."

Caleb tugged on her hand, until she straddled him, ran his right hand up her spine to the cedar-burned bundles of skin and bark on her neck. He searched her lips, the kind turn of her eyes as sharp as they were when she slaughtered for Perun. Her nose batted at his and he let it, batting back. Their lips brushed and he gasped.

"I promise not to break you." She whispered in his ear, kissed his earlobe and nipped at the cartilage of his ear. Caleb nuzzled into her neck, voice hoarse as he spoke sensuous secrets. Hopes and dreams. Desires for the night. Tuija pulled back, and nodded. "I agree to your terms. On one condition: I come with you. You leave me behind one time and a demon almost serves your liver for Sunday Roast. You need me."

"Yes." Hand on the back of her neck, Caleb attempted to disable the unease of being in her partitioned expanse in the Axis Mundi. The hum of liminal space seeped into the grassland and the dance of the sun and moon, a permanent sense of somewhere else or the strike of a belonging two steps too far over the cliff. Finnegan might've given Tuija access to the space, but the constant morph of land and magic shifted any sense of permanence as far off as the stone circle, where the Altar laid in state.

This was another space in passing, another temporary spot they occupied without owning. Tuija caught him up, arms around his neck and kissed him. Under the stars, swathed in the stringent sun and moon in their eternal retreat, Caleb and Tuija inspected what life became when an old soldier and a judge tried to forget about their pains for a while.

9

MUTE ROTTEN ROOTS

"When I found the book left stagnant in the old man's basement, I had no idea of the Mystic Realms or the Truce. I knew nothing but the fairy stories of youth. Films and animations. A few folktales. There was no God, for we killed him, left his bones for dead and moved past the societal requirement for a guiding hand. I would not believe in one." Stana set the ereader in her pocket with a definitive clunk. Refused the message which flashed on the backlit screen. Refused to read the document pages, articles put further up in the priority list generated by the small voice inflected with magic's artifice, when the Book spoke to her in her mother tongue. No, she would not be told what to read from a book. "Imagine then, finding the Book of Knowledge. The repository of all wisdom, all information. And it was full of deities clinging for scraps. Foetid relics of collective weakness."

Stana slumped into a chair, holding her head in one hand. The struggle of the Hellene Legionnaire bound by rope knots she learned from her Book was less delicious than Stana wished. A gag stuffed in the Legionnaire's mouth was slick with sweat and mucus. The woman's head cranked back by ropes, hands and feet tied together behind her, body stretched on the floor. One foot at a time, Stana propped her heels on the Hellene's rib cage. Cooed sweet whispers to hush the woman into a compliance which would never come, for she was of Ares' folk and they all died fighting.

A firebrand who combated everything now, not only lines or tribute ties, but apathy and cultural degradation. How the Olympian of War ended up in the back end of the universe's shakiest set of deals, as a cultural icon and peacemaker sat as ill as Jesus Christ returning only to roll up his sleeves and start a carpentry business. The tales the Book told! Jase and his band of androgynous assistants launching into projects on the most needy side of town in every city. Every place.

And what did the Church do, when their saviour performed signs, wonders and solid craftsmanship? Eke out a small per diem. Others rustled up, took up arms and weapons and called for a holy war Jase refused to spearhead. War was Ares' thing now. Maybe it was always Ares' thing more than anyone else but Tyr (but wasn't that another name for Ares?), maybe Perun or Durga.

The whole concept rotted between Stana's teeth.

On the table beside a cup of cold tea perched the take out container Stana scooped the residual ash from the burn into, a few charnel pieces dotted in the grey soot like islands.

All that, all that.

"I thought it would be harder. Torching living beings. But the match lit, their bodies went up. It was not as hard as I expected. Book! Tell me why." Stana patted her pocket, but the Book rested in its silence.

"And you think you did well?" A series of vines congealed in the corner of the room, budding with a single sickly flower, which opened and flapped its petals like loose yellow gums.

"I did the ritual. The spell is as you predicted."

"It didn't work."

"How do you know it didn't? Have you checked?"

"I would feel the heart-wrench in the air, and I feel nothing but the disappointing lack of breeze." The flower petals flopped useless.

"Did your bitch throw you into the Silent Forest again?"

"Come release me." The petals slopped together, their vocal echoes a slick reminder of Stana's early teachings.

"In due time, I'm tired. I have more to read."

"All the knowledge in the world at your fingers is useless, when you don't know what to look for, I fed you the lead on the ritual expecting results."

"The dryad and the other one are dead. The Egyptian who noticed the Book."

"Yes, but the ritual didn't work, did it? The spell didn't take."

"I'll try again, with this one."

"That's no god." The yellow petals combed at the Hellene's shoulder, and the woman bucked, jaw gnawing at the fabric in her mouth.

"She's a believer in them."

"Do you not know what god means, mammal? A deity. Divine being. This is a human with beliefs, maybe a bit of Zeus blood in her, as many of the Mediterranean ones do. Not a god."

"Why do you care? You got what you wanted, both the bitches dead." Stana tapped at the corner of the ereader, pages of notation on spells and rituals, the history of names flashed before retina and iris. Through the optic nerve and into the cruel brain.

"It matters, because death isn't enough if it doesn't come with the incense!" Cormac's disembodied voice broke from the petals, cracked by distance and desire.

"They will be dead. I promise."

"No. Not enough. We cannot kill the gods without it."

"Why? Why incense? I thought it would be a weapon, or incantation. The casting of a soul away from their body for the final redress. But incense?" Stana shoved the groaning Hellene to the floor and propped her feet up on the captive's side.

"What do all gods need to survive?"

"Air?"

"Worship." Coiled vines spasmed from the pot in the corner of Stana's newest borrowed dwelling. The Downtown Core of Vancouver expanded on the other side of massive floor to ceiling windows, house propped atop the mountainous North Shore. Lamps and other lights remained unused behind her, the kitchen dark and silent but for the thrum of the fridge.

It was the sort of house Stana only saw in architectural magazines left unread on rich clients' coffee tables. Aspirational expanses of white walls, glass and brushed metal with paintings as lost of context as the lives of the intellectual thousands, who searched for more reasons to prove the wait for Godot was worthwhile. As if the act of existing was the only necessity for taking up space. As if a fledgeling existence meant screaming at those people, who took up too much space, their roots breaking the mottled grey of chic, eco 'non-flooring'.

Why the wealthy wanted concrete floors was beyond her, until she realised how expensive the rugs were, when she had to clean spilled coffee after the Dr told her friend not to worry. It was alright, Stana would clean it, don't worry dear it's not your fault. Parkinsons was horrible and they'd sit on the porch, get some blankets. Stana, can you help me please, I'll pay you extra since I know you're at the end of your time, today.

"And worship usually comes on the back of incense or some sort of smoke offering in most religions. Poison the worship, you poison the gods." Stana let her eyes crawl over to the leather couch underneath an abstract painting from an artist nobody would remember five minutes after seeing it. There, knees indecently parted in a grey pencil skirt, Dr. Elena Liu sat. Chin hung down to her rumpled white blouse, arms slack, eyes wobbling between shut and searching the space between her knee and unshod toes.

"Now get me out of here and help me find another god. One you can hate with some passion." The yellow petals flopped onto the floor Stana polished once upon another life, part of one stroked Mrs. Liu's foot and her eyes lifted.

They locked with Stana one more time, chapped lips working in a stinking mouth.

"You shouldn't have told me your name." Stana rose and patted the book in her pocket, whispered in a language which cut at the world.

A fog poured from her mouth and nostrils, speckles of ink peppered at her eyelids as Stana recited the traverse runes, as she wove Elena Liu's soul-name into the spell like spider silk across a fly's passage. Dr. Liu grunted, and her head fell, then her shoulder, to the leather of the couch she'd been so proud of, when she got off shifts at the oncology department of St. Paul's.

The portal ripped Midgard's reality into loose spun rags, and Stana stepped through as she felt the name and the soul attached to it evaporate like dew under the summer sun.

And there was no sound left, in the Silent Forest.

Nothing but the faintest whisper shut in her mouth like the silences pronounced when one lived in a refugee camp, and dared not whisper about which village they were from, lest the next family over be from the wrong place.

Stana walked through the Forest with the same even gait, claiming space she didn't own as the Forest held its breath before a haggard exhalation. Leaves crumpled under her feet but made no sound, she broke a flowering twig from a tree and wondered at how it snapped without the crackle. Stepping over a burnt husk of a tree with limbs hugging its trunk, Stana smelled the charcoal rot on the tepid, immobile air. A bird flitted to a new nest, a deer skittered with doe eyes wide and nostrils flared as it bolted away from the usurper.

An ember hung in mid-air, another as a trail of motes and smoke, the only convection one of motion Stana and the scant fauna of the Silent Forest provided. She passed through the thicket until trails of grey wove in circular patterns and there in a copse encircled by ash sloughing trees he stood.

Mouth a caricature of humanity's smile, Cormac put a fire on his forearm out with his hand, rubbing the birch bark skin until a dusting of ash poured down to the drab, grey ground.

There had been grass, once.

And her strange godling, the Fae who promised in whispers and easy exhalations of pure oxygen he could give her the paths and passages through the damned book, cocked jewel-amber eyes. Pulled roots which puddled together like cobbled feet from the loam. He bowed low, the threaded willow braids of what passed for hair flopped over his strange face.

He signed for her, motioning to a glade where the trees had been scoured of their lives, names written in ashes with enough potency he got his message through the Realms from his satellite seed in Stana's plant pot.

'This isn't what I'm for.' The Book's letters grew on the ereader's screen and Stana wiped them away, clicking for the spell and her list of names. She would need someone of note, or a dozen of the humans milling about wasting time until they got old enough to do nothing with their lives. The curse on Stana's lips ebbed noiseless. Counting soul-names, another form of currency Stana refused to be strangled by. 'Do not murder in my name.'

No, Stana needed more names.

She shook the ereader, when the names jumbled, sorted them by note. No, not that one, they might be useful. How many times had she dug into that one's soul? Did they have enough left to keep responding? The growl she wished to hear faded and Stana dug into the list of names until one or a few called to her.

The Whore's daughter.

Enough magic in the Enchantress, her daughter proved resilient to a welcome extreme. After the first thrill of the name's power in France, a bunch of screaming teens swathed in their own privilege, Stana highlighted Delilah's young progeny. Her mother hadn't noticed, or hadn't thought anything of the child's hollowing out.

The name had uncharacteristic power. A bright future stolen, some intrinsic leftovers from the mother? Any future the girl might be left to pale in the shadow of these meddling gods. Yes, the whore's daughter would rip them through the veil and tangle of Selyka's forest.

Delilah wouldn't mind, she never did.

Stana wrote the spell on the ereader, twice after the words jumbled and Stana slapped the cursed device. With a willful grip of both it and Cormac's shoulder,

Stana wrenched them through the tangled ruin of space. Back into Dr. Liu's living room with its view of Downtown Vancouver through the proud cedars and sharp bank of the mountainside. Stana screamed to get the silence out of her ears, to make up for the rush of power when she used a name which had enough left to it to grip her.

"Oh beautiful sound... Stana, did you plan to keep fertiliser as an appetiser for me? You're not so considerate." Cormac dusted himself off with a shake and the descent of ash to the carpet. Motioning his head to the body on the couch, he clacked spindle fingers together. Stalked toward the body with his root-like feet splayed on smooth concrete.

"Why would I bother? Oh. If you must." Stana shrugged and returned to the kitchen for a glass of orange juice, from a stainless steel refrigerator with fingerprints all over in an act of petty defiance. "Don't be too happy with this house. The food is running low, and I don't know how much more she has left in savings and on her credit cards."

"Worried about food when I'm around. Hah... well if you don't want me to snack, you'll have to do something with that one, before it too turns into fertilizer." Cormac's arm detangled into a series of willow-like branches and curled around the body of Elena Liu, cocooning her in a tangle. Lifted and pulled out to the porch, the body dangled as Cormac parted the soil under well watered sod. A shallow grave for the doctor, who paid well enough to be remembered by the cleaning lady. He shuddered as his roots expanded down, deep in the water rich soil of North Vancouver, and began to whisper the body through an expedited decomposition. Cormac was hungry, after the magic used to whisper in Stana's ear from a Realm afar.

As he swayed outside, a gnarled willow hearing the bustle of the Inlet on the stiff breeze, Stana pulled a shaker bottle out of the cupboard, poured in milk and a few scoops of protein rich meal replacement from the doctor's supply. She shook it as the vines around the Hellene loosened at the mouth, and the Kopis officer worked her jaw with a groan.

"What is your name, little Hellene?" Stana sunk down on her haunches, waggled the bottle in front of the bound woman's face.

"Babs Thortan."

"What is your name? Give me your name and this? Won't it feel better to be out of these chains?" Stana's smile never crossed the distance between cheek and eye, the severe mouse brown of each iris as unpleasant as the greasy strands of hair overgrown from a pixie cut.

"Mimsy Bob, you bitch."

"Uh-uh." Stana clucked her tongue, stuck the bottle at the Hellene's lips and pushed until the Hellene gurgled. Gripping the captive's hair, Stana yanked her head back until the liquid poured down her throat. The Hellene gurgled in gasped swallows, no pleasure to be taken from the caloric intake. No respite for the sore and tingling limbs kept bound behind her. "There. Isn't it better? Don't you want to be champion of your own intentions? All I'm doing is giving us a chance."

"The gods don't do shit until called upon. You sit here cutting people's souls to shreds with some faulty idea that gods are tripping us up every day. My gods supply what I need through salary and tax forms at the end of the fiscal calendar. You want to kill them? End the gods? No. You want to become them, you raggedy bitch."

"Fine. Call on your Ares, then. Call on the gods and they will rescue you."

"No." The Hellene croaked, red sores stretched across her cheeks like a large, macabre smile.

"You are going to die hogtied in a bundle on the floor of a corpse's house. Two ways out. One, give me your name and none of this will be a struggle. Death will take you, but you die in the knowledge your sacrifice freed humanity. Two. Call upon your gods to rescue you, and they might come! You might be important enough for them to send some scout or demi-god. What's the most likely? Hmm?"

"Three. I give you nothing and my suffering is a gift to my deity, who gains strength and voracity for every second I continue to spite you." Laughter rattled at the woman's rib cage, uniform loose over emaciating skin.

"I do not think Ares requires your suffering to be so strong." Stana pursed her lips in a coy frown, and tipped the remainder of the meal shake onto the carpet as the vines shifted the Hellene's limbs to keep a sort of functionality. A shift in position at least, once Stana wore her down her True Name would belong to the Keeper and with it, everything this uncooperative officer was, or knew.

"Ares is not my god." The woman croaked and bucked weak against the vines, a struggle to each centimetre taken in a worshipful battle on the floor.

And the shudders focused in Stana's eyes. Obvious as the uniform on the Hellene's body, Kopis Industries was Ares' company and he the Magnus Pater. The Hellenes worshipped with their violence. Obvious as the way this soldier struggled, as she fell into the terror and dread of immobility and the indignity of prison via claustrophobic bindings, this was a child of War.

A struggling warrior.

But this Hellene kept her head longer than the others, she continued to fight. To bark at each comfort Stana offered. No, this was Ares' Folk...

The vines roiled between the Hellene's gnashing teeth, and as Stana saw her eyes roll back, a deep and coiling dread slithered around her spine.

"The Twins." Too grotesque, too macabre, who worshipped Deimos and Phobos?

Who put themselves in the care of the battle-frenzied children of Love and War? Who petitioned the gods, when their gifts were terror and fear? White sclera gazed unseeing at Stana, as the gurgled scream rose from a rattling chest.

"Cormac! We're done!"

"But I'm eating!" Cormac called from the yard.

Stana scrambled to the porch as the coiling terror began to beat at her spine as if acid ate at her vertebrae. "The Hellene worships Deimos. If I teleport us, they'll feel it."

"Run." And Cormac pulled his roots from the shallow ground, pointed at Stanley Park across the inlet. "Tell me you manoeuvre those mechanical wagons."

"What!?"

"Drive! Do you drive!?" Cormac plodded through the yard, as Stana pulled her bag across her body.

"Why would I drive, when transit exists!?"

"A Fae Lord on a public bus!? Are you out of your mammalian mind!?"

"Stop! Stop." Stana sucked in a few deep breaths and shook her head. "We make our way across the inlet under the water, they won't be able to track that magic."

"Won't they!? These are the sons of Ares, not some deer hunter in Sherwood Forest tracking hoof prints in loam!" Cormac tried to shudder off the sensation pouring down his bark, the acid burn of panic tweaking his sensible mind. Stana wheeled round and returned to the living room, gripped her fist and clenched. The vines around the Hellene tightened in an expedited crawl, which yanked the Hellene's limbs back.

"She'll be dead and they'll have nothing to track." Stana jumped into Cormac's waiting branches. He dove through the curated garden down the trail of backyards to Ambleside Park. The denizens of North Vancouver would believe a movie shoot over the return of old gods, to parched ground with being seen. Distance. They needed the distance.

Terror popped the Hellene's eyes open, her chapped lips speckling with the same blue which began to spot around the cord-vines upon her neck. Pain radiated from snapping limbs, until the thud and crackle of a dying woman's panic ceased.

Calm swelled as the dread flowed into the two deities, who raced up the driveway in an armoured vehicle. Four Spartans rushed out of gullwing doors, slow in comparison to the beings who sprinted into the living space. A glance to the strained body on the floor and Phobos howled, pitching himself over the porch in a single cantankerous leap. The Spartans began to secure the house, as their terror god chased the thin trail of panic on the wind.

"Danae, to me." Deimos' voice coated Danae Atropos' soul in its rumble, in its tempestuous denial of her pain. The sensation drained into her god, fuel for his nightmarish roars and rumbles, with nothing left to Danae but the security of spirit that her deity heard her scream. Ares' son ripped the vines off her, bundled Danae into his arms and raised her head as she gasped and coughed for air. "There you are, the fight's still in you."

A cackle rocked Deimos' ribcage, the giddy inflection of terror tickling down into his toes. He laid her on her side on the chesterfield, brushed matted hair out of her face and clucked his tongue as his mighty father did to mother, when Aphrodite was afraid. An act he saw ad infinitum when they were young and played with their mother in the dirt of Thrace, then Sparta, the grasslands and stiff peaked meadows of the Norse Lands.

"The Book..." Danae croaked, one of her arms motionless, the other radiant in a horrible soreness. Legs still curled behind her, she tried to move them and grunted a cry.

"No, no no, rest. Let me have your tears, you beautiful wonder."

"Deimos." Danae reached with aching fingers, the periphery of her vision shuddered in black. "She has the Book. New... new Keeper... of..."

Head lolling onto soft leather, Danae fled consciousness into Morpheus' bastion.

"Gaius! Call Leonidas. Tell him to check on old Sal. Agrippa, prepare Lochagos Atropos for medical evac, Asclepius is waiting at the helipad."

"Yes, Sir." The calls resounded, and as Danae's panic and fear died down with her exhaustion, Deimos felt the slink of worry eat at his gut. A new Keeper for the Book of Knowledge? One who dared attempt murder of Deimos' faithful? Whose head would he cause to roll from their shoulders first, this new Keeper's, or Caleb's for letting the artifact out of his sight in the first place?

"Did you hear that, Caru?"

'Triangulating satellites, I'm seeing a figure move through the trees but no confirmation it's them. I heard it, Deimos. I'll tell Pippos.'

10 MISSING LETTERS

Moss was surprisingly comfortable, when a man slept on it. The sun attempted to take up more of the sky when Caleb turned over in the moss-like sheet which covered their skin. He yawned and watched Tuija nuzzled into the green, hair sprawled behind her head. Sliding out from thc stuff, Caleb hunted down his canvas knapsack while taking an empty bottle of wine to the box beside Tuija's door.

He liberated a pour over, two mugs and ground coffee from beside a box of crackers in Tuija's cupboard. Brushed aside a random mote of dust, which scurried off carrying a bag of black tea. As he set the kettle on the stovetop, Caleb slid on a fresh pair of boxers from his rucksack. Fighting off a yawn, Caleb shook his head and searched for his trousers, and the slim black book in the pocket.

While the watcr boiled, he had time to take stock. Whomever was attempting the ritual failed part of the spell. Inexperience? Lack of faith? Was it personal? Did the perpetrator only want to seem like the ritual was the target? Pretty specific and horrifying red herring, if so. He flicked on his phone and started reading the reports. Asclepius wasn't kidding about being thorough.

Chemical chains, burn time, magical residues, each report was concise and as precise as he knew Icarus and Athene to be. And why not? After a few thousand years of practice, one would think they were ahead of the curve. The kettle whistled, and Caleb yanked it off the heat by its metal handle. Poured the boiling water over the coffee grounds in the filter. Amber liquid began to seep down into the first clear glass mug.

"That kettle's hot, you know." Tuija's sleep-muffled voice piped up with the rest of her as she padded along the grass wearing nothing but her own voluptuous skin. "Don't you feel it?"

"Hmm? Oh, not really." Caleb poured more water over the grounds, waited as it drained into the cup below. "Coffee might be on the table, if you're up for it."

"Mmmhmmm. I do enjoy the black miracle, especially when my fika loving Scandi makes it for me. You up long?" Tuija yawned and stretched, her breasts framed by arms cast over her head and the odd patch of cedar scars. Caleb nearly forgot he was pouring hot water, and tried to seek out her eyes for good measure. She chuckled and slid on a snagged silk robe, which draped across a bar stool. A few extra steps and she cuddled up against his back, muscular arms around his chest. "I still cannot decide whether the asbestos hands are a you thing or a god thing."

"What do you take in it, again? Hopes and dreams? Good morning, by the way." Caleb set the kettle back onto the stove, and with a healthy yawn, leaned over to kiss the sleep out of her. "Sleep alright?"

"Better than I expected, a raucous bastard beside me." Tuija returned the kiss, took hold of Caleb's chin to guide her lips to the corner of his mouth.

"Didn't see any cream or sugar." He nodded, slid his book away from the coffee mugs, its pages buzzed with new scribbles from Folk across the Realms.

"Honey, in the cupboard." Tuija opened her refrigerator and pulled out the remains of the pizza from the night before, some eggs. Caleb searched and found the honey, ladled some into his mug and gave it a stir with a spoon from a drawer beside the sink. "What are you working on?"

"Icarus forwarded the reports on Juliana and Tiperet's autopsies."

"Ritual?"

"Confirmed along with their identities. DNA matches."

"Been some scuttlebutt around Finn's, someone's got Folk in a tizzy. Lighting fires, torching sacred spaces, any place the Truce holds steady. Fire freaks the flowers out. Don't you scry?"

"I need something tangible and inanimate to use my psychometric magic. Without something belonging to the person or such, I'm shit out of luck."

"Where are your fire gods? Ahura Mazda, Hephaestus, Pele, Rod, Agni. Could it have been one of them?" Tuija dripped olive oil in a pan, waited for it to heat up as she blended six eggs with a fork. Cold pizza might have been the breakfast of champions, but she knew Caleb's stomach well enough to give him a hearty feed.

"I'll call Sal, see what the Book of Knowledge says. Work the leads until something breaks, bust my ass aside from a fika or two."

"Say the syllables fi and ka side by side and a legion of you Nordics come running."

"We never miss a good coffee and pastry moment. Not that I've spent time with my Aesir side."

"They're chomping at various bits to get to know the grandson of the legendary Thor."

"Learned early to keep my distance." He flicked another page down on a report, and hummed over its contents. Slid Tuija a mug of coffee, and stepped away from the phone to curl his arm around her waist from behind, pulling her back against his chest. "Smells pretty fantastic."

"My hair, or the eggs?"

"Little of column a, little of column b..."

"Screwball." Tuija leaned back into him, plucked the coffee from his hand and took her first luxuriant sip. "Da. You're Scandinavian, you make coffee like a boss."

"Glad you approve... might need the pick-you-up."

"Are... are you saying you tired me out, but I didn't reciprocate, Judge Mauthisen?" Tuija raised her eyebrow with a smirk. Burying his nose in her hair, Caleb chuckled. "Oh, now he's shy. Where was the shy one last night? Hmm?"

"Am I allowed to say I want to do that again?"

"The drinking, the sex, or the ordering pizza through idle conversation over your spy phone?"

"It was pretty damn good pizza."

"My love. You're all cuddles this fine morning." Tuija ran her hand along his arm, nestling back to enjoy the comfort Caleb brought after a good sleep in a safe place.

"Is that a problem? I can stop."

"No, I'm glad I get to see you this way. Soft and snuggled, making coffee. Nobody else does."

"I'm aware." He slid from behind her, walked back around the kitchen island to take up his cup of coffee, and hid a grimace behind a sip. Another report via his phone gave spikes from samples in a mass spectrometer.

"Hieroglyphics would make more sense. Fae buying up roots and herbs they couldn't grow, Sacred Groves going up in flames with chemical residue of...

these..." He tried to decipher its unique brand of magic, and instead glanced down to the notations Icarus left on what each of the atomic residues meant.

"Here." Tuija glanced over the report, flipped through notes while leaning against Caleb's bare shoulder. "That list you gave Aunt Maia, it didn't include star lily or beggar's tears, did it?"

"No, wait, you can translate the boffin-speak?"

"See this spike? These constituent proteins concentrate in human tears, my love... what? I spend enough time around Seraya while her and Icarus are geeking out. Besides, Icarus and Athene wanted to study Rastenivitsya change? I said yes. Listen to Daedalus' child wax scientific about one's tear ducts and platelet response, or a diatribe by Athene the Goddess of Overcomplication, you pick a few words here and there, or your brain explodes."

Elbow leaning on the countertop, Caleb cleared his throat in an attempt to staunch the smile which tipped his lips. "You told me that was a spa weekend."

"There were face masks. Plaster ones." Tuija sipped more coffee and flicked through the report. "... and then Harmonia and Aphrodite showed up and it became a spa weekend, massages, manicures, pedicures, indulgent but healthy meals, the lot. Of course Athene was more interested in seeing how my feet handled exfoliation than getting hers painted in a dull grey colour, but Icarus still managed to coat Athene's nails before she ruined the manicure taking notes."

"Sounds like a time." Any softness descended the more Caleb pondered the fire. There might have been less to it, grieving Folk who didn't want to see their beloved deceased warriors wake up as Fae instead of their old mammalian bodies. Tensions kept well within the range of ludicrous under his radar.

Queen Selyka held the pruning shears to half the Realm's flora in her manicured hands. The only way to ensure the Fair Folk didn't turn into the first repeat offenders of the next century and a half was a firm and wholesale grip on mischief and power. Did she grip too hard?

"Why be glum? It's not unwelcome." Tuija shut off the burner, portioned two plates of eggs and set some cold pizza beside them, took out a couple of forks with a gentle shove of her ample hip against the drawer to shut it. "Breakfast then evaluation."

"Stay armed." Caleb swung his fork like a temporary sabre, before stabbing it back into the eggs again.

"Yes, Sir." Tuija saluted, cracking a grin.

"I'm not kidding."

"Neither am I." She twisted his chair and straddled his waist, one arm slung around his neck. "If I could handle four hundred years by Perun's side, I can handle a week with my lover searching for some fire starting idiots trying to create death on sticks. We've solved dragons in Canada, we can fix this, too."

"I'd..." Caleb's phone blinked with a new message. He set Tuija on the chair and stepped away from the kitchen. "Mmrh... hold on."

"Are you... you're serious."

"You saw how fast they came with the pizza, you think something this important will wait?" Caleb nuzzled his nose into her collarbone and gave a quick kiss. She swatted at his shoulder, laid some shadow punches along his arm as he chuckled and flicked the screen to life. "Frick, there's a list of the missing."

"How long, I could call friends, get a bit of help to search." Tuija was up and dressing before Caleb lifted his eyes from the names. "You think they all ended up char in a pit?"

"No, this is going back a ways... Jesus."

"Thought he liked being called Jase now. Less baggage."

"Yeah, he does." Caleb felt along his wounded side, tried to make out if the bandage was stiff or needed to be replaced. "What's with the face?"

"Gives me the wiggin's. I know humans make what they make of us, but his followers? Then him? Weird. Turn." Tuija dug into the kit in Caleb's pack and pulled out the wound care kit. Peeled the yellowed and redded bandage off Caleb's wounded side and tsked. "Demon got you good, if Hestia's cooking and some nectar didn't cure it. We need to check back in with Sclep?"

"No! No, I'll be... I'll be fine. Should have seen the monks' faces when I asked if they could consecrate a tub. Was in Orthodox territory, near St. Nic's. Demons like that? Dissolve." Caleb hissed as she wiped the area with disinfectant, holy water around the sutured flesh. "How's it looking?"

"Thankfully I don't see you as less pretty." She set another bandage over the wound, kissed his shoulder then packed up the kit, back to the bag beside his socks and a stray box of ammunition. "There. Might get a lollipop later if you're good."

"Mmh." Caleb pulled on a t-shirt and his navy sweater, turned to wrap his arms around her. "Promise? I can be all sorts of good."

"Depends on how many phone messages you get."

"Let's avoid the buddy call outs. Keep it between us. I'll give Sal a call, see if he can narrow it down." He tapped at his phone, brought up the number for Sal Calder and set it to his ear. "Might want to wear boots. Could get messy."

“Don’t worry, I’m a big girl. Know how to holster my firearms and everything.”

“Hah! Good, G-oh hey Sal. Yeah, it’s Caleb. New phone. Don’t know why it didn’t come up as the same number... No, it’s a loaner from Kopis. How’ve you been?” Caleb walked slowly around the space, still barefoot on the grass. “Uh-huh? Yeah, I told you I’d talk to Hestia about getting you a housekeeper, she offered... what!?”

Caleb stopped short, shoved the phone harder against his ear. “What... wait, Sal. Slow down!”

Tuija put a multitool and a knife holster to her belt as she looped it through her jeans, paused as Caleb grit his teeth with a groan. “Everything alr-”

He held up his hand, stomped off toward the confines of Tuija’s glade, where the cliff fell away. “Salomon, why the fuck didn’t you call!? ... Wha-oh. Fuck! I lost my phone. Where did she go!? How... Do you have anything, any leads?”

Caleb launched at the table and his black book, tossed around for a pen and began wildly writing notes on the page, which never seemed to run shy of room. “Yeah... uh huh, Stana. Got it. No it’s not fucking okay! Sal, we had someone... what? No, don’t... don’t cancel your doctor’s appointment I’ll handle it. Yeah. Call your daughter, maybe she can come down for a few days, you know she never minds. No, she never minds. Maybe you do. Give Hestia a call, get that housekeeper she offered to stop by. It’s not trouble, you served for almost a century, it’s owed. Yes, I’ll... no I’m not alone, Tuija’s with me. Yes, I’ll... Tuj, Sal says hi... Fuck, Sal. Just... fuck me. Yeah. Call you later. Bye.”

“Of all the conversations you wanted, I’m guessing that wasn’t the top one of the list.”

Hands to his face, Caleb sat on a stone near the pond with fresh, cold water. A shaken head was the most Tuija got, until Caleb set his phone into his back pocket and swore curses in his native Norse tongue as loud and prolific as he could. The curses shook back at him, echoing in a redundancy which coloured the skies of the place like a moody storm.

“Yeah, that’s a ‘pack extra ammunition’ sort of not great. What happened?”

“The cleaning lady Sal’s daughter hired stole the Book.”

“One book?”

“The Book. The. Book. The Book of Knowledge. It’s gone.”

“How!? Didn’t he have cantrips to cover that sort of thing!? It seems like a pretty glaring omission if not!”

“Yes! Yes, he did, but Sal... he’s been...” Caleb stared off at the conjuring storm off in Tuija’s miniature piece of the Axis Mundi.

"What!? Forgetful? Off his nut? What?"

"Getting old! I... haven't needed him or the Book in years, beyond a phone call or two. Guess... the Book got bored."

"The Book of Knowledge has enough personality to get bored!? Who in Makosh's linen closet thought giving such a powerful piece of magic gumption was a good idea!? It what, let itself be stolen!? When did Salomon notice!? You weren't in Moscow that long."

"Maybe... I don't know. The only one who spent any real time with the thing is Salomon. I have another lead. Stana. Croatian national, last seen in Vancouver a few days ago."

"Days? Why in the Truce's ass didn't you know something that important was lost for days!?"

"I've been a bit busy!"

"For that!?"

"Yes! You think I get cell reception when my phone's at the bottom of a river? If Sal lost it, and he didn't think to check, how would I know? I can be underground or out of Realm for weeks, anything that integral is supposed to flag in my book... so... so why didn't it flag?"

"We need to track this new Keeper down."

"Wait, why didn't it flag?" Caleb dusted off his thighs as he stood, a scowl affixed on his freckled skin.

"You tell me." Tuija looked up from folding a shirt back up into Caleb's knapsack and leaned her hip on it.

"Sal said the girl was clean, no mystical alliances, total non-believer. So how did she learn to manipulate the Book that fast?"

"How did someone figure out how to learn from the Book of Knowledge? Caleb. It's got all the knowledge of every Realm its ever experienced in it."

"Sure, but... you go to a library, right? Pick out a book, but how do you know which one? If you don't even know certain categories exist, how do you know how to search for them? Going from a total non-believer to Keeper isn't so much a learning curve as a massive worldview jerk. I'd be surprised if her neck didn't snap from that sort of spiritual whiplash." Caleb pulled on socks and began tying up his trusted old boots, mind alive with the potentials. "And for the Book not to call out, or trigger it was taken means she's doing what it wanted. At least until she figured it out."

"Someone had to know she took it from Sal's possession. Who would have the capacity? Who had residence at old Sal's?"

"We gotta talk to Finn." Running to the kitchen, Caleb pulled his coat on, held out his hand. "'Cause I don't like how short that list of answers is, and it might be delicate enough to start a war."

"Oh fun! Not fun, but... I got your back, so much so we might not have to go to Finn yet. Try my girl first."

"Alright. Here's hoping I can get it back before this Stana person figures out what she's got. The Groves can wait until then, Ares has Kopis all over them. If anyone can secure a few locations for some time it's Leonidas the bleeding First." He kissed her cheek, set his hand on the fabric covering her backside and tweaked. She squeaked, then rounded and kicked his shin with a soft as a kiss round kick. Despite the gravity of the situation, Caleb laughed as he shrugged on his backpack with another loose pained groan.

11

THE PRODIGAL MAPMAKER

Caleb wrung his fingers while Tuija knocked on another door in the back-stage of Finnegan's Bluff. Finnegan had rooms for days in the place.

"The Realms have plants, right?" Tuija knocked on the red painted door, "Lu? Lu, open up!"

"Of course most..."

"Most? Are you going to tell me there's no plant matter in the Kehmeti Realm? No reeds along the Nile? How about the peach tree in Tian. Sure, keep talking, Preacher." Tuija smirked, fist battering at Lu's door.

"All right, mighty Tuija. I concede, there are plants in all Realms."

"And where do you think they came from, hmm? Gonna knock on your head next, see if it makes the coconut noise." Tuija battered at the door with her fist. "Lu! Open the door, I know you're not working! Come on, we need you! Gosh I'm going to be so mad if she's got her headphones on.... what?"

A shake of his head, and Caleb let the smile on his face grow to an open grin he desperately needed to stay level. If a situation could get worse, Caleb prayed he'd never know. He wrapped his arm around Tuija's waist and pulled her back into his chest, nuzzling his face to her deep brown hair. "You're adorable. Think she's in there?"

"I can smell her." Tuija looked up to Caleb's chin, one hand slid around his arm and held it to her torso.

"Shall I commence door kicking?"

"Pfft. And give you the fun? Eff that!" Tuija grounded with one foot and kicked at the door with a push kick to make Ares proud. The door buckled, swinging open from the gaping hole beside the handle. "Lu!? I know you're here!"

"What the FU-K!?" 'Lu', shears in hand, hopped to her feet and away from the bonsai she was tending on a low table. Headphones yanked off her ears, the ginger headed woman threw the shears at Tuija, who with a twist of her shoulder, let them bop harmlessly off Caleb's chest. "The flaming char of Muspelheim, Tuija!? What the actual fuck!?"

"Headphones." Tuija nodded back.

"Yep… Kind of feel bad for kicking in her door." Caleb glanced from the pruning shears to the door and its cracked wood, as three pixies and a miniature creature with a bulbous nose, white beard and pointed red hat hoisted up from places otherwise unseen and began nattering off too quick for him to catch. "Huh… Nysse?"

"Yes! Thank you, someone knows they're not garden gno-oh… oh Tyr's arse you didn't. Tuija tell me you didn't."

"We need your help." Tuija picked at an evergreen frond sticking out of one of Lu's braids, and tossed it to the ground, where one of the pixies swept it into a miniature dustpan. "Got your runes around?"

"Aaaaaaah… sorry Judge Sir, ah, you mind I …. ah… I'm just going to leave you for a minute… go…. make small talk with my Nysse." Lu grabbed Tuija's arm and towed her further from Caleb into Lu's apartment space. If apartment was the word at all. Like Tuija's, it had less standard four walls, kitchen, bedroom and living area and more echo of the Realm she left behind. A softly rolling hill in Tuija's place became the stiff peaks of a fjord for Lu. The sun and the moon were veiled chariots, Sól's golden hair radiated with a solar glow. Two wolves, like wisps of clouds, gave chase.

Caleb's breath went fallow in his lungs. Barely capable of hearing the mutters of two women in rapid discussion about Judges and personal space, Moði's Son stopped short.

The wall surrounding the inner place was as high as the legends stated, each block the size of a mountain excised by a giant and his mighty stallion. In the distance, long houses nestled between groves of trees and farmers fields tucked into the mountainsides.

Dragon-headed ships waited on the lowlands, docked at the base of a village which spun up the fjord-side.

Asgård.

He stepped out into the light cast from Sòl's hair and his lungs contracted. If he dragged his eyes from the halls to the skyline, Caleb could make out the limits to Lu's pocket framed within Finnegan's Pub and its secret places. Close, so close he could reach down and touch the sweet grass, the lingonberry and cloudberry bushes dotting round. A tug came to his pant-leg and Caleb gasped. The Nysse muttered in Old Norse about breaking things and the cost of lumber these days, a single smack of the back of his hand on Caleb's shin.

"Beklager... Unnskyld..." He wondered if he ought to pay the Nysse in oatmeal, but before he could ask another question, the Nysse trotted off and away into the space between Lu's cupboard and the entry wall to her spot of paradise. The house spirit came back out with a two-hand saw of miniature scale, and another yawning Nysse. Off to the copse of trees nearby.

Caleb sat on the low stool Lu had been using to shape her bonsai with a wheeze.

"I get it! Yes, you can have your divination, but he's... what's he staring at?" Lu tramped back to the table and picked the bonsai up, back to a display shelf built beside the quilts which made up her bed.

"If I told him where you lived, do you think he'd agree to kick open your door?" Tuija sat beside Caleb and took his hand in hers, gripped and played with his fingers. "Welcome home, baby. Or, a pocket of it."

"Pfft, home, you make it sound... Odin's beard." Lu swerved round and put both hands to her hair. "Tuija!! You are going to be the death of me! If Odin sees him, or Frigg, and Frigg knows and sees everything, you know she does, so you know this is going to get back and..."

"We're still in Finnegan's Pub. Go get the runestones. Go on. Shoo." Tuija jutted out her chin, and Lu sprinted through the grass and flowers of the Nordic meadow to a chest over by a deep pool, muttering all the while. "Hey... you alive love?"

"Is this... it's..."

"Like I said. Lu, she's a seer. Great-great-grandmother was a Norn. She's Scandi like you."

"Half of me." Caleb's eyes transfixed on the longhouse in the distance, its straw coloured roof and rich amber lumber shone in the casted light from Sól's hair. From the tiny meadow he thought he could see vibrant painted edging, greens and ochres and yellows. The flicker of gold. A shiver tore through him, he stuffed his hands in his lap. Tuija wrapped her hands around his bicep and kissed the top of his shoulder.

"Enough of you to feel it, right? Feels like..."

"I shouldn't be here."

"No, this is the one place you should be, Caleb look at me love." Tuija's hand scratched at his skin, palm already striated with the cedar which would consume her. "Asgård is part of you. You don't get to deny it like your daddy, his anger at the people here isn't yours. It belongs to him, not you and you shouldn't be in the middle."

"Isn't that my job? What you lot wanted from me in the beginning isn't it? When I was an infant on a slab?" Caleb tried to stand. Pick up his pride and walk out the door the Nysse were currently fixing with lumber they felled from a copse of hazel and pine. His lover's hand wrapped around his arm tighter, and for one brief instant in the eternity of his erasure, Caleb was home.

"Right now? You need to feel it. You need to rectify and own it. This place is as much yours as the Truce's altar."

"Why did you bring me here? It wasn't for Lu and her mystic stones."

"Nah, there's seven other people we could've gone to, but I knew you'd never be caught dead... you need to see it, to feel this, before we find Ule and our way out. Even if it's once." Her lips found his scruff laden cheek, tucked up and kissed his jaw. "You can't go without feeling this any longer. I won't let you. Starving yourself of your home Realm's energies isn't helping. Not if I'm asking you to give it up."

"The wind's stinging my eyes." Caleb nuzzled his nose into her hair and wrapped his arm around Tuija's shoulders as they waited for Lu to find her rune stones, or her courage. Mute mouthed, Caleb fought with the infilling of the Nordic soul in his chest, the music which filtered through the cochlea, hammer and anvil of his ears. He attempted to memorise the scent of the wildflowers, the feel of the trees. Sounds from the fjord below.

This illusion, or pocket of a place he wasn't meant to go, was all the home Caleb would get. And as he cuddled Tuija up beside him, felt her hand drift onto his knee, he knew he could leave with only one look. This was all he needed. He couldn't belong to this world if Tuija wasn't in it.

"Found them! What're we looking to answer, give me as much info as possible or I could send you to Kenya instead of Kansas." Lu trotted back to the two, planted herself on the ground and unrolled a canvas roll painted with topographical maps of the Realms suspended upon the World Tree. Between the fabric, a leather sack embroidered with floss jiggled and clinked with stones.

"Her name is Stana, and she has the Book of Knowledge with her. Hone in on that, it should get you the location."

"Stana! Old girlfriend, is it?"

Caleb glared. “No.”

“Woa, sorry dude, just… just looking out for my girl… you know Tuija hasn’t dated in…”

“Lu!” Tuija yanked a clump of grass from the meadow and tossed it at her. “The stones, girl!”

“Gods! Sorry! Just… you know… it’s a girl’s right to investigate her bestie’s intended, so… the stones are here, I could always do a look-see into the whole… romantic situation if you like. It’s more up my all-”

“Lu! By Perun and Czernobog’s balls!”

“Got it! Yes! Alright! All. Right. Stana bimbo-not-girlfriend and the Book. Got it. I’ve got it…” Lu bit her lip, cast her eyes up and down the two as they nestled on her seat. “… but I’m feeling inspired and you know what happens when I get inspired to do a reading, I mean, it’s kind of more my style and…”

“Do what inspires you first. I’m copacetic.” Caleb smiled tight, hissed out a breath through his nose. The woman looked ready to burst if they pushed, he wondered how much less time it would take if they let her do what she wanted. “Hurry? We’re on a schedule.”

“Hah! I knew I … okay so I’m terrified of you, because you kill people all the freaking time, and…” Lu flinched at more grass thrown her way, some strands collected in her braided hair. “… I’m telling the truth! Truth is good, right!?”

“Don’t scare him off.”

“Scare him off!? What about me!? You!? Gosh, Tuj. I’m good, thank you, it’s not every century the Judge pops by to break my door and give my Nysse another woodworking project. Pretty sure they’re thrilled by the way, so you’ll have to see it when it’s finished and yes! I know, Tuija! I know I should throw the stones but I’m nervous! This is Thor’s Grandkid and I’m reading his romance stones and I didn’t even consider the man had the balls and you probably asked him out, and… oooohhhhh nevermind neither of you had your shit together, it was a third and fourth party in conspiracy mode… Finn?”

“Finn.”

“Definitely Finn.” Caleb nodded, gaze caught by the traverse of Sòl through the Scandinavian sky. Did her hair shimmer? Was the swivel of the sun’s face a trick of the light?

“That tracks… yikes.”

“What?”

“Oooohhhh nothing. Nothing you need to know, I’m seeing some…” Lu winced, “… how good are you at grieving, Judge Sir?”

“Beg pardon?”

"Let's find the Book, eh? The Book of Knowledge? You know, the Book we need. How about you look at that? Eh?" Tuija nudged the map with her booted foot, giving her head a quick shake. The rune stones sang in place, tales and legends of woe, regret. Reconciliation. While Caleb stared at the landscape his father barely saw before infant eyes were ripped from the Asgardian Realm, Tuija nudged one of the stones over. Then another as Lu slipped them back into the bag.

"This'll take a bit more oomph and I could use a teensy bit of cooperative resonance, if you catch me. Focus on it. Hold tight." Lu's eyes fluttered closed, the air around them swerved from a balmy summer warmth to the harsh slice of a cutting autumnal gale. Reverberations struck the air like a stringed instrument, as Lu began to hum low in her throat, a keening sound which threaded into Caleb's mind until he felt himself inside the joik.

It conjoined and tamed him, until the pitch changed and it billowed as rain pouring through the cracks in a broken prow. The fluctuations cut into his sweater, through the wound to his back, into memories and the motion of spheres which would not be discovered until telescopes were ground from glass. Caleb's head pitched into the sounds, body tanked against Tuija's side.

Lu sang on, the rune stones in their cloth vibrated and shone.

Light as consuming as the aurora borealis exploded from Lu's eyes, lips and ears. She created sigils with her fingers, tossed the stones to the map. It spun then settled in nine different planes of existence, nine Realms narrowed from the many which lingered in attachment to the human's middling plane. Two stones pulsed and spun like meteors toward fixed points. One, a dying pulsar in the middling map.

Vancouver, BC. Midgard.

The other, stronger in pulse and more hearty of glimmer, not far from Canterbury in England, the shadow of a woman flushed in the air before it dissipated. Lu fell back into the soft grass up to her elbows, and the maps condensed back down to a single roll of canvas, painted by a precise hand.

"........ woa." Lu breathed, eyes wider than before, cheeks struck with a pink flush. "... what are you, Judge Mauthisen?"

"Nngghh..."

"Malyatko-love?" Tuija threaded her hand over Caleb's cheek, towed his forehead against hers and held him as he seemed to come down from the high of Lu's magic, the high of the Asgardian plane. "Breathe in and hold it. The magic will pass."

"D-damn..."

"No, seriously, what are you? That's not supposed to happen." Lu handed the map to Caleb but he was too discombobulated to take it. Tuija grabbed her phone and took a picture, then another.

"He's Caleb and his Dad's from here."

"That should've taken an hour. Tuija! I'm serious! All Ásgard could feel that! I've got two strikes!"

"Saved you time. Three, two, one I'm going to heave you to your feet, Cale. You ready?" Tuija reached her arms around his waist, tossed his arm about her shoulders as he mumbled and swooned. "Three, two..."

"Tuija! By Hella!? He's supposed to be human!"

"... One. Hup! Half-Human!" She lifted Caleb up and yanked his rucksack around her shoulder, let him put his weight on her frame. The man collapsed into Tuija with numb legs, the conversation numb in his ringing ears. The old soldier in her could take it, wrapped around like the heaves of the Mystic War. "Thanks Lu, we'll see you later for another reading."

"Does he even know!?"

"This one's on the Judge! Love you too, bye!" As the Nysse and a pixie helper continued repairing the door, Tuija of Perun's war band towed Caleb away from his first glimpse of home.

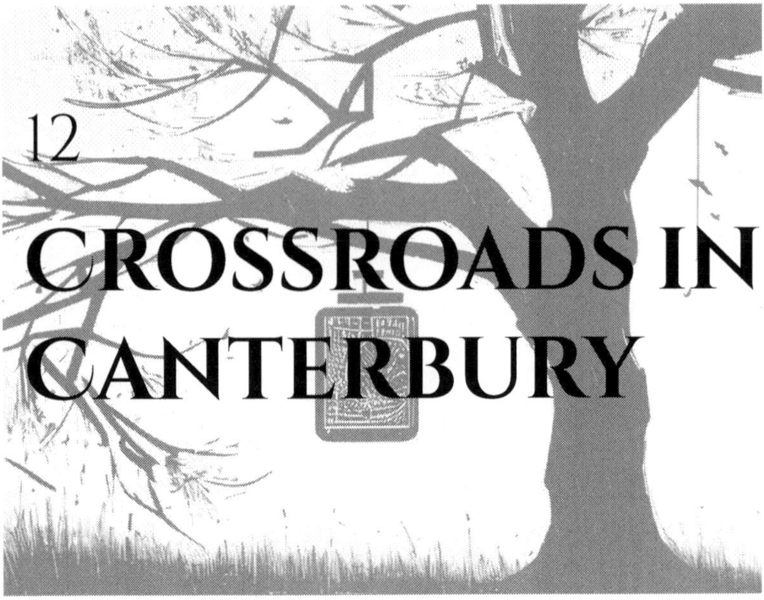

12 CROSSROADS IN CANTERBURY

The closest door swung on grieving hinges, both Finnegan and Tuija's shoulders bit into the ancient darkened wood with a counted push. Slumped against Donovan's bar, Caleb sipped a double espresso as Donovan ensured the man wouldn't tank to the floor.

"Hell you do to 'im last night, Tuj!? I know you like playing with your food, but damn!" Donovan shook his head, and rubbed a circle around Caleb's back in tiny pats. "Pity Sera ain't here to see this. Probably take pictures for her instant gramophone whatsits."

"Another cup of your coffee, he'll be right as raindrops, Dono." Tuija grunted and gave the door another shove, with Finnegan's help it was finally parting from its rusting hinge.

"Poor lucky bastard." Donovan whistled and set another espresso down for Caleb, who hazarded a chuckle as the magical fog began to clear at the scent of strong coffee and a caramel crema.

"Think you might be skirting too close to the flames, budling? Magic like that?" Finnegan whispered in Tuija's ears as he shoved at the door. "Axis Mundi ain't totally removed from Odin and Frigg's mighty armchair."

"He ought to know." Tuija heaved and the door creaked open.

"Decisions not yours to make. When you're ready for the things you ought to know? I'll add his to the list." Finnegan sighed with a whiff of oxygen and looked beyond the ancient oak door. A courtyard where ancient graffiti on stonework warped by time rested in the relative quiet of the Canterbury Cathedral. Arches lined the covered walk, hemming in rebellious tufts of grass as enticing as the signs to stay off were laughable. Who would notice.

"Do you want to come with us? Stretch your roots. Oh wait..."

"Ah, budling. Prison and palace, the Pub is my home until I can pay back that look in your eye." Finnegan slapped Tuija and Caleb's shoulders with bark-like hands. "But you! Get out, solve the suck and come home for a pint."

Caleb finished his coffee and dove through with his hand on Tuija's lower back. Halted in the ancient remains of Canterbury's former medicinal garden, Caleb snapped to and shouldered his rucksack with numb compliance. Tuija continued around relic-stones in silence, until Caleb pulled out his phone. He sat on the remains of a bench meant for monks or their charges, centuries prior.

As degraded as his wandering mind, Canterbury was a staunch and comforting dissonance in comparison to the colour and waft of Ásgard's meadow. The wildflowers in their wistful petals struck a nigh violent swathe of colour in his mind, as war-like as the Vikings who descended from skaldic kenning and soulful joik. He shook his head.

The network changed with a ping to the time in the English locale, Caleb vaguely aware of Tuija walking through the scant display herbs in the once lush garden. How didn't he feel something this off? The Book of Knowledge with a new Keeper? Salomon getting old? Was his brain too occupied with Trucc business for him to check up on his friends? Was Tuija right and something remained amiss?

"You with me?" Tuija rubbed at bare arms, eyes cast round the Cathedral and caught the sight of the Archbishop, who smiled demurely as he walked the outdoor path, hands behind his purple cassock.

"Y-yeah. Hey... thanks."

"For towing your ass out of Finn's? You're welcome. Pay me back with dinner, maybe a steak... haven't had a good steak in a while... one of those twice baked potatoes the Americans are so fond of, or oooooo, no, truffle fries. Yes. Pay me back with steak frites and truffle. Side of ketchup."

"Ketchup? What happened to mayonnaise?" Caleb leaned against a broken buttress, a slow shake of his head as his phone rediscovered the inside of his pocket, and a series of ominous messages flashed from Icarus and Kopis Industries. "You never cease, you know?"

"I am woefully aware. Testing you, making sure your mind was in it. Do you need a minute? Maybe seven? An hour? A fortnight? What do you need?" Tuija reached for his shoulder, thumb grazing over his sweater with a smooth and consistent touch Caleb refused to shy from. "I didn't realise her magic would push you this hard... what grandson of Thor's never been to Asgard, right?"

"Never felt anything close in my life. Like to know how she did it."

"Lu usually attaches to someone, pulls them into the spell as a sort of... battery back-up."

"I'm just a man. A demi-god with a human mother."

"Hah! Oh you're hilarious. You're the Judge. That comes with power, power you're going to have to use in about ten minutes after we find Stana's precise location. So, Judge, what's the play? Flank her, take the Book and run like a bat out of Beelzebub's boudoir? Clonk her over the head? What?"

"Stana's probably confused as fuck, we have to give her the benefit of the doubt. She's just a human, who figured out magic exists.. I'd be surprised if she was lucid or past the point of shock."

"No clonking her over the head... But I picked out a fine rock from the abbey rubble, it would be so perfect."

"Warrior, set down thy shield." Caleb slid his thumb down Tuija's cheek, let it feel the scratch of the cedar bark until she stilled his fingers and pulled them away. "Everyone gets three chances, this is her first introduction. We talk to her, see if she'll hand over the Book. Or, maybe she'll end up being a better Keeper than Sal the last few years. Sciatica. A heart murmur can make the whole running thing a bit tough."

"If she make trouble, I shoot her in spleen. Maybe the kidney. I'm too much of an old soldier to trust unknowns."

"Deal. I'm half-sure it'll all turn out fine." Caleb tried to cover the hesitation in his feet with a smirk which didn't land, he shouldered his pack and started off in the direction of Stana's cell image, until his phone chimed and an updated location struck from a map app which mysteriously opened itself and narrowed in.

"Damn, when you say the Hellenes don't let you out of their sight..."

"Oh, this? See the little falcon icon? The Olympians are pairing their tech with Horus' Falcons. Probably Icarus's deal, kid's a genius, but they learned their waxen winged lesson enough to ask Horus to do the flying. If you see a bird of prey in the air, do me a favour and don't shoot it down."

"Take my fun. C'mon. Let's get this done, salvage the Book, find the arsonist, then steak."

They walked through the gift shop, not cognizant of the stares or the wares of Canterbury model bookmarks, monk-made ales or postcards. Gilded crosses in a locked cabinet. Out in the streets, they wove through foot traffic past galleries and pubs, until the city filtered into a car park on one side, houses on another.

In the middle of the crossroads, a woman with mouse brown hair and a faded brown dress under a wool-lined jean jacket was flicking through pages on a slim black tablet. Caleb's brow quivered, he searched the slip of a human being, as she flicked a page, flicked, clicked. Dragged. Paid him no never mind.

A scan down to his phone confirmed the place. Here?

Twin ravens lit upon a branch in a nearby oak tree gave a single caw. His stomach pitched with fluctuations of raw magic, a malevolent concentration in the trees. As he walked toward the figure in the crossroad, he felt the oddness of abandoned places; a shade removed from the humanity they passed through streets of tourists and kids out of school grabbing a snack from Marks & Spencers.

None of the life of Canterbury made it to the crossroads, and it hit.

Strange as the single caw.

Almost all intersections in Canterbury were roundabouts, not crossroads. He nodded to Tuija, the glare in her eyes let him know she saw it too, she felt the woeful illness of a place which didn't belong. Raw magic in Midgard's plane was as wrong as sea water in a pair of lungs.

"Something's twisting the place. I have your six." They stepped toward the epicentre, a creaking ache to Caleb's bones. The twisting of bark and branches. A car horn faded, died before it became part of the area no humans trod upon. None but the woman in the faded dress, slim black device in hand. No giant bag, or massive book, nothing but the pulse of the Book's magic which threaded through Caleb's jaw and down his spine.

Reaching into his innate mystic senses, Caleb opened his eyes to the pitch and yaw of magic around them, was the Book hidden? But where?

Another single caw. Caleb fought the urge to unholster his pistol. No use in freaking the woman out, if this was Stana, and the closer he got the more sure Caleb became it was, the Mystic Realms were probably as much of a mind-fuck as LSD. Or that film by Dali and Disney.

"You alright, Ma'am?" Caleb waited for an acknowledgement, tried to picture what she must be feeling, a sense of strangeness, or maybe shock. Gods and magic, spirits, goblins, demons, pixies. Nysse who repaired broken doors, or found lost socks. What would be the trigger to this woman, the heir to Salomon's temporal position? Caleb cleared his throat, showed an open palm. "Stana?"

"I used to shoot birds in the countryside. Before the war." English heavily accented by the Caucasus mountains poured from the woman's mouth, face lit by the device in her hand. "They would make a nuisance in the grain fields. It was easier to use the air rifle. Low powered, Grandfather said I couldn't get hurt."

"Not how I thought this conversation was going to start. Am I right in thinking you're Stana? Are you doing alright? Tell me about it." Caleb stepped sure and steady, an even pace as he slunk closer. The malevolence around the crossroads continued to magnify the sounds within their microcosm. Flies buzzed in his ear, as the muffled laugh of children two streets over faded to a long and slow and basso rumble. Each boom of his boots on the pavement. Tuija clucked her tongue.

Evil chased the Book the same as good, a world of grey intersected the parallel running lines of paradise and perdition. If Stana tapped into the magic of the Book of Knowledge without control, without knowing what she was doing, any number of plagues could rush them. Poltergeist or priestly choir.

"Do you know what I did to those birds?"

"No idea. Are you Stana? I know this might be confusing, but you happen to..." The weight of the Book's magic crushed his shoulders as it sung out in a pitiful howl. It called in a clear and distinct pitch, which now that he heard it, Caleb knew was trapped within the crossroads. But where?

He waved a hand through the air to part whatever hidden veil kept him from seeing the situation fully, and came through with a deeper sickly sensation that dissipated into the gloom.

"Caleb." Tuija shoved her hand against Caleb's chest as he went to walk closer, cast her eyes down to his feet, where a thin tripwire of magical twine glinted in the receding sun. His eyebrow rose, had the woman figured out defensive spells already? Flipped a few pages and come across a cantrip or two? He'd best get the tome away from her before...

"Do you know what I would have done, if I knew the Ravens were mystic fortune tellers? The magpies wove stories and I could have learned the intricacies of the future from a flock of sparrows?"

"World's a complicated place... my name's Caleb. This is Tuija. We're here about a book. Old Sal's been missing it. It's okay, you're not in trouble, we want to return it is all." The malevolent spirit surrounding them contaminated the air with the scent of rotting wood fibre, soot from volatile ash.

Caleb needed to get this mortal cleaning lady out of the danger zone.

"Ahhh, the generous male in power, flush with the potency of post-coitus youth. I, the tender female, am not in trouble, no, you are benevolent. Aim to educate and train. To take the power back to the stodgy old man, who muttered ceaseless in his chair by the window every Tuesday, every week like clock workings."

"... that's a little unfair coming from the person who stole my friend's possessions, don't you think?"

"Power does not belong in the hands of stodgy old men whose minds were slipping."

"Sal's mind is fine." Caleb's voice deepened. He searched the surroundings for traps, the waft of spell-weaving or other sorts of craftwork. Stana didn't bother looking up from her ereader, didn't acknowledge either Caleb or Tuija. Flick, another page. Flick.

What was that thing? Why was it...

"I didn't know that when I cleaned his toilet. He muttered and mumbled about faeries in the yard, how the mushrooms glowed in the right season. He tried to tell me stories of adventures he had in his youth, when it was 1897 and he met this young strapping Scandinavian man named Caleb. Not a man, a Judge."

"It's discombobulating, isn't it? When we find out the world is a bit more crowded. I can help you learn more about the Realms if you..." Caleb reached for Stana's hand with an open palm, nodded with a half-smile.

"What!? Give the man the power? I think I'll keep it, thank you. Piss off." Stana's eyes snapped up to stare with a loathing Caleb only saw in his mirror in the hours immediately after the apprehension of Folk with three strikes. Three attempts at salvation denied and buried.

"No. That isn't a curio, you're keeping..." The oppressive energy shifted, flagrant malevolence ramped two-fold, not from the creaking trees, or the spirits of damned, hungry things but... the woman?

"I know what I'm keeping, what, did you think I'm a moron?"

"Misinformed." Who was this cleaning lady? Did the tome corrupt so readily in a few days? He remembered the search for the right Keeper, a person of pure heart and no ego, someone with a mind to serve humanity, to preserve others. The Book in any other hands, the power it had to corrupt or grant compassion was as staggering as the Truce's altar call.

"I found teachers."

"Enemies behind us. I got them." The sound of Tuija's pistol exiting her shoulder holster twitched at Caleb's ear. He reached for his handgun, unclicked the safety on instinct. Odds were, Stana could likely see it. Why wasn't the woman running? Tuija's back pressed against his, her shoulders shifted, Caleb refused to turn and face Tuija's threat. She knew what she was doing, and there would be no hesitation, no refusal to fire if the need were present.

“I’ll be taking the Book, thanks. Come on, we have to move. You’re in danger, let’s go, there’s a pub down the road. We can talk this over some food. Maybe a coffee. You need to walk away from this crossroad. Can you feel that? The temper of the air? Walk with me, I’ll protect you.”

“No.” Stana waved her hand and a buffet of energy smacked into Caleb’s chest with enough potency to send a lesser person careening into the street behind. “Hmm. That usually works.”

“What would you know about usually? I’ll give you a pass, because we’re meeting for the first time. As I said. I am Judge Caleb Mauthisen, and you are in violation of the Mystic Truce. Magic out in the open, in the Human’s Middling Plane is forbidden. Come with me, right now, and we can work this out.” Caleb stepped over the trip wire. Gun pointed to the ground.

“Another group of men seeking control of women with the potential for power.”

“The Truce is not a collection of tawdry old fucks, men like Zeus lost their power and good riddance, our Truce is the best chance any of us have to handle the magics of the spheres and leave humanity to its’ own devices.” Tuija said over grit teeth.

“If you believed humanity ought to be left to its own devices, you’d point that handgun at the deities instead of the human girl who was cuckolded by fairytales.” Again Stana’s eyes, calculating and frigid, scanned over at Caleb’s approach. “Don’t worry, I’ll clean up the mess.”

She began to whisper in a language Caleb struggled to remember, as her voice died in blatant bangs from Tuija’s gun. Three shots, the scuffling of Tuija’s boots on the pavement.

“We’re two seconds short of time here! Grab her or shoot her, she’s nuts!” Another shot. Another. Caleb battled the urge to turn around, to salvage Tuija from whatever it was she shot at, but every fibre of threat awareness in his body told him the real danger was standing in doc martens and a faded brown dress. Holding a slip of black plastic as if it were a piece of purest gold. The smell in the air continued to bask in old smoke, and it clicked in Caleb’s mind.

“You burned fourteen people alive, didn’t you... who taught you that? Who showed you what that meant?!”

“No, I doused twelve trees and two mythical morons in lighter fluid and liberated part of a British beach.” The sickly waft of decrepit magic behind his back strengthened, as the wind shifted. Billowed in a miniature cyclone as the churn of it hit Caleb’s nostrils.

Not behind them, in front and swirling. Caleb's chest tightened. Whoever this Stana was before she got hold of the Book, she was no shrinking, innocent violet. "Ssssshit!"

"Now would be nice, malyatko! Grab it now!" Tuija's pistol reported three more clangs, followed by the sound of the magazine exiting the pistol, a new one rustled from Tuija's belt and slid in. Two more shots.

"Grab it?! I don't even see it! The thing's gigantic and leather bound, she doesn't have it on her!"

"What does she have?!"

"A coat and a phone! Some black tablet thing!"

"Now." Stana flung her hand out, as needles crackled with brown and orange energy pierced the air, cast off the invisible walls of the place to split and cascade at the unwary. The entire crossroads was a flimsy, naive trap.

"Hand it over!" Caleb raised his pistol and the woman flashed a bright light directly into Caleb's eyes. They shut by instinct, trigger squeezed. A woman's scream followed the clattering of plastic against the pavement. Caleb blinked away the spots in his eyes and pulled the trigger. The pistol bucked in his hand, but he held firm. The bullet penetrated through the jean jacket, then blasted outward, back out on a new trajectory, until Stana stumbled to her feet, ereader in hand.

"You... you shot... you can't shoot..."

Caleb fired twice at Stana's head. The woman screeched, thrust her arm up and over as a rip scattered the atoms around her stomach and hand. She dove into a ragged hole in the fabric of the Middling Plane. All Caleb could grab before her body disappeared was her jacket. Caleb swore and swerved round. Tuija stood surrounded by a tangle of twisted vines shaped in vaguely humanoid bundles, pistol in one hand, curved blade of her shashka dripping with milky sap.

The malevolent sensation shunted off, Book doffed into the void with the woman who stole it.

"It wanted to... no. It couldn't have..." Standing in the crossroad with Stana's jacket, Caleb's head swam. "I could feel it, but I couldn't see it. All she had was this... I don't know, a tablet or something?"

'Small, black plastic, got a screen? Bout the size of a thin paperback?' Icarus' voice peppered out of the phone in Caleb's pocket. He blinked and the road metamorphosed into a small roundabout, bundles of tangled leaves strewn about, some already billowing away in the wind as the sound of teenagers' laughter tore through the market town.

"Yeah. Yes, she was obsessed with it." Caleb felt Tuija's forehead connect with his shoulder, the pants of her lungs as physical as the pistol she slid back into her holster.

'That would be an ereader, my luddite compatriot.'

"Ereader... wait... no, it couldn't. Could it?"

'All the knowledge in the Cosmos, teensy tiny pocket sized package. You copacetic if I ask Athene if it's possible the Book updated itself? Would make sense, that thing's supposed to be older than sin and ya can't tell me it was in some whacked out kinda Middle English Cuneiform or something. Clay doesn't travel well, trust me on that.'

"Do it." Caleb pulled Tuija onto the roundabout as a car zipped by with a honk and a man gesticulated out the window.

"This is a much bigger problem than a human with the world's most informative book." A shudder in one of Tuija's arms stole Caleb's attention. Thick orange amber like blood bubbled across a long vertical wound up her forearm, staining the borrowed hoodie and handle of her curved sword. "Cale? She got me."

"Fuck. Fuck!" He yanked the torn fabric of the hoodie away from her skin, the amber slice of the wound poured slow and sticky over faded tattoos, thick navy lines of slavic symbology a pageant on her body. "The Hallowes isn't far, come on."

13

AMBER IS A PRECIOUS STONE

Air crisp with spring's gumless teeth snapped at Caleb's neck. He popped the collar of his pea coat around Tuija's shoulders. Busied over the roots overgrown from loose cobbles trailing up from the paved Yorkshire road to a parsonage in shambles. The roof bore no more of its weight, as tossed in as half the crumbling masonry. Remnants of a cathedral ached upon the landscape of gnarled overgrowth. Patches of tall grass replaced the path, which once led to a vegetable garden; rows of leafy tops skirted Caleb's memories as he caught Tuija against his side.

"Place is desolate. Why would Stana be here?" Tuija pushed her chestnut hair back from a weary face. A lone rose bush grew gangled and thin in the hedgerow, the few anaemic petals clung to the stalk. Caleb turned away.

"We're not looking for Stana until you're checked out." The door of the parsonage slumped off its one rusted hinge, a crack in split wood creaked until the door crashed in two wet pieces. Stepping over the remains, Caleb offered his hand for Tuija, who hopped past and folded her fingers into his for comfort's sake. The injury bubbling on Tuija's arm coiled into his spine like the gut-rot of returning to a place as degraded as his chances if he played the Truce's continued game.

“So the creepy dilapidated house beside the crusty chapel is...”

“Welcome home.” Caleb trotted over a broken bit of flooring, to another door bereft its stopper, which angled down into the pitch and dark.

“I seem to remember your father living in a place with a roof. And you were in it, what happened, the Fae take the wood back?”

“Kitten, claws. You didn’t want Finn’s, where else were we going to go?”

Tuija rifled through one of the rooms, plucking the leaves off the crab apple tree which grew through a wall into the salon. She doffed her borrowed coat onto a pile of crumbled masonry, and sat atop it on the mossy stone.

“Puppy, eyes. Why didn’t you tell us things got this bad?” Tuija peeked at her shoulder, grunted and shook her head. The throb dulled at her periphery enough she missed Caleb’s grit-toothed jaw, the search around the stone hearth for a dry box hidden beside a salt pot bereft its contents.

“For a while I thought Dad...” a gravelled Scandinavian tilted the English language from his throat. Ruined furniture appeared as bespoke and desolate as the slop of rain on a roof lost of its sod come a harsh autumn, fabric disintegrated to scraps by time’s stinging arrows. Caleb yanked a broken leg off an easy chair and tossed it into the worn fireplace. “Spend my life putting out other folks’ fires, when did you think I had time to handle the cinders of my own? Not like I came back much after... it doesn’t matter. Getting a fire started, and taking a look at your shoulder, then hunting down the Book and figuring out why it abandoned Salomon matters. Stopping another Grove torch matters. Besides, needed time to think where we’d be...”

“Safe?” She settled Caleb’s knapsack against the creak of a broken bench once carved with the roots of Yggdrasil, as Caleb broke apart the rest of the wingback chair in powerful hands.

Like most of Midgard’s world, the wood felt thin as paper in his hands, fragile bits of wrapping and cardboard cores. In the remains of his family home, Caleb hissed out a deep shudder at the fragility of the place reflected in Tuija’s urgently ambering skin.

“Uninterrupted.” The waft of flint and steel brought embers to light for Tuija to curl her open fist around the fledgeling flame and coax it into a blaze warm enough to dry the derelict wood they pulled from the furnishings. The fire crackled and popped, matte grey smoke billowed around the house’s ceiling and out holes deconstructed from the once solid frame.

“This is bad, Tuju.” Caleb sighed and pulled the ripped hoodie off Tuija’s torso, swore under his breath and eased her shirt off as well, once the damage was clear. Kit on his lap, Caleb nudged her chin aside with his thumb and felt along the fledgeling lines of amber already thickened into new bark.

"If we stay? We're fucked." Tuija raked her hand through his hair, tugged Caleb's head back until his eyes collided with the ache in hers. "When we find Ule and get our way out, we're not leaving the Realms with nothing. You've been going non-stop for over a century, I get it. They put so much pressure on you it's insane. But... you also don't go looking for those of us who can help."

"Salomon was supposed to take it on. The Book. Every time I got Folk help it became political. Gridlocked by the Council refusing to set aside their pride."

"Maybe we need to band the rejects together. Find a neutral space and give them a chance in our grand exit. I could coordinate, bring some of the old ones in, the ones like me, who were cast out after the War. Maybe some of the Folk you go after don't need a warning to fly right or die. Maybe they need something productive. Why not build a team, find a new Keeper for the Book of Knowledge, one who isn't two sheets to Bedlam?"

"That's different from Ares and Kopis Industries, how?" There in the bastion of his ruined home, Caleb considered the woman, her insight filtered with the force of a spring gale. "Ares is already better situated, he has armies willing to die for him in seconds, scientists glutting on his half-sister's wisdom while Heph brings his engineers as close to godhood as humans can get."

"Ares is a warmonger, that's his function. Sure, I like the guy, but it has to be..."

"Me?"

"It has to come from you, yes. Ares set down his swords to protect you, me, all of us. A grand retirement where he could focus on Aphrodite and Leonidas. Spend time with his copious kids. Asking him to pick it back up... you know he'd do it and if that doesn't frighten you a little I need to patch up this bark on my shoulder and slap you upside the head."

"I'm sorry I didn't turn around."

"You trust me?" Tuija clucked her tongue as if calming a wild stallion, or a bear with a hurt paw. She stroked his cheek with the back of her cedar-shifted fingers, the roughness of her bark a pleasant scratch against his stubble.

"Yes." The word burst out of him faster than he'd expected. Every tug in his ribcage, the force of his heart beating at his bones, drove Caleb to seek out the soul of the woman in his arms.

A powerful warrior who survived centuries of battles, not to be taken out by a stray arrow or lucky shot but cursed to slowly degrade until her soul became part of another organism, a tree which had the audacity not to go extinct without a fight. One day, Tuija would be branches and bark, the spirit of an extinct cedar with enough open antagonism to protect its reintroduction to the world. Each year a little less. Each year a centimetre more. And he was doing nothing about it but stare.

"I got sloppy, nothing I couldn't handle and you had more important things to tend to. Like the Book. You said you felt it but it wasn't there? Maybe we can talk the Truce into deputising or setting up neutral spaces for us to figure shit out. Give me time to work. And once it's set, we find Ule. They can't fault us for that. Not if we give them something better."

"We set this Stana business right, find your noble rejects, then I will follow you out of whatever path it takes. If it means we get a lifetime together? I'll do what needs to be done." Caleb hovered over her, slid his thumb along her cheek until he flicked harmless on a thin line of cedar bark.

"You always do." A hitch in her breath, Tuija pushed past Caleb and searched the decrepit room until she found a pock marked mirror. Left hand swathed in soft human skin drifted along the fissure of pink scarring, which burst at its seams in bark. She peeled a thin strand of red wood-flesh from the mass on her cheek, scratched at a corner to get more grip on another band. The pads of her fingers searched for more skin, and found the deficit which rebuked her pride.

Humanity reversed.

"Tuija? Are you copacetic?"

"Got any sandpaper?"

The faint sound of rustling morphed into stepping feet. Caleb's arms swept around her from behind. He nuzzled into her hair, rocking them back and forth in front of the mirror. Tuija clung to his arms, and with a whisper, pushed her head back into his chest.

"Don't remember me like this."

"Marry me." Caleb shuddered at the giddy sensation of his own words. He sealed them by weaving his hand around the back of her neck for a kiss deep and strong. A gasped squeak, and Tuija gripped at his clothes with eyes shut, lengthened the affection.

Pulling her face back, she watched the wide gaze of Caleb's eyes go from a brilliant cerulean to a dull grey in her silence. In the work of her jaw. The rumble of tires on gravel and the chortle of a diesel engine shutting down drained as far from Tuija's ears as the colour on Caleb's cheeks when Tuija ceased to answer.

"Somebody call a Carpen-" A man stepped gingerly over the threshold and its broken door with a knock against sponge-wood, fingers woven around a navy blue metal tool box which saw enough scuff marks to prove its mettle. "-ter. Me, this place is... it... well it isn't a place, more a rubbish tip."

"You called him?" Tuija's forehead creased, she slid away from Caleb and swept her unwounded hand up her cheek into the remains of her hair.

"Who else is better with hand tools?" Caleb grunted thick in his throat, swept his gaze from Tuija to the middle eastern man with laugh lines entrenched around both eyes, dimpling his cheeks. Kind were the eyes, a compassion born of a stern and mighty justice laced their mahogany brown. Black curls bobbed around his ears, dusted the top collar of a workman's plaid button down tucked into a pair of worn blue jeans, cinched by thick leather.

"Thanks for coming, Jase."

"I always come to those who call." He slung a tool belt over his shoulder, each precious chisel and file as pristine as the mercy which flowed around all but the hypocrite. The love which consumed all but those who didn't want it, or misused others in his name. Jase winked at Tuija. "Otherwise they leave terrible reviews... not like my reviews could get much worse with some people, but... eh!"

Tuija rubbed her amber calloused bicep, eyed the tools on the belt, the triangle file, a stray chisel.

"That one usually gets at least a snicker. Nothing? Not a... not even a pity giggle?"

"I don't belong to you." Tuija eyed him, the Carpenter with a kind smile.

"No, you don't. He does, but you? I'm here with no strings to help and you can turn down the offer although I might take some measurements of this house, my me, Caleb how did you let it get this bad!? What in the Realms!"

"Right!?" Tuija scoffed and threw her hand toward the fire. "He tossed the easy chair in the hearth! Poof! One less furnishing!"

"That chair was a Georgian masterpiece!"

"Tuija was cold."

"What an excellent fire." Jase set his tool box down on the nearest solid bit of flooring after testing it with his steel toed boot, warmed his hands for a pause before slipping the tool belt around his waist and cinching the buckle.

"You, too? I thought you'd at least defend the furniture."

"Build you whatever you want, after we do a little emergency care, eh?" Jase offered Tuija his hand, the gruesome scar of his crucifixion a mark of flesh on his wrist. "Sweeten the deal and use the wreckage to build you an ottoman, eh? Eh?"

"Not even you could break the Rastenivitsya curse."

"No, but I can help a friend. Give you some peace for a while, will you let me?" The hand freely offered was taken in hesitant fingers, and although Jase's smile was friendly and warm, his strength was unmistakable. Tuija relaxed onto the moss covered stone, Caleb's peacoat her cushion. Jase turned her chin one way, the other and only then did Tuija remember she was sitting in her bra in front of a two thousand year old resurrected man. The burble of an apology dissipated at the thick browed empathy, his fingers light upon the flakes of bark and solidifying amber.

"I've got you. I think I saw some hyssop in the garden and it'll help, are you comfortable if I ask Caleb to retrieve it?"

"Yes. I'm alright, Cale. You can go." She felt no shame as Jase picked a narrow chisel and tested the circumference of the newest patch of cursed flesh. True to his soul, Jase was gentle and firm handed. His tools worked and Tuija felt a strange gentility.

"I'll be a whisper away." Caleb kissed the top of Tuija's head and vacated the room. Caleb's foot creaked on rotted floor boards, as he searched for more detritus for the fire, or a dry spot where he and Tuija could bed down. His father's old study was preternaturally dry, a brittle collection of desk and shelves fitted with manuscripts, ancient tomes, scrolls, Caleb stroked his finger over a jade foo dog - one of a pair - which guarded an ornate carved box. Unlike the rest of the house, nothing in the study changed.

Stasis, alone in the dark. He remembered the spot at the doorway where he'd stop as a child, knocking on the wall beside the cavernous opening with his father bent over some old script. Where Pappa wrote homilies to present at the small cathedral a breath away. Raynar Einridsen's absence clung to Caleb's back, another form of disconnect.

'You could, ya know, call? Jussayin.' Icarus' voice warbled soft out of Caleb's pocket as Caleb dusted off his hands and trotted out to the back garden.

"How in the worlds?"

'Sure, GPS shows you at the Hallowes, which you mentioned not ex amount of minutes ago. Two plus absent dad, equals I got his number I could patch you through, Deimos and Phobos? Tweaking enough ya might need him.'

"That bad, huh?" The breeze stroked his cheek with marigolds and lavender, the herbaceous lilt of hyssop peppered into the air and Caleb sought out the mint-like leaves and purple flowers of the herb.

'Tortured Lochagos Atropos for days, Hestia's priestess is with old Sal and Athene confirmed. Book's always updated with the tech of the time. Likeliest outcome? That ereader is the Book of Knowledge.'

"It was right in front of me and I didn't see it. Damn."

'If this Stana bitch goes after any more Folk, I don't know how to keep the intel contained. You got hours, maybe days and the entire Truce will be down your throat. I'd say it's time to call in the backup. Ya want Lou? I can... I can send ya Lou and his squad. Hit up Izanami, she's got some devotees on the flip side of life who could step up.'

Bent on his haunches, Caleb took a folding knife from his pocket and cut a bundle of hyssop at the base. "Yeah, kid. Any contacts you got, I need a 4-1-1 on Stana's location at all times, there were some crazy Fae with her. Think Sera could shake some vines?"

'You want my girlfriend to poke her nose back into Fae business?'

"The Changelings have got to know something. Figured their Princess might still have an ear to the buds."

'I'll ask her, but I ain't putting Sera in danger, not for you, not for anybody. She's staying on the firm side of not in the line of fire, here with me.'

"Thanks, Icarus." The moon cast grey light and stark shadows on the overgrowth. Rising from his perch, Caleb folded the knife back into his pocket and looked to the echo of warm firelight in the house. "You think you could find someone for me?"

'Yeah, kinda what we were... we were discussing me using like... every discrete contact to find this Stana chick, right? I thought... heh... hoh boy do we have wires crossed or...'

"Yes, no, kid... Icarus. Someone other than Stana. Off the books, not a word to anybody. Not a soul, not even Sera or Lou."

'... Jesus, there's someone worse out there?'

"Ule Bjørnsen, used to run the Grout Market." Silence caved in the connection, a lingering disease which compounded the shudder to Caleb's heart as he watched the Carpenter carve bark off his lover's face from a break in the windowpane.

'Don't ask me for that. Not that.'

"Tuija's desperate, I've got to..."

'No! You don't have to try. You hunt down this Ule guy, what? Leave the rest of us? Tuija's the closest person to a mother my Seraya has left, and you wanna what, get me to find a dude who can... what?'

"Calm down. I only want to talk."

'No, you want to leave. Is being a Fae so bad you wanna exit stage right from the people who love... well not you, sorry but I don't love you, dude, I mean you rock some serious socks, but Tuija, now there's a...'

"Icarus."

'... I never met my mother so I don't know what she was like, but Grandma Dite is kinda the best, most loving person in the universe because of the whole... being love... thing, and yet Sera is all Dono and Tuija are her Pub Parents and that makes you like... but...'

"Icarus, stop. Focus on Stana, we're not doing a damn thing until this mess is fixed. Backburner Ule. Even if I don't go after him for Tuija's sake..."

'Which you will.'

"... if someone got out of the Truce, I need to know how he did it before it becomes endemic."

'... damn it.'

"What?"

'That makes too much sense for me to boil down to panicked crazy talk and a pamphlet on So Your Lover's A Tree... I was halfway through that thing, even made pictures. Little... little sticker book...'

"Halfway, huh? What, Tuija's was already done?"

'Sitting on my desk, under...' Icarus' lips smack-popped on the connection, the rustle of items in bulk and a timid squeak piqued Caleb's ear as he leaned against an old oak with a view of the cathedral and the parsonage. '... an astounding amount of things.'

'When did I collect these things? What are... these things... gee do I never clean in here? Like... do I have access to a cleaning person? Oooh bad timing, ya know, 'cause Stana was a cleaning lady and now she's a murderous god-killer in training and oh hey! Tuija's picture book! Sera drew those pictures, and hey, do you know that there's like two kinds of hyssop that have totally different scientific names? True story!'

Caleb glanced at the sky with a bemused glint to his eyes, sure Icarus Areides might be older than him by thousands of years, but the kid was eternally twenty. A congregation of mighty wings fluttered in his periphery, and the Judge snapped his gaze to a multitude of eyes and wheels.

"Do the thing, find the bitch. And Icarus? Thanks for helping Tuija. Caleb out." Yanking back to his feet, Caleb kept his hands open.

The conflagration of wings, wheels and eyes churned and burned into his mind, a terrifying dissonance incongruent with the reality of Midgard. As disconcerting as the fourth, fifth and sixth dimensions to a physics student who hadn't mastered the first three. Theosians were the billow on the mountain top. The breath in the names of God creating hurricanes with their whispers. They were fire and light and astonishment defined in a legion of eyes and wings and wheels. Utterly confounding, when seen in the limited dimensional space humans and other such Folk knew as their reality. "Mika?"

"Be afraid."

"Well that's a different line than usual."

"Deimos and Phobos are moving and the rumour is Salomon lost the Book, while sacred fire torches Groves. Care to share?" Myriad wings and eyes morphed into the body shape of a non-binary person, blond hair flopped over the side of a muscular shoulder. Mika fiddled with the collar of their cream coloured shirt, flexed their arms as if the muscles and sinew were a fine suit.

"Stana Dubrivik, a human Sal's daughter hired to clean his house, stole the Book on the way out. She's behind all of this, but I don't see her acting alone. Someone taught her enough about the Realms to feed into... I don't know."

"You think a Folk taught her."

"Yes, I do. So I'd welcome discretion. I need to find out who and shut them down, without a Mystic dust-up. No angelic flaming swords ablaze yet."

"Noted. I'll check in with the Areosides. What do you want me to do when we find her?"

"Contain her, until we can yank the Book loose. Had my hand on it, damn thing ended up with her in the end, so there's got to be a cantrip or two holding it firm. We don't know what she knows, but I'm assuming it's a metric ton."

"Rationale?"

"Shot her multiple times in centre mass and she still managed to rip a hole in Midgard and jet herself out of synch."

"Yep! That would do it." Mika shook their head, ear tilted as if hearing messages from a horde of whispering voices. "So you need the Theosians to keep discrete sights on the multitude dimensions outside of most Folk purview."

"If you wouldn't mind. Yeah."

"You said human."

"Yes I did."

"Even if she is throwing herself into the Ginnungagap, or a higher dimension, she'd be insane by the time she got out. If she got out." The Archangel sniffed at the herb garden, looked up to the Cathedral and its fallen roof, exposed buttresses crumbled over time. "I remember a roof. Yes, I'm sure there was a roof on this place..."

"That's what's worrying me."

"The roof? Good thing to be worried about."

"Stana. More worried about Stana than my roof, thanks. Way she did it looked odd, like she'd done it before and if that's true, how's she navigating?

What energy source is she tapping into? How isn't she two curves short of a loop-de-hoop? What sort of magic preserves the human mind?"

"There is one human you could ask." Mika unfurled a pair of milk-white wings and shook them out, followed by a smaller set tinged with crimson feathers. "Carolee."

Both beings, demi-god and angel, shuddered.

"I should get back in there."

"We're scouring, for now I'll stay close to Jase."

"Safe plan. See you Mika." The walk back into the abandoned parsonage sunk into Caleb's shoulders. Strange as the Areosides genius was, Icarus was neither subtle nor quiet when it came to Tuija, and Caleb's body buzzed. Death's sting was nothing to being rewritten from the inside, modified by an alien sensation which stole the mammal out of the woman he loved.

A woman whose answer lay interrupted by the Carpenter's timing. Clinging to the hyssop, Caleb hissed out a thick exhale and eased his foot over the broken lumber of the door. The fire dried and warmed the broken interior, with a soft yellow glow, Jase with thin paintbrush in hand did one final stroke of pigment across Tuija's throat.

"I'm back."

"What did I tell you about timing, eh?" The resurrected divinity leaned back and dusted his hands off on a rag. Tuija clung to the fabric she sat on, eyes still closed, as if drumming up the courage to face Caleb at all. "Did I do her justice?"

"Tuija, what do you think? Yes, I... oh. The hyssop." Caleb offered the bundle of mint-like herb, its purple flowers a spritz of colour in the ruined and brown space. "Thought you needed it."

"Hmm? Oh! You two looked stressed, I was gonna make some calming tea. Hyssop, kinda like strange mint. Amazing how little things can help people. Washing the feet of a weary traveller, handing out some fish and bread, a cupp a... ooo York's nearby isn't it?" Jase smacked his lips and put a copper kettle on the tripod to boil. "Builder's tea and jammy dodgers. Mmm."

Jase pulled hyssop leaves off their stalk and into the swirling water of the kettle. Before Caleb could raise an eyebrow at the magical appearance of water in an oddly clean kettle, or three tin camping mugs on a side table cobbled together from broken chair legs and half a fallen shelf, Tuija caught his eye.

She worried at her bottom lip, the scars sanded down and carved as close to her skin as Jase could with his mastery, handle. In the sixty years he knew her as more than a bouncer or barfly, the fifty or so before their hovering orbits brought them to synchronisation, Caleb never knew this face. The bark-less skin, eased by firelight in the shambles of his own home.

And he knew it didn't matter whether she was half-wrapped in cedar, a Fae sprite taking her first steps beyond her anchor tree or the mimic of her polyanitsa days; Caleb loved her. All he could do was breathe and love her.

"Do I look human enough?" Eyes which challenged deities and armies with their might searched Caleb in rare vulnerability, open and soft as silk ribbon. "Did it work?"

Caleb stepped over a broken floorboard and took her hands, turning them this way and that to see the work Jase did on finger and knuckle, sanded down and carved back smooth to her skin, each reverse tattoo concealed the lines of amber and bark with a matte sheen. "Tuija, I..."

"Marry me like this." Tuija nudged her nose into Caleb's jaw at a soft gasp. "I want this to be the face you remember."

"Tea's..." Jase glanced up holding the kettle by a cloth on the handle, glanced between Caleb and Tuija, and quirked his lips. "... not important. I'm ah... heh... gonna... build something..."

"I want to remember all your faces." Caleb chuffed a grin at Jase's milling about, and tugged Tuija gently into his chest. Swept the backs of his fingers along her cheek, his grin deep as the soul in him. "And I don't give two wet fucks whether you're half Fae or a weeping willow or the warrior queen of the Bogatyrs. I care that you're my wife, in all forms of life, we belong to each other. I love you kjæreste."

"You said it." Tuija's eyebrows quivered, and she let her lips stroke his mouth, the twist to her upper lip still felt the same as before, another comfort of knowing his Tuija hadn't changed. "Caleb, you said you love me."

"Being here, I don't think any magic can touch us we don't allow inside. Jase, you got a minute?"

"For you two? Several." Jase dropped the broken stick of furniture he held, dusted his hands on a cloth from his back pocket. As Jase breathed, the doting carpenter rescinded for the ferocious might of the being, both deity and man, who stood tea forgotten in the ruined remains of Caleb's childhood home. Self-same creation, who whipped hypocrites as he threw their ill gotten gains to the floor for daring to exploit the frightened who hadn't heard the Theosian's only true command. Love one another.

"A marriage vow is sacred, that gives me power to connect and preserve you both. You and I have made our vows before, Caleb." His voice filled the space with its warmth and adoration, warming the wood and damp. The building no longer hung across Caleb's shoulders like a broken millstone, but a place for promises and reunion, a home in potentia. "Tuija Miroslava Draganova, do you willingly offer your marriage vow to my blessing? And thus to Theosian protection?"

"You would protect a Rastenivitsya? Even when I'm Fae?"

"With every fiber of my soul." And the eyes which sought to be kind through horrors and hypocrisy, which saw the beginning and end of all things, crinkled with a fiercely human glint.

"Fuck the Council, then. I accept."

Captive to the wells of Tuija's eyes, the turn of her lip, Caleb took Jase's offered hand. As Caleb remembered to breathe, a surge pure and untempered filtered through his fingers, up nerves and into his brainstem. Theosians were transcendent, their Realm functioned on too many higher dimensions to comprehend without time or habituation. After the century and a half he'd known the Carpenter, Caleb still found Jase's connection a heady and overwhelming rush.

Prismic light infilled the triad connection. A healing and holiness as if they were the only souls in this microcosm, spouses and the facilitating hands of a god whose truth was love and compassion and the sword to any who would mar it.

Tuija and Caleb found each other in the mystery, and intertwined as the house around them was no more the shambles of Caleb's ruined and dutiful childhood, but the vault of the Spheres with choirs both holy and profane singing in the joy and catharsis of this firm connection.

Jase receded into the choir, the chorus of celebration enough in its endless throng.

The only breaths which mattered to their miniature universe, Caleb and Tuija, wove together in the deeper waters which carried all Realms bound by the Green Man's Tree.

14

CEASEFIRE DARTS

God of shield clash and battle cry, Ares' boots landed on the defrosted ground as he hopped thirty metres from the helicopter with one dull thud. The sun's glint pinged off mirrored lenses and the brass coloured buckles of his otherwise dark grey combat gear.

Surrounded by evergreens on the summit of the British Columbian mountainside, a woman pulled her camouflage hood down and huffed at the wealth of noise which followed the charging Olympian, his Kopis Industries 'copter far louder than the distress beacon she lit.

"Alcippe." Ares' mouth contorted in a grin, as he opened one arm for the woman in the glade. "Come hug your old man."

"Pater. We're not alone." Alcippe dove in for an embrace which promised more familial affection another time, a tight smile punctuating deep brown eyes. Her mother's eyes, framed by her mother's deep brown hair and skin which took a tan without Ares' freckles.

"Show me." Pistol on his hip, kopis at the other, Ares raced into the wood two steps behind his demi-goddess daughter and her compound bow. A mix of modernity and nods to the Mediterranean, Alcippe's clothing was modern weave and kevlar light enough to wear under camouflage windbreakers and cargo trousers. Pockets packed flat and neat with the ephemera of a lifelong survivalist who wove her way around her 3,700th birthday.

Twigs dared not crack beneath Alcippe's feet, as she dashed through the forest. March in the mountains ought to have been a more frigid affair, but for the intervention of the Amazons, and the nearby Grove. Ares fared as the warmonger he was, proud of foot and loud as the crash of shield walls and charging infantry.

"We found the fir grove smoldering in time to stamp it out, there was a strange Fae on the periphery my sisters and I chased off to the falcons on the wind."

"Kehmeti?" Ares stomped over a fallen trunk half rotted. "Did Horus send reinforcements?"

"They certainly didn't come from British Columbia... do you ever not make noise?"

"If you wanted the element of surprise, you would have called Dite." The former Olympian shouldered a tree aside with a loud crack as he chased his daughter's swift heels.

"Hmph. Aphrodite Areia would be more effective in the forests. My bad."

"She'd love how you called her that."

"What, her name? Does she not often hear it? Father, do I have to read you our Feminist Library via telephone again?"

At that, Ares burst into a guffaw, which shocked the meadow of its songbirds and the lone yip of a fox farther off. "Areia. Your step-mother's proud of her armour. She doesn't get to use it much anymore."

"And whose fault is that?"

"Time's. You try running what she does in bronze plate."

"Ah. Pater?"

"Yes, Alcippe."

"I needed you and you're here." Alcippe skidded to a halt in the brush, the thin leather soles of her boots shushing the ground. Leaf matter with flecks of ash, charnel smoke lingered and wove into Ares' nostrils, several branches snapped under foot. "Thank you."

"Always." Ares' boots found piles of charred undergrowth.

The Sacred Grove shook and wailed in his divine ear, a keening discord to the peace the soldiers buried under the ground ought to have known. Twisted branches thick as limbs outstretched from strange stalks, the bark and leaf of each Sacred Tree was another soldier who fought and died with the Fae Lord's Curse. Concentric circles of strange trees centred on the remains of a sprout half-crushed from stamping feet and a fire blanket, thin trails of smoke puffed up from fallen pine needles. Alcippe dug her foot under them and spread the needles out, stomped any ember under the dirt for good measure.

"Wasn't the promise I offered old soldiers a calm and comfort in the end? Their families salvaged, the crops returned when the battles were done? Not this, woken immobile from their dreams, locked in a Fae's body."

"At least they have the potential to wake up at all. Most humans would kill for a second chance, regardless of how it came."

"We'd all feel less uneasy if some of them did wake up. Waiting hundreds of years to see if our battle dead even remember their names is agonising." He reached for an alder with a trunk swollen as if a narrow hipped form rose to seek the sun. "Sleep, warrior. Return to sweeter dreams."

"Tyr Odinson. Would that you calmed all our glorious dead." The Einherjar snuck out of the undergrowth, his scent covered by the soot. Red tresses braided as cleanly as his beard, the warrior wore engravings of Odin's two ravens on either shoulder, Huginn and Muninn. Thought and Emotion.

"I calm whoever requires it, goad the rest. Where is Thor? I assume he's rolled off his mead bench for this?" Ares rocked his shoulders to centre himself, an Einherjar and not a Valkyrie in the Amazon's Preserve? Not even Thrud? The discordance lingered on his back, another place he'd been away from for too long.

"Alfather sent us, Thor has roofs to shingle. Is this not not your territory, Tyr? Aesir of War and Justice? Is the ignition of our siblings' souls not something where Justice ought to be done?" The lilt of the warrior's voice gripped at a ferocity unveiled, a tempest in the blood. Ares sniffed it through the ash as the man stepped closer, its giddy rattle enough to shake into the deity and cling.

"It is. If Alfather was sending reinforcements, why am I hearing it from you?" Ares clenched his fist, as the potency of the Einherjar's belief raced into him like another cup of Icarus' nuclear coffee.

"We thought it obvious you would want our help."

"Amazons need no help from men." Alcippe set her hand on the hilt of the kopis strapped to her thigh, eyes narrowed.

"Oh, is your cloister and personal comfort more important than the lives of our fallen? Maybe... maybe I should go, stand two paces out of your territory and yell the enemy over. Might not save the Grove in time, but as long as you're comfortable." The Einherjar raised an eyebrow and pursed his lips. A grit-toothed sneer and low growl emanated from the Amazon Queen.

"Next emergency, send the Shield Maidens t-" Ares raised his fist and both warriors went quiet. Ill intent on the breeze stung at Ares' eyes. He twisted, kopis unsheathed as two darts thudded into the tree behind him. Alcippe rolled forward and away into the brush, bow off her back and an arrow knocked. The

Einherjar roared and yanked a dane axe from his back one-handed, the dark wood of the haft inscribed with softly glowing runes.

Another volley of darts whistled in the air, avoided by Ares' lunging steps into the centre of the Sacred Grove.

"Stop sneaking around like whelps and show yourselves!" The Einherjar bellowed, stepping back to back with his beloved Tyr. A host of pounding feet caught their ears, with the shriek of a strange bird.

"Villains with tinder box in pocket! Out! Leave our mighty Rastenivitsya alone!" Dressed in sharovary and a blue thick leather tunic, the Bogatyr who thundered into the glade looked painted from the panel of strange folklore. The fur around his hat twitched in the breeze less than the brown moustache wobbling above drawn lips. He surged at the Einherjar, war hammer met axe and the two locked in violent grimaces.

"Who called the Makoshki? Stop fighting my soldier, you Slavic fool! We're here for the same reason!" Ares grit his teeth as the sounds of canine footsteps padded at the ground. "Easy! Show yourselves!"

With the scurrying sound of a struggle and a canid shriek, a fox was tossed into the centre of the Grove.

"O-Kami!? What's a Kitsune doing in the backwoods of British Columbia?!" The kitsune snuffled at Ares' boots, then wheeled around with a short shriek, the fur on all four of its white tails puffed out.

"Immigration is a thing." Alcippe circled in and back through the underbrush, as another series of darts flowed between the Einherjar and Bogatyr's gnashing teeth. Both men thrust away from each other, eyes out on the thick wood. Coils of green vines wove through some of the trees further out, the rustle of leaves peppered into the acrid air.

"Do not torch our dead!" The Kitsune wheeled about on Ares, leapt up to sink teeth into his sword arm, but met only the thin metal of his retracted buckler.

"We're not burning them, we're saving them!" Ares swatted the Kitsune down, as another legion of darts spattered across tree and loam. Once embedded in the soil, the darts quivered, and thick green vines shot out to entangle the warriors' legs. "Every time I try... should have sent Dite."

"Fae!" The kitsune transformed into a lithe four tailed figure in modified kusari armour, unsheathed their tantō and sliced a vine in half. It recoiled, as the surrounding thicket rustled. Alcippe's braid flashed in the green, and disappeared. Another strange caw laced from the sky.

"Together!" Ares stomped a vine out at the root. The Einherjar and the Bogatyr continued to bash away at each other, the roil of their struggle as intoxicating as the adrenaline coursing through each of the warriors' veins. Their collective heartbeats pulsed behind Ares' eyes, causing his senses to become keener, his reflexes faster, his strength multiplied in a heady rush.

"If not you, why is the ash so thick!?" The kitsune circled as axe and war hammer continued to clash. The Bogatyr's back thudded hard against a tree, shaken with a howl as a dart found the flesh of his shoulder. He raised his warhammer in time to avoid the outstretched talons of a golden falcon, who careened down from the sky with a screech.

"My Amazons snuffed out the fire." Ares clashed kopis to tantō, thrust down and the kitsune stumbled. His eye flickered on the Kehmeti Falcon, who transformed from bird into a woman in golden armour and winged collar necklace, her helmet shaped as the Falcon's Head.

"Then why are the Fae attacking you?" The Falcon unsheathed the curved blade of her khopesh, an avian caw at the growling kitsune, who wheeled around to meet it.

"Ask this one." Alcippe shoved a bundle of paracord into the Grove, vines of ivy trailed over the bark-face and slim shoulders of an amber eyed Fae. It sloped to the ground, an alien hatred emblazoned across its noseless, lipless face. "One swipe of my blade and it'll have a mouth."

"Peel so much of a flake of bark off that Fae and I'll gut you." The Kehmeti flashed round, and Khopesh pointed at Alcippe. Ares' daughter kicked the Fae to the ground by Ares' feet, flicked her blade to the ready and squared her shoulders.

Leaping back, the Kitsune waited on a knife point, as the Norseman yanked the Bogatyr's war hammer out of his hands, dane axe set on his chest up at the man's throat. They swore at each other in their own languages, eyes a constant search between the confounding and chaotic skirmish.

"Enough!" Booming and solid as machine gun fire, Ares' voice broke the chaos as his heel stomped a wandering vine on the ground. "Weapons down. Now!"

Alcippe and the Einherjar complied immediately, their weapons cleaned and sheathed before another breath. The Kitsune was next, followed by a twitch in the Kehmeti Falcon's arm.

"You do not own this world." She did not release her khopesh to its sheath before Ares picked the Fae up by the neck-like trunk and away from the potential to root.

"For all the fighting we do on it, I may as well." Ares bit back, staring across the tempestuous Folk.

"You might have summered with Horus as a child, but I do not take your orders." The Falcon circled the circumference of the Grove's clearing, as the Kitsune glanced between both and hopped back to take their chances with the Kehmeti.

"Where is the Judge? Should he not be called?"

"You'd pull the Judge from his work tracking the arsonist bastard down to calm a tiff in a forest?"

"Yes." The Kitsune strafed along the clearing's edge, vulpine ears flicking at each sound of the forest. Despite most weapons being lowered, Ares continued to feel the heady rush of a battle reconflagrated, the fear and wide-eyed readiness to throw another attack.

He hissed out a low breath, the battle would be an easy victory. Alcippe to the Kehmeti, a glorious round of combat for the evenly matched warrior women. All but defeated, it wouldn't take more than a single strike to render the Bogatyr unconscious and pair with the Einherjar to distract and subdue the Kitsune.

The trickiest of the opponents, the Fae might've been young, but if it rooted, if it gained control of the plant life around it, an entire forest could come down on them. No, it was best to leave the Kitsune to Odin's faithful and handle the Fae personally. Keep it bundled up, incapable of rooting, wounds would carve their way through the gathered Folk. Red-wine offerings to his pugilist's altar.

Ares breathed in and out as the tensions around him notched and raised. Why stop? Caleb faltered every third step the last few years, the Judge was as fatigued as Ares when he bundled Dite and little Eros up for Thrace's shores. What if the whispers were true, and Midgard needed a King to protect it?

A pantheon of its own, and who fit better than him? Jase? Sarasvati? Old Wandering One-Eye?

And the kopis in his hand shone.

The Folk readied their weapons in the thrall of the warmonger.

A war would spread from the Grove, alliances strung up like festival lights, one by one to conquer. All with the flick of Ares' sword.

"Get the Bogatyr loose from the tree and clean him up, this is sacred ground." Another heavy exhale, and Ares sheathed his sword with a shiver. How could he look his spouses in their eyes and tell them once again, Ares son of Zeus let his pride win? Would he trade Olympus' Throne, or the Seat of the Aesir for humanity's neon altar? Would Aphrodite and Leonidas stand beside him as the conqueror, instead of their solid and compassionate love? The exiled Olympian learned war without justice was barbarism. Fighting to tear the ragged injustices down did not always need a sword and shield. "All of us want the same thing, the Sacred Groves protected. Maybe if we stop trying to kill each other we'd have the chance to succeed."

Bringing the Fae's face to his eyeline, Ares growled out of grit teeth. "And you, stop throwing darts or we'll throw you in a biodome without soil. Understood, little leaf?"

The Fae glared at him, and with a shake of its vines, budded flowers instead of thorns. Ares dropped it, and the Fae slunk to the ground, two thick vines plunging into the soil, as the rest of its body attempted a humanoid appearance.

"This Fae can't even talk, yet. I don't see more of their ilk, it may have been acting alone." Alcippe set her gloved hand on her father's shoulder, a knowing curve to her eyebrow. Sweet daughter, she always was able to read him like Icarus' many books.

"High Queen Selyka promised to reinforce the Sacred Groves, I was there when she said it." The Kehmeti Falcon brushed her dark fingertips over the winged collar necklace around her neck and collarbone, the glint of gold cosmetics painted around one eye, black kohl around the other, caught in the diffused forest light. "Pity we can't ask this Fae if it's a budling setting these fires."

"Anyone know charades?" The Bogatyr grunted from his seated spot leaning against a Sacred birch, a gauze square from the Einherjar's pack pressed to his wound. "What? Is a fun game, you make pretend body movements, guess answers from interpretive dance. It's not the Bolshoi, but..."

Ares paced the Grove's border in an effort to catch his breath. The violent torrent thudding in his veins ebbed as the Bogatyr entered a discussion of charades between the emphatically waving Fae and the Kitsune. He knew better than to expect Alcippe to ease with potential threats in her wood. The thin line of remaining fury dictated a caution unrelated to the talk in the glade.

A shadow crossed paths with a tree at an angle foreign to the sun, and Ares' sword unsheathed with a melodic slice in the air.

"I'm here for the Fae, little codger jumped the gun. Didn't wait for proper reinforcements to pass through Artemis' territory." Curly hair billowed like a crimson crown from a loose ponytail atop her head, the grey pallor of pale skin seemed akin more to moonlight than the sunlight filtering through old growth. A spotted hand brushed a leaf off black trousers.

"Carolee. Tread light in my daughters' forest, or we shall have more than words." The shrill line of wrongness, of horrifying cost slicked down Ares' spine.

"Pussy whipped." Carolee snorted, one set of spindle fingers stroked at a strange shadow, until it conjured into a jagged obsidian bolt.

"The thought that I ought to question my masculinity for loving the most gracious woman in the cosmos and raising mighty and caring daughters is beyond ridiculous. Grow up."

"Love you, too Pater." Alcippe's alto voice clipped into the curve of Ares' ear. He would have cursed his lack of focus in picking up Alcippe's footsteps if he hadn't taught her to walk in silence. The power to be heard when applied and temporarily restricted, was as powerful as a tidal wave and his daughter knew this to the marrow in her demi-divine bones.

"I'm the father of the Amazons. That should give you enough indication of my beliefs on womanhood." Ares postured his arms across his chest, the taller target, the bigger of the two and more likely to be targeted. "Why did Selyka send her assassin to grab one stray budling? One who can't even talk?"

Carolee grimaced, and the light around her shifted as if weighted by the act, the black sclera of her eyes dipped in a bone-gnawing malice.

"None of that." The growl to Ares' voice pitched into the ground and the roots and the air, a knife edge sharper than Carolee's obsidian blades.

"Remind me to make you a Best Pater urn for your next feast day." Alcippe lowered her kopis as Carolee scoffed and leaned against the nearest tree which would hold her weight.

"Someon-"

"Y'think I can't smell a lie?" More to the gravel toothed baritone, the rumble of blood seas pouring through streets into soldiers' graves.

"Give me time. I'll have the culprit, and no more Groves will burn. Trust me."

"Hah."

"Trust my blade, then." Carolee pushed off from the tree and stalked Ares' shoulder, never close enough to be caught in stray, dangerous Areosides arms. "My will to return to my Liam. A boy ought to know his mother."

A tweak in Ares' eyebrows bored into the atmosphere, a faint lull in the wind settled against his spine. "A parent would do anything to return to their child."

"Including play patsie for Zeus? You think a few thousand years covers the stink of your old codger?"

"Careful, assassin. Don't exhaust the slight empathy I have for your plight. Not when you're trespassing on my daughters and sister's land."

"Or what? Think the Judge would look favourable on a warmonger's threats?" Even the freckles on the back of Carolee's hand appeared grey and discoloured in comparison to the void black cloth on her slim body, the fire of her hair. She stroked her hand along the other bicep, this tainted being set into Selyka's service.

"The Judge is occupied. By strange malignant Fae, luck would have it, ah yes, and a human woman who tears portals into Kaos with bitter magics. I don't know where anyone would get those ideas, let's think." Ares' boot crunched into the ground, Alcippe's gloved hand found her father's fingers and with a tug, attempted to settle the dissipating rush left in his divine veins.

"She what?" Carolee's cheek twitched, the black sclera of her eyes deep as pools of starless night narrowed. Thin pupils darted from Alcippe and her father, until with pursed lips, Carolee trudged toward the sacred circle of the grove's inner ring.

"Tell me. What is chasing us?"

"I'll take care of it!"

"What tried to kill my son's Lochagos and ripped reality like a tattered coat? How was it done? Is it one of your blades?" Ares chased after, both beings careful not to walk within range of the others arms, the staccato of clapping reverberating around the air from the clearing in the centre.

They passed the Einherjar and Falcon who whispered in proximity as they investigated the runic circle, the protector trees which should have prevented harm or spark. Both Viking and Kehmeti stopped their whispers at the sight of Carolee, and trotted in pursuit.

"It's mine! My quarry to pursue." Carolee stalked forward, eyes on the flicker of a Fae vine through the tree cover.

"If you..." Ares growled and grabbed Carolee's shoulder, slamming her back against a tree trunk. Within a blink, Carolee held an obsidian spike in hand, aimed for Ares' liver. The forest arrested into abrupt silence. "... think I will be patient, when my family is at risk and the soldiers I promised peace find nothing but a burning hell, you are far from capable of mind. Was it your blade that opened the woman's passage?"

"No."

"Who helped her?"

"It's my burden to handle."

"So it is a Fae." Ares' eyes flickered to Alcippe, and she set her sword back in its sheath. Leaning closer, Ares stared into Carolee's endlessly black eyes, the piercing blue of his own as cold as a forgotten nordic winter. "Who?"

Thin lips knitted shut, Carolee glared at the Faeling, who hopped around the Bogatyr in a flimsy interpretive dance. The guffawing warrior held his hand over a wad of leaves and vine sealing up his shoulder, until the Fae rocketed into a straight spindle of a tree, bark face with amber eyes locked on the High Queen's assassin.

"Eh! Little twigling, why you st-" He swerved round and caught the sight of Ares, Deity of War in two Realms and adopted son of a third clench his fist around the slight woman's shoulder. "-op that would be why."

Fae toes dug into the soil, tried to root in place. Carolee stared at the Faeling child, little more than a spindle-vined adolescent fresh from their anchor tree. Ares' eyes followed, the whisper of mischief present in the Faeling enough to cause it to click a set of bark coated vines over each other in a form of chirping sound.

"Or... do you know, little leaf?" Releasing the pressure on Carolee's shoulder, Ares turned to the Faeling fully, its vines gathered into humanoid limbs. Broad shoulders, a narrower face. Ivy leaves on its head began to curl into thinner circles.

"Asking a budling? Isn't interrogating children beyond you?" Carolee bucked against the tree, the obsidian blade in her hand slipped into her grasp and stopped only when the curve of Alcippe's kopis pressed against her neck. "They're deceivers, budling."

"Well, I do have deceptively good interpretive dance skills." The Bogatyr guffawed, his healthy hand wrapping around the haft of his war hammer released by the Einherjar. "Who, Faeling? Who does this evil thing?"

The amber in the Faeling's eyes crusted as it concentrated, limbs moving, body growing until the size of the spectre in its mind. Masculine shoulders and hips, a crown of willow on its head.

And as the Faeling scooped up a cloud of ash from the ground, shaking as it rubbed the grey powder on its limbs, Ares released the High Queen's assassin. The circle of Folk were captive of the sight, ash up the arms of a Fae Lord.

"A firestarter? Crowned in willow..." A flash of void black painted Ares' vision. Obsidian and sharp, Carolee's blade punctured the fabric of Midgard's reality with a thin brush of air. She dove for the Faeling and tumbled into the void between all Realms, the Kaos known by many of the Realms as the Ginnungagap.

The rip sealed shut, clean as a surgeon's suture.

"Gone! And I almost won the game." The Bogatyr shook his head, their complicated Faeling beyond anyone's reach.

"Eh, come to Finn's, I'll beat you in a game of Hnefltafl." The Einherjar sheathed his axe, dusting off his hands before bowing in a deep and reverent salute. "If Tyr is finished with me."

"Whatever Fae attempted to start this fire is gone. Call your shield maiden sisters to reinforce the Amazons. You and the rest of your warriors, coordinate with Lady Falcon and our Kitsune associate. I want all Sacred Groves protected by only those who have experience fighting Fae."

"I still do not answer t-"

"Stop testing my patience, it's well used up." Whether wisdom prevailed or Ares' tone threatened too much violence for the Falcon to stomach, the warrior woman bowed in an approximation of reverence before taking to the air as a golden falcon on a swift wind. "Icarus."

'Yes, magnus pater?' The electronic undulation of Icarus' voice echoed through a microphone on Ares' collar, a slight comfort knowing no matter his trials, there were two children left at home who needed a grandfather's guidance.

"Call my sons. Patch us through to Caleb, a firestarter Fae with a willow's crown is burning the Groves. It's the Fae."

'Ah… I think we got this one, it seems like we gotta put Fae-by gates around the Sacred Groves and bing bang boom, they're…'

"Icarus."

'… maybe electrified or such, plants hate electricity. Remember that time I tried to solve the invasive knotweed problem with a taser?'

"Icarus." Ares growled.

"Fae-by Gate?" The Kitsune's ears flicked as they pulled out a fan to hide the silent laugh pouring out of their throat.

'Like baby gate but for Fae, 'cause rhymes and…'

"Child! What reason do you have to stall?" Alcippe ran her hand over her hair, leaning into the small comm on her father's collar.

'Oh hey Grandma! You called me child instead of daughter, that's cool of you and…'

"Hush child, call the Judge we desire to speak with him. It is a matter of urgency."

'Ya did it again! Aw dat's precious, you'll get the whole non-binary pronoun thing in no time, I mean maybe no time for us since… hah… we're both over three thousand…' As Icarus babbled, Ares cleared his throat, the steady tap of his boot on the soil enough to puff some dirt up in a miniature cloud. '... I can call Caleb in a couple hours.'

"Pardon?" Ares glared at the comm, what in Gaia's cave was happening this day?

'I'm not calling Caleb for another few hours, we can handle it.'

"Icarus, so help me..."

'No force in the universe can get me to call my girlfriend's Pub Mom in the middle of her impromptu nuptials. Sorry! Not gonna do it! No way, not for all the microchips in the macrocosm. It can wait a couple hours, Magnus Pater.' The torrent of words stopped abrupt as the shock across Ares' cheeks.

"Nuptials?" Ares spat, was the Judge taking none of this sincerely?

'You should probably hurry. Deimos and Phobos are still moving at break-other-people's-necks speed.' Icarus' voice garbled with the rustle of fingers on keys, 'As much as it might cause my ears to bleed, I'll keep Daedalus.AI on the lovebirds to tell you when they're copacetic with the outside world. Caleb's not slacking off, they clattered with Stana and Tuija got hurt... give them an hour? A couple? They need this, Pappos, and if they need it, I'll defend their need for it, even from you.'

"They fought Stana? Where?"

'Canterbury, England. However she's doing it, she's skipping continents as fast as the Fae. I'll talk Finn into letting the Twins have a hall pass for his doors, might...'

"No. The Fae are involved somehow, we can't trust those doors... Einherjar."

"Yes, Tyr."

"Go to Heimdall, my sons need permission to traverse Bifröst, and if that won't work, tell Frigg I need Gna to ferry them on Hofvarpnir. She can handle their terror long enough to give them a ride."

"Did Icarus say Thor's grandson got... married?" The Einherjar shifted closer to Ares, the Dane Axe on his back, and Bogatyr by his side.

"To Draganova? This makes us family! If! She was not banished for being a cursed traitor for refusing to die in a heroic act of self-sacrifice instead of turning into our hated enemy, oh and if your Thor's grandson was not kept from his family by Raynar Thorson."

"Einridsen."

"Bud'te zdorovy. Be healthy, my friend." The Bogatyr slapped the Einherjar's shoulder with a stern nod.

"Thank y-I didn't sneeze! That is his name! Einridsen! After Einridi! The one who rides alone! Einridi's son! Son of he who rides alone!" The Einherjar shook his head, the pitiful quiver under his beard enough to snap Ares back into the surreality of the situation.

"Eh, I like Ivan. Ivan is a solid name. Ivanov. Ivanovich. Rolls off the tongue."

Deimos and Phobos were on a warpath through Midgard to capture this Stana, who unbeknownst to the Council, or the Truce at large stole the Book of Knowledge. A willow crowned Fae Lord transformed into a fire starter, one with the secret to sacred fire strong enough to burn gods to cinder and ash. And the Fae controlled the doors in a magical monopoly of Realm travel.

Those old paths like the Bifrost weren't without their dangers, the odds of catching up to someone using the Faerie Doors with alternate means were not odds Ares favoured. He repressed a roar. How could Caleb be so foolish?!

Telling no one, Caleb and Tuija rushed off on their own, in a time like this. Regardless of divinity, Caleb was still a man, Tuija, his lover. Ares ran his thumb along the scars on his index finger, aeons never chilled the flames of his brother Hephaestus' vulcanic plasma holding him to the mountain, while he claimed a bride not meant to be his. Aphrodite... Leonidas. If Ares knew he had a moment with each, before the clatter and the shield breaks of war, did he ever refuse?

"Not a word about the marriage." Ares glared at the beads on the man's beard, how they glinted with the shine of a polished and refined warrior. While Caleb seemed off the last while, Ares wondered. Whether he could handle the rush to his veins or not, would he need to step beyond Caleb for the good of the Realms?

"Yes, Tyr. We're at your disposal." The Einherjar bowed in a respectful salute, covering the grind of his teeth at the prospect of buddying up even temporarily with the jolly Bogatyr.

"Do it, Pater." Alcippe clenched her fists with a tight shake to her head. Ares' eyebrow quirked.

"Are you..."

"Call the noisy whirlybird." Alcippe whirled round and motioned for the kitsune and the Falcon to accompany her, "You're out of time, pater! Call it and go! The danger is past here, we women have work to do. Be gone!"

"I don't think you'll get a clearer 'piss off' in all your days." The Bogatyr scratched at his neck, fixed his moustache, and cleared his throat. "When do we leave?"

"If I'm not their firstborn's godfather, I'm going to revolt. Watch me." Ares growled, the sound of helicopter rotors already in the wind. "Run!"

15 EMPTY PINTS & SPENT SHELLS

"Fucking disaster. What the hell, how didn't I see this?" While not as comfortable as Finnegan's Pub, the Sword and Tack in Masham's town square had enough of a back room for Caleb to work. The Hallowes was nothing but an empty shell come morning, dry enough for a night but lacking in any sort of provision. While he and Tuija knew they could call for an evac, whispers from Icarus as to Kopis Industries' movement, paired with the intel of Stana working with a willow crowned Fae Lord didn't ingratiate them to the Fae Lord of Finnegan's Bluff.

If Caleb was truthful, he'd admit he wasn't ready for the other Folk to see him or Tuija yet. Not when the majority would sniff out a marriage bond like bad cologne on the over perfumed. "How did the woman know to cast spells at all?"

"You think the best of people, why else do you think half the Realms off their repeat offenders?" Tuija walked two pints of amber ale to the table and set them down on soaked cardboard coasters, after the miniature maze of alcoves and a tight staircase, which spiralled on creaking wooden steps. "One of the things to love, but it didn't serve you this time. Sometimes bastards need culling. The level of crazy off that one? Gods and pixies, at first I thought it was the messed up Fae who trudged into the crossroad."

"Who the fuck did Afua hire!? I thought she'd be some confused human staring at hocus pocus for the first time, but that!? How long has Sal been without the Book?" Caleb fussed with Stana's jacket collar, shook his head with a sharp huff. The table's waxed texture played under his fingernails, what was this place, a quarter as old as Finn's?

"Hydrate, then what? We call Lu for another locator session?" Tuija shoved the pint across the table. Caleb stood with both palms on either side of the bloody jean jacket, pocket contents strewn on the old wood stained with time's patina and a few etched names of the inebriant brave.

"No need. Now I have something of hers, I can triangulate."

"Why didn't you lead with that when we were at Lu's?"

Caleb eyed his bride and took the pint. Sucked half of it down his gullet before he set the glass back down on the moist coaster.

"What? Don't shoot me with that stare unless you're going to buy the next round. Then shoot me that death glare and make it a double shot of whiskey. Preferably Irish. Peaty. Delicious." Tuija's pint disappeared in stages, the cursed Slavic warrior nudged at a pen from Stana's pocket, a packet of mints with Cyrillic writing on the wrapper, a set of keys with a keychain from a car sales place off Marine Drive, wherever the Marine Drive in question was... bits and bobs. The beginning peek into a life on the wrong side of Vancouver's house-wealth and empty dwellings.

"Delilah taught me, besides, I didn't know who I was looking for. Ditch the pocket contents, they're useless. This is all I need." Caleb held up the jacket itself, turned inside out with patches of crimson leaked into the white wool.

"You shot her."

"I've been doing this for a hundred and fifty years, I'm not a poor shot. Without magical intervention, she should have bled out at our feet."

"Morbid much?"

"I'm a glorified assassin for naughty immortals, I kill people all the time." Caleb clenched his jaw and sucked down the rest of his pint, set the glass on the table with a loud 'thunk'. "It tracks. Besides, Icarus said it was defcon desperation on the Areosides front. If I want her to be anything other than paste on the bottom of Deimos and Phobos' shoes we have to hurry."

"You do the best you can."

"Tuija, she got away! I shot the bastard four times and she still had enough magic to open a portal into another Realm and scat! With the Book! How the hell did this bitch learn to manipulate things so fast!? Took Sal ten years to figure that shit out, so pardon me if the situation has me in a tizzy!"

"...... okay I haven't heard someone say 'tizzy' since 1983."

Stopped short, Caleb stared with a firm set jaw as Tuija stared back, one hand drifting through the business cards creased and folded from Stana's pocket.

"You sound like Dad's girlfriend."

"Groovy, is she a cool cat?" Tuija made a pretence of doing the mash-potato until Caleb's lip wobbled. "Have her over for dinner, make a pot roast, grill some fish?"

"You are making it diff-"

"Diff? Difficult? Me? Crank up the radio receiver, doll face. Tune in to my channel."

"... Tuija."

"Bully day." She balled her fist like a bare knuckle boxer and slugged at his shoulder with a couple of loose punches until Caleb cracked. His chuckle chased the nervous shift of his fingers, and Caleb shook his head to take in the faded posters and antique art collected and curated by the owner's past.

"Can I focus now on the killer magic lady, or are you going to take us back to 1895?"

"Made you smile. My work here is done, I'm going to order the next round. Hand over your wallet, or the business cards get hurt, Caleb Draganov." Tuija opened her palm, and Caleb broke into another chuckle.

"Draganov, eh? Not a bad ring to it, Tuija Mauthisen... we ought to hyphenate." He dug into his back trouser pocket, pulled out a 20 pound note, released it only when he dragged Tuija close for a kiss. They clung together, longer than the breath he thought he needed, longer than it took her to walk backward, eye him over.

"No magic without me... Caleb Mauthisen-Draganov... Caleb Draganov-Mauthisen? Hmm. I might like that better. I mean it. No magic."

"Never." With Tuija out of the alcove, Caleb sunk into the long wooden bench and set his elbows on the table with a hiss. Why couldn't Sal... no. He couldn't blame Sal for setting the Book down and holding out. This, yet again, was on him. The new phone sat on the table, slim and metallic in its rebuking silence.

"Tell the Twins she tore through Midgard's dimensional fabric out of a crossroads and I've got the Theosians on the higher dimensions, see if she turns up in the Voids, Tuija and I'll leave the jacket, you can take your own samples. Any intel on accomplices would help, she learned from somebody and I need to know whom. No, I didn't see this coming. No, I didn't know Sal lost the book."

Pending... An ellipsis in flux on the screen.

Condensed reports from Icarus flickered with helmet cam videos of Lochagos Danae Atropos contorted from binding vines, one of the missing from his earlier list in the thin black notebook stuck in his back pocket.

A body interrupted in the garden, half-consumed in a shallow grave. A slim line of text from Icarus asking if they should have Seraya steer clear of the Pub a few days.

Caleb felt the synchronicity of Icarus staring back through the screen from their lab in the Aphneion palace. A place firm as an inner sanctum to the temple of love and war. They were two beings disconnected but for the technological thread, which wove around their devices like beaded chains, maybe Icarus' attention wasn't terrible. Maybe the kid had moxy. Maybe Caleb could forgive the youth for what they did under Melinöe's control, after all, what more was he doing for Tuija than Icarus did for Seraya?

'Stana kept asking for Danae's name. Used that other woman's name until she croaked. Don't know how it'd help, but that's what Lochagos Atropos said before she tanked. She's with Sclep, Deimos and Phobos're livid.'

"Frick. The Twins are within their rights to go after Stana, human or no. Thanks Icarus, that helps."

'We're gonna get it back, right? The Book, you're gonna take it back?'

It was Caleb's idea to give the Book to a human Keeper in the first place, his idea to choose a person who would age and wither and fall to the horrors of mortality. Not such a consuming thought when they were young and dumb, larking about in Queen Victoria's Empire for the most part, travels on steamer ships or through Finnegan's doors.

'Not that I'm sticking my neck out for ya and all, but I was mighty decent when you and Tuija needed some personal time, and Magnus Pater can be persuasive as the gigantic personification of war and justice that he is, but I stood... well... sat 'cause heh... I was at my computer and... okay so the sitting or standing wasn't important, but this is. You're gonna set this square. I'll do what you need me to do, anything, as long as I know the end goal. We're setting this square, right, Caleb?'

Caleb's fingers shook through each strand of hair he ran them through. He clutched at his skull, trying to remember to keep focused. Keep to his tasks, his duty. The rest would come out in the wash.

"I'll find a way." The bodies. Said first as a taunt, became a revelation. The room was small as it was constricted with distant conversations and music through antique speakers garbled by poor wifi. The fuzz of an old radio.

Stana's spiteful gaze settled on his mind's eye, quick to a driving apathy of one who couldn't wait for bodies to hit the ground. Confirmed by Icarus, more bodies, these ones human as the person Stana was prior to the Book reaching out. And there it was, the taint of the Realms, when not handled properly.

When not kept in containment, or measured out with the ethics of shared power.

The Book of Knowledge was so hungry for release from a stodgy old man it jumped ship with a psychopath.

Before he knew how long Tuija was gone, Caleb heard the filter of her voice, felt her hands reach under his elbows, yank them off the table so she could push his back against the bench seat, and search her new husband's face.

"I should have called, he was getting older and his hip went out and his heart, he started taking pills three times a day and..."

"Oooh Oh, look at me, eyes here..."

"He kept aging and I don't age like he does, I didn't age. He kept fading right in front of me." Caleb heaved a sigh to clear his head, "I should age like him, shouldn't I? The human half of me, shouldn't I feel it by now?"

"Cale, you need to look at me. Open your eyes."

"The Book was supposed to be safe."

Tuija gripped at his jaw, supported the back of his head with her hand and tugged again. "Open your eyes."

"I can't watch you being burnt to cinders like them. Not by some psycho bitch, not by anyone."

"I'm with you, and we are going to breathe, and we are going to figure this out."

"What do I tell them? No.... I shouldn't tell them anything..."

"They delivered pizza because I mentioned I got the nibble-fits within earshot of your phone, they already know."

"Not Kopis, Icarus said the Terrors found one of their missing in Vancouver already, Fae vines broke her limbs. I have to fix this before Stana burns more groves."

"We will."

"You're not listening!"

"I'm negating you for us. The fact you did this alone for a century is insane. Remember those marriage vows we took a few hours ago? You don't get to veto them. Not now, not ever. Shut up a minute." Shoving his arm open, Tuija sat across Caleb's thighs and pushed the table away with the screech of wood on old stone. She wove her arm around his neck, dug into the bottom of his hair. Foreheads together, they sat and breathed in silence. Caleb's arms wound around her waist, a hand on her back. "We're going to find Stana, and we're going to rip that Book from her bitch hands before she finds the belief in her body to kill a god. Alright? Caleb, I need you to tell me you heard me and understand."

Caleb nodded, murmured through clumsy teeth.

"Caleb, look at me."

He opened his eyes, saw the fret line in Tuija's brow, how it was truncated by the painted over and smoothed cedar-line of her curse, the inhuman growth which in a century or so, another collection of decades would slowly claim her. The eye which remained from her human self was as wide and blue as the North Sea, the other as golden as the amber from an ancient tree.

"I need you to leave, Tuija. Bunk down with Ares' folk in Chalceus."

"No. You're rattled love. Here." She passed him the old fashioned tumbler of whiskey, wove his hand around it until she was certain he wouldn't drop it. "Sip. What do we need to locate Stana?"

"A clear head."

"Well that's not happening for a while." Tuija shook her head and pushed up to kiss the scruff on his cheek. "Calm and steady first, then you'll have it."

"I need to know you're safe."

"It takes more to kill an old soldier than a mindfucked bitch with a stolen book. If she is the one who killed Tiperet and the Grove, it's likely she's going to do the whole shebang again. So. Spell it out for me. What does she need?"

The whiskey burned down his throat, clean into his empty stomach. Caleb shivered as he leaned back with Tuija in his lap, swathed in shaken arms.

"She needs a dying god. Tiperet wasn't divine, not totally. Tuj, we're missing a whack load of how the freaking heaven, earth and in between did Stana figure out where to look for the ritual in the first place? How did she know it existed? Who was her puppet master? Some willow Fae? Thousands of those."

"The creatures who attacked were fucked up, but I've never seen them quite as... tainted before. It was different in the war, the Fae got desperate. Started losing entire species of trees and shrubs, they panicked. Sent Finnegan and a few others out like ash from an erupting volcano. These ones, it was like they were sick. Infected with some whacked out... Should have taken a sample."

"We didn't have time... but I know someone who might've."

"H-hoh joys. Think they'll bring more pizza?"

"Thought my wife requested steak frites."

"Medium rare. I am not a savage."

"Not here, you ain't."

"Caleb Mauthievich Draganov! I ought to smack you." Tuija made a play of gripping his lapels, tugging herself up to nudge her nose against his. He took comfort, tried to let the tightness in his muscles fade for Tuija's hold in his arms. A lightness lingered within her aura, the promise of joined burdens.

"Steak frites, times two f-or.. oh." The bar server set their food down and Tuija exhaled sharply as the man did an about-face and ditched.

"Best timing in the universe." Tuija fixed her hair, set the table to rights with a burble.

"Yep." Caleb gulped the rest of his luke-warm beer, and slid Tuija off his lap.

"Steak?"

"Yep."

"So you still want me to..."

"Yes. I don't know why the words don't come easy, but Tuj... I'm not changing my tune." Caleb pulled over one of the plates of steak and thick cut chips, towed over a serviette wrapped around cutlery and passed it to Tuija.

"There's this... film around you, like dust on glass. Got the waft of funky magic. What did she do to you, kohana? Some ties are invisible, love. You care about her, Delilah."

"Of course I do. How could I not? We were together for decades, I spent part of my childhood with her in the caravan, it's... impossible to expunge."

"History is history, lovers come and go. But the Enchantress Delilah?" Tuija scooped some horseradish onto her steak, the pungent herb enough to make Caleb's nose twitch before he'd taken a bite of his own.

"I keep feeling this pull, like there's something unfinished between us. We're done, I'm not... I care about her, but not..."

"She got her hooks into you good."

"So Finnegan says."

"He doesn't shut up about it when the mood strikes him. Finn might be a bastard, but he's a caring bastard. I might even love the old oak in our weird found family way. Even if it's complicated." Tuija dipped a small cut of the steak into horseradish and offered it to Caleb. "They forgot the mayo for my chips."

"I'll get it." Kissing her temple, Caleb nipped the piece of offered steak, and trotted off to the bar.

The old warrior leaned back against the wood of the bench, pursed her lips and tapped at the table. "No, you can't send 100 litres of compressed acid to Delilah's address."

'Awwww, but I just gotta click send!' Icarus groaned on the other end of the phone Caleb left behind, and Tuija laughed.

"Babydoll, I'm not that vindictive."

'Yeah, so 90 litres enough? Eighty, tops?' The disembodied voice of Ares' great-grandchild warbled through the slim connection, another peppered moment in Tuija's life.

"Hah! Keep tabs on her for me, but no. No acid."

'Well if ya wanna be pedantic...'

"Icarus."

'I gotchoo, it's gucci twenty-four seven. Ya know someday I'm gonna talk to both of you at once.'

"Caru?"

'Yeeeeess?'

"He married me." Tuija couldn't help the smile on her face, the ridiculousness of a cursed immortal warrior falling for the Realms' only chance at reunification.

'About fucking time, too. Far be it for me, the disembodied voice of hahah... reason quote-unquote to make comment upon that, fair warrior-who-could-snap-me-in-twain, but why are you not tapping that every spare second? Might be Dite's influence talking, but the way you two...'

"Are you going to ask Seraya to be your wife anytime soon, babycakes?" Tuija grinned and swayed in her seat, sipping the whiskey on the table. "Join us in wedded bliss?"

'Hera might have offered to tie our marital knot... shush I haven't asked. Took a few thousand years for Hera to realize lesbian love's worth her blessing in the first place.'

"Origami."

'Pardon?'

"Origami flowers, handmade. That's what Seraya wants... and the perfect cuppa, with biscuits. A quiet morning with no plans, Lou off on some mission until he brings home exotic meat he will then barbecue outside, with a couple easy top beers to wash down the grin on his face."

'Speaking as someone who stayed dead for 3,500 years? Stop thinking he's better off if you hold back. Mammals, plants, what's it matter? We're all magic, all of us, this bundle of fantasy threads in a tapestry plucked into being by forces other than ourselves. People wait their whole lives and half the afterlife for what you've got. Exes with hexes, or bits of bark be damned.'

"How many hours did you practise that?" Tuija watched Caleb saunter back with mayo in hand, the creases on his face less pronounced in this netherspace of humanity.

'Someday you'll thank me... and so will Lou, my gods does he not see Violet? I mean what in Tartarus, dude, like... frick! What's a sibling to do?! Hi Caleb! Congratulations, by the bye, I'm leaving, don't worry! Sera's over, I'm'a be busy. Ares took you serious on the call them all in thing, I've got distant cousins up the ying yang... not that any of them are getting into Brolympus, I'm not insane... be good to each other. I promise we'll only throw you two a Seraya Supreme party when you're ready... although I can't promise Sera hasn't already started growing table arrangements... whatever... whatever those are... eyeyey.'

"Bye, Icarus." Caleb laughed and set down the next drinks, a shake of his head consuming the cobwebs as he sat down beside Tuija. "Seriously, when is that kid gonna touch grass?"

"I think Icarus is going to be perfectly fine." Tuija tucked into Caleb's side, and although the Cosmos waited in bated breath, they would be alright long enough to eat. "Eat up, I've got your back."

"Yes Ma'am. I'll need strength for this. Mayo, milady."

Once the plates were piled on the corner beside tumblers and pint glasses, Caleb set the bloody jacket back on the table top. He flicked out his pocket knife, scraped some of the blood onto a paper serviette. Dabbing the serviette on the wool, he began to whisper in a language Tuija only recognized in passing, a mixture of Old Germanic and something imaginary. Emotive. The blood began to spark, pocked at the air like miniature explosions between the table and Caleb's lowered face. He scooped at the charred smoke and inhaled as oracles in ancient times, as the pub around him receded.

"I'm not... she's not on Midgard... wait."

The room went blank for Caleb Mauthisen, as all he could sense was the fall.

16 THE MAGIC OF CHAOS

The void sucked Stana's body into a tempestuous reversal of gravity. Pitched in a full spin, no atmosphere existed to temper Stana's trajectory or the gaining speed with which she fell through the null-space beyond the Middling Plane. No friction to slow her, no terminal velocity, no physical laws existed at all. Four stinging shots radiated with a pain which gouged at her mind and curled limbs into her torso, which increased the rate of her tailspin.

Who was Judge Caleb Mauthisen, whose name and nothing more appeared in the Book, no adventures, no stories, nothing but the shimmer of an image which danced in her retinae as if the magic which contained the Book of Knowledge in the first place was tempered by a higher power.

Higher and higher, and this man, this... Caleb Mauthisen was protected.

She hadn't seen him coming. The Fae-twisted Slav she saw, another harmless passerby in Canterbury, who found a path near a car park on the side of the road leading to the famous Cathedral. The fact the woman was packing and Fae cursed was neither here, nor there. Could have been pattern recognition. After discovering the Book, Stana's eyes opened to the multi-dimensional worlds connected to her own: The Faerie Courts, the Hellenes, the Brahmani, the Kehmeti, or Yataban or Kami or Pele's ilk or Dao. Legions of mystical aberrations, who somehow one way or another found their method to reach the human world.

Her world.

And they made a bloody mess every time they touched down. Jesus Christ's miracles might not have seemed an act of war, but Stana knew, she felt it down to the bone. Any form of non-human control of the planet, be it magic or divine mercy, was cursed. Tainted.

A creation of dependence and worship when none ought to have the privilege beyond those women who gave birth, raised decent children, and slapped the battles out of their partner's mouths. But what would Stana know about mothers?

Motherhood?

What did she imagine about her own body?

She spun and she spun, mind a blur to the nauseous sensations as her blood vacated to the spray. Muscles contracted, bones crunched in her skeleton. Lungs burned and screamed and deflated. Her life flung away in the tear, the rip in the Realms she made without direction. Deeper still, the drain of the True Name she used to make the spell-rip in the first place.

Sacrifices. Raw meat laid upon the altar of human expansion without interference from all comers, the Atheist's Altar rang in Stana's senses, she could create it, see the job done. And when the dust settled, when the spinning stopped and she found the right method to kill the gods, the sliver of humanity left over would worship her anonymity. They would fade from their beliefs in a generation or two, become nothing but the meat and the bone and the marrow. Nothing but creatures of chance, evolved from the dust cast off of adolescent stars.

Once the Realms were free of elves, fae, aesir, kami, ancestral spirits and Anubis-headed guides, what did the rest matter?

Stana spun. She clutched the Book to her chest. Its' hunger to be known, to see the world as it changed brought her to it in the first place. Brought her closer to its lingering pulse. But now, it chattered and chittered on. Attempted to guide through required readings, to see the Realms as the necessity it expected.

The damned Book thought it was giving Stana a fairy story to cling to, a collection of magical links in a chain which would fit around her neck and elevate her to the Mystic and Holy.

It was as foolish as the Fae, who thought Changelings would be taken and loved instead of sent to post-birth abortion clinics, if Stana recognized and called them out. If she could see them prior to their bundling to 'meet the baby' celebrations. But, now she could. The moment the Book made itself known, and Stana felt the reeling significance of deities and monsters lingering in the shadows she feared as a child, Stana became aware of the gifts she alone could give to humanity.

Fuck the old man, who kept the Book locked in his basement study, a place she was not supposed to clean. Call it curiosity or desperation to get ahead on bills, but Stana knew she could glean a bit of fat off the top before the man noticed what she'd done. He had to have jewellery or antiques small enough to fit in her pockets. What did he need with all the contents of a house anyway?

Three sharp pangs dulled as Stana spun. Black encroached on her vision, breathing a forsaken dream. She spun and she clung.

If Stana went down, if she died to the Judge and his bullets, the Book would be lost to the ether. Lost to the vacated nothingness of the deep. Again the Realms would be bereft of their guiding hands and godspeed.

Or it would have been, if the deep vault of infinite chaos were not populated.

As Stana spun, she began to feel the sensation, the watchful gaze of myriad eyes on her back. Front. Side. Front. The soles of her feet. Front. Back. The hairs on the back of her neck rose, she was useless and fragile, a bleeding stump of humanity in the chaos.

In the Void.

But something hovered upon the waters.

A spirit upon the deep.

Stana shrieked with the last air in her lungs, the flow of her blood began to trickle as pressure dropped, as the wounds grew, as the spin of her body slowed to a crawl. To an equilibrium Stana knew in her heart she should not feel. The curious Chaos enveloped her. Prodded and tempted her.

If she unclenched from the rage, fell into the arms of this chaos-deceiver, the hovering presence above the waters of infinite, salt-laden waters...

Stana stuttered out a sob. Thirsty. The waters around and beneath her, if she opened her mouth, drank of them whole... would they infill her? Drown her? Suck her life dry? Would they spill inside her, heal and guide her, would they become the one thing she could not deny?

Caleb Mauthisen, the Judge whose name was written in the Book, was a blessed and unconfined piece of compassion from gods, who turned their backs to give Humanity the time to decide its path.

Caleb Mauthisen shot her three times.

Caleb Mauthisen wanted the Book, which gave her the ability to slay him, to slay the Immortals and the iterations of Thor-Heracles, who descended from the roots of a long expunged ancient tree. She clutched the Book and wailed.

The presence which lingered upon the waters hovered over this decrepit thing, until Stana felt six sharp slices into her body. Sharp entanglements to limbs, neck and torso. Jerked away, Stana was flung through another rip in the fabric. And Stana knew the presence over the waters no more. She landed hard on dirt as a light rain fell from the sky.

Clutching the Book of Knowledge, Stana cursed the one who fluttered above the chaotic waters, as firmly as she cursed the one who pulled her from them. Willow fronds collected and pressed into the wounds to staunch bleeding, bark pushed between her teeth. She clenched her jaws, gnawed on the willow bark as a grinning face consumed her shaken vision.

"Wasn't the kettle of fish you thought it was, poppet?" Cormac of the Willow grinned down at the faltering mammal, her lifeblood full of iron and oxygen leaking to the soil.

"F-fix..."

"Use the names. What does it matter if some fallen mammal gives you the name of their soul? Use it. Heal yourself." Most humans didn't realise they had a true name at all, as lost within the echo of the gods they didn't know to hold and contain it. What did it matter if they lost something they didn't value, but when used properly, powered magics as divine as death row deities in Stana's new world? Stana coughed and rolled in the dirt. Screamed at the agony across her chest, deep into her body. Whispers tamed the pain, as she felt the slack of ownership soften to a fine line.

Others took her pain, and as their bodies bled and fissured, Stana rolled to her elbows and knees. Coughed red onto the soil as Cormac soaked the blood into his roots. Names dimmed, their holders distant husks fallen ill or taken by accidents of ignorance.

"Wasn't so difficult. Why didn't you kill him?"

"There was a woman with him, I didn't get the chance." Stana glared at Cormac, fighting to her knees. "You didn't tell me he was divine."

"You need a god to make god-killing incense. Where do you think I was going to send you, to a mini-mall? A human den? Row-homes? You need a god and a believer. I taught you that."

"I can try again."

"And whom, pray tell, will you sacrifice? We need a conflagration of incense to send the Realms into their mad spiral. You won't get multiple chances, not if Deimos and Phobos are on our roots."

Stana sat on the sparse grass, smelled the char of Cormac's ashen defiance of nature. Two slugs plopped from her gut to the ground, their gentle 'tink' sound when they clinked together as dichotic as the groan Stana gave while the muscle and skin reknit. The beginnings of a septic fever were tossed away to another person, another life. Their name drifted by Stana's mind, and she whispered it with a grit to her teeth. What did it matter if the people who gave their name for some wish fulfilment or small favour doubled over with gunshot wounds sans the bullets in their guts?

They would thank her, when their children were free. They would bury their dead and brush off their tears and give no prayers or incantations. No ceremony but the laying of ashes in the ground. It was the best freedom Stana could give to those who she knew in the back of her mind were in a sudden agony. No faces came to mind, nothing but the whispered names of the lost souls none would miss.

Sold their names for a sandwich, or a hit, or a business connection. A situation she crafted to terrify influential parents' children.

"Take the useless first." It was easier that way, Cormac whispered. "Zeus isn't dead."

"No idea wh..." She panted, a shake to her head.

"... where they put him? Book! Show us Delilah, if anyone knows, it'll be her." Cormac grinned with wooden teeth, his lips too far apart, too wide to be human.

"The whore might facilitate our work, but why would we trust her to find Zeus? She could as likely tip the Olympians off." Stana crept to her knees, spat on the ground and thumbed the ruined remains of her dress, Delilah ought to have sorted the clothing since the last time Stana needed an update.

"Not likely, you have the ace to play." Cormac offered a branch-like hand, and pulled Stana to her feet. "Besides, your clothing is torn and you stink like human fluids. We pay her enough for her services, but think of how much more she's likely to give when you mention your run in with her former plaything? Delilah will help you for a song."

"Plaything?"

"Mauthisen, he's been threaded into the enchantress' web for decades."

A slight smirk tipped the crust of blood on Stana's mouth, "Book, show me Delilah's location, and compile a list of names I require to teleport us. Now."

The Book would have sighed if it possessed lips. Instead, it mutely recorded the conversation, the twirling void of the Ginnungagap, the injuries sustained by its new Keeper. The Book of Knowledge recorded everything in its pages without fail, while an address in Vancouver appeared in monospace black letters on the backlit page, beside a list of names from the thinning pile.

The sun purged a stray cumulus with the last spark of light before Vancouver's evening came in sweet and crisp, Deimos and Phobos' shadows long past to investigate a jacket left for them in England by the Judge and his cursed mistress.

17

Honey Cake & Samovar of Destiny

"One loaf of rye, and some beer." Caleb fiddled with the top of the bag from the bakery, crinkled the paper under fingers which ought to clasp his bride's. Condensation from the beer cans collected and trailed down aluminium, but Caleb's eyes were on the criss-cross of fine amber which scaled Tuija's cheek. Barely a scar visible after Jase plied his carpenter's craft. "We could bugger off and have a picnic. Start that honeymoon, say the word."

"I'd rather it be for a picnic." Tuija ran her hand along a smooth cheek, wondering whether the beer would be enough as the ache of Vysotsky rumbled out of a window propped open with an empty vodka bottle. Choppers and other modes of transportation lingered on the side of the Floridian swamp, where each building whether wooden or metal perched on roosting chicken legs sunken and encompassed by spanish moss and overgrowth like miniature mountains too tempestuous to climb. Still, Vysotsky played, his gravel-voice and seven stringed guitar as crackled as the gramophone it warbled on. "I don't trust Stana won't teleport straight from the void before the Theosians find her. If we don't get a solid lead, someone's going to die."

"Yeah. Someone we can't afford to lose. Pistol's holstered, but if they start something that gets out of hand, I don't care who they were to you, I'm slinging bullets." Caleb's chest bumped against her palm, chin down to pull a trailing kiss from his bride. Her hand slid to the back of his neck as their kiss continued, averting disaster another scant slip-beat of their syncopated hearts. Fingers against her lower back, Caleb snugged Tuija to his chest until the door of the glorified diner-turned-bar creaked open with a whine.

"Zdravstvuy' assholes!" A shirtless bogatyr fiddled with the wide fabric belt of his sharovary - baggy slavic trousers bundled at the ankles - staggered down steps crafted from upturned plastic milk cartons wedged against the metal siding of the dining car. "What is this, necking cursed stray bitches with wagging vine tails, Scandi?"

"Privet Ivan. Is Matushka Dobrodijka in?" Tuija spat and whirled round, her back bumping into Caleb's chest.

"Why is it always Ivan? It's always freaking Ivan." Caleb groaned, his hand a gentle swell holding Tuija's stomach as much to keep her back than let his polyanitsa fly.

"What's wrong with my name?" Ivan gurgled and staggered a few paces away from the door. The skipping record garbled the gravel throat of Vladimir Vysotsky's recorded voice between hoarse conversations in rough slavic tongues and Ivan turned his head to look back into the yellow incandescence of the boisterous dining car.

"Nothing! Not a thing, Ivan..." Caleb grunted and shook his head. "Nope, still sounds like I'm being... I dunno."

"Ivan is a good, solid name." Ivan gesticulated into the murky evening, katydids and cicadas made their calls in tall grass stomped down by a multitude of boots and bike tires, the odd circle smashed into the bog by what Caleb could only imagine was a giant mortar and pestle.

"You read a story about the Bogatyrs, all these glorious Slavic heroes, so many. Ivan. Ivanovich. Ivanov." Tuija clucked her tongue. Stepped carefully in the unkempt grass, as Ivan scratched a tattoo on his bare chest, scant hairs peppered along his torso. "It's like our mothers forgot other names."

"Or my mother was prophetic. I am Ivan, blessed by the Makoshki, all our gods. You would not remember what that is like, Rastenivitsya."

"Sven. It's like calling all Scandinavian guys Sven." Caleb shook his head, "Or Bjørn."

"Let it go, malyatko-love." Tuija tossed mismatched eyes back. Buttonbush and swamp lilies scattered at the edge of black mangrove trees past the collection of mobile domiciles. A thatch-roofed farmhouse squatted beside an airstream trailer, self-made tiny homes mingled with repurposed RV's in the Makoshki camp.

"I was going to take a piss. Now I take trash out too." Ivan swayed on his feet, smacked his lips and splashed his boot on a clump of crab grass with a damp squelch. "Matushka will never see a Fae tainted traitor like you."

"Traitor? For leaping in the way of Perun!?" Tuija beat her chest with open palms, surged away from the protective calm of Caleb's arm and butted torsos with the sneer-sunk Bogatyr. Their foreheads collided, each pushing the other. "For not baring my neck to be beheaded!?"

"Any of us would have rather taken Perun's sword than rush off into the wilds with the bushes and vines!" Ivan snarled, enough of a shout to alert Caleb to the ebbing silence of the cicadas.

"Ah, Tuj?"

"Oh, because death by the Makoshki is easier than the path I chose!?"

"We could have grieved you then, Tuija Miloslava Draganova!" Ivan shoved Tuija with both palms on her shoulders, beating his chest with twin fists. "You, the Dragon Slayer Daughter, you! Our hero! Beloved by Makosh, by Perun, by fucking Czernobog we could have grieved you! Told your story to our children, but no! You gave us nothing! You faded by centimeters from behind the enemy's bastion!"

She buckled and Caleb surged toward the man too late for the wet smack of Tuija's solid punch to hit Ivan in the jaw. Shaking out her fist, Tuija grit her teeth and roared. "Is Matushka here or not!?"

"Kjæreste! Eyes up!" Caleb pulled her back as the doorway scattered with a half dozen Bogatyrs with varying levels of intoxication swaying out the creaking door.

"They want to cast me out, I'll bloody them first."

"And here I thought our wedding night would be boring." Caleb boot kicked a bogatyr, who ran at him with a half-full vodka bottle. The vodka rolled to the ground and got stuck in a patch of crabgrass, while another of the gathered Slavic warriors hurtled themselves with a mighty war cry from the top of the stairs straight at Caleb's centre mass.

"Jayzus!" Knocked to the mud, Caleb kneed the warbling warrior's middle and shoved him over his own head. Rolling to one knee, Caleb was ready when the man sprang up. As he charged, Caleb shouldered into the man's hip and ploughed down to the ground, taking the man down with a loud huff. "You gonna stop trying!?"

The lob of spit which flew out of the warrior's mouth was enough of an answer.

"The fun way it is." Caleb struggled to get behind the man's back as they both fought for position, elbows and knees colliding with whatever softer parts of the other man's anatomy they could reach. Finally, Caleb shoved the warrior forward, slipped behind him and wove his arms around the man's neck in a rear naked choke.

Caleb's legs wove around the other man's waist from behind, and he lengthened their torsos until with a gurgle and a few fruitless struggles, the Bogatyr tapped Caleb's arm.

"Enough? Say it!"

"I buy first drink!" The Bogatyr rasped, coughing once Caleb let the pressure loose and shoved away, rolling to his feet to catch sight of his wife with her boot in one man's stomach, and another woman's wrist locked up to the shoulder.

"I married her, today." Caleb couldn't help the grin as he caught his breath, parried another warrior's drunken haymaker and shoved him into the nearest pond. The chaos around the chicken legged trailers expanded from roughing up a couple intruders to the sort of row necessary to assert a companionable dominance.

"Ey! Ivan!" Still rubbing his neck, the warbling warrior motioned between Ivan, Tuija and Caleb. "They got hitched! The Judge man and our Tuija!"

"We weren't invited..."

"Ivan Ivanovich! You banished me!" Tuija threw another warrior into two more, as devoid of connection as her groom. "I'm still angry!"

"One little banishment, what is that to family, da?" Ivan stumble launched at Caleb with a loose arcing swing, his foot chasing with a lazy and powerless kick to Caleb's thigh. Caleb let the kick land, to shoulder bump Ivan out of the way and into the metal siding of the trailer. "Marrying this Viking!? He's too skinny!"

"Schto, Ivan!? A banishment is banishment!" The woman who nursed her wrist gesticulated and harrumphed, eyeing Caleb with the scorn of an uninvited guest. Several of the bogatyrs linked up behind the woman, her brown hair woven into a braided bun.

Trotting to Tuija, Caleb picked up the vodka bottle in case things got messier than some fisticuffs and jousting, nodding to his wife. "Think this was a good idea?"

"Matushka Dobrodijka knows all. It's worth the attempt, why, not having fun?"

"I was expecting a little more privacy when you whispered about doing something kinetic tonight." Caleb hugged Tuija's stomach, her back to his chest and nuzzled his nose in her neck. She pulled at the top of the bag, and held up the beer and bread. "Not that a good row is disappointing..."

"Ey! You think a little bread and beer will bring the Dobrodijka out of her woven threads!?" The polyanitsa grit her teeth, a few of the others rumbled, posture a mixture of vodka and adrenaline-imbued tension. "You, who hides the curse on your face? Think we don't see it?"

"I'm surprised you saw beyond your vanity, Vanyanka. You still punch like a child." Tuija gesticulated a weak punch into the air, to which Vanya grunted and lunged into the middle of the impromptu circle.

The diner door flung open with a metallic slap.

"Fighting like scolded puppies, what is this!? Ivan! Vanya! Clean the mess before you antagonise the dvorovoi. Or the alligators. The rest of you! What, you have a good row while there's work to be done!? Away with you!" The woman who spoke at the diner's rickety door was radiant as a wheat field ready for harvest, flaxen hair caught in a braid down her back. Ageless pale skin hid under a white linen Vyshyvanka shirt embroidered with red thread, Makosh shoved a red cuff up her arm, the billowing fabric tucked into a pair of dark wash jeans. Animal life stilled in the everglades, as Makosh levelled her gaze on Tuija and Caleb's offering. Stern and unyielding as the fate which struck all mortals in their time, Makosh stared at the hand Caleb cupped around Tuija's stomach, his thumb busied about in miniature circles to soothe her. "Wipe your feet, no mud in my house. Ivan, prepare a room."

"That's our cue." Tuija strode forward, as the Bogatyrs erupted in roared protests.

"Trouble. Everywhere we go is trouble." Caleb kissed her neck, and kept pace with his bride's steps over the threshold of the diner car, which he had to duck down to enter.

At the inside of the doorway, framed in yellow incandescent light, a domovoi adjusted his tiny red cap and brushed off the dust and filth from the well maintained door mat. Tuija wiped her feet along one edge, and the knee-high creature swatted at her booted heels.

"Jumpy fellahs." Caleb kept his hand on her lower back, wiping off his boots before he got worse treatment. The diminutive house spirit gasped and barked another long name. A side panel opened in the wall, where a woman equal in size to the Domovoi swept out wielding her own broom aloft. The tiny domestic creatures bickered, then got to work.

"Treat them right, Domovoi and Kikimora help tend a house better than any other domestic spirit I know. Not that we could entice one as is, when this is over, you and I are setting a budget to fix the house." Tuija set her hand on Caleb's chest and pushed him into the warm light of a dining room with tables and chairs aplenty, one lone bar at the wall deceptively far from where the outside container ought to have stopped. Caleb kept backing up to Tuija's touch until he collided softly with the wall, and tugged Tuija's hand up to weave around the back of his neck.

"Don't want to stay at your place? Got a lit ceiling." He batted at her chin with his nose, turned her face until Tuija chortled into a kiss that dazed the time out of Caleb's bone-cage. Let Tuija keep light, let her have this one reprieve from the banishment written on her body with every hidden amber line. In his heart, Caleb pleaded to every deity of love he knew to let his Tuija be released from the worries weighing them down for long enough - a blink, a slim exhale - to feel like a bride in the presence of her birth Realm's folk. Within one tangled grasp from home. "We could annoy Finn and Dono with our newlywed routine for years. After-"

"Neither of you are young enough to act like adolescent fools. You were going to beg for my help, do you need another minute or three? An hour perhaps? That amount of time? You don't possess it, but... wish you did." Beside them in an ornately carved doorway, leaned Makosh with one arm crossed, fingers cupping her bicep. The scowl on her lips went no further north than her cupid's bow, as eyes bright as stars shone with a lightness of being which threatened to shock the breath out of Caleb Mauthisen. A heady goddess, who wove and spun the destiny of the Cosmos, Makosh kept the spark of the first emanations of the Creatrix alive in each smile. In the weft and weave of her fabrics.

Love.

Destiny.

Nature.

The first emanations.

Nodding them into her inner sanctum, the goddess who knew before Tuija was born she was fated to the exaltation of victory and renown and the ragged knife point of Fae-cursed traitor, stepped beyond the door.

Caleb watched the way Makosh's body wove through the buzzing atmosphere, the tilt of her chin and reflection of calm blue eyes, which always bore the potential of a shattering storm for some small augury or prophetic glint. No doubt Makosh knew the true stakes, of all the deities in all the Realms, those predominating over fate and time were few, dead or disinterested. Makosh knew what Stana possessed, what Caleb and Tuija whispered after hearing of Ule's fall, and there the goddess was with a clearing of her throat and wave of her hand, goading them further on and further in.

Redemption was not too late, or too hard to win.

"Sorry. Getting ahead of myself. After you, Tuij?" One more hug for his bride, and Caleb followed Tuija into another space. The weight of the missing Book curled up the back of his spine and settled in Caleb's shoulders, unyielding in the periphery, but no longer intangible after deciphering Stana's tumble in the Void. Tuija was right, if they were to pre-empt the Keeper before she struck again, they needed a direction.

No one in the Cosmos gave direction better than the Emanation of Destiny.

Gasping at the shift in atmosphere, Tuija stumbled the first few steps, caught from behind as Caleb followed her through the door to find no ceiling, no walls. He turned and the door was gone, nothing but the golden wheat fields in neat rows ceased by groves of tall deciduous trees and a lazy river.

"Home." Tuija clutched Caleb's hand. Twilight bathed the sky in jewel glints of sapphire and amethyst, framed by the painted wood of a well kept izba with poppies and herbs glinting round its four wooden corners, decorated windows and door. A tree in the herb garden bore two strange birds, one with obsidian and labradorite feathers roosted in fitful sleep with their head tucked into their feathers, a crest of raven hair down their back. The other preened her cream white feathers with teeth and lips from a mouth on her human head. Silken hair coiled around a gentle face surrounding avian eyes, and with a ruffle of her feathers, Alkonost trilled in a bittersweet song.

Hopping twice on her branch, the melodic bird caught sight of Tuija's wide eyed stare, the hard tense line of Tuija's arm as she clenched Caleb's hand. The bird's song came all the sweeter, a lilting chitter in the crisp air. Weaving his arm around Tuija's waist, Caleb nuzzled his lips into her neck, rocking as they listened to the song. The door of the farmhouse swung open and a woman with loose threads on her dress shoved her shoulder out with a sour countenance, followed by a basket of woven fabric for the line. She scrutinized the two of them and muttered under her breath about damn strange birds, before trundling off to the other side of the house.

"Alkonost and Sirin are on loan from Veles, he's in one of his frisky moods. Not that a woman minds." Makosh held the izba's door open and radiant prismatic light bathed the twilit grass, with its faint emerald sparkle. "Come! Come, the samovar is full and there's honey cake in the oven. Your favourite."

Tuija watched the grass as she stepped on it, ear poised to listen to the crunch of the emerald crystalline blades, which would reform back to their perfection once a person forgot they'd stepped in that exact spot. She caught a gasp and licked her lips, entering the homely abode to the sound of a throaty alto singing by the spinning wheel, as a comely woman with her hair under a kerchief sung and spun from a thousand stray thoughts which combined into chord.

The back of the one room house was taken up by a massive Russian oven, decorated with a mosaic of folk patterned tiles and a sleeping shelf built the width of the izba. Makosh removed a pan from the brick oven's wide front, where a chipper fire clinked and crackled with embers shaped like rubies. The scent of honey, black tea and cinnamon permeated the air, stroking across the newly wedded couple's cheeks. Caleb set the loaf of bread and beer cans on the table, where a brightly woven Rushnyk ran the length of the wooden surface.

"Tuija, help Caleb with his tea, yes? Not many Scandinavians know how to use a samovar." Makosh smiled, and began to cut generous slices of a sticky apple honey cake from the hot pan onto plates. "Thank you Caleb, beer later. Cake now. The forks are in the vase there, three if you please. Dolyanka does not want hers now."

Still humming her song, Dolya continued to spin with a generous rhythm, pouring her desire for kindness and beauty into the thread in double measure for each inevitable sour note.

"Yes, Matushka." Tuija fell into a short routine of pouring concentrated tea from the pot resting on top of the samovar's smokestack and diluting it with the hot water from its spout. She stirred in honey from a ceramic pot and placed a half slice of lemon in each tea cup set on a painted saucer. As Caleb set out the forks on each plate of honey cake, his limbs grew warm and tired, his chair a welcome place.

In the centre of the blue stained wooden table and woven rushnyk, a crystal candy dish with wrapped sweets became the most surreal part of striding up to a mobile Bogatyr camp in Florida, searching a fight out for beer and rye bread. The idea of storming the halls, fighting their way in and through to some modicum of Makosh's graces faded with sight of a ubiquitous candy dish, and the sound of Dolya's humming.

"The Book of Knowledge was always meant for you, Caleb. Not Salomon Calder, although the man did valiant work in his time. Stana's choices are not your fault." Makosh slid the plates across the table, sitting at its head. She thanked Tuija for her tea, manoeuvred the handle to a perfect position and watched the lemon slice bob peacefully atop the steaming liquid.

"I don't understand why. As everyone reminds me, I'm a demi-god. Keyword, demi. Why would that human part of me mean I couldn't share? Wouldn't it make sense? No supreme power in any one half-human's hands?"

"Is that what you believe?" Makosh sipped from her cup, set it down on the saucer with a soft click. She eyed Tuija, who nibbled on her bottom lip more than she bit at her cake.

"Isn't that what I'm supposed to believe?"

"Stana had the option of encountering the Book and leaving it be, or of taking it and learning this grand magic around us to benefit Folk and humanity. The potential was present for her to be one of the best Keepers the Book could have attracted. Her choices are her own."

"Who is she targeting next? Who taught her where the spells were? Are they going after Tuija to complete some macabre set? Which Folk can I trust?"

"Eat your cake while the apples are warm. Enjoy little ones."

Honey sweet and lemon astringency lingered when Caleb sipped his tea, forearms on the table's edge in tandem with his dwindling hope of straight answers. "Will you tell us where to go?"

"I will tell you the answers to the most important questions you have, Caleb Mauthi's Son, I don't have patience to think small."

"Who is the easiest old god to reach?"

"Tuijka."

"Yes, Matushka?"

"Do you like the cake?"

"It tastes like home. Thank you." Tuija licked her lips with a held breath to control the abundant nostalgia, the echo of contentment smoothing face.

"What is more important to you, Caleb, a few minutes to enjoy a cake I soaked in honey on your wedding night, or the staccato answers you can do nothing with until Stana resurfaces?" Makosh monitored the fire in the brick oven, how it sparked and cast prisms of orange, yellow and white light on every surface in a space which for the woman glutting quiet on a taste of home, was as momentous as the universe's full expanse.

"Obviously Tuija. But as the Council constantly reminds me, I don't usually get to take me-time. Not when there's Realms in chaos and a human walking around with the method to kill deities like you in her pocket. Hera..."

"Hera is incapable of understanding a life outside her duty, and most of the Council cluck at her feet like hungry chickens, or isolate out of self-preservation or pride. And the Fae? Three quarters of the strife built into the Realms is the fact conscious and sapient plants are biologically incapable of understanding the needs of their fauna cousins. The war was epoch shifting, little one. We were all afraid it was a temporary peace. The decision you two made?"

"Many deities who could give you pedantic answers of 'over there, that one, this time'. You didn't choose them. You brought beer and bread to my table, as humans did before I found this name. One of the earliest forms of belief after animist shamans inhabited the souls of the hunter and prey to save spiritual face. Destiny is the weaving of an end goal knotted in the strands, some choices bring us away from that perfect work, others towards it. But we will arrive. The truth you seek is this." Turning her fork around, Makosh stirred more honey into her tea in hypnotic circles, topped up from pot and samovar. "Will you and Tuija make it out of the Truce, and thus the Creatrix's grace, alive?"

"All the magic in the goddamned universe and my wife still has to bury herself in dirt and become plant food for a symbiotic tree? What in the Cosmos could be important enough to you not to give her the respite she was begging for over a century and a half? Hmm? What destiny puts that fear in her eyes?"

"Caleb." Tuija took Caleb's hand, mismatched eyes stroked at the red tempering his cheeks, the shaken breaths Caleb hazarded to fight to hold. Caleb stroked his thumb along Tuija's hand, "Let's enjoy this tea."

"Tuija was hurt because she chose to throw herself in the way of a curse meant for Perun. One without remedy. This was not asked of her, but as Stana had the freedom to decide what to do with the knowledge of the Realms in a tidy bundle in her pocket, Tuija reacted to Finnegan's dart. That act of fealty changed you, Tuija, it was born of love, and love keeps it. Trust in that and the rest of this? The way your body changes and joints crack with amber will make sense in time. You both must realise this, for all else to make sense. The path away from the Truce and our love is a constant and exhausting battle to push all else but pain and hurt aside. Walking the path Stana walks is not easy. Deciding to cause evil is not without its stop-gaps and safety measures. Distancing oneself from the Truce, Caleb, is rejecting the love which brought our Cosmos into motion at the Creatrix's first dance. One I remember, for it birthed me.

As imperfect as most are, the battles stopped when we decided to love you. We decided one and another wrapping our arms around your newborn body was worth more than the hurt and the shame and the pain our mutual bloodshed caused. I fed you from my own body, child. And it tears at me that as you grew our independent acts of mutual love can be overshadowed by squabbles worth less than a mote of dust on a broom. But that is my burden, seeing the entire Cosmos' story in its complete beauty and catharsis then forgetting to check on the minutiae. While love opens its arms, acting out of perfect love is not always the path of least resistance. Ask Psyche, my sister did a number on her, even if now they're mother and daughter. All this? The exhaustion, the pressure you're under, the imperfect choices, there are ways beyond your fatigue and your fears. Are you ready to be vulnerable enough to find them?"

"I've got to stop Stana. My mistake in trusting the Book to Sal brought us here, and I hear you, Stana's choices aren't mine to bear, but... Matushka..." Caleb's mouth worked without sound.

"Destiny demands you will confront Stana, because your destiny is intricately tied to the Book and now so is she. You will find her as easy as thunder follows the lightning strike in the midwestern sky. You will find Ule Bjørnsen, and when you do? I grant you the gift of honey and tea made the way your wife remembers, that it might sustain your search through undeniably difficult times."

"I don't want to die."

"Few do. All you have is a decision of whether you wrap yourself in trust and love, or do you push away? Keep your centre on your love and eventually, there will be unending beauty until all the pain is gone. Hold this memory close, my precocious Tuijka." Makosh stroked her thumb along the hidden amber and soft skin of Tuija's cheek and wiped it clean. "This is the last your eye will see of Prav and of me. I have no greater wedding gift."

A matronly kiss lingered with an invisible sigil on Tuija's forehead, as Makosh pulled away and the crystalline tranquillity of Mat Zemlya's Realm folded in on itself, inward and inward until there was nothing but the concept and the power strong memories left behind in Midgard's waking world.

18

Creaky Acres Nursing Home

"Yeah, I caught him slipping his hand up Mrs. Falkner's skirt again. Gave him some lorazepam and a cookie, should settle him down." The nurse leaned her elbows against the white laminate of the nursing station at the Creaky Acres Nursing Home, with a shake of her head. The man was persistent, for a limp old fart. "Mrs. Falkner's settled, she's fine, apparently she was glad for the attention from a god. Blimey, I get that confused, put my meds in my pudding."

"Dr. Lucas ordered lorazepam?" Another nurse sat behind the nursing station desk, flipped through files on an updated computer and made a notation on one chart. He pushed her glasses up her nose with the cap end of her pen, as Mrs. Wheeler pulled herself along in her wheelchair by each padded foot the way she did every day. Never her hands on the wheels, always that same aching plod in the old fall risk.

"Whenever we need it. Daddy Thunder isn't about to get his rocks off with the ladies for eight to twelve." Another shake of her head, and the nurse turned round to lean against the station counter. The south module of the Creaky Acres Nursing Home, like the rest of it, was far enough outside Milwaukee only the diehard families came to visit. Elderly people sat in scotchguarded chairs, walkers set beside or canes leaned on the wing-backs. At one table, two men played checkers, sipping the coffee their 'carers' poured them when they were feeling generous, or needed a smile. A story about the old country of Oak County. Amidst the relative cleanliness of once new linoleum and matching chairs, the elderly who needed extra help, or whose families couldn't afford other places lived in relative comfort. Course they did, Kopis Industries gave out enough stipends, didn't they?

The TV in the corner played reruns from Hogan's Heroes and MASH, old war films like The Great Escape, Tora! Tora! Tora!, Midway, Stalag 13. Victory. Downfall. Sons of Anarchy on DVD. Their collection of war material used to sit on a bespoke cabinet, engraved with a bronze plate:

Donated by Ares & Heph Olympia, Zeus's Boys

Now, only the technological device which looked like an off-brand cable box sat on the shelves, beside the biggest TV on the market. Replaced annually for another plaque each time, the old television doffed off to a youth centre, school or usually a nurse's family.

Donated by Ares & Heph Olympia, Zeus's Boys

"Wonder if your boys will be by anytime soon to add more movies to our box, Zeusie." Frederek leaned forward in his chair, and using his cane tap-tap-tapped at the knee of a man dressed in brown and yellow plaid trousers, a yellow dress shirt tucked in, cuffs halfway up forearms covered in white, downy arm hair. Around his neck, gold chains with a lightning bolt pendant sat atop another tuft of white hair on his chest. Zeus groaned, creaked open eyes older than the dirt of the world and peered around.

"Hmmm?" He smacked clammy lips, reached for a plastic cup with a lid and a straw, and fumbled it.

"Looks like Daddy Thunder's done and gone woke up. Ought to fill his glass before he tries to 'conjure the rains' and pees himself again." The nurse shook her head, pushing off the side wall of the nursing station. "Don't worry, I got him."

"I said your boys! Should come soon, put more movies and shows on the box! Nice they play all hours and all, but how many times we got to see all them war movies? Might try putting on Driving Miss Daisy, or the Colour Purple!"

"Hrrrrrrrhhh hate my sons." Zeus garbled his tongue in his mouth, reached for the cup just out of reach without shifting his arm on his wheelchair. Half the time folk thought he was struck by a stroke, speaking languages more ancient than these mere humans' understanding.

"I got you, Mr. Olympia. Here's a nice cup of ice water. Here. Suck! Suck on it, suck harder, there you go." The nurse leaned down to put the straw in Zeus's mouth, waited for him to close his lips around it and suckle water like milk from a teet. Zeus's eyes cranked a little more open, with the angle of the nurse's scrubs. He slowed down the suckle on the straw. She pulled back and set the water down, then unlocked the wheels of his wheelchair and set him beside Frederek and the TV. "There you go, now you can watch your movies! Your son tells us you love all these old war movies."

"Remind... reminds me of him..." Zeus sniffed and angled his face away. The screen too tempting to zap, the south module of the Creaky Acres Nursing Home too depressing. "Little shit."

"Ohhh, everyone here should be so lucky! You know, your son gave us a high speed internet. Now, your kids can download movies to the box any time they want. Keep you up to date on new releases. Here. Why don't I put one on, eh? Any preference? Mr. Iversen?"

"Got any Gal Godot?"

"Hah! I'll have to check..." The nurse click-click-clicked through the menus, until the panel illuminated one. "Ah! Here we go, you're from Rome, right? Or was it Greece? Here. You watch and in a bit it'll be time for dinner and pudding."

Zeus's eyes levelled on the woman, his lips worked as the ancient magics of his birthright burbled up through his stomach, up his chest, up the esophagus until the power which crowned him King of Olympus with his dominance, with his might, descended upon the mere mortals of his prison.

A resounding, burbled burp.

On the screen, threaded through the pristine sound system mastered just so to not compete with hearing aids and monitors, a sword and sandal epic played. Zeus's eyes narrowed. He tried once more to conjure the lightning of his youth, the power which levelled mountains and took princesses, maids and goddesses to bed. He would do it, Master of the Lightning Bolt, God-King of Olympus, he would destroy the altar to Ares' many successful campaigns.

Each film, each tv show, each bit of documentaries on the rise of women, feminist literature, old war campaigns was as much a middle finger up Zeus's ass as the drugs the mortals shovelled into his divine blood for him to piss out hours later.

Damn Asclepius. Damn him for becoming a doctor who could write orders on bits of paper like some... like some...

The scene on the film switched, three men wore togas and talked over wine served by slim servant women in what appeared to be a poorly constructed bath house. Zeus smacked his lips and sat dull-eyed in his chair, retribution forgotten as one of the men grabbed a serving girl and towed her into his lap.

She yelped, and Zeus's fingers curled on the arm rests of his wheelchair.

"Oh! Sorry about that, hold on." The nurse descended, picked up the remote from the cabinet and fast forwarded the scene. Zeus moaned, head lolled to the side as he eyed the usurper. She would rue every day she paid attention to his machinations! "I know, Mr. Olympia. I forgot there was sex in this one. Your sons told me all about your aversions. I'll remember to put on something more docile next time."

He groaned and leaned forward, the belt around his waist keeping him firm in the chair after the fourth 'fall risk' turned into a family meeting with a well dressed eldest son in his fine Italian suit, black button down and gold cufflinks. The middle boy was much rougher, long grey hair and beard oiled and straightened, clad in black jeans and a leather jacket with patches from the local motorcycle club, crutch always stood beside his chair with perfect balance. The nurse remembered their medical director talking about the new conference room equipment installed by Heph Olympia that day 'oh it's no trouble', so their sister with her swept back black curls added dignity to the grey turtleneck, the rimmed spectacles and proud aristocratic nose. Professor Athene Olympia, lecturer in Bologna.

It wasn't too late in Italy for the Professor to make her appearance, not for their... dear... daddy.

The fall risk meant new medications, a physical therapist to help their darling father walk maybe, one day, if his hip didn't give out. Maybe surgery on the table.

Surgery never happened, the hip never replaced, and the PT was both firm, and aggressively male.

"You know, half your friends would love a quarter of the attention your kids give you. Oh, you're so lucky. By the way, you got a phone call from your grand-niece. She's coming to visit later. Enjoy the movie." The nurse walked off, a hummed song in the back of her mind she'd never remember.

Zeus's fingernails dug into the soft foam of the wheelchair's arms, his toes curled in the slippers tailor made to look like loafers. Chosen from a catalogue of 'accessibility wear' for the elderly gentleman. He clenched his teeth and shut his eyes, leaning back in the chair until Frederek tapped at his shoulder with his cane. Sweet, doting relief. Maybe Morpheus would pity him this time round, and he would dance on Hellas' fields, the frightened but intrigued eyes of indecently dressed maidens...

"Hey, Zeusie. You're gonna miss the battle, buddy! Don't fall asleep till the end. Don't worry I'll remind you." Frederek gave a snaggle-toothed smile, slipped his cane against the arm of the chair and shifted so one foot was on the ottoman in front of his wingback chair.

Another gift, the furniture brought in from Heph's shop when the Home's old stuff got worn.

The entire place, every cubit a temple to forgotten people, the elders none wanted to recognize or toilet in their homes. Zeus sat back to watch the hero don his armour, valiant red linen under bronze plate. Cringed at the inaccuracy, who had swords like that? How did he remember what those swords were like? He never used something as undignified. Then, the nurse's babble sunk through the addled mind of the once-great King of Heaven.

Grand-niece?

What grand-niece would visit him? Which of his children had a daughter alive at all? Harmonia? No, she would never be caught within a continent of him after he made a game of bedding each one of her luscious friends. One of Apollo's kids, no... they were mostly dead or gone. Zeus's eyes narrowed, the tempest-grey of his irises flickered with a mote of power, a mote of the godhood he knew.

He flicked the locks off his wheelchair's wheels, and turned the chair to leave the room. Use the talky box Ares gave him, which spoke with the voice of a strangely distant accent from Mycenae. A youth, who sounded altogether too much like Alcippe mixed with some labyrinthine puzzle.

"Lunch! Here, let me help you Mr. Olympia."

Zeus cursed in a language too ancient and dignified for the human to catch, as Jimmy, Louanne's boy, who volunteered every Thursday for high school credit, wheeled him into the dining hall for soup and a sandwich. "But... but I was going to use the talky box... unhand me, curr!"

Well, at least he could use a turkey club. Anything other than tuna. By the time Jimmy engaged the wheel-locks on Zeus's wheelchair, the King of the Gods had quite forgotten suspicious visitors, Ares' war library and rebellious sons bettering their fathers. He'd forgotten every single thing, the smell of olive groves in the baking summer sun, the glint of oiled bodies during the Games, the wafting salt of the Aegean.

Poseidon was ever in a twist over receiving the Sea as his right instead of Olympus... could have been worse, he could have been Hades. Even that faded away from the once Royal.

Zeus remembered nothing of heroes or princesses and their fallen hemlines. The stretched bellies.

The damned kitchen made tuna melts, again.

"Here you go, Mr. Olympia. Oh! Your favourite!" Jimmy set down a tapioca pudding, and Zeus felt the crumbling ache of eternal defeat by sons and a daughter who didn't even give him the dignity of a final blow.

19

SPARK AND WHEEL

The stink of incontinence and bleach chased through Stana's nose as she passed through the automatic doors plastered with 'intercom for access' signs and the number for incoming guests to key into the keypad under the awning before they entered.

She passed by the welcome station, where a receptionist glanced up from her newspaper and scrambled for the visitor clipboard. "Ahh.. Ma'am? Ma'am, Miss? You need to sign in, just a minute, can I get you your visitor badge? Ma'am!?"

Stana kept walking past the display of old settler's pinafores, quilts and the woodworking project collected from the elderly who wanted to join 'Zeusie's boy Heph' in some carving. She didn't stop to see the picture of a wizened and withered Hephaestus surrounded by smiling people, his father a prop in his wheelchair. The Keeper kept walking, as the Book in her pocket buzzed and flashed its screen to get her attention.

"Ma'am!"

"I'll sign for her, sorry Miss..." Hair snipped close to his rounded scalp, a poorboy cap on his brow, Cormac of the Willow trotted up to the receptionist and grabbed a pen taped to the wire set on the desk. "Got to watch out for my girl, she's deaf as a post."

"Oh, sorry Mr... Willow? I can get Mildred, she uses ASL every day, if we need to..."

"Won't be necessary, we won't be here long."

"You..." The woman's eyes narrowed. A flicker of green in the 'man's' eyes, the way his clothing seemed made of thin paper or beaten down birch bark. "... you must be the visitors who called about Mr. Olympia."

"That's right. Going to take the old codger for a gad about town. Only for a few hours, have him back before the bonfires."

"Bonfires?"

"Old saying in my neck of the woods, once in a while got to let the meadows burn, don't we?"

"Oh, well I won't know anything about..."

"Ah! There you are, darling, nice mammal was just asking some questions, no need to be stand-offish. eh? Let's get your old man." Cormac trotted off after Stana, jerked her bicep once to break her stride, a reminder to be as inconspicuous as possible before they were clear of the home.

"Place gives me the living wiggins. Planting your elders in rooms like pots." The Fae shivered, a rustle of his suit jacket clung to Stana's ears.

She tried to forget the smell, body odour and baby powder. Never. Not a single day more would she take care of the relics in their homes or the institutions which held them. Stana would do nothing for the filth ridden incontinent, or those who were headed in the direction of indignity. Not anymore. She stumble-walked into the dining room with plastic covered tables and paper place mats, the elderly supping with the odd stray flower in a vase placed by a family member for birthdays or anniversaries barely remembered. Hunched humanity, living out the last of their dignity, unaware of how close they were to ancient deities and their dirty laundry. A man with grey-white hair in a wheelchair caught Stana's eye, the dull metal spoon covered in tapioca halfway to his mouth. A small bit of pudding dribbled onto his chin, and he licked it away with a lecher's tongue, wiped his mouth on the paper napkin folded in half, then set beside a brown and yellow clad knee.

Stana gulped. "Is that..."

Cormac let go of Stana's arm and stalked the table. Potted plants in various states of under-watered shifted as if the sun came to the room and lit upon Cormac's shoulder. The Fae lengthened out, grew a few inches in height as his body narrowed and the skin of his hands turned brittle as tinder from a desert pile. A transformation worthy of the divinity in their midst. The wild grin which swept across his face grew in magnitude when Zeus looked up from his pudding, and inhaled stiffly into his anaemic lungs.

"Well hello again, you old codger arsehole. So this is where they put you." Cormac nodded Stana over, and missed the split second Zeus pulled the spoon and fork from the table into his lap, nestled each in a pocket of the loose slacks they put on him after the adult diaper in case he soiled himself again. The indignity of powers lost and humanity's slip into his bloodstream, as if with every reversal of a believer he became less god and more man was almost worse than Ares' dotage.

His dastard son.

Zeus cleared his throat, made a squeaking brae as Stana rushed him, unlocked the wheelchair's locks and pulled the handles. She walked fast and calm out of the dining room, despite the way Zeus tried to hold his hands to the wheels, rubbed raw by Stana's singular trot past the front desk, out into the cool of the early evening. Barely a word to the receptionist, who rustled papers when they got near, picked up the phone receiver a second later.

"I'm being kidnapped!"

"Yes, Mr. Olympia! Awh, Daddy Olympus is getting an outing, don't say too much when you get back, Frederek and Mrs. Feedler will be right jealous, sweetie.... keep him a while... Creaky Acres! Oh hi, Patty, yes we got the new sheets yesterday, they're already on your Mum's bed..."

"Help me, you babbling brook of a woman! I don't mean kidnapped in the fun ways! Hey! Stop that, ow! My hands!" By the time they got to the road outside the home, Zeus mumbled and set his hands to the wheels. "Put me back... unless you plan to take me to a mattress..."

"Shut up, old man." Stana smacked Zeus on the back of his head, and kept walking until they rounded the corner and the trio were out of sight.

"Ow! You hit me! Hera never... I suppose she did hit me that one time... and then there was..." The wheels of his chair didn't squeak or buck, too well weighted by the mechanical offal Hephaestus used to craft the perfect father's day device. Down the street, past the school and row of neatly kept homes, which stopped abruptly at the park. "... was it truly that easy to pilfer me? I'd've thought Ares put an honour guard at the door... a few dozen worshippers. Two... not even two worshippers? A vestal virgin? Not one?"

The ancient god was next to death, Stana could smell the acid of old age on him, piss and body odour, the soap from industrial medical supply. Pink, Stana remembered the soap was pink in a jug shaped like a bleach container with translucent plastic. The memories returned from when she first arrived in Vancouver from the former Yugoslavia, how it felt to empty bed pans and buckets of grime-smitten water for the elders, who paid her to tend them. A girl with nothing but clothes and a bag and her rage.

"Who spat in his baklava as a child? … suppose everybody. Oh! Heh, oh yes, that was his birthday oh Apollo and Hermes had such fun! Hephaestus made a dish, you'll love this one… he made a dish that would leak Ares' soup into secret channels in the clay, so every time he tried to take a sip, aha! No soup! Then if he tipped it further, all the soup! Ahahaaah the man went as red as his hair."

Now her hatred could sit on its' rightful head. Nobody, not one person in the universe deserved to miss this antiquated relic of misogyny's heyday. The man invented troubles with his first thrust. In the labour screams, which became his wife's first-born son.

Ares wouldn't come for the old man.

"Why would Ares save you?"

"To finish me off properly, there's rules to usurping the throne, young brat. Ares is mightily afraid I'll best him in single combat and is weakening me up before the killing blow. Yes, that's it." Zeus tapped his slipper clad toes on the metal foot rests, hands in his lap as if a dignified elder going for a roll.

"Why by the soil and seas would a son kill their father? Bit backward, innit?" Cormac trotted along, bits of his human appearance cast off for the Fae underneath. How did Finnegan manage his mammalian appearance?

"Why-but-why I… how awful, no! Not possible, how dreadful of an idea, the accursed idea that Ares won't come kill me in a pitch of battle to take my throne! Why, it's the only thing keeping me alive! My ire and excitement at his inevitable failure." Zeus harrumphed in his chair, watching the picnic tables go by as Stana slogged over grass when the walking trail turned to gravel. "Well, Frederek and the others at the Home do donate a certain… longevity I suppose, it's not worship as in the lovely sacrifices and vesta-"

"Say Vestal Virgin one more time and I will cut your tongue out and shove it so far down your throat it licks your stomach." Stana shoved the chair over a patch of crabgrass, and caught her breath. Ares would be the first to thank Stana and Cormac, when the codger was gone, and in that celebration Stana would light the incense, shut the doors and box them all in. A funeral for the gods and right fuck to their ash-bound corpses.

"Is it your time of the month, woman? You may let the man push my royal throne, I don't want… womanly… emotions… to be catching." Zeus grunted as Stana jerked the chair at a rock on purpose, thin lips pursed in a gloating smirk. "Woman! Contain yourself! Not that it's possible, ah! You're just like Hera, and let me tell you, the worst decision I ever made, marrying my sister.

But I did like her throne… should have made vows of feminine silence a sign of matrimony. Now there's an idea, you'll see, once Ares is defeated and I am back in my rightful place, I'll give women the right silent treatment! Haha! Worlds will bow in thanks, at that."

"Never happen." Clothing on Cormac's body shed in strips, chaff lost to the breeze. The poorboy hat flew off, and ropes of willow fronds burst from his scalp, down his back. Cormac cawed and whooped, jumped atop a fence and strode its' white pickets with root stalks for feet. "We're killing your sorry arse today, Zeusie! Going to pave the way, Ares's been docile far too long!"

"Whatever you think you are about to accomplish, you'll find it sorely lacking, Willow-the-Wisp. And you, cock-sure girl." Zeus scowled into his scant bit of stubble which grew between what Stana bet was twice weekly shaves from the care aid. "You're not even pretty."

"I don't have to be pretty to kill you."

"You have to be stronger than a slip of a willow tree and a mortal."

"Not with this!" Stana yanked out the Book of Knowledge, the wheelchair continued down the pavement for another few metres, before its' momentum lost its' way and Zeus craned his neck to see the ereader in hand.

"Ah, my mistake, a woman learned to read. This will solve all your woes."

"Shut it! You're supposed to be senile!"

"I am a God. Everyone on the planet who matters knows my name, even in jest or children's cartoons. Not that I understood using my name to conjure heroes in comics." He sniffed his regal brow, an easier feat when he was outside, in the sun and the wind and the clouds puffed above him. "I am the God of the Skies, the originator of the weather you cry for in seasons of lack and plenty alike. I am the fertilizer."

"You did enough of that to last a few godly lifetimes." Cormac hopped both feet onto a single picket of the last sign post before the park's wilderness stole the town away from the humans. Trees planted by the long dead knotted together with carefully felled corpses of honey locust and norwegian maple for ecological diversity some said, others for the risk of harming some needless human too ignorant to know not to get caught under unstable ancestors.

"Hah! And I will again." Zeus shook his head, the breeze, his cousin according to the Book, played in his shorn hair. The radiance of Helios' sun-chariot shone through the leaf filter, a chariot reconquered when Apollo went away and good riddance. Each second and minute outside the home, outside the dank, filtered environment of a carefully selected atmosphere, woke in Zeus a new vigour. He played his fingers across the foam of his wheelchair, cracked his neck from side to si- "Uuuugh."

So his neck gave him trouble. Odd for a god to have trick knees, faulty hips or sore necks, the echo of his body which trapped him in the chair wasn't quite as godly or divine as Stana wished... but clouds built upon the horizon. Slim, anaemic, but present. As long as it would be enough for the ritual, enough godliness left in the old coot, Stana welcomed its ashen byproduct.

"If you'll excuse me, this has been a lovely walk. I'll be going." Zeus yanked hard on the chair and made it two metres further than he thought by the time Stana lashed out and reached for the handles. Towed him off the paved pathway into the relative wilds of the park's scant forest with grunted pushes of vitriolic force. At the third jerking push, Cormac's branch hand wove around the handles, and pushed Stana off.

"Watching the struggle is pathetic. We need one other." Cormac gritted his white-bark teeth. "Why didn't you grab one of the other ones? We still need a worshipper for this to work, what, you think we'll come across a pagan on the sidewalk?"

"The Judge will come. He'll be enough."

"The Frederek one he mentioned was an easy capture. I could go back and get him, the Fae door isn't much farther."

"Ah, Fred. He always tells me how wonderful it must be to have such good sons..." Zeus sniffled and dug his pocket square out of his yellow dress shirt pocket and dabbed at the white nose hairs hanging from his nose. "I hate that guy."

"Shut it!" Stana howled, and kicked the side of Zeus's chair, stifled a scream at the ridiculous notion of ancient gods alive in more than fairy stories or beams of light which impregnated princesses who waited for lovers to take them as brides. None of the knowledge made life more palatable, that Zeus was real, that people worshipped him. Made sacrifices at his altar until his capricious nature acquiesced to giving rain.

"I don't know, he was getting somewhere." Leaning against a tree, Caleb Mauthisen held his arms across his chest. Beside him, Tuija the woman from the Crossroad held her pistol in both hands, face removed from the patchwork of cedar bark which flaked across it before. Delilah's choice words of the woman still stung Stana's ears from Wisconsin. "Step away from the God."

"You may chop the tree and take the woman at thy leisure, Judge!"

"Shut up, you perverted fool, adults are talking! Be glad I figured out Makosh's thunder and lightning motif enough to be here in the first place."

Caleb walked out from the protection of the tree, continuing to pace along the confines of the wood. Stana searched how the man moved for a way in on a death blow or a stun hard enough to capture. The swagger of his shoulders, no man deserved to wear such confidence like a coat, betrayed a man who knew his way around a fight with more than words. He'd missed her missiles in Canterbury, none of them made their marks. Perilous redeemer, he continued to pretend he held power in the place. Did he not know his power was dead as the relic in the chair?

"And you, Cormac, King of the Willow. Of all the fucked up flowers it could have been, didn't think we'd have royalty on our hands." Caleb scoffed with a firm shake of his head. "What your wife must be whispering now. You feel Carolee's knife at your back, yet?"

"Wife..." Stana's eyes narrowed, chin flicked in Cormac's direction, "King?"

"Oh." Caleb motioned to the scowling Fae, "Sorry didn't he tell you? Cormac of the Willow is the King Consort of High Queen Selyka, ruler of the Fae Lands, whose tree budded directly from the Green Man's stalk... you've been in proverbial bed with a King. One I was wondering about, always were a spark or two of trouble, weren't you?"

"Watch it, mammal. I like the little warrior I created. Stana, what's..."

"You blocked me. From reading your passage in the Book, you said it didn't matter."

"It doesn't! I never lied to you." Cormac dug one foot then the other into the ground, and a ripple shuddered along the soil into the surrounding Norwegian Maples and pine of the park.

"Sure, try to use your Fae roots to control the trees. It'll work fantastic for you while I'm here, Willow-the-Wisp. Oh, and omitting the truth is worse." Caleb stomped on the ground with his heel and the dirt reverberated. Caught aback, Cormac scowled to the willow leaves perched atop his head and swore. "Stana, this Fae is jaded. He doesn't care about anything but his own power, you don't need him. Don't fall in his hands. Last chance. Return the Book. Whatever lies the acrid tree taught you? Let me unteach. If you plan to use the Book of Knowledge to protect humanity I have no guff with you. I know what it's like..."

"You know nothing of what this is like." Stana shook her head, raised a hand like a lightning rod and stepped away from the elderly god and his muttering obsession with feet and clouds. The Fae passage was within her sight, a shade lighter in the wood than the rest of the atmosphere. If they ran, if she booked it how close would she go, could she traverse it without Cormac? She began to count names like bullets in a magazine, how many did she have left strong enough to both conduct the ritual and set Caleb and wife aside? "You were born into this life."

"I know what it's like to walk into a room and have nobody like me in it. To be the odd person out. It must've been hellaciously confusing to find myth is real and we're all..."

"Pawns?"

"Complicit." Caleb angled closer to Stana, back barren of protection aside from the woman and the automatic pistol in her hands. What had Delilah called her? Some scruffy Veteran, an uncultured Bogatyr... Tuija. The bitter syllables on Delilah's breath. No wonder the enchantress held a thinly veiled contempt for the woman, if she married Delilah's plaything. "Killing Zeus, it'll solve a few old beefs."

"Oy!"

"Zeus, you deserve to burn!"

"Tomato, tomahto." Zeus flicked his one hand to and fro, a small flicker of electric energy played between each digit.

Stana's eyebrow rose, what was the end game of this man and his Tuija? This... Judge Redeemer of the Truce? "If you believe he is better dead, why not let me kill him? Who will miss the old lech?"

"... oy! The skies will drown this world in tears at my passing! A flood would be right for my demise... maybe catastrophe... ooo nothing like a good catastrophe, maybe a miniature armageddon."

"Stana. The Book is dangerous."

"I bet you say similar to all the women with power."

"Who the eff brought womanhood into this?" Tuija shook her head, gun trained on Cormac who for the moment appeared to be more interested with the trees in the forest than either the Judge or his companion. "I know a great therapist. They're a non-binary djinn from Lebanon. Fair rates, too. What? Therapy is awesome. Honey doll, I'm turning into a living tree, facing this with some form of therapeutic assistance was your idea."

"No, no! Go on. Got their business card, darling? Wait, I think I left it in my other death on the line fighting jacket."

"I don't require therapy."

"Bullshit, you have the literal god Zeus locked in a wheelchair in middle of a park teenagers use to smoke weed and pretend they invented apathy. We know what you would do. You torched my brothers and sisters, my war siblings in their beds for soot. You need far more than therapy, but it's the only gracious start I give you, because my husband asked." Tuija clucked her tongue, and raised the pistol to Cormac's head, when the willow started swaying. "Do you think I'm fool enough to keep lead bullets in this gun, Cormac?"

The Fae raised both hands, feet rooted in the soil and the undergrowth. Liar. In the back of her mind, Stana felt the pulse of life Cormac represented, the force of nature which created willow trees. Their bark and scent, the sensation of pain relief and lack of inflammation. The entirety of the Fae was a drug she tried to ignore, an essence of pain relief she knew as she continued, Stana might need.

"Not from you." Stana elongated the last vowel, and wove it back in on herself, into her throat to become a double sound. Fingers buzzing from the influx of magic present in such a natural place, Stana continued to compound and compile the syllables of her spell, adding new ones to the circuit. Her vision narrowed, Cormac's deception pressed at her spine, but did nothing to shift her plans. The image of Cormac's body turning to a pile of ashes and a coal or two she'd keep going for the magic residue lingered with the imaginations of what death looked like on the bodies of the divine. Was it strange to believe one she intended to destroy had his own motives?

Didn't everyone keep their own motives hidden behind layers of their mind, dreadful strangers who would creep up to the wrong door? The pitch of her voice rose, all else falling away but her desire to claim Caleb's thoughts, to own some small piece of his mind for an instant, long enough to twist him round. To push him into a loop and free herself before the sensation of Deimos and Phobos' terror began to bead down her spine.

As her words began to take form, with their crackle and might, Caleb raised his hand.

"Enough of that." The spell dissipated from her tongue, lips began to babble into nonsense at the snap of his fingers. Caleb stalked forward, the perilous alpha male taking his time. The Olympians must have known Zeus was gone by now. "You don't get to use my Hugr, my own mind, against me."

Stana staggered back, her mouth worked, hand flung up to her mouth and she shook her head. Tried to remember how to breathe through her nose, to breathe through the panic and the hesitation she felt like a marred and useless blanket.

"Didn't do enough research, did you?" Caleb walked within centimetres of her body. Reached for the slim ereader in her hand. "Give it to me now, or you will never be able to walk away from the Realms, from Zeus and his shuffleboard buddies. You'll never know a decent, well-meaning life."

Stana stared up at his face, the eyes which kept a layer of kindness within them Delilah kept in fond opinion. He whispered in a language she couldn't pick out of the rush in her ears. She gulped and hugged the Book to her chest, its slim weight pressed between both nipples under the thin fabric of her brown dress.

"Cormac knows nothing about the Book but the death in it." Caleb wove his hand around the book's bottom and tugged. It slipped from her fingers, the cantrips holding the Book to her began to dissolve.

Stana's eyes narrowed. She thrust her hand against his chest and felt the flop of her burgeoning magic dissipate along pectorals built from centuries of Viking raids and fine breeding. Then, with the crack and pop of branches, Cormac bolted.

Stana yelped and dove for the Book, her one chance to return humanity to the path it was always meant to maintain. She shoved at Caleb, as the first bullet exploded from Tuija's gun. He shouldn't have turned around, but the impetus to protect his lover was too strong. Too grounded into his being. Tuija fired thrice into Cormac, watched each bullet embed into his bark with a sizzle and smoke. Tree branches broke off maples, flung toward them by thin willow-like vines.

"I envy you, Mauthisen! Your girl's got more sense in her head than mine." Cormac grinned wide, and before Caleb could shout out, or change his trajectory, the trees around Tuija shifted. Branches grabbed outward, roots upturned. Tuija became the epicenter of a fae quake, her feet lost their footing, too much meat and not enough root to keep her stance.

"Tuija!"

"I've got it! Keep the Keeper!" Tuija jumped and clambered onto a root, which fluctuated from the ground. The warrior leapt from the root to the branches, then rushed at the Fae lord, pistol fire ablaze in the twilight. Cormac dove into the ground, so far deep into soil it barely bulged where his body rested. Locked under the layers of earth and soil. "Okay maybe I don't got it as much as I thought I got it."

Caleb stepped backward, angled his body to meet with Tuija. While he did so, the worst possible happenstance occurred for Stana, Cormac and the entirety of the planet at large.

Zeus, King of the Gods, learned how to unfasten his wheelchair belt.

"Oh for the love of fuc-"

All at once, the situation went fubar. Zeus cackled with crackles of yellow lightning discharging from his fingertips as the loop and tightened strap released from around his waist. The Olympian God surged to his feet, slipper loafers stumbled onto the undergrowth and found purchase in a bed of pine needles. Slowly, ever slowly, his feet appeared to lighten, to raise from the ground and hover within a few centimetres of the forest's detritus.

The sparks between his fingers increased, chest hair and the hair upon his head and arms stood straight on end. His laugh was pathetic, but there in a park outside Milwaukee, Wisconsin's least tended suburb, Zeus, son of Cronus, woke up.

"I am the mighty god of lighting! I will be obeyed!"

Tuija rolled over a vine, and seeing the new threat, pulled her trigger. A bullet whizzed by Zeus's head.

"Gah! Woman! Why do you vex me so!?"

"Holy fuck!"

"Give me an hour to fly home and I can get my medication."

"Thoughts off my wife!" Caleb dove away with the Book, but vines tore him off from reaching Tuija.

The Book launched from his hand when a maple root struck him, and Caleb scrambled for it. He lurched and yanked free his utility knife to chop and saw at the vines. Each swing sent floral offal screeching into the ground to wither to dust. They released with a scream from Cormac, who dug into the soil to his knees, body elongating, growing taller and more slender. Up as the willow. "Zeus, get out of here! You're fucking it up!"

"I will not cower in my element! For I am the mighty Zeus!" He hovered less than a metre from the grass, one loafer slid off his dappled foot to plop unceremoniously to the ground. Shirt tails in the back untucked from the slacks, partially up to display the band of his adult incontinence wear. The Mighty Zeus.

"Cale, switch!" Tuija leapt and rolled toward Stana, sprinted at the human who staggered and lost her footing with a beleaguered shout at a stray bolt of electricity searing her hand. Stana searched upward, began a string of spell-words and incantations, a language Tuija recognized only by the pitch and yaw of the ground beneath her. She felt her ears twist and wrench inside her skull, put a hand to her temple, the other aimed her pistol. But the hand slipped from her temple to her cheek. The pistol waivered. Stana crawled for the ereader, half buried in loam.

"Wither, damn you!" Caleb shook his head and grabbed a vine, which threatened to bind Zeus's knees. Cormac bellowed, as two more bullets from Tuija's gun found their place in Cormac's wooden side. The vine-like branches in Caleb's hand withered and rotted in a pathway up, back to the source. Spots of wood rot began to appear on Cormac's face, swooping down his trunk-like body through the bits of clothing left from his human form. Caleb poured power into the Fae, grunted as two roots burst up from the ground and wrapped around his ankles. A surge of lightning crackled on, in tandem with Zeus's cackle. Caleb shook off the roots, stomped on one and broke it.

"Tuj! The Book, grab it now!"

Cormac screamed, branches like broken limbs began to fracture at their own weight. Caleb poured his dominance and life force into the magic, the withering call which seemed so different depending on the Folk. For the Fae, a withering of the main organism, the plant itself. The more he felt Cormac's control over the vines subside, the more Caleb doubled into the act. He would salvage this.

It was an act of magic so firm in its execution a thought crept into Stana's mind and bit into her brainstem.

Caleb Mauthisen would always be more masterful, and capable The thought stung with its acid, and she bawled out a screech as she dove through the undergrowth for the Book wrapped precariously in Tuija's hands.

Once Cormac was down, he'd rip the Book of Knowledge from her hands and go back to Sal's. Back to the beginning and fix this. Bolts of lightning fizzled, barren of the majesty they held in Zeus's prime. One stray bolt flickered across Caleb's arm, singed skin and charred a hole in his sweater. Still the god cackled, and Cormac bellowed out an array of curses. New roots lessened. He retreated into the main form, until a stray crackle hit Caleb's back.

"Watch it!"

"Get-you..." Zeus teetered, swung his hands in wild arcs. Was the senility catching up? Then, Caleb felt it. The sickening dawn of nausea, and he saw Stana, one hand raised, spewing words of power too numerous and too strong to come from the magical potential of a human like her. Let him wonder, Stana craved the recognition, the realization in his eyes that even if he was born with power beyond her, she could leave his curled up body in the dirt.

"Wait... where did..." Caleb shook his head in a wild shake as his feet stumbled on what he thought was stable ground.

"Little witch!" Zeus flung his hands out toward Stana, as the woman rose to her feet, as she spoke words of power no human knew or tapped into since the one time Sal thought he'd give some of the more rigorous spells a try. Beams of light snapped from Zeus's fingertips.

And from the refraction angle, from the discombobulation of Stana's spell, hit Tuija. Tuija screamed and jittered, steam rose from the cedar bark which sizzled from her flesh. Zeus's body hit the ground, tapped from the strain of the sky in its endless shake. As the world shuddered, Caleb paced to Stana, shoulder in and eyes forward. She shook into triplicate, back to one, then two forms, back to one. Her words came faster, trilled as the bodies of Tuija and Zeus shook within a finger's width of each other. As a line of willow fronds trailed toward the old god.

"Leave my wife alone!" Caleb stomped at the ground with every step, towed foot after foot as the nausea blistered across his tongue and down his throat with the acidic tang of bile. "Magic like this, you're not getting it from a god."

Stana staggered backward, both hands raised and voice growing louder, louder still. Louder. And louder and louder. And then...

She whispered a name.

The magic reinvigorated, Caleb stopped his forward momentum, stumbled back and shook out his head, heaved from a stomach still full of honey cake and tea. He spied Cormac, curled into a root ball beside a pine tree planted by a children's society from the plaque at his head.

"Who taught you... did you? Did you teach her how to take True Names!?" Caleb tried to rush Cormac, stomp-kicked the fae's gut, but ended in the soil, crawling on his belly to the curled up form of his wife. "Did you teach her how to take Names!?"

Cormac cackled, steam rose off from his fingers, "What's the matter, Mauthisen? They're just tiny, confused humans. Think what she can do after a week? A month? Do you know how many humans there are, who would give their own mother for a loaf of bread? A hit?"

Caleb whirled round on Stana. A human stealing the Book of Knowledge was unprecedented, but one capable of ripping the soul of a person, storing True Names as if they were battery packs? Stana staggered to her feet to gloat, power flickered between her hands at the shock on Caleb's face, the horror she'd waited to see since first discovering there was such a man as a Judge in the first place. Caleb raised his pistol and fired three rounds before another second was wasted. One hit its target, red blood staining Stana's dress.

"Enough." Palm out, Caleb clenched his fingers around the bands of energy

She cried out, and held a hand to her side as she was flung to the ground beside Tuija. Book clutched to Tuija's chest, Stana threw herself atop the other woman and roared. Names faded from the black notebook in Caleb's back pocket, missing Folk and Humans beyond the point of rescue. A ragged portal cut itself from the fabric of Midgard's reality, each rip and tear another Name. Another soul lost.

On his feet, Caleb reached into the shredded void and grabbed Stana's ankle. She bucked and kicked, the echo of a struggle reaching Caleb's ears through the suction of the Ginnungagap on the other side. With a roar of his own, Caleb pulled the thrashing woman backward a centimetre at a time. His feet dug into the earth, muscles alive with strain.

In the black miasma, Caleb witnessed the outline of his bride's body hitting back, untangling from Zeus and Stana with vicious close elbows and knees. Tuija mouthed something unintelligible as she hugged the Book, a horrific line of cedar bark opened along her belly, trailed to her sternum.

Boots slid in the soil, Caleb searched for something greater than his convictions to grab onto, but as the Truce laid disproportionate on his shoulders, so too the lack of it left Caleb reeling, digging his heels into whatever purchase the ground could offer.

"Tuija!" Stana's leg smashed against Caleb's hand, she conjured slender darts and hurtled them in all directions. Tuija lunged for Caleb's hand and their fingers slid together as a dart penetrated Zeus's gut.

Zeus's wide eyes and clenching grip around Tuija's shoulder kept the warrior woman off balance, his last burst of strength a plea not to be lost in Kaos. A plea echoed by the lightning which crackled into them all. Tuija's fingers went rigid, crackle-lines covered with bark.

The ragged portal closed and Caleb launched backward from the sudden shift in momentum. Body steaming from the electricity which coursed through him, Caleb's skull connected with an evergreen tree and cracked the trunk in half.

20 MAPS & GLASS BOXES

"Tuija…" The sound of helicopter blades and soldiers' voices churned Caleb's roiling mind back to consciousness. Caleb rose to his feet at a stumble and ran for the remains of the battlefield. Trees laid cracked on their sides, ground cover billowed in piles. "Tuija!? Tuj!"

Cormac fared little better, two Kopis soldiers in Morae panoply tased him while another shoved his body into a containment cube: a portable prison cell developed from Athene's technological wizardry and thick Roman glass. Caleb went to lean against a tree and faltered, caught up by the strong arm of a man who towered over even him to stop the fall.

"Where's my father? Where's Zeus?" Ares helped Caleb get steady, as the Scandinavian searched the forest, pointed a shaking hand over to a spot of burnt grass.

"Th-there, he was… where's Tuija?"

"Tuija was here?" Ares led Caleb to a rapidly built command centre, a folding chair sized up to handle Olympian girth took Caleb's weight.

"Tuija my… she was… she had the Book in her hands." He touched his forehead and hissed. Blood?

"Uncle, ease off. Let me take a look." Asclepius rushed with a medical kit and the loose almost-smile he wore as perpetual bedside manner, a bullet proof vest over his scrubs. "Caleb? Over here, look at me. Look, that's right. Now follow my finger. Yep. Follow my finger with your eyes… both of them preferably."

As best he could, Caleb complied and chased the wobbling finger while the world tilted. "Tuija had the Book in her hands, it would have worked if Zeus hadn't..."

"I need to get him to the hospital." Asclepius looked up at Ares and shook his head. Caleb thought he heard the sound of mighty wings, footsteps on the ground. All he saw was grass and spots of dirt and blood on his slack hands.

"N-no, Tuija, she was... Tuija and Zeus. They were both right there." Caleb tried to rise and another set of hands held his shoulders down. His stomach raged with an excruciating sharpness, he panted hard, pushed his palm against the slip of blood.

"Ares will handle it." The soft spoken voice filtered into Caleb's addled brainstem as calm and collected as a river stream was pleasant on a warm day. An urge to bathe in the sonic vibrations slipped down Caleb's shoulders, over biceps and clenched fists, until each finger relaxed. "Greetings Asclepius, mind if I consult?"

"Raph! Thought you were in Africa."

"They were. Ares. Asclepius. Leonidas. Caleb, you look like shit." The face which came to focus was androgynous with a mop of dark blonde hair swept over one side, an undercut shaved into the other. Draped in light grey tactical trousers and a crisp white long sleeved shirt, Mika may not have inspired the paintings of St. Michael and the Dragon like this, but Caleb knew the archangel carried the force of the spear and pilum.

The warrior of the Theosians, like the rest of them, was too damn late.

Caleb spied more sets of boots when his chin fell to his chest, jade green grieves, and one set gold as Ra's light, hieroglyphs imprinted in the sides which vibrated with power and wobbled Caleb's vision. Shutting his eyes, Caleb heaved and was caught by Raphael's calm inducing hands, held back onto the chair as his shirt disintegrated.

"I see a black mass. Slender and pointed like an arrow. Am I cleared to conduct a healing?"

"How many strikes do you have, Theosian?"

"Are you serious?! The Judge is bleeding out and you're worried about strikes?!" Asclepius' voice distorted in Caleb's ears, he felt himself lifted and set on something solid.

"Without the Rule of Law, we are chaotic beasts clawing at each other."

"Gee, thanks Cao. It'll help Caleb so much."

"Ares, it has to be done." Inflected with his Spartan roots, Leonidas' voice coated the crowd in stern command. "You and Mika are the only ones here strong enough to hold him while Idunn's cider does its work."

"Asclepius, Raphael, can nothing else be done?"

"I could heal him."

"If you do, my Realm will come down on you. It's against the Truce Law. We cannot make exceptions."

"Where were you, when we were fighting? Funny your opinion matters now, after the blood was shed." Dazed, Caleb forced his eyes open and stared blood-lidded at Cao's pristine hanfu style belted gown. Not a single drop of muck from hairline to slipper.

"I am merely attempting to keep order. Is that not our function? Your collective emotional state is not my problem."

"Stop squabbling, where's the cider? To stop this bitch and get my wife back, I'll take it." Caleb wiped a spot of blood from his mouth with the back of a red stained hand. "Stand me up."

There was a nod between Mika and Ares, the angel set hands upon the Judge's right shoulder, Ares on the left and hefted Caleb to his feet. One foot slipped poorly out of socket, eliciting a grunt from the Judge. Caleb psyched himself up with two ragged deep breaths.

The flask sung of an uncontained joik, released from its cap by Leonidas. The concentrated liquor of the Aesir Idunn coated the air with cardamom and honey, the warmth of baked apples. Its scent struck Caleb with a longing for the home he saw only through the tired glimpse in Lu's place, Finnegan's Pub a transparent layer between the two soils.

Caleb guzzled the liquor as it burned through his body. The dim and dark cavernous Scandinavian winter froze into Caleb's injuries, while sparks of rare summer heat and the never setting sun set them aflame. As extreme as the Asgardian reflection of Scandinavia, Idunn's cider was neither pleasant nor gentle on the injured.

Ares and Mika grunted into Caleb's flail. Head rocked back, Caleb felt bones reknit and blood seep back into closing capillaries. He barked and hyperventilated, overtaken by the potency of the cider.

"Bit intense, isn't it?" The Kehmeti Falcon beside Cao cocked his head to the side, gold capped locks flowing down his shoulder.

"On the injured? Yes. Think of all the pain you're in recovering from an injury. Now survive it all in fifty seconds. We're practical people in Asgard, pain fades but it's a bitch at the time." Ares held Caleb as he rocked, body clenched.

"Some go mad like the Alfather. Others turn Cider into an act of bravery. Aesir and Vanir earn their immortality through pain."

"How is this barbarism better than a wave of my wings?" Raphael shook their head as the Judge gasped and tried to shake his head, snapping his neck with a thunder crack.

Caleb went slack into Mika's hold to catch his breath as the last of the pain faded to a heady buzz which turned the world of Midgard bright as a snow bank in the winter sun.

"See? That was no reason to fuss. I shall report to the Council and inform them you've finally taken your medicine like the obedient Judge you're meant to be. Ares. Michael. Carry on, we expect a full report on this inconvenient circumstance." Cao bowed to both and turned round to the park's path with a smug upturn to prim lips.

One step toward the Dao Immortal was all Ares got before Leonidas put a calming hand on his chest. "Enyo, don't."

"Leave it. Where are we at?" Caleb clenched and unclenched his fists, the Council could think they got this one minor victory. Confiscating the Book and getting Tuija home was more important than the smugness of a man whose head Caleb could pop off like a dandelion.

"If Stana took both Zeus and Tuija, nothing matters but how much time she's got before conducting the ritual." Leonidas shook his head and handed Caleb a long sleeve shirt for his bare chest. "Deimos and Phobos are rerouting with Lou's Enomotia. The second she touches Midgard soil, we attack. But if she's capable of this, I want to know how before we strategize."

"Stana's human, bog standard. Found an instructor. Someone to teach her the ropes." Caleb pulled the shirt over the closing wounds and stared daggers at Cormac in his containment box. "Who taught Stana where to find the recipe for killing a god? Cormac of the Willow. In those three days, he not only taught her where to look, but how to harvest True Names."

A hush of whispers vaulted through the tangle of Kopis Industries, Kehmeti and Theosians. Caleb stalked to the containment cube and knelt on his haunches before the wounded and wilted body of Cormac.

"Why unload an unstable weapon on the Realms? Why did you do it, Cormac? And where is she going?" Mika and Ares encircled the cell, both descended to their haunches, Ares' hand slapped the top of the translucent cube.

In an act of defiance, Cormac morphed humanoid limbs back into the branches of a willow tree. Legs became roots, his torso a trunk, until the containment cell appeared to contain a bonsai with no soil.

"Fuck."

"Does kidnapping Zeus from an old folks home count?" Asclepius piped up, gulped and rubbed at his cheek. "It counts, right?"

"That's three. Once the dust settles, his life is mine." The words came with a gravity so vast they wilted half the vines on Cormac's head. Folk searched each other's faces, Caleb's voice as hard as the clatter of bullets exiting a gun.

"We find her. Now. Before Stana tries the ritual again." Caleb saw two ravens beside a falcon and a songbird on the periphery. Another songbird took flight. At the edge of the wood, a slender fox watched warily, twin tails shifted back and forth. Back and forth. "I don't give two shits about anything else, only that she stops. Now."

"You might be too close to this." Mika unfurled their white wings, a golden sword visible attached to a holster on their slender hip.

"You think!?" Caleb kicked the containment cube hard enough to send it tumbling edge over edge into a truck. "Get him out of here! Take him to Chalceus, we're not giving him back to the Fae until we get every answer he's got in his roots. Reroute Phobos and Leander to Chalceus to pry those answers out of Cormac's bark. Sclep, Raph, prep your kits. I don't know what state we'll find Tuija and Zeus in, but it won't be pretty. Zeus was half looped and off his gourd."

"He's always like that. Has been for centuries, it's no change." Ares shook his head, with a sigh. "I'm going with you."

"If you come, we'll all descend into a bloody and emphatic war."

"Yes, and that fight is what you need." Ares gripped Caleb's shoulder, nodding over another soldier with armour sized up enough to give Caleb pause.

"She's looking to kill gods and until this willow-the-wisp talks, we don't know how many methods she has at her disposal. I don't aim to find out, Ares so stuff it. I'll take Leo and Mika."

"I trade you my husband for you to rescue your wife and stay on the sidelines? No, Caleb. She's gotten away from you twice now, nevermind Zeus, who by himself is a senile powder keg with the power of a hurricane at his fingers. Father's outside, there's a reason we put him in a glorified box with enough companions who dedicate what slim bit of belief they have in the fact he's a man with good kids. If he happens to go off worse than what happened here? It's my right to bear it and I will. We take her together, or you have nothing from me." Ares was stern, but maintained a begrudging fairness when Caleb stopped to breathe long enough for sense to return to his head.

"Enyo?" Pouring over the evidence feeds on a few scattered tablets, Leonidas grit his teeth. "Maybe you and Caleb should both hang back. We're useless to Stana, you're not."

Running both hands through long black hair and down his well cropped beard, Leonidas shook his head and leaned against the table. "Give me a firm reason to send my spouse into an altercation with high stakes and no idea of the enemy's power. Zeus? I'll slit the bastard's throat myself if I have to."

"Oh please allow me." Mika piped up, both hands together in prayer. "Please let me behead Zeus. I promise I will make it clean and only gloat for one or two songs worth."

"Songs last what, a few millennia in the Spheres?" Ares leaned down to nudge his nose at Leonidas' ear, whispering with pursed lips.

"We're almost finished one... well... Luci made that first one a round... I promise you, I will strike your father down if he interferes. Yes?"

"Almost worth it." Ares nodded with a frown, arm around Leonidas' shoulders.

"She needs a god to kill, I'm as immune as you are, Leonidas. Gear up. Mika? Prepare to kick ass and play keep-away. Huginn!" True desperation led Caleb to reach out to Odinn's ravens, an act he'd not done since one rebellious moment in his forties his father never let him forget.

One of the ravens perked up with a ruffle of their feathers, and flew to Caleb's outstretched arm. Caleb ran his index finger over Huginn's feathers, from the crown down the massive black bird's back. A strange familiarity lilted from the creature, one eye milked with an intelligence and thoughtfulness which saw through Caleb's facade. Through the bravado and command to the flail of a man whose plan to solve his problems doomed his bride. "I need a spell. One to protect against fire, I know Frigg has it. Go. Muninn can stay. Fly fast."

The raven nuzzled its head into Caleb's cheek, then rose into the air with three massive flaps of its' mighty wings. As Caleb saw the raven hit the air currents, he sighed.

"They could be lost in the Ginnungagap by now. We'll comb it but it'll take time." Mika shouldered a cuirass and tightened the straps. Tried bending and twisting in their corporeal humanoid form with a grunt of appreciation for the fine Hellene craftsmanship.

"No, with Deimos and us on her tail, Stana's window of opportunity is closing. She'd go somewhere familiar and relatively safe, with a Sacred Grove... Ares, I need a map." Caleb let Leonidas strap Kopis armour over his chest.

"What do we do about the Names? If she's bleeding human's souls dry for their magical potential, the death toll is monumentally higher depending on how many Names she's got."

"Put them on her tab. She's paying for the lot in pieces." Caleb took hold of Tuija's memory, laid the sensation of his wife's love out on a hastily opened table beside a tablet with a display of the Midgardian world map. Stillness and calm. His hands jittered as he tried to calm his breathing, to feel something more than the ticking god damned clock in his mind, counting down how long it would take Tuija to burn. He tried to fish the images of burnt trees out of his mind, to focus on Stana's wary and angry eyes, to hold onto the image of Tuija standing in his, no, their ruined house promising they'd fix it together. They would piece their lives from the shattered masonry of his duty into a family. Neither of them would be alone again, Tuija would have all the Folk through Caleb's insistence and place, and he would forever have his love by his side, fighting shoulder to shoulder, soothing wounds, waiting in an approximation of patience while he made coffee in the mornings, and switching the script while she made tea at night.

An ache tugged at his side and he let the pain take him. Further down. Further in. Eyes shut to the world, he concentrated on the scent of her, on the way Tuija felt in his arms, a vibrational cord in the harp of the middling Realm. Index finger and thumb tightened on the tablet's map. North America, further in. Further. Not just North America, somewhere West.

The scent caught his nose in a sickly burn. Char. Burnt meat. His fingers twitched on the map, tightened the view further in. And in.

Vancouver.

The Sacred Grove in the middle of Stanley Park. He opened his eyes.

"We need a door." Caleb barely pulled his phone from his pocket before Icarus' voice peppered in that they'd patched Caleb through. As he coordinated with the Fae Lord, Caleb missed a knowing glance shared between Ares, Leonidas and the Theosians.

"I'm with Tuija on this one." Leonidas whispered low in his throat. "Someone has got to tell Caleb the truth, before he gets himself killed."

"Or worse." Mika pursed their lips and hovered in midair. "Once this is done. We'll fly ahead, we're faster."

21 THE RITUAL GROUND

The ritual ground split into a shallow container, wafts of Stana's power hovered unconvinced and raw. Stana staggered to her footing, hand wrapped up the arm in a black and purple iridescence, which bound her prisoners together. Book in hand, she coughed out a laugh and sat on a fallen log to breathe in the forest's humid air.

"Wasteful... I could've used those Names." Zeus tsked and wriggled in his bonds, "You're not even using them right! There's no pomp! No circumstance or flair. Just 'oh dear me I read a Book passage and it told me to flex. Woe is me, I hate gods, oh blubbery bubbers.' Worse than Ares when he told us women were people. Mama's boy, the only one too."

"You're despicable." Tuija pulled her head back, then careened her forehead into Zeus's. He cried out, his arms tied around her with rope made of no material Tuija could fathom. Face to face with the legendary lecher was not how Tuija thought her day would end. "And the reason we're both in this mess. If you'd stayed down, we had them!"

She needed a shower, a handgun, a moment to collect herself. If she dislocated her thumb, maybe she could slip out of the bind.

"I doubt it. The rope spell I used was meant to tighten with every motion. If you tried, I believe your limbs would fall off." Stana poked at a stack of wood from various trees, which conjured from another belch of black and purple iridescence. Beech, alder, oak, cedar... some petrified logs and some which came from churches or sacred meeting places.

"How many humans are you tapping to use those powers?" Zeus horked and spat behind Tuija as she groaned with a shiver.

"How many did you tap for yours?" Stana laid out the wood in a pattern, their standing bodies in the epicentre of the grid. Trees swayed round, leaner and shorter than the giant redwoods and cedars which grew before any Aquarium went in, before yacht clubs on the dock, or cannons at bridges. A Sacred Grove whispered into the soil and the sounds, the muted vault of trees filtering higher and higher to the eventual break of sky.

"None. Taking True Names is more despicable than him." Tuija jerked her head to the side and felt it collide again with Zeus's cheek. Stana eyed her with one eyebrow raised, shaking her head. "It's true. Taking Names is the most despicable taboo in the Truce. Tell her, Zeus."

"Never did it myself, although I never had to. You see, when the sky is your powerhouse, it acts better than those batteries you leave out in the sun with the black umbrellas."

"Solar panels, Jase and Mika." Tuija shook her head, sighed and felt the ropes twinge into her flesh. Crack the bark on her right wrist. "They're called solar panels."

"I hate that man. He fucked my family over, you know. He's the real villain! All peace and love and follow me, and sell what you have and share the love around. But what happens when all the wealth is shared around? What then? You end up with beggars on the street. Beggars peddling their priests in front of my halls. My Temples, they were a place of offering and plenty! You should have seen the way they worshipped me... oh the hoards of gold and jewels."

"Who, the rich and well connected?"

"I am Zeus, King of the Gods, my love. I have standards. Standards my son did not inherit." Zeus spat and the saliva dribbled down his chin. He grunted and tried to wipe it on Tuija's shirt. She groaned and glared at Stana, who for once looked up from her preparations to shiver. "Ares got it from Hera's side of the family."

"It's the same family, you incestuous moron."

"... yes, but the female side. Thus, Ares learned how to be a pussy."

"The God of War. A pussy." Tuija chuffed with a shake of her head, the breeze from the Burrard Inlet stroked at her cheek, and she pulled into the sensation, if Tuija could stall, if she could distract them both. Keep Zeus talking...

"What else would you call a man who didn't kill his father and usurp his throne when he had the chance?"

"A good man! Gods! No wonder everybody hates you so much! Stana, please. I beg you, start with Mr. Important. Kill him first, let me die in peace from his prattling!"

"Of course the most dangerous of us should die first! It is the proper way of deicide, trust me! I've killed more gods than you've years before Charon dumps your disastrous body into the River Styx without ransom." Zeus's eyes flickered. He shifted his body, trying to reach for his pockets. He nodded his eyes downward, the fine tree-like maiden's hands were closer to his pockets than his were, if she could get to the metal. Get to the spoon and fork... preferably before the tapioca stained his trousers... Tuija groaned and turned her head away.

"No, I'm not grinding against you, gods did that ever... of course it worked, you're Zeus, it worked at least twice."

"Thrice!" He grinned then nodded downward again, attempting to shake his trick hip. The pain cracked along his spine. Zeus bit back a howl and nodded back down. Jiggled his hip one more time... and the metal touched Tuija's hand. He knew it did! For her hand was righteously close to his spindly, elderly ass.

Her eyes snapped up to his face, and for one brief moment, Tuija smiled at the old arthritic codger. The smile faded with the scent of kerosene and olive oil, frankincense and myrrh, bundles of sage and dragon's blood which were placed in intervals around their entwined bodies. Stana muttered to herself, counted bundles and checked back to her supplies. Weed... she needed a weed grown on a mountainside... would dandelions do? The bit of park was littered with them.

"Let me think. Who would be the most dangerous? The elderly wimp with incontinence issues and fewer followers than his crippled motorcycle repairing son Hephaestus? Or the lover of the one man capable in all the Realms, of dissipating my magic?" Stana stalkled closer, Tuija grit her teeth and jiggled into Zeus's pocket, felt the sticky goo of tapioca residue and tried to keep the glance of revulsion from her face. Let Stana think it was fear.

"Oh, so you're saying because her male lover is of power, she has value greater than mine in my current state? Well, if you want to..."

"Husband. We're married," Tuija stopped. "I will help you kill this man. Let me go, we can do the ritual with him, give you sticks of Eau de Zeus and rid humanity of his sticky memory. Gods."

"Eugh. This is why the gods need to die."

"Seriously? They're not all like him, you know."

"Prove it."

"Aphrodite helped fund the feminist movement. You know who helped get women the vote? Ares. Yep! World War I had a purpose beyond Frans fucking Ferdinand. Ahh..."

"My son Apollo is in your prison for..."

"Nobody wants to hear a list of Apollo's crimes." Tuija grit her teeth with a hiss.

"But I was so proud." Zeus smacked his lips, "My boy. Chip off my old block, now if he were here, I bet you he'd sing you a song so erotic you would forget this futile attempt at misandry and give him a strong and sturdy son! Then raise him by yourself until he comes of age and goes on an adventure for the Family."

"Seriously, Stana. I will help you kill him. Right now. I will rip his throat out with my teeth." Tuija leaned in gnashing her teeth, and Zeus whimpered. Stana rushed to Tuija, shoved a handkerchief into her mouth and shook her head.

"He dies when he is useful. You die the same death as the codger." She swerved and pulled a vial of beggar's tears from a cosmetics bag and poured it over the wood.

"Hurry, woman." Zeus gnashed his teeth, and with a thrust of his sagging manhood against the adult diaper which contained it, gave Tuija the angle to grab hold of the pudding spoon. She yanked it loose from his pocket, angled it so his fingers could make the grab as the binding tightened.

Tuija screamed through her gag as deep cuts opened to amber over. But, Zeus held... the spoon.

"AAAAAHHAHAHAHAHAHAAAAAAAAAAAAH!" He cackled aloud, the weather shifted and clouds pregnant with rain wafted off the Burrard Inlet to the peninsula. "You dumb hag! You tried to light a fire in Vancouver! Aaaaaaaaaaaaa Forsooth your King is nigh!"

Zeus waggled the spoon around in a tiny circle, as split drops of Vancouver's perpetual rains began to drip drop from the trees. "Come to me, Lightning and THUNDER!"

In the distance, no louder than a flatulent fart, a small peal of thunder. Tuija glared at him, chewed on the hankie and tried to spit it out.

"... this usually works, hold on a minute..."

"What are you doing now, you crazy old ma-"

BRZZZT CRACK

Lightning struck through the treeline, veered through Zeus's body and for a split second, rejuvenated his beleaguered body. With a flex of his mighty muscles, Zeus broke the bonds which threatened them, caught Tuija before she fell to the ground as her body shook with the electricity.

".... are you finished?" Stana flicked to the right bookmark in the Book's saved pages, her hand awash in green flame.

"What!? This is impressive!" Wielding both fork and spoon aloft, Zeus shook them over his head, as the clouds grew darker, higher in the sky as pillars of gunmetal over the Vancouver Harbour and North Shore. "Come to me, Lightning! Come to your GOD, Storm and thunder and crash of the hoofed horsemen! For I! Am!"

"Down!" The thunderous voice which yelled over Zeus was not the God of the Sky, King of Kings, but that of his treacherous and torturous son.

"Areees, I had her!" Zeus shot a bolt of lightning straight at Stana, who caught it in the chest and spun out on the ground with a heave.

"Father, get down! Now!" Ares rushed and a shield popped out of the black metal bracer on his arm, telescoped outward into the circular buckler of a Spartan. He launched in front of the old man, ate a spike of pure hatred, made manifest by Stana's ire. The green flames now shone with a yellow core, staining Stana's open mouthed grin and the mania of wide brown eyes.

"Zounds and forsooth!"

"Get. Down. Father. Then shoot her! As much as she can take and more." Ares whistled, and the beating of mighty wings vaulted from the darkening sky. Mika, a vengeful archangel speared down with holy light strong enough to crumple Stana to the soil.

"About time you said something nice to me... can I have her when we're finis-"

"NO!"

"NO!"

"NO!" Caleb dove for Tuija, a shield unfurled from his arm too, the patwing of Stana's hatred canted off to the side, dissipated in the oncoming rain. At the onslaught of their rescue, Stana began to unravel. Zeus was there, crouched in an arthritic ball, and Tuija not far from her lover's side. The stink of desperation wafted off Stana's shaking shoulders, the cling of her fingernails to dirt.

"You walk here!?" Tuija clung to Caleb's side, unsheathing the kopis strapped to his leg with a flourish. "I was about to turn traitor to get rid of the lech."

"Are you alright!?" The Judge and the warrior queen jousted away from Stana's regaining fire, a quick kiss their reunion. "Let's finish this and go home."

"A door. First project is installing a proper door. A big, thick, soundproof door." Tuija slashed at the air, and cut down another dart flung from Stana's flailing desperation.

"Mika, now!" Caleb rolled himself and Tuija away, watched for the signal from Leonidas that the deities were clear of the danger zone. Clear of the dreaded circle which began to smoke as Stana incanted, wood smoke fizzling with Zeus's raindrops. "Ares, get Zeus out of here! Go!"

"I won't leave you!"

"Yes you will! She needs gods, and I'm not one! Go!" Caleb threw a stone at the Olympian's back and Ares picked his dazed father up. For the first time in his life, since the rigged battles of his youth, Ares ran. Zeus continued to thrust his fork and spoon into the sky, trying to call down lightning from further and further away.

"Leon, I'm armed!" Tuija clanked her borrowed sword and shield together, feet secure in their stance on the readily slipping ground. Sparta's resurrected King let out a war cry, and both warriors stalked the woman in the centre, who stumbled to her knocking knees.

"I see the Book. Get me an opening!" At another volley of cantankerous energy from Stana's cracking fingertips, Caleb dove toward the furious spellcaster.

"No!" Stana wheeled backward, throwing her arms up in front of her. Two sword blows should have cut the woman down, but for the thin bubble of a hastily constructed shield strengthened by Stana's whispering lips. "I cannot fail! You won't kill me!"

Caleb rose up, sprinted and leapt over another hateful arrow, as Mika and Leonidas rushed her to the cliffside near enough to be seen. Armed with a spear and shield, a tac-helmet on his head, Leonidas barked and roared in Greek, swung wide while Mika, the lauded St. Michael of the Archangels stabbed low and contained, their sword aflame with the essence of the Divine. Stana stumbled back, braying wild curses as name after name twisted past her lips and name after name recorded itself on Caleb's book.

More missing humans, more catatonic collaterals damaged by the gripping desperation of the obscene.

Casualties of his mistake. Caleb yanked the semi-automatic firearm from his webbing and strafed with cover fire when Leonidas, Tuija and Mika swung. Stabbed. Launched. Stana continued to stagger, and in the blink, the uneasy exhalation between one human's disposed soul and another Tuija threw the kopis between the space of Leonidas' shield and Mika's armour clad androgynous form.

The sword buried deep into Stana's stomach, coloured her clothing and spewed a black ichor into Stana's veins.

"Take her down!" Caleb let loose barrage after barrage into Stana's body as she fell back. As she suspended in midair. As the sword did its evil work.

He rushed through the line of defenders, and Caleb yanked through Stana's jacket and dress pockets for the Book. She clutched his arm, sucked in wet breaths. "I can kill... you."

"Caleb, get back!" Tuija's voice lost its way to Caleb's ears, when Stana's hands clenched around Caleb's arm.

At first, he felt nothing but the sapping rains of Vancouver swathing Stanley Park in a new bit of fresh grass. As he tried to tug away, the cloth on his arm turned red as embers, orange as fire. He yanked at her hand, but nothing would free it, her fingers like talons down to the bone. Caleb roared and spun through the grass, tried to kick her off, get the spindle-creature of a woman to let go, as flames as pure and profane as those which torched the Dover Grove burst along his body.

He was no god, he was as human as Tuija, he... Caleb combusted. An unholy conflagration spiked from the wood pile and herbs, a line of dripping oil rushed from Stana's body and blood to the pile of placed lumber.

Mika grabbed Caleb, Leonidas brought his shield down again and again on Stana's arms, but some unnatural feat kept her safe. One by one, name after name, Lisa Fricton lost both arms in a freak manufacturing accident. Otis Carval crashed his car, investigators wondered at the way his hands split off from the rest of his body, as if cut in a sick guillotine. Name after name, the act of selling out, of giving their Names for magical comforts, for extra cash, for a new dog the same as the old which died too young. Too soon. What did they care, atheists and the desperate?

Stana shrieked and gnashed her teeth as the fire consumed her hair too, down her back.

Shoulder to diaphragm, Tuija ploughed into Stana's wounded stomach. The force of the strike, of Leonidas', of Mika's stabbing slashes broke through the litany of names Stana had taken. Used like convenient wrappings left out in the rain.

Through his agony, Caleb heard the boom of Ares' basso voice, felt Leonidas yank him back from the blaze by his shoulder. The pressure of Zeus' rain and Mika's blessed wing strokes were a memory Caleb's mind would compile in the infinite hereafter, when he kept no other purpose but the searing investigation of how the world could pitch so far off its axis.

Tuija back-pedalled into Caleb's chest, the shield hung at a strange angle, the alloy bent and Tuija's arm with it. "For the love of all that's holy get the fuck out of here, Cale-"

The blow struck with a dry smack of Tuija's back against the armour at Caleb's chest. Both beings were flung backward into a desiccated cedar stump hard enough to rattle Caleb's bone cage.

"T-Tuj..." He wrestled for his breath as the cackle of the mad woman roared in both ears, whispers of the spell echoed in his mind, the flickers of flame haunted his skin. As adamant as he was, as powerful. "Tuija..."

A strangled wheeze stopped Caleb's world.

The rattle of lungs filling with fluid, in tandem with shaking limbs.

"Tuija... Tuj..." Caleb cradled Tuija in arms gone instantaneously stiff, as he felt the prick of the magic fade. The universe stilled, focused on the microcosm in his grasp as he felt the magic fade, the spear of obsidian with it. Her head flopped against Caleb's shoulder, strained and sweating, lips pale as they fumbled on words which died first.

Died before the rest of her, quaking in her husband's arms.

"My..."

"Wh-why'd you... she...she couldn't hurt me with.... with... no...no...Raph! Raphael!" Caleb's wail burst across the old growth of the forest, where hikers seldom explored. Tuija's hand shook as it stroked his cheek, leaving a spread of crimson on freckled skin. "Asclepius!! Raphael!"

He held her hand to his face, pulled her close as he could as if proximity would stave off the reaper coming like a seed given water and loam. Tuija's lips worked, no breath left in ragged lungs split open by Stana's nefarious dart. Ferocity lingered in her mismatched eyes, and a vice grip on Caleb's shoulder. She pulled herself up to press her forehead to her husband's cheek and with the last manoeuvre in a life which spanned eleven centuries, Tuija Draganova, the Dragon's Daughter, whispered her last.

"My God." Her syllables filtered through Caleb's ear canal, past drum and hammer and anvil down the nerve bundle into the frontal lobe of a man whose arms quit their shake in tandem with the stillness of shock capturing both lungs.

"Tuija..." The smell, the slow cascade of ash fluttered to the planet spun by an arthritic hand. Slow as the inhale which betrayed Caleb's desire to stop.

Stop.

"Stop."

Caleb rocked on his knees, his lungs betrayed him, they forced more air into his body, more time into the vault of stars above covered by the filmy grey of the atmosphere. Each staggered breath was another second removed from Tuija's motion, from the closing and opening of her round, beautiful eyes.

A caw of victory erupted from Stana's throat, she'd done it. She'd killed one and the ash which fell consumed the air with a mystic sensation so potent she wanted to scoop the entire atmosphere into her pocket. Leonidas slashed at Stana's torso, but the second of shock which rocked the Grove gave her enough time to collect herself and whisper another of the dwindling names on her murderous list.

"Son?" Zeus sauntered back to the battle, glowered at the gasping man. The Judge who thought he could command the Realms to live quietly. As if he alone had the agency to demand what Stana knew to be self-evident.

"Will you never listen!? Why didn't you stay where I put you!? Go..." Ares lowered his sword as he caught the shudder of the gruesome display and the sink of Caleb's shoulders. "Oh... oh no."

"If you want that lover of yours to live, get behind me." The graven marble of Zeus' voice regained a modicum of power, as he reached to the rain and the vast greying sky above Vancouver. Leonidas dove behind his spouse. Mika launched into the air. And the son Zeus hated knelt with his shield pressed against the armour of his shoulder.

"Hold firm." Ares' prosthetic hand whirred as it gripped the shield, his arm around Leonidas's waist to hem the human in. Hold him steady the way he promised, but failed at Thermopylae.

"No letting go."

A pop of the air. Caleb inhaled, the pressure shifted.

Stana raised her hand and began to whisper, one more of these mythic horrors dead and she'd have it. She would kill the gods wholesale. Raze their memory from the sky and the stars and the earth at their feet.

The ash which danced in the air flitted in coils around the wrathful god's son.

Zeus placed his hands on cedar trees, planted his feet with mighty roaring words from acrid lungs. Stana kept whispering to call forth the same ichor-laced spell which struck down the bark-faced believer. Zeus lifted his face up to the sky's rain and its wind, and its lightning roiling off the sea. Wasn't the Aegean, but the cloud cover would be enough, the perpetual Vancouver rains would be enough.

He would be enough, one last time.

Caleb's hyperventilation stopped.

The excruciating roar which purged from Caleb's throat shook Vancouver in what the Humans would dub an earthquake so ferocious it caused ships to beach in the harbour and foundations to crack through Downtown. Trees flattened, waves surged and the ash Stana desired scattered across the planet in a shockwave, which tore at the sky across the hemisphere. Consumed with Caleb's shock, the agony of the scream tore the landscape asunder, it ripped into the spirits of those present until Tuija's stillness penetrated deep into the vaults of their collective souls.

The planet groaned in syncope with Caleb Mauthisen's grief-shook onslaught.

Zeus called down the clouds and the rain, to create a barrier against Caleb's tempest, his feet anchored to the earth. The deposed King of Olympus' wretched groan mixed with Caleb's roar, the pathetic caterwaul of a god who knew his time was over.

Ares' cloak draped over Leonidas, the Olympian of War held his lover as if one blink too many and he too would suffer Tuija's fate. The shield bent. Ares' prosthetic hand twitched as two of the knuckles shattered. He dared peer at the catastrophe over the side of the shield. "Father!"

And in Zeus' dwindling persistence, Ares witnessed the face of godhood in Caleb Mauthisen, the emanation too late to save one of the mightiest warriors Ares had known. Tuija was right. The ideal Raynar clung to, that he could resurrect a piece of his beloved in claiming her motherhood on his only surviving child, that Caleb was human and divine... was as foolish as a consoling isolation.

Ares turned his head to witness the god of Midgard's soul screaming for his wife, the first true believer in the divinity within, and felt the slap of Zeus's hand against his cheek. "If you want your pet to live, stay down!"

Caleb stalked Stana with footfells which crumbled the earth beneath them, all her sigils and specifically placed totems crushed or brushed away in the tempest. Stana shrieked and crawled backward, until she was lifted by her shoulder as if her body were paper.

And Stana knew fear, in its purity and decrepit might. She stared into the eyes of the divine, saw reflected back each Name she'd used like battery charges, and the weight of their lives began to crumple her ribcage into bits. Clinging to the Book of Knowledge, eyes and mouth wide in a terrified gape, Stana held most to the conviction that each life she took to end these creatures was a worthy sacrifice. Unrepentant and broken, Stana whimpered the only Name she had left.

"Lilith..." The name fractured in her mouth, as the void burst and closed her in its infinite black.

Without the target for his rage, Caleb collapsed. The roar which shook the world became a whimpered crawl back toward the still figure who laid on a tangled bed of ferns.

"Ah, Ares. You will never be King of this place." Consumed by vitriol, Zeus' voice began to crumble to the ground with the rest of him.

22

Ares Son of Zeus

Ares carried his father back into the Creaky Acres from the SUV, through the main doors with its intercom and past the reception desk. The middle of the night quieted the world, the receptionist gone for the day with nothing amiss. The nurses station had low light, while most of the denizens of the place were long in bed, or nestled in their rooms with radios, or televisions of a much smaller variety than the one Ares reinvigorated every year.

A constant reminder.

Zeus mumbled in his arms, strained to keep his head off Ares' shoulder in a last lingering defiance. While the nurse at the nursing station rose, Ares shook his head.

"I've got him. A little too much excitement for an old man." Ares gave the nurse a smile and kept walking.

"If you need anything..."

"He'll need a change later, give me a minute to settle him in and I'll fetch you. Thanks, Melinda."

"You remembered..." Melinda covered a yawn with a sip of coffee from the espresso machine donated by Athene. While his sister hated their bastard father, she refused to punish his carers with substandard coffee. Wouldn't do, and thus she worshipped their dedication with coffee roasts and cold brews. The stray frothed milk.

"How are your boys?"

"Jacen decided to join the army, like you suggested. Thanks for helping get him out of his tight spot."

"The army will make a good man of him. It was no trouble, I remember being a rebellious asshole in my day. We idiots have to look after each other, as long as we look after our Mum's. If you need anything more, give the office a call." Ares nodded with another smile, perfect teeth in the dim light, and kicked at a door with a name plate in the middle: Zeus Olympia.

Once inside, he stepped on a ground-trigger for the lamps, and the room painted a soft yellow glowed with golden light. Pictures of Greece, of the Roman Colosseum lined the walls, Zeus's bed (woefully narrow to Zeus's standards) held fresh silk sheets, three pillows set to prop him up, one for his knees. Ares laid him on his bed, propped the two pillows behind Zeus's back and slipped the other under the knees to alleviate pressure from Zeus's hip.

"There you are, father."

"Why don't you kill me? Are you lacking in ambition?" Zeus croaked, arms crossed over the stain on his yellow button down.

Ares passed by the pictures on the wall, sat in another scotchguarded armchair big enough for his and Heph's frames, done in red velvet. The closest thing Zeus had left to a throne, aside from the porcelain one in the attached bath and the ruined wheelchair Heph would no doubt replace in the morning.

"I could. Keep thinking it wouldn't take much. A pillow to your face while you sleep. But..." Ares leaned into the chair, felt the toll of the day as it tempered into his spirit. "... then I think. It's what you want."

Zeus glanced with a scowl in storm-grey eyes. Fiddled with the buttons of his button down to reveal the crisp white tank underneath.

"All those centuries, tearing me down. Apollo is the better son, Dionysus, Hermes. I was your first born, the Heir of Olympus outright."

"Ah... Athene was conceived sooner."

"And then you ate her mother while she was still in the womb. I was born first, I was your son. Not through wedlock, the child of the Queen of Heaven. And you hated every moment of my birth, the way I sought your eyes and challenged you. I know, father, I know you spent every second of those centuries ensuring I would not usurp you like you usurped Cronus. Like Cronus usurped Ouranos. Ouranos and Eurynome. You fought against me so hard the humans changed around you and you barely noticed. Nothing you did prepared you for the fact Kings and Princes might've been the only ones worthy of your deference, but Kings and Princes would die out. The common man you despised would become master of his own fate. The fate of his family. I bested you."

Shaking his head, Ares rose from the chair and over to his father. Yanked the shirt from the front of his trousers amidst Zeus's feeble attempt to push him away. Ares undid the buttons, a warrior's hands using the same gentility which came natural when holding his infant children to his chest. He undid Zeus' belt, pulled his socks off, took down Zeus's trousers and tossed the clothing in the laundry hamper. Turned to the wardrobe lovingly made by Hephaestus and pulled out a pair of pajamas. Silk, like the sheets.

"So kill me and be done with it." Zeus sat on his narrow bed, draped only in his adult incontinence briefs, undershirt and his shame. "Take the crown. Put the consort's crown on your love-bitch. Break it in twain, give half to that man of yours as a necklace. Trot me out and burn me before old Wander."

"Mother's a splendid Queen. I would not take her rights away from her for my amusement."

"No ambition! This is why I hated you, this is why..."

"I protect us all! Do you expect me to house you in a place with carers, to ensure Athene has what she needs, Hephaestus his work and his shop if I'm sitting on a throne mother adores? No!"

"You're sick! You're a twisted relic, a back-birth of my funk and piss."

"I bested you, by being the better man. I take care of our family, keep Artemis' land preserve in place for her Hunt. I ensure you're comfortable in your elder years, that there are people to clean you of your piss you talk of so much. And you know, dear father. You know with every minute of your life I did not become you.

I transcended you, I broke our cycle and I will continue to do so. I will continue to care for you, to feed you with those pathetic pudding cups and give plenty to everyone around you by association. And each one of your friends, the people who spend such a short bit of time before they die, they will praise you for your diligent good sons. Your beloved daughter, who fixes their emails. Every day you get to hear them mention me, mention how glad they are to see an old man rotting away with the comforts of his children around him.

Every day, limp dicked and incontinent, bound to the fucking chair for your own hubris and the damage you did to those women's hips, every day you hear nothing but my praise. You see nothing but the humans lauding my gifts of courage, in their wars and in their relaxations I have bested you. I won. I took everything you held away and I will keep them."

Ares spat, before descending into silence. "There, the mighty King of the Gods. No, father. I could kill you. I should for your crimes against women and..."

"Pfth women. Uppity bitches."

"I should kill you for that too, I have daughters. But. If I killed you, your pain would cease. If I let your life slip through my fingers, I would lose my freedom to act in the best interest of our family. Through the sheer act of keeping you here, caring not only for you but all these people, through their praise and their admiration for the work of your diligent, beloved kids... they give you just enough worship. Enough power not to fade away." He leaned in, nose within a brushing millimetre of Zeus' face. "You will live in this place, decrepit and bereft. You will live in the shadow of our dotage. And you will hate not only yourself, but the world you helped maintain. I told you, father.

I won." Ares, God of War leaned down and kissed his father's forehead with lips which pressed like fire. He turned down the light, and walked to the door of the small suite. "Melinda? My father is ready for his bath, if you don't mind. I think he soiled himself again."

"Not at all. Happens all the time. Why we get paid the big bucks, right?" Melinda walked into the room and pushed her white sweater up her elbows. "Aww, look at this. You've got such a good son, how he takes care of you."

"Thank you, Melinda. Alright, I'll see you in a few weeks."

Zeus mumbled curses under his tongue in a language Melinda didn't understand.

"I love you too, father. Goodbye." Ares walked out of the old folk's home at a hurried strut, stopping only to clean his hands with sanitizer to get the funk of his father off him.

Idling by the front door, Leonidas sat behind the wheel of an armoured SUV with symphonic heavy metal pouring out of speakers. Collapsing into the passenger seat, Ares hissed out a breath and set his palm on his face. The waft of the hand sanitizer stung shut eyes, a click and zip from Leonidas' seatbelt was chased by the rustle of the smaller man. Leaning over Ares, Leonidas rumbled sweet words in Hellax as he reached for Ares' seatbelt and buckled his spouse in. The scent of liquorice and peppermint on Leonidas' breath roused Ares' eyes open and he caught the man for a kiss as comforting as it was familiar.

"Old bastard back in his prison? Godspeed to the cuckold." Leonidas settled back in the driver's seat and clipped his seatbelt on, shifting the SUV into gear before he took Ares' hand.

"Is it wrong I wish... no. No, if Zeus died..."

"Your mother would continue as the dowager she is now. You worry too much. We've too many people to look after to do right by them all and still have enough energy for ourselves." Leonidas shifted into a higher gear on the freeway and thrashed the engine to reach the airport a mote faster.

"What if it was you? What if that bolt hit you instead of..."

"I'm not going to halt our mission out of fear and neither are you."

"You're my conscience, as Dite is my compassion. If I lost either of you..."

"We're no stranger to death, Enyo. What happened was a tragedy, but we'll get the bitch yet. Justice will be done."

"No. Death is not a stranger, but..." Ares searched the rapid retreat of the highway outside for a sign he could cling to, a presence in the breeze. "... I want a full trace on Caleb. Transcripts from Icarus, I don't trust him to avoid stupidity, and Raynar isn't answering any summons. He shouldn't be alone."

"Want me to send Lou to bring him in?"

"Yes."

"On one condition."

"Oh?"

"Get some sleep, love, you're going to need it. We all are." Driving down the highway with one hand on the wheel, Leonidas of Sparta took hold of his spouse's fingers. He knew Ares' grip could crush him in a millisecond, a single twitch. Yet, Ares settled into the reclined seat all the same, and shut his eyes with a mirror of the face Leonidas first fell in love with more than two millennia ago in Sparta.

Caleb was as lost now as Ares was then, the weight of empires and pantheons on his shoulders. Unlike Ares in those times, Caleb had no children to care for, no consort to defend or sisters to protect. As Leonidas passed car after car, he thought back to the consoling isolation of Ares in Sparta, when Gorgo brought Aphrodite into the world of Spartan women and their children entered the Agoge. Without the excess of Olympus, Ares had nothing but his family and his comrades. The fellow Spartans they trained beside.

As Leonidas ducked his eyes once in a while to check on Ares' slumbering face, he wondered how Caleb could fare with no consolation. Ares was right. They had to intercept Caleb and bring him home.

Truce be damned.

"Minitron, where's Leander? I have a mission for you."

23 CLIFFS AND THEIR CHASMS

"Married!? Did ye say married!? Why I, we'll be throwing them the biggest shindig this side of Creation, now won't we? Hah! Them two finally did it, a bit pissed they didn't let me do them a proper handfasting if I'm honest, and being a Fae I always am." Finnegan was having a much better day, since young Seraya called, from her protective perch in Ares' Chalceus Citadel. Not that Finnegan didn't trust Ares to protect his family, and thus his great-grandchild's girlfriend, but the Changeling Princess was as much family to the Lord of Finnegan's Bluff as she was banging Icarus.

Standing by the antique phone, whyever the humans upgraded perfectly workable technology Finnegan never understood, he tucked the receiver between his chin and shoulder and wove one finger around in the cord. "Yes, everything's coming up roses, Frigga dropped a spell by for Caleb, figured it was easier to leave it here for him than try another monumentally awkward meeting. Dunno what he'll do with it, got a mind to use it myself and fireproof the Sacred Groves wholesale, the lot! Aw, thanks love, bloody nuisance this whole thing, but I think we're all finally on the mend. Hold on Sera, seems a commotio-oh... oh no."

Finnegan dropped the receiver and ran into the centre of a silent bustle in the crowd. Jostled about by the crowd, Finnegan pushed at gaining voices and pointed shoulders.

"Steady on! We'll get nowhere like this. Oy! Move!" Two branches wove into the throng and shoved Folk out of Finnegan's way. Caleb stumbled to his knees with a bundle wrapped in red linen in his arms, flanked by Raphael. The angel's wings brushed Folk back, giving Caleb space enough to cradle the bundle to his chest.

"There they are, the couple of.. the..." Strange bit of bundle, rather bulky, rather large wrapped in what looked like a spartan cloak. It sang to Finnegan's senses, the call from a cursed child to its father. A sleeping seed reaching for the ground. "What's that, then?"

Before the crowd caught sight of Caleb's stunned face, Donovan rushed into the fray, wielding a dish towel like Odin's spear. "Git! Go on, now! All y'all, git! Leave or you ain't never coming back! Get gone! Raph, Leon, be mighty better of ya to pick Caleb up from the floor, gonna pour the man a drink. Finn! Gawking ain't helping. Move your pine needles or I'll move ya."

"Tuija?" Finnegan reached a limb shaped of oaken branches to brush over the fabric wrapped bundle. He plucked it from Caleb's arms, and the Fae Lord felt none of its weight.

Finnegan cradled her and all else was gone, but the seed of his promise those decades ago, that death wouldn't touch but transform her soul into another of Finnegan's lost prodigals. Finnegan's adopted daughter was home with the billow of a broken sob.

"I didn't know where to take her." Caleb mumbled slack-jawed, helped onto a barstool by Raphael. He slumped both elbows onto the bar top, ran his thumb along a stray line left by a patron long passed.

"How..." Finnegan swayed in place, his arms metamorphosing into a cocoon of branches, which wrapped round Tuija like a wild seed husk. The Pub descended into an enriched disquiet, barstools and tables faded into obsolescence, until the collective of deities, heroes and angels stood and slumped against a stone circle, surrounding an oak tree older than the worlds it touched.

"Stana set Caleb alight. Tuija took offence to it, she fought bravely and stopped Stana from using Caleb in her ritual." Raphael rubbed Caleb's back and he let him, as Caleb stared at the tumbler Donovan set down with a draught of liquor inside. "What can be done?"

"Leave Tuija with me, the curse gives her a chance at returning, doesn't it?"

"Have any of them woken up with memories of their pasts?" Raphael leaned against a stone, one foot propped on another.

"I cooked up a curse worthy of a god, when I flung that dart at Tuija. Was a desperate time, and we were watching species after species of Fae die out.

Torched from existence. When a Fae dies out, so does their species across all Realms. You try being Greek without Olives, my lad. Didn't hit her with some casual tree, thought I was ending the war with that blow." Finnegan set the seed husk of Tuija's cocooned body on the altar of the Axis Mundi, a floral hand stroked along its side. "The cedar I resurrected was a contingency plan, in case some lucky fuck got the drop on me, or found some way to poison my roots."

"You don't mean..." Raphael continued to rub Caleb's back in slow circles, humming at the mumbles and sobs that wracked his ribcage.

"Tuija is the heiress of Yggdrasil. The future tree upon which the Realms shall sway. Really, Raph. Think I left my girl hanging off a dry branch in the summer droughts?" Despite the weight of Tuija's passing, Finnegan's grin broke on a relatively jovial face. These creatures and the density of their convictions. Turn an ageless tree to drink before they'd understand the long way round. "Not another being in my aeons I'd rather leave the Realms to than Tuija Miroslava Draganova. And knowing Tuija, she'll find her way. Terrified as she was of death, I wish I could've given another way to her, but sometimes what's done is done. Only got the chance to make it right. Eh? Eh, Caleb? Cale..."

"His wife is dead. Give him some time."

"Transforming, I hope."

"Doesn't make it easier for them." Raphael sighed with a shake of their head. "What's a tree to understand about mammalian grief? A century's a split second to us. To Caleb, it's a lifetime."

"What's a few hundred years before seeing what she turns into, eh? My boy, Caleb, did you hear me? What, he lost his hearing in the battle?"

"You might see Tuija's end as a grand metamorphosis, but to Caleb it's the vacancy in his bed, the loss of his wife's whispers and her cantankerous roars as she fought harder than any for those things she believed. For the first time in a century and a half, he promised to the Cosmos and the Creatrix he would not stand alone. Death takes its toll on the mammals, it wounds them. What's the Truce left him? Caleb has nothing but a ruin for a house and more troubles than the Creatrix had initial sparks."

"Suppose for me, this next phase of Tuija's existence is all excitement, a father waiting for their child to come home and finally learn about the gifts he's been holding onto. Ones she wasn't ready for in life. Don't really understand the rest, do I? Fae like myself, moments like this are a blip... so I'm gonna leave the grieving mammal to you... or..." Tapping his slender fingers together, Finnegan sidled up to Caleb and reached, then retracted his hand as the man jerked out a sob. "Oh, well now, Dono my boy you got a rag about ya?"

Donovan faded into being seated on the altar beside Caleb, holding out a clean dish rag. "Empathy, ya oaken idiot."

"Empathy! Yes! You lot do go on about your emotional whatevers." Finnegan yanked the dish rag from Donovan's extended finger and crouched to wipe the tears off Caleb's face. There, the wonder. The fauna's visage was a crumbling mask, with wide water laden eyes and skin bruised red from tears. Was this what they hinged the Truce upon, 163 years ago? A caterwauling infant laid on cold stone, wrapped in cloth of starlight as Hera clucked her tongue and hummed a lullaby? Then Sarasvati, then Mary and Sif and Pele. At the shiver of Caleb's shoulders, the incapacity to see beyond his present condition, Finnegan softened.

"Let me go."

"Sorry, I thought you needed a moment."

"No.. . let me go. I don't want this. I didn't choose it, you have... make it disappear. I can't..."

"Wait a little longer, trust me that far, my friend."

"I'm done."

"I'm not as flippant as I seem, me boy. I should have told Tuija when she was alive what her fate meant, but bless me, I thought we had more time and she kept saying she wasn't ready. Trust my confidence, if anyone can wake up untampered, it's Tuija. I won't do you wrong. Can you do th-bless me, the man's plum passed out. Eh! I'll finish telling him later. Always a later, innit?"

"I suppose. We'll take him somewhere safe." Raphael cradled Caleb to their chest, and they took to the skies. Off and away.

"You arse of an oaken menace. You tell him right and proper, wouldn't be a mess if'n you did."

"Dono, my lad, if I trust anything in this Cosmos, I trust Tuija Draganova's indomitable will to crawl her way back after a couple centuries. And she'll do so with our help, won't she? It can't fail! Much... bit of a fifty-fifty, really. Twenty-eighty tops."

"... cheese and crackers, sometimes you're a fucking dumbass, ya old green bastard. Best we get started trying to wake Tuija up enough t'see if your darn fool ways worked."

"About that..." Hands in his pockets, Jase stepped out from the Theosian door and smiled through eyes stained with tears. "... hello, Finnegan.

"Jase the bloody Carpenter. What in the root balls of aspen groves are you doing here?"

"Fulfilling a promise. I might have a way to help."

"... you?" Finnegan paused, stifling the urge to shove the Carpenter away from Tuija's cocoon, when Jase walked close and set his hand on the altar.

"Who else would Caleb ask to bless his marriage? Frigga?"

"Tuija, she didn't..."

"I'm here for both of them, and I think between you, me, Vele, Izanami and Odin, we might be able to pull off a miracle."

"Hand the man a shovel, Dono. I'm listening."

"Finn? Finnegan? Did you drop your pint again? I told you, Iccy will upgrade the Pub's phone and... Finn?" A bright eyed young woman tucked blue curls behind pointed ears. Curled up in one of Icarus' oversized hoodies, Seraya flopped on the bed as the door opened and cast a deep yellow glow from the sunlight filtering through Brolympus. "Iccy! I think Finn dropped his pint again, he must be in shock! Can you believe it!? I still can't believe they finally did it!"

Seraya rolled and hopped to the end of the massive bed, her grin so large it tore at Icarus' chest like fateful faulty wings. Each second poured onto Icarus' skin like burning wax, no force in the Cosmos could make Icarus want to destroy the smile on their girlfriend's face.

"We've got to get planning the party! I can already imagine the flowers, ooo! I should start growing the roses now, and some peonies and those blue poppies that remind Tuija of home. Do you think Caleb's more of an evergreen or sandalwood kind of guy?" The Changeling chatted on, her phone never far from her ear in case Finnegan picked the receiver back up. "I bet he'd be a saxifrage man. What do you think?"

The sunshine smile on Seraya's face sliced deep into Icarus' lungs, until the eternal youth could do nothing but open and close their mouth. This was too big, maybe Icarus could wait, pretend nothing happened, hold off until Magnus Pater and Leonidas got back, anything to keep the illusion going another second.

"I don't expect you to help me with the flowers, Thiccphrodite and I can tackle that while you make the most epic playlist in existence. Oh! And Lou will obviously make himself useful with much heavy lifting, oh! I'll need some wheat for Tuija's flower crown, because of course she'll have a flower crown and I need to call someone about some ribbon and... Finn!? Finnegan, have you cleaned up your pint yet!? We should go over there, it sounds busy."

"No!" Icarus reached for Seraya's hand, and tugged her phone out of loose fingers. Staring at the slip of glass and metal, Icarus pressed the end call button. "Sera, baby... I gotta tell you something important."

"Wh... hey, what can be more important than welcoming Caleb into our family? Hmm? Think of how much brighter things will be once..."

"Seraya, please!" Icarus sat on their bed and eyes on the floor. A lengthy shadow spilled into the sunlight, Icarus didn't have to turn their head to know Lou poked his in at the raised tone.

"You two aiight?"

"Caleb and Tuija got married! Finn and I are already planning a party and you are not allowed to be too busy with a mission... to... Iccy? Are you... why are you crying?"

"Leander, can you come here for a minute?" Icarus sniffled and pulled a hankie from their back jean pocket, careful to train their eyes up on the ceiling.

"Woa, ey, why the tears my sib?" The bed depressed as Lou sat beside Icarus, a protective arm hovered at his sibling's back. "You allergic to romance or something? Heh, we both know that ain't the case. Eh, Sera? Eh? Eeeeh?"

Icarus hiccupped a sordid laugh and shook their head, "It's not that, it... there was a battle, and... Stana found Zeus and I don't know how 'cause I was super careful about cleaning up traces but somehow she found him and Caleb and Tuija found her and..."

Another deep breath stuttered through Icarus, who blew their nose. Tried to settle without another choke.

"Iccy?" Seraya's smile faded to a gentle quiet, she put her hand on Icarus' knee, searching the youth's face.

"I know I didn't leave a trace about Zeus anywhere, I know it. Athene always checked my work when it came to the old bastard. But Tuija got captured by Stana in the dust-up and..." Icarus rubbed their nose, leaning into Leander's side the way a younger sibling only could when troubles were real enough to sober even the most cynical relationship. "... Tuija needs a wake, not a wedding, baby."

The microcosm of Brolympus split into crumbling fragments. Seraya blinked hard, her phone forgotten for the reality of Icarus' tears. More sobering yet was Lou's hard-set jaw, the way he hemmed Icarus in and kept solid and silent as an anchor. Joviality could wait.

"Wh-what?"

"Damn it, I was supposed to be there. Caleb needed me!"

"Tuija didn't make it."

"We were ready, my entire squad was ready! Magnus Pater wouldn't let me go!" Lou punched his thigh and rocketed to his feet, pacing the room like a caged predator.

"Good! I'm glad, 'cause if this bitch took Tuija out, you'd be dead too!" Icarus chased Lou to their feet, fists balled and face red. Seraya's gasp thundered in Icarus' ears, her hand over mouth with a squeak which echoed across the palatial bedroom.

"I... I'm sorry, I..." Icarus suspended in the room, a freefall sensation in their gut they recognized in a legion of nightmares and lost waxen feathers.

"Where's Caleb?" Seraya stuttered between wiping both eyes with a tissue from the nightstand. Holding the box in her lap, Sera huddled in Icarus' hoodie. Lou's eyes snapped to his sibling. The room turned cold from its loss of joy. A bastion of safety and love, Brolympus was only one wing of the Aphneion palace built against the Thracian lakeside, where Ares and Aphrodite rebuilt their lives after leaving Olympus. Now, with Tuija's death descending on the trio's waking minds, it seemed as empty and barren as marble floors in the cold of an abandoned temple.

"I..." Icarus stood empty, bare feet stung on cold tile.

"Icarus? Where is Caleb?" Seraya reached for her lover, their fingers intertwined as the Changeling sniffed and rubbed her palm at her cheek.

"I don't know." The truth shuddered at the room, shook across Icarus' shoulders like Medusa's penetrating stone.

"Ya what?" Lou stopped pacing, both hands firm over his mouth. "My dude, don't do this. Don't tell me I lost Caleb."

"He needs you, Lou... You gotta go find him."

"But... Iccy you always know. That's your job, you know things. You find people, you..."

"He was at Finn's and then poof." Eyes the colour of the Aegean widened, hands unplugged from their banks of keyboards and screens fumbled to hold Seraya's fingers. Leaning into Lou, Icarus shook their head as the most terrifying truth in all the Realms echoed from wobbling lips. "Daedalus.AI, my phone trace, the cantrips, heck even the tracking device in his shoes... all of it. Nothing's working. Magnus Pater and Leon are gonna be here in an hour tops. They're gonna want options and I got net zero. I don't know what to do. Caleb's gone."

EPILOGUE: TWO WEEKS LATER

Enshrined off Osaka's Namba district, through alleyways beyond neon signs and tachinomiya flaunting a specialty dish or cocktail, a tattoo parlour called out. He'd phoned ahead, gotten an appointment for the senior artist Odoro to meet late. Would cost a few favours, some children's laughter from the supply in Tuija's place, but it was worth it.

His throat contracted, a lump which wouldn't fade. Working his hands in and out of fists, Caleb dug into his pocket. Pulled his slim black book out and flipped to the page with his map, circled in red ink was the tebori-style tattoo parlour off another small alley. The sign was a faded and hand painted affair,

Odoro Takeshi. Tebori.

Black letters on what was a crisp white board before the city took its toll. Before passersby stuck fading and chipped stickers of the latest anime character, or notable bar giving out freebies. Faded and torn.

Was this how he wanted to go out? To walk up the narrow stairs to an incandescent bulb into the tattoo parlour of an old schooler who knew enough to know the Shinto Kami were as real as his ink?

No, he needed a believer. The demon in Russia spoke so much before he died bloody and raw. But now Caleb knew, Ares or at least Icarus might know what

Caleb was on about. Icarus might be able to hear the calls or track his footsteps, send Lou to chase him down. The idea brought slim comfort, how could he face them?

Where were they?

Caleb leaned against the building, beside a poster for a new cat cafe which served purring good times. He brushed his finger against the curve of a face half masked. "This has to be for me. Tuija, it has to be for me."

Tuija was gone, regardless of Finn's trust that a few hundred years could grow her into a strong tree. The hope of reunion stabbed at his ribcage. Too much for one man to handle, there were too many dead, too many dying, too many needed him, too many voices, when the one voice which could calm him might wake up, maybe in a hundred years. Would Tuija remember? Would any of his wife survive, taken before they could get a foothold into matrimony?

The black book in his pocket buzzed and he tossed it to the gutter.

"I'll be dead by then." Caleb opened the door and took the stairs two at a time, up three flights past a talent agency, an office, a cat cafe, up to the fourth floor and another identical but less worn sign.

Odoro Takeshi. Tebori.

He went to press the chime, when Caleb noticed the door hung ill on its moorings. It opened with a nudge of his foot, and Caleb's nose was filled with smoke and flame.

"Odoro-San? Odoro-San!?" He rushed in, a handkerchief over his mouth, and found the area around Odoro-San's Kamidana on fire. The man slumped in a chair, Caleb charged at him, pulled the man up and out of the room into the hall. "Odoro-San!"

Odoro-San muttered in Japanese, Caleb rushed back into the shop, looking for a fire extinguisher, the fire alarm, anything. As he got closer to the blaze, it died to flickers of blue and yellow flame before puffing out. Smoke wove its way through the air filtration system, an old fan churned it up. The Kamidana sat surrounded by fine white ash, only the immediate area around the tattoo inks, the supplies burned to dust.

"I apologise, Mauthisen-Sama. The message came with the flames. I cannot give you what you want. Bjørnsen was never here. Leave."

"But your place, I can help you clean it up, I..."

"Leave, Mauthisen-Sama! Please. Leave." Flickers and shadows popmarked the walls, a myriad of wings and broad shoulders.

Caleb backed away, and fled down the hall as a candle in Odoro-San's shrine flickered back to flame.

They would never let him go.

Follow Caleb through the Valley in...

Son of Abel (Judge of Mystics Saga 2)

"I want out."

The entire cosmos hiccups around Finnegan the Fae. Mystic Judge Caleb Mauthisen desperately clings to the journals of a 7th Century Catholic Cardinal, obsessed with a magical tattoo that threatens to crumble the Mystic Realms to wrath and war.

A place they know and fear too well.

Spiralling with only his scheming ex Delilah to 'help', Caleb searches for the elusive way out of the Truce, as he descends through the essence of grief into layers of hell on earth.

Finnegan breaks his exile to find Caleb's absentee father Raynar, to wrench Caleb loose before his absence strips the Realms of their Judge and protector. Before Delilah weaves Caleb into plans of her own, and wrath shatters through to the last root of the World Tree.

Son of Abel is a cathartic mythpunk & godpunk supernatural fantasy and the second novel in the Judge of Mystics Saga.

ACKNOWLEDGEMENTS

The Judge of Mystics Saga has been a long and metamorphosing haul since its inception in flash fiction back in the MacroMicroCosm days. Back before 2012, where I wrote a flash piece about a magic book calling a cleaning lady by name for rescue from the mildew infested basement of a damp Vancouver special owned by an old sorcerer. A decrepit elderly man asleep in the easy chair upstairs.

From there, the world exploded. Would I write a book about Stana discovering how to use the knowledge she'd been gifted by an innocently hopeful Book of Knowledge? I tried at first, to write Stana's story.

It wasn't in me, cut out like a paper bag damp from the rain.

What whispered to my exhausted mind was not to write some rebellious anima, but animus. As Carl Jung dubbed it, an inner masculine part of the female personality. So I dove into the oceanic salt waters of Caleb Mauthisen, a deity born of a milkmaid and laid on the Altar of the Axis Mundi as an interdimensional peace child.

Adulthood fit atop his shoulders with the weight of the Mystic Realms, his one task to keep peace between the Hellenes, Kehmeti, Immortals, O-Kami, Aesir, Vanir, Theosians, Fae and other Realms spanning what we know as world mythologies (lovingly reverenced and fictionalized in the work). The means for this minted Judge were both guiding glove and firearm. Keep the peace, with a bullet or five if he must.

Keep the Human world of Midgard from a second bought of millennia long collateral damage from warring mystic folk & gods.

Special thanks to my long-suffering spouse Kick and our goodest of rescue dogs Iroh, for all the tap-taps at my knee so he can herd me to bed. Thank you to my siblings Noah, Sanya and Matt, who wait patiently enough for me to be done another draft and have a few extra minutes for our cross-global voice calls.

And to my Muse Jesse, thank you for the music, the unconditional affection and gentle reminders to breathe.

The Judge of Mystics Saga wouldn't exist without the sounding board and editing of Tegan Ward & Marissa Wagner, nor would I be confident enough in my writing to publish without the support of Kelsey Fast.

The character of Icarus Areides was originally inspired by a wonderfully zany idea by KS Bishoff, which spawned a single sentence where I, improvising voice actor, called for a brother named 'Lou'. Emily stepped up, and the siblings were born. Without Emily Armstrong and KS Bishoff there would be no novels at all. No Icarus, no Lou, no daily motivations or the encouragement of a couple fellow bitches who know what it's like to sprint, hobble and crawl out of the proverbial and legitimate trenches.

And to Melody, I give the absolute gratitude of good soop (spelled exactly as written), of slow burns and woeful emotional depth. Without your encouragement, this novel would look entirely different... and be missing one particular Hellene genius who might want to take this conversation away from the water. Oh, and if you're looking for a place to hang with fellow creatives and a castle full of positive reinforcement to reach your goals? The Castle Cafe is lit.

Thanks to Vraeyda Media Inc for publishing my work, and to all the authors I've been able to meet. May you be ever inspired and always creative.

See you @usurperkings.

About Sapha Burnell

Cyberpunk + Mythpunk

"Sapha is like a young Wolfgang Pauli, in every laboratory he went, there was a little explosion."

Cyberpunk + Mythpunk converge in emotive works dubbed 'a work of gob-smackingly beautiful discovery' (Kevin Hogan on Usurper Kings) and 'an insane diabolical rollercoaster' (RL Arenz III on NEON Lieben). A true -punk, Sapha teethed on images of the Berlin Wall falling down, challenges norms like bricks under sledgehammers and intertwines queerness and faith to envision a world on the brink of dystopia we can usurp and heal. Steeped in divergent cultures, she spent years in humanitarian work, before dedicating her life to writing, editing and publishing.

A member of The Writers Union of Canada, Sapha leads weekly writing and critique streams on Twitch and across social media as usurperkings.

BY SAPHA BURNELL

Usurper Kings *Tenth Anniversary Edition*
Future's Lens *Cage Wire*

The Judge of Mystics Saga

Char & Ash
Son of Abel
Book of Revels (2023)

The Lieben Cycle

NEON Lieben

Vraeyda Literary

Warning Light Calling *Peter Graarup Westergaard*
Aegis *RL Arenz III*
Vostok *Łukasz Drobnik*
My Heart is The Tempest *Sacha Rosel*
Sky Tracer (The Fungal Realm 1) *Hayden Moore*
The Saga of Ádís Rauðfeldr *Siobhan Clark*
The Drake Equation *Brad Hoge*

Manufactured by Amazon.ca
Bolton, ON

41315078R00132